Teddy Dee: In the World of Shadows
By Mark T. Sneed
An Original Piece of Fiction

To my mother, who always encouraged me to be a better man and do my best in the face of injustice and unfair challenges.

Teddy Dee: In the World of Shadows
By Mark T. Sneed
An Original Piece of Fiction

Prologue.

"How long?"

"Can't say."

"Can't say? Or won't say?"

The doctor chuckled despite the seriousness of the situation. He shook his head.

"There is no exact science to your question." He paused and narrowed his dark eyes behind his thin rimless glasses. "Use the time you have left to do something for you. I have always believed that if I was in your particular situation I would want to do things that I have never done."

Teddy Dee hated how simplistic people could be, at times. He knew that the doctor was going to ask him if he had a "bucket list" of things that he had not done.

"Are you familiar with the concept of a bucket list."

Teddy Dee nodded, suddenly bored by the conversation. He listened and pretended that everything that the doctor said was new and significant. Then he climbed to his feet and walked out of the ten store shopping mall where he had been directed by his handler; Roberta.

He was in Arizona. More specifically, he was in Phoenix, Arizona. He had been doing a job when he began to black out. He had been in his hotel room, thankfully. So, no one had seen him wobble and tilt and nearly fall on his face.

Teddy Dee had made it to the hotel bed and sat down and tried to compose himself and do a mental check. Had he had a heart attack? Was he having a stroke? What could it have been?

The last time that anything unusual had happened to him was in Kulani. Teddy Dee was thirty-seven days out of Kulani and finishing a job for an electronic company when he felt tingling in his fingers. He had driven to the airport hotel and barely made it to his hotel room before he felt the black curtain of nothingness envelop him. When he woke up, he was lying on the floor of his hotel room his car keys and hotel key card just out of reach. His phone was cracked for some reason. He had a headache. Teddy Dee had fallen and the fall had shaken him.

In Kulani, less than one hundred days ago, Teddy Dee had been found having a seizure in the showers by a guard and taken to the prison doctor. The doctor had run a few tests and determined the issue. Teddy Dee was not long for this world.

Teddy Dee was told that he would be released once the doctor talked to him. The doctor, a brown haired, white man with a slight slouch appeared with a guard to talk to Teddy Dee in the prison hospital ward. The doctor looked to be thirty something and harried. Teddy Dee watched as the man dressed in a lab coat approached with one of the prison guards.

"I ran a few tests once you came into the hospital ward. We noted that you are sensitive to light. The seizures seem to stem from that light sensitivity. Having done a cursory physical examination, you look as if you have been hit by at least three trucks and your body has sustained some severe physical damage. I noted no less than half a dozen bullet wounds and," he studied the clipboard. "At least, ten knife wounds."

The doctor smiled. He had a clipboard in his hand and pressed to his slight beer belly. Doctor Thomas reached out and shook Teddy Dee's hand awkwardly. "What is troubling is not the physical trauma but the psychological trauma you must be dealing with."

Teddy Dee prepared to hear the doctor recommend him to a psychologist. It only made sense but Teddy Dee did not want to sit and share his feelings. That was a no-win situation for him. Teddy Dee had to lock his feelings and emotions away like the various secrets he had been privy to over the years as a corporate blooder.

"I have only the most basic of examining equipment at my disposal here. I want to recommend that you get an MRI so that we can see if that seizure came as a result of symptoms that are not visible."

Teddy Dee did not respond. He was thinking. An MRI would determine what exactly. He tried to recall the purpose of an MRI.

"You have sustained some severe concussions and I have to admit that I am surprised to see you standing in front of me." He paused. "Do you have migraines? Do you ever forget things?"

Teddy Dee did not respond. Instead, he listened, not knowing if he should tell the truth or lie. He was so used to lying about everything. Lying was just a part of his personality.

"Teddy, you are one punch, kick, or slap in the face from a massive brain aneurysm. That is not good. If anyone hits you in the head you could die."

Teddy Dee had nodded and tried to think what the doctor was saying.

"You look like a man that is used to solving problems with your fists. You have a lot of scar tissue, everywhere. The worst happens to be around your eyes, nose, and temples."

Teddy Dee listened and not hearing a recommendation for a psychologist nodded to the MRI test. The doctor was knowledgeable and bright. He had heard the prison doctor's report of his health and been surprised at the detail and extent that the prison doctor had gone to check and recheck the information before telling Teddy Dee that he was living on borrowed time.

Act One.

"Good evening Miss Robinson, I would like to talk to your son," Teddy Dee announced, dressed in a dark blue suit, bleached white collared shirt, a blue and green silk tie, and comfortable Italian leather shoes.

Erica Robinson's eyes widened. She was a broad hipped woman with glasses and small brown eyes. She was dressed all in black as she stood in the doorway of her apartment.

"You want to see my Eric?"

Teddy Dee nodded.

"What has he done?"

Teddy Dee smiled at the question. He understood where the question came from. Any time a man came to the Jungle and was bold enough to knock on doors dressed like Teddy Dee there had to be a problem.

"Eric hasn't done anything," Teddy Dee admitted. "It's quite the opposite. I am here to offer your son a job."

For the second time Erica Robinson's eyes widened in disbelief.

"You know that Eric is only fifteen, right?"

Teddy Dee nodded.

"Miss Robinson I know how unusual this may seem but there is no age limit on talent. If someone is talented and distinguishes themselves then they should expect to get the attention of people that need those talents and eventually get offers of work as a result."

"Wait," Erica Robinson said from the crack in the door as she spoke to Teddy Dee. "You think that my Eric has talent?"

"I do."

"You want Eric to work for you?"

"I do."

"You are talking about my Eric."

"I am."

Eric Robinson's mother looked at Teddy Dee from the other side of the door curiously. Teddy Dee did not blink. He waited. He waited knowing that Eric Robinson's mother was trying to figure out the angle on this man that had appeared out of nowhere at her door dressed like a banker or businessman.

"What is the job?"

Teddy Dee paused. He allowed the pause to drag out just a little longer as if he were pondering the question. Teddy Dee was not pondering but eyeing the apartment and the people in the small apartment over Erica Robinson's shoulder.

"I am more than comfortable talking to you about your son's potential in the hallway but I do not know if you want everyone in this apartment complex to know all the details of my potential job offer," Teddy Dee explained noticing that a neighbor had their door open and was listening to the conversation.

"Can you show me your identification again?"

Teddy Dee pulled out his wallet again and showed Miss Robinson his identification. The identification that Erica Robinson read stated that Teddy Dee was an executive at a made up company named: WynnCorp. WynnCorp was located, according to the card, in Los Angeles. There was a phony phone number that if Erica Robinson called would be answered by a switchboard that had been directed to tell whoever called that WynnCorp was one of the nation's most reliable corporate recruitment firms since 1959.

Teddy Dee had crafted his recruitment persona from several sources. He was a little bit Banacek, a little Columbo, a touch of Shaft and a sprinkle of a dapper Dan and a bunch of Low Down Dirty Shame. His title, according to his identification card read: Recruiter.

Teddy Dee stood in the hallway of the jungle apartments patiently. He checked his three and nine occasionally, casually. He had been trained to always be on alert and in any situation.

Erica Robinson, single mother, no husband, no boyfriend, was the mother of four. She was high school educated and hard working. She worked at the school district as a custodian. In her spare time, she was also a seamstress.

"Okay, sorry, can't be too careful," Erica Robinson smiled and opened the door to her apartment enough to allow Teddy Dee entry.

"Thank you for allowing me entry," Teddy Dee smiled.

"Yeah, I am sorry about all the questions."

Teddy Dee smiled to himself. He knew the routine. He had grown up with his mother and aunt. At the tender age of eleven Teddy Dee found himself the man of the house. It was an awkward position to put a pre-teen but one that Teddy Dee did not grouse about. So, as Erica Robinson tried to regroup and redress the stranger in her home Teddy Dee did not take offense at being made to earn his entry into the Robinson home.

"Quite understandable," Teddy Dee smiled. "WynnCorp is interested in Eric's mind. He has showed incredible talent at parsing out details that no one else has been able to do."

Erica Robinson stared at the man dressed in a suit and tie.

"Your son's mind sees things that others overlook," Teddy Dee continued nonplussed.

"Is it illegal?"

"No. I would not come to your home and offer your son, your only son, an illegal job. No, ma'am, I am offering Eric a job to utilize his genius." Erica Robinson brushed one of her braids from her small round face and smiled for the first time in the conversation at the door of her apartment. She had a buck tooth smile, Teddy Dee noticed. She looked at Teddy Dee, the man she had allowed to enter the cluttered apartment that housed four children, curiously. Teddy Dee noted that there was a hint of a smile on Erica Robinson's brown face. He had done his research.

Teddy Dee noted the oldest daughter, Tiffany, taller and darker than her mother but facially very similar, lurking just to the right of her. Tiffany was a teenager and dressed in a hooded sweatshirt of some designer, blue jeans and Nike basketball sneakers. Sitting on the couch were Tiffany's two younger sisters: Emma and Ella. They were in their first year of elementary school. They were dressed exactly alike and had the exact same hairdo. The one on the right had a scratch on her nose. That was the only noticeable difference Teddy Dee saw.

Erica Robinson looked from Tiffany to Teddy Dee and back. Tiffany mouthed something that Teddy Dee missed. Teddy Dee figured that Tiffany had to be the fly in the ointment. She would be the hard sell.

"You think Eric is a genius?"

"I do," Teddy Dee smiled.

"Tiff, get your brother," Erica Robinson commanded her daughter who was just behind her watching everything happening at the front door of the apartment. Tiffany, tall and athletic, spun on her heels and walked deeper into the apartment.

"What kind of work do you want Eric to do?"

Teddy Dee took in the twins: Emma and Ella, sitting on the couch watching television. They both had notebook computers on their laps. Their small hands were busy on the keyboards. They were dressed in collared blouses and jeans. One of the girls was wearing mismatched athletic socks of a football and basketball team. The other girl was wearing fairy socks with an outline of a fairy in midair.

"Well, I am faced with a predicament that needs a new set of eyes and possibly a genius to figure out. It is a puzzle of sorts. It is a puzzle and riddle and mystery that I cannot, for the life of me, unravel. It is for this knotty situation that I want to hire your son."

"You believe that Eric can solve your problem?"

"I believe if there is anyone that can solve my problem it will be Eric," Teddy Dee confessed.

"How do you know Eric?"

"I don't," Teddy Dee smiled.

Erica Robinson narrowed her small brown eyes and studied Teddy Dee evenly.

"Let me back up, a bit. Twelve months ago there was a note given to me. That note suggested that there was a particular problem that if not solved would end the life of someone I did not know. For four weeks I grappled with the problem to no end. So, I tried to find the brightest and most brilliant. Miss Robinson I have been asking schools in the district to offer their students, at any level, my problem. Well, I have given them part of the problem with hopes that I can find someone to solve the bigger problem. I have been waiting for a reasonable answer that merits discussion. I only wanted reasonable answers to follow up. I am following up."

"How many students answered your problem?"

"Hundreds answered. Only one answered with a flare that surprised me. That is why I am here."

"Wait a minute," Erica Robinson said as Tiffany and Eric Robinson stepped into the small living room where Teddy Dee, the twins, and their mother were all gathered.

"Hello, Eric, I am Teddy Dandridge. I am the man that asked you to answer a problem in class that was not one thing or required one skill to answer. It was a word problem, on its face. Yet, that problem was so much more." Teddy Dee paused. "You recall the problem?"

Eric Robinson was dressed in Converse tennis shoes, faded blue jeans and a black cartoon T-shirt that read: Tokyo Atom. He looked nothing like his mother or sisters. He had a round head, miniscule shoulders, long arms and legs.

"It was a problem about lies and truths and knights and knaves." Eric looked from Teddy Dee to his mother and back to his mother before answering, yes.

"Can I sit down?"

"Yes, I'm sorry." Erica Robinson looked around and pointed to the kitchen and the small table there. Teddy Dee walked into the kitchen and sat down at the kitchen table. Eric stood and allowed his mother and Tiffany to sit.

"First, I want to make sure that your son offered the solution. I do not doubt his ability but he is not the brightest student in his classes but he offered the solution."

"It was my idea," Eric finally burped. His voice was low and squeaky.

"How did you come up with the idea?"

"Well, the problem was really three problems in one. The first problem was the king and his protectors. The king did not trust his protectors. So, the protector needed to prove his trust in some way. The second problem was the princess and her love. The third problem was the brave knight and his quest. They all were in the same kingdom but they all had different issues. To solve the king problem there were three elements to address: the king, the queen and the protectors. The court seemed not to care or seem to care enough about the king's problem to get involved," Eric explained his squeaky voice taking a more commanding voice the more he explained the problem.

Teddy Dee smiled. He raised his hand satisfied that Eric Robinson was the one student in the whole district who had offered a novel solution to his problem.

"Okay, as I stated I have this problem and I need someone much smarter than me to try to figure it out. If Eric can unravel the knots of this problem, then I will pay him handsomely."

"What are we talking about," Tiffany asked, suddenly curious.
Erica Robinson narrowed her eyes and Tiffany fell silent.

"Why me?"

"Because you hit on points that no one else did. You looked at the problem in a significantly different way."

"That's it?"

"I don't have a lot of time to waste. No one does, really but I am aware of the time constraints on all of us. So, I will not and do not waste time. I was told that you exhibit these flashes of brilliance in school. I was told that you are incredibly bright but that you do not apply yourself. I don't really care about that. I just want results. If you can unlock this problem, then your life and your family's life will be forever changed."

Teddy Dee laid out a plan for Eric on the kitchen table in the midst of South Central's jungle.

"Forever changed?"

Teddy Dee spoke. Eric was to meet Teddy Dee at the Beverly Hills Hotel in Beverly Hills every Friday, after school. Teddy Dee had arranged a car to pick up Eric and drop him off on Friday and Saturday. They would meet in the conference room of the hotel and discuss the problem that Teddy Dee was facing. Teddy Dee was putting Eric under contract for eight weeks; two months.

"Unlike school, I am a businessman. If you do not hold up your part of the bargain, then I will not give you another chance. Life doesn't give anyone second chances," Teddy Dee noted. "I need solutions. I want solutions."

"What if I cannot solve your problem?"

"Then you will fail. You will return to this life and life will go on. Things will return to the same shit sandwich you have been eating for the last fifteen years. Nothing special."

"What if Eric solves your problem?"

"If he produces, if you produce, I will sweeten the pot and give you and your family a weekend at the Beverly Hills Hotel any month of the year. Of course, this is a contract and contracts are binding. Sixteen sessions should suffice. If you solve the problem earlier Eric, I will give you a bonus. Is that fair?"

Eric Robinson stood and measured Teddy Dee. He did not rush to answer. Teddy Dee liked that about Eric Robinson. There was no rush to impress or feeling of being impulsive when he answered.

Teddy Dee smiled. "I am a generous man. I have learned that praise alone is not enough. We all are in need of things to make our lives better. So, I will offer Eric, and by Eric, I mean your family a better life."

Eric and his mother signed the contract for eight weeks. They read and reread the contract to make sure that they had not overlooked anything that seemed essential.

"Get a good night's sleep and be ready to go on Saturday. There will be a car waiting for you at eight o'clock. You should be at the hotel by nine. Eat. Relax. Think. I'll meet you at ten o'clock. You should be home by three. Fair?"

Teddy Dee stood and removed an envelope from his jacket and handed it to Erica Robinson.

"Open it," Teddy Dee insisted.

The mother opened the envelope and Teddy Dee watched the various expressions roll across her face: Surprise. Disbelief. Gratefulness. Erica Robinson looked at Teddy Dee with a newfound sense of appreciation. She was suddenly all smiles. Teddy Dee had given her three thousand dollars in cash to retain the services of her son for two months.

Teddy Dee extended his hand to Eric Robinson. Eric Robinson reached out his hand and the two shook.

"See you tomorrow."

Teddy Dee walked out of the Robinson apartment and down the hallways ever aware of his surroundings. Teddy Dee walked down the stairs instead of taking the slow elevator. Once on the ground floor he made his way to the lobby and out of the jungle apartments past some of the most hardened gangsters in Los Angeles without batting an eye. The gangsters did not move or speak.

For the first time, Teddy Dee thought that he knew how it felt to be Oscar Easton and be given respect, without word or action. The gangsters who rarely allowed anyone unknown entry into the jungle without a bracing gave Teddy Dee a wide berth. They, Teddy Dee imagined, must have been aware of Teddy Dee's ease and disregard of the gangsters posturing. At the same time Teddy Dee knew that he was not some small or insignificant individual. He walked down the stairs of the apartment complex and to his waiting car. He climbed into the back seat and the car slipped silently into the dark.

Teddy Dee, ever vigilant, looked back to see if anyone was following him. After the sedan swung onto Crenshaw Boulevard headed toward Westchester Teddy Dee relaxed, just a little.

In the back of his mind Teddy Dee could hear Oscar Easton, his mentor, talking about the harsh realities of working in the shadows of corporations.

"We don't get to fall in love."

"Why not?"

"We don't have the rights, I suppose."

That answer stung. It was painful but true, Teddy Dee knew. It took him a moment to regain his thoughts. He studied the older man dressed in a thousand-dollar tailor made suit.

Oscar Easton was everything that Teddy Dee was not. He was a shorter, thinner, older man with a neatly trimmed moustache. Not six foot tall. Not two hundred pounds. Easton was a legend in Chicago and in the shadow world that he had brought Teddy Dee.

He was maybe ten or twenty years older than Teddy Dee. It was hard to tell. The telltale signs of aging were missing on Oscar Easton.

He had no pot belly. He had no visible aging marks that screamed out forty or fifty or any age really. His hair, short and close to his head had some gray in it but that did not give away his age. Teddy Dee had seen many men with a sprinkling of gray in their hair, like Easton, as early as thirty and as late as sixty.

Teddy Dee studied his mentor's hands but they gave nothing away. His hands were veined and brown and long. Oscar Easton had big hands and small wrists. That did not give away his age.

"Haven't you ever been in love?"

"Yes, more times than I like to admit. But the difference is that I have never been selfish enough to do anything about it."

"What would have happened if you had been selfish?"

"She would have been..." Easton did not finish.

"What if, whoever that woman was, she had been the one person that changed you."

"Whose to say that she wasn't," Easton concluded. He added, "There is no fairytale endings for us. We don't get the princess. We aren't invited to the dining table. You have to remember; we work for them. We are not them."

Chapter One.

The hum of the engine faded. The pain in his body subsided. Suddenly, Teddy Dee was falling deeper and deeper into the embrace of sleep.

On the other side of sleep Teddy Dee found himself suddenly strapped to a doctor's examining table. The table was sturdy and overhead was a singular light shining into his face.

Somehow, he had loosened the straps and escaped the table only to find himself trapped in the austere examining room. There were pictures in frames on the wall but the pictures were white. Those pictures of nothing were disturbing and made Teddy Dee fearful in the dream.

He tried the door and it was locked. Teddy Dee, in the dream, looked for another escape. There were no windows. The walls were all smooth.

So, he returned to the door and tried the locked door again only to find it turn under his hand. Teddy Dee pushed open the door and walked out and into the barren white hallway. The hallway went left and right. He went instinctively left.

Teddy Dee walked down the quiet hallway following the pathway until he passed one then another door before coming to the end of the hallway where a door stood. He tried the door and of course, it was locked. Teddy Dee reversed his course and tried the next door only to find it locked also. The third door on the left was unlocked.

Teddy Dee entered the dark room and the room stretched out before him. At the far end of the room was another door. Teddy Dee opened the door and found himself again in a barren white hallway.

The dream shifted and suddenly Teddy Dee noticed that a brown faced beauty with glasses was beside him. She was beautiful. The nameless beauty was wearing a gray hooded sweater over a blueberry colored V-neck T-shirt. She was wearing matching blueberry and lemon splashed skort that looked more suited for tennis than anything else. On her small feet were nob nailed work boots.

"What?" The beautiful stranger sneered half joking, half serious. "You can look at me all longingly and puppy dog found his bone all you want but we are trapped. We have to get out of this." She motioned to the hallway and Teddy Dee slowly looked from her near perfect skin to the hallway.

"You have to concentrate," the gorgeous woman wearing glasses advised. "This is serious. It is all fun and games until they send in the guys with the shotguns."

Teddy Dee suddenly narrowed his eyes, in the dream, and looked past the brown skinned beauty to see shadowy figures moving quickly down the long hallway.

Teddy Dee and the stranger began to run, trying every door as they ran down the hallway away from the shadowy figures.

Another door opened under Teddy Dee's hand and he and the stranger entered. The room was similar to the examining room except there was a couch and coffee table and several chairs in it. On one of the tables was a magazine. On one of the chairs was an umbrella and hat.

"Look," the beauty pointed to the right and Teddy Dee saw a set of stairs leading up and into the white of the wall.

"Let's head for the door," Teddy Dee countered and he and the black beauty ran to the door, opened it and exited the room as the shadowy figures entered.

Once again, Teddy Dee and the bespectacled woman were in a hallway. Teddy Dee paused and leaned against the door that they had just exited.

"What now?"

Teddy Dee cut his eyes at the stranger and for an instant thought about strangling her. That mad moment dissipated. He smiled.

"We are in a maze," Teddy Dee announced.

The beauty smirked as if Teddy Dee's revelation was old news. Teddy Dee found himself battling with his madness again. He smiled and the rage that had been momentarily aimed at the spirited beauty was redirected toward the shadowy figures chasing them.

"Okay, so the quickest way out of a maze is to move toward the middle and then look for an exit."

"Says who?"

"Says me," Teddy Dee said as the door he was leaning against pushed hard against his back and then like a heavy breeze hitting a barrier faded. Teddy Dee looked left and right surprised that he had held back the invisible threat. He knew instinctively that there were people trying to come through the door that he alone barred.

"So, we are heading left until left runs out."

The beauty had stood in the hallway, her hand on her hip, all pouty and sexy. Teddy Dee had no time to appreciate that pout or sexiness. He was focused on getting out of this maze.

"Move," Teddy Dee shouted as he ran headlong left and down the hallway. They, he and the beauty, moved quickly away from the door. The woman was a great runner and easily kept up with Teddy Dee. She weighed half as much as the giant, he figured.

"Dammit, stay focused Teddy," the beauty yelled in his ear.

At the end of the hallway there was a growling were bear. It was a man in combat boots, jeans, no shirt and a gigantic bear head; a were bear. Teddy Dee, always a fighter balled his fists and stepped forward ready for a fight.

The were bear swiped at Teddy Dee with claws and raked his knife-like claws across Teddy Dee's chest. Teddy Dee recoiled. He grabbed at his chest feeling the intense pain suddenly.

Teddy Dee sat up on the hammock in the small room and replayed that dream again in his mind. A maze. A girl. A doctor's room. Trapped. Hunted. Escaping danger.

Teddy Dee recalled. He was no psychologist. He didn't put much stock in dream analysis. He thought most of the people that believed in zodiacs, horoscopes, fortune telling, and the like were weak minded. Yet, as he rethought the theme of the dream he could see some recurring ideas. His life was complicated. It was a rat's nest of problems that rarely had simple solutions. There was always a girl in the mess that was his life. He was trapped. Teddy Dee had lived this cloak and dagger life so long that he couldn't imagine a life that didn't involve the high risk and reward that had become his life. Escaping danger was just a part of the business. That was his life.

The corporate blooder blinked and considered his present situation. Teddy Dee was once again a wanted criminal, he thought in the close quarters that was his cabin on the Ghanzou Shipping and Freight cargo ship. Teddy Dee imagined that the cabin he was in had been a makeshift room, just off the galley. The captain had given Elijah and him a few foodstuffs to survive the twelve-hour sea voyage.

While Teddy Dee sat on a small hammock that was secured by two eye bolts in the ceiling of the cabin he found himself recalling the last three days of his international adventure that had begun nearly nine months before after he was released from Kulani Correctional Facility on Hilo. One name came to mind as he looked back nearly a year to the various and seemingly random events that had lead him to the Ghanzou Shipping and Freight cargo ship; Elliott Winslow.

Roland Cambridge, Katherine Rogers, and Samantha Morris, and Tanaka Fujinaka had all played their parts. Roland Cambridge had been the friend who had given Teddy Dee the chance when no one had given him a chance. "Alabama" Fleming, the curvaceous beauty that had met Teddy Dee after his return from Ecuador, intrigued Teddy Dee. He knew that she was trouble from the start but her endless curves and infectious smile and lilting laugh held him like the mythical Sirens. Samantha Morris had surprised and intrigued Teddy Dee when he thought that was no longer possible. Even Fujinaka had played his part but it had taken Teddy Dee nearly nine months to realize the connection between all of them.

Less than an hour from the port and Yu Li knocked and poked his head into the cabin.

"We should begin offloading in forty-five minutes. You can leave as soon as we begin," he said in broken English.

Teddy Dee nodded.

The Ghanzou Shipping and Freight cargo ship docked and the gigantic ship was suddenly busy. There were men everywhere doing everything to secure the mammoth ship to the Hong Kong dock. Ropes were thrown. Men ran here and there. Yu Li escorted Elijah and Teddy Dee to the gangway and gestured for them to leave with the four crewmen already lined up to climb down the gangway.

Elijah and Teddy Dee fell in line behind the four crewmen as they arrived in Hong Kong. The pair walked the dock following the crewmen. At the far end of the dock Teddy Dee noticed that there was a man dressed in a suit.

On the dock waiting for Teddy Dee and Elijah Graham was a small square faced man with a crew cut dressed in a green checked business suit holding up a placard in English that read: Theodore + One.

“Think you are the plus one,” Teddy Dee smiled at Elijah.

"I am Theodore," Teddy Dee said.

"I am Cho," the driver dressed in a green checked suit and white collared shirt, wearing an earring in his ear said and bowed reverently.

“You pick up a lot of people at the cargo docks?”

“No, but Mister Kim wanted to make sure that you knew that you were safe.” Cho smiled, awkwardly.

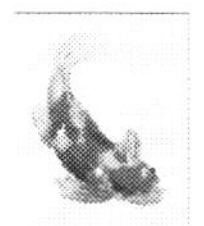  

The clouds were gathering off the coast of Japan. The coming storm had been forecast for days but the storm had dangled in the Sea of Japan for days threatening to come to ground but then turning and returning to sea only to build more power. This storm because of its behavior was called: Yo-yo. The predictions of Yo-yo's intensity were varied. Initially, the unnamed storm had been thought to be a drencher and nothing more. Yet, after three days in the Sea of Japan and building intensity Yo-yo seemed to be the first possible hurricane level storm of the season.

Asami Fujinaka, dressed in a red kimono, walked into the conference room silently as the men gathered, chatted amongst themselves, and adjusted in the chairs to watch the video. The daughter of Hiro Fujinaka, President of Signet Industries, smiled as she took in the boardroom filled with familiar faces. The dozen or so members of the board and their security details all knew Asami Fujinaka. She was the niece of most. The ones that she was not blood related to she knew from years of interaction with the business of one of Japan's largest herbal companies.

So, as Asami Fujinaka walked slowly and deliberately into the boardroom noting the swish and whoosh of her silk kimono's movement the daughter of Hiro Fujinaka counted the members of her family in the conference room. There were six members of the Fujinaka family present. One of her uncles was absent. That absence surprised Asami Fujinaka. All of the board members were required to be present on the first meeting of each quarter. It was the meeting that detailed the financial outlook for the multi-national company.

Asami Fujinaka found her place beside her mother and tried to think what could cause her uncle to be absent from the quarterly meeting.

"Did you check on your father?"

Asami nodded.

"Mother, aren't all the members invited to the board meeting?"

"Of course," her mother said dressed in the traditional kimono like herself.

"Then why are there only six members inside?"

"They are sometimes a little slow to arrive."

Asami nodded.

There were voices suddenly being raised as the gathered talked.

Hiro Fujinaka sat in the conference room with his son, Tanaka, who had been named the US delegate of Signet Industries. In the room sat the seven elders of the Fujinaka family and board members of Signet Industries. The only people in the conference room other than the Fujinaka family were the three members of the advertising firm tasked with creating the video and Daiki Kirasawa, managing COO of Signet Industries.

The dour Akimitsu Fujinaka, who looked like a miniature sumo wrestler, sat at the conference table dressed in a striped three-piece suit that made him look like an overstuffed candy cane, was flanked by his two sons; Fumihiro and Gakuto. Next to Akimitsu sat the dapper Arashi Fujinaka.

Arashi Fujinaka was reportedly in a relationship with one of the national Kabuki dance troupe. His sexuality was always at issue, especially with the publicly reported tryst with a still unidentified Kabuki performer. Next to Arashi Fujinaka sat the be-speckled Bishamon Fujinaka, who looked as if he should be in a bank somewhere, instead of at a board meeting for one of Japan's biggest pharmaceutical manufacturers.

Bishamon Fujinaka had tried three times to become the chairman of the board of directors and failed. He was a cold and calculating individual and no one to play with. Next to Bishamon sat Aito Fujinaka.

Aito Fujinaka was the peacemaker. He got along with everyone for some reason. He posed no threat to anyone. Aito was an average looking individual with black hair, a slight potbelly and a friendly face. He was the first cousin of Hiro Fujinaka. He sat the closest to his cousin. On either side of him were his brothers; Choukichi and Eiichi Fujinaka.

Choukichi, the eldest, was a dull witted bully who drank too much and gambled recklessly. He liked fast cars and fast women. Too often Choukichi had brought shame upon the Fujinaka family name. Choukichi was the bad boy in the boardroom. He had been arrested a half a dozen times for drunkenness and belligerence. Aito Fujinaka had admitted to Hiro more than once that he wouldn't shed too many tears if he got news that Choukichi had been found dead in a gutter somewhere.

Unlike Choukichi, Eiichi Fujinaka had graduated from university and become a manager for one of the peripheral businesses created by Signet Industries. Eiichi Fujinaka had decided to open a sushi bar at one of the offices for the pharmaceutical firms. He had begun humbly and after five years had nearly a dozen sushi shops catering to the influential and powerful in Japan's corporate world.

The lights went down.

The gathered suits and lawyers mumbled until the video began.

The video began with a black screen. The screen faded in. The Spring blossoms were the first things that were observed.

Japan was a mysterious place to the outside world long ago. The ways of Eastern healing were still rumored. Some believed that Eastern medicine, with its lack of medicinal products, was backwards.

Yet, the herbalist was a very noble position in most villages in Japan. When anyone fell ill they called first for the elder and the leader and then the herbalist. The elder of the village was the most respected individual and sometimes, by default, the leader of the village. It was the elder that usually requested the herbalist.

In the village of Osa the herbalist that everyone depended on was Hiro Fujinaka. He was a short, stout man with black hair and dark eyes that seemed to burn with a distant fire. Hiro Fujinaka was a farmer. He was also the village herbalist.

Hiro Fujinaka had learned the power of herbs when he was a rice farmer in a province in Japan. He was a farmer like his father and his father before him. Through chance and misfortune Hiro Fujinaka had stumbled upon a chance to utilize his herbal knowledge and assist a wealthy businessman.

Hiro Fujinaka had gone to Okayama for supplies and to visit a sick cousin. He rarely left Osa. Yet, he had made the journey to Okayama and in that city he had changed his future.

The story of the creation of the Royal Family Remedy Company was legendary. The Fujinaka family knew it from their great ancestor Hiro Fujinaka. The story seemed impossible and mythical at times.

Chapter Two.

Teddy Dee had been in Atlanta when he got the job in Hawaii. He had flown to Hawaii from Atlanta. He had signed on to help the shit heel, Elliott Winslow, who had screwed up in Hawaii. Teddy Dee should have known better. Just reading the synopsis of the problem Teddy Dee learned that the shit heel, Winslow, was a vice president of a corporation in Hawaii and that he was the typical rich kid. He had been groomed early to take over the family business. He had gone to some of the best schools. Teddy Dee noted that in college Winslow had been arrested a number of times soliciting prostitutes and nearly expelled for lascivious acts. When he had left college he had returned to Hawaii and all the hijinks had continued in Hawaii.

Teddy Dee should have, right then and there, with all those red flags turned around and returned to Atlanta. Reading the background information on Elliott Winslow on the flight to Hawaii Teddy Dee realized that the man that he was trying to keep out of prison had a history of being caught with his pants down.

The arrest had come after Winslow had roughed up an escort named: Gemini. The possible prison sentence revolved around Elliott Winslow and his threats of violence in the presence of others to said underage she male. Gemini was reported to be sixteen and higher than a kite when Winslow was arrested for statutory rape. The statutory rape had been pushed to assault and battery when Winslow decided to get tough with Gemini before the police arrived. Winslow, based on the criminal report, had been drunk and belligerent and fought everyone that dared to look at him that night, including three officers.

Teddy Dee did not cherry pick jobs. He liked challenges. Yet, as he read the mission synopsis, Teddy Dee found himself liking the shit heel less and less. He should have run in the opposite direction of Elliott Winslow. Instead, he had a face-to-face with the shit heel to finalize details.

So, Teddy Dee had flown to Hawaii and met with Elliott Winslow. The meeting had been in the Royal Hawaiian Hotel. The Royal Hawaiian Hotel was one of the oldest hotels on the island.

"I love this bar," Elliott Winslow, tanned and blonde, remarked sipping a martini, in Teddy Dee's memories. He was dressed in a Tommy Bahama Hawaiian print shirt, khaki trousers, and casual brown dress shoes. On his wrist was a Rolex, the only thing that stated that Winslow had money. He might have been another tourist come to the Royal Hawaiian Hotel from the mainland except for his tan and Rolex. "I don't know if you know this or not but they say that heads of state, Hollywood stars and international jet-setters have mingled with kama'aina to sip cocktails while taking in Diamond Head, Waikiki Beach and the Pacific," the blonde haired man that smelled of wood and lavender smiled waving his hand to take in the seaside bar.

Teddy Dee did not know anything about the Royal Hawaiian Hotel. It was a hotel. Dressed in a suit jacket and trousers, Teddy Dee was sweating in his collared shirt and tie. He did not give one whit about the Royal Hawaiian Hotel. Hotels were places to rest your head, nothing more, to Teddy Dee. There were hotels that cost more than others and had more amenities but the differences were lost on Teddy Dee. What did it matter to Teddy Dee that the Royal Hawaiian Hotel was a 1927 landmark? He was not born during that time.

Yet, Teddy Dee had listened to Elliott Winslow studying the two men that Winslow had brought with him that night to discuss his delicate situation. The two men did not speak. They sat and watched Teddy Dee.

The pair of intimidators, both younger than Winslow, were dressed in Hawaiian print shirts. One was wearing a print shirt that had sea turtles swimming across the fabric from front to back. He looked as if he had played some sports. The sea turtle had broad shoulders and a thickness of neck and forearms that seemed gym created. He squinted his watery blue eyes, as if he might need glasses, and sat and sipped on a Belgian beer.

The other man at the table was wearing a pineapple and coconut dominated print. He was taller than Winslow and the sea turtle and carried himself like he might have been a boxer at one time. He moved more fluidly than the sea turtle. So, Teddy Dee calculated that of the two pineapple and coconut would be the tougher opponent, if it came to a fight. Teddy Dee listened and idly played out scenarios where he had to disarm one or both of the men at the table.

"There is a little bit of a sticky situation that you were asked to assist me in," Winslow smiled as the sea turtle and pineapple and coconut juniors watched the beautiful people sitting in the bar with their toes in the sand.

Teddy Dee did not like that Winslow wanted to discuss the matter in the open. Then again Teddy Dee thought that there was less of a chance that the

Mai Tai Bar would be bugged by anyone that could use the conversation against Winslow or Teddy Dee. So, he listened.

"There is a court trial that is imminent and we cannot win. So, we have to figure out a way to make sure that I do not walk into that courtroom or that there is no trial."

Teddy Dee nodded, thinking.

"Any questions?"

"Can you give me a list of everyone you have already used?" Teddy Dee asked. He thought and added: "Is there anyone still working to resolve this?"

Elliott Winslow tilted his head slightly and narrowed his ice blue eyes just a little, measuring Teddy Dee. It looked as if he was trying to decide if Teddy Dee was kidding but not sure. He smiled finally.

"Yeah, my assistant will get you your list and anything else you need. Just call the office tomorrow." Elliott Winslow narrowed his eyes again. "Now, on the other subject," he twisted his thin lips, trying to find the right words. "We cannot put all our eggs in one basket," Winslow smiled. "So, we are attempting a number of avenues to stop this madness from moving forward." Winslow paused, he seemed to lose interest.

Teddy Dee followed Winslow's eye line and saw that he was looking at a table with three women that looked as if they were in Hawaii to celebrate someone's birthday or wedding engagement. Winslow smiled at the table of women. He turned back to Teddy Dee. "Is there anything else?" Winslow asked, suddenly more interested in the table of strangers.

He should have known then and there that Elliot Winslow was toxic. Toxic relationships, in the hive, usually ended badly. The client was usually high maintenance and could not be pleased even with a successful effort.

Teddy Dee did not care what was the crime that Elliott Winslow had committed. It wasn't his concern. All he cared about was stopping Elliott Winslow from going to jail or in this case for the trial to proceed to its conclusion. That was the job. He was tasked to extricate Winslow. It seemed an easy task.

Five minutes into the face-to-face and Teddy Dee had Elliott Winslow figured out for a snake. Teddy Dee did not care that Winslow was a snake. Teddy Dee did not discriminate. He worked for snakes and non-snakes everyday but Elliott Winslow was a particularly slimy snake. Winslow was a sleazy, perverted, condescending, unapologetic snake.

Looking past the negatives of Elliott Winslow was easy for Teddy Dee. Everyone had negatives. Teddy Dee did not look at the person. He could not. He looked at the job and not the individual. The executive, whoever it was, was meaningless to Teddy Dee. He needed their name, picture, face and vital details but little more. When Teddy Dee stepped from the shadows he was a man on a mission. Extricating executives was nothing new for Teddy Dee. He was always pulling executives bacon out of the fire. It was part of the job.

Teddy Dee smiled at Elliott Winslow. He looked at the coconut bodyguard. He checked the sea turtle intimidator.

"No, that's all," Teddy Dee said and climbed to his feet and stepped away from the table with Winslow and his two mute friends. Teddy Dee walked out of the Mai Tai Bar, listening to Elliott Winslow loudly talking to coconut and sea turtle.

"You know that the greatest aphrodisiac on earth is being rich and powerful," Elliott Winslow laughed. "My tastes are rather exotic," he continued as Teddy Dee reached the hotel and the noise and Winslow's voice faded. The three women had been seated with Elliott Winslow and the coconut and sea turtle when Teddy Dee climbed the stairs and made his way to the lobby of the Royal Hawaiian.

So, Teddy Dee walked away and tried to figure out how to succeed and complete the job given to him by Elliott Winslow. He did not know at that moment how he would grapple with the problem. He needed more information. Teddy Dee crossed the oldest hotel in Hawaii and made his way to his rental car.

As he drove to his new digs, in Hawaii, Teddy Dee tried to imagine a scenario that ended with Elliott Winslow not doing any prison time. Teddy Dee thought through several ideas but every time he came to a roadblock not knowing what had been done prior to his arrival.

He usually stayed in hotels close to the airport for convenience. He liked the ease of location. He could get in and get out quickly at an airport hotel. It was his signature. It was a part of his routine.

Hotels, and particular airport hotels, rarely asked a lot of questions. They were built on the premise of short stays and privacy. They prided themselves in those two elements. So, they were cleaned regularly and secured always.

Yet, every once in awhile Teddy Dee treated himself to five star hotels when staying longer than a week. In that case he preferred high-end hotels because he could do anything there and not have to worry about police showing up unannounced. High end also meant that there was security and security made most rethink the idea of doing anything stupid.

In Hawaii, Teddy Dee rented a beachfront condo near the Waikiki beach. It was, according to the advertisement, the vacation rental was an oceanfront panoramic view suite.

Teddy Dee drove to his beachfront home and noted that though it was already night the streets were still bustling. As he got closer to where he was staying he noted that the foot traffic lessened. There were a few people on the street but nothing like when he was downtown or at the Royal Hawaiian. He was in one of the hottest areas in Hawaii and next-door neighbors with flash in the pan celebrities and starlets. Teddy Dee had come upon the location quite by accident. When Teddy Dee had been asked to come to Hawaii he had done a quick Internet search of rental properties that were in Teddy Dee's agreed upon price range and came upon the beachfront location.

Teddy Dee arrived at his beachfront condominium he was renting for the month and walked through the suite trying to imagine who lived there regularly. He knew that it was a couple. They were young, compared to Teddy Dee. He estimated that the couple was in their thirties. From the books in the bookcase it seemed that one of them liked comic books. One of them liked cooking.

Pulling a graphic novel from the bookcase Teddy Dee took the book and walked to the balcony to think. He sat in the dark of the night listening to the waves crashing on the beach below and the occasional sound of laughter from couples walking on the beach and opened the graphic novel. The balcony railing was lighted and gave off just enough light to read.

Teddy Dee read the first couple of pages and found himself interested in the novel. The story was about a hero that was fighting an unknown villain who seemed to know the hero somehow. The villain had left a list of twenty people and that list was a list of the hero's closest friends. The villain told the hero that he was going to kidnap, torture and kill one of the people on the list.

The story was complicated because the villain was toying with the hero. The villain had left a cryptic clue about the first person that he would kidnap and then torture and finally kill. The hero who was gifted with incredible intelligence and resourcefulness had to decipher the clue and thwart the unnamed villain. The hero was given an impossible task and what kept Teddy Dee turning the pages was that the hero could not contact anyone he cared about for fear that the contact would signal the kidnapping and eventual torture of that person. So, the hero was doing all the detective and hero work in the shadows, unbeknownst to everyone he cared about.

Teddy Dee read halfway through the graphic novel before stopping and replacing the book in the library. He stripped off his work togs and donned his workout gear. It was nearly ten o'clock when he walked into the gym in the condominium and began his two-hour routine. Teddy Dee was a physical force and to keep himself sharp he trained to that end. He confused his body with constant, varied, high intensity efforts. The workout was a little weight lifting, some aerobic work, interval efforts and pushing his body to its limits.

One hundred and twenty minutes from the beginning of his workout Teddy Dee made his way back to his condominium. He showered. He cleaned up. He ate. He went to bed.

Teddy Dee woke for the first morning in Hawaii and noted the slight differences of Hawaii compared to the states and other places he had visited. The sun was smaller for some reason Teddy Dee noted. The beach, in the morning was already a hive of activity. There were men and women and children already out on the sand enjoying the morning warmth. It was a mild morning.

So, while the waves crashed on the beach Teddy Dee noted that there was a chin up bar placed in the condo. Teddy Dee did a non-weight training session. He began with the simplest and easiest; sit ups and push ups. He finished his first morning training with twenty-five pull ups.

Teddy Dee heard a knock at the door.

On the other side of the door was a bespectacled black man wearing a Hawaiian shirt and headphones. Teddy Dee opened the door and studied the twenty something in front of him.

"Need you to sign for this," the messenger smiled extending his hand and producing a thin electronic notepad. He had a shoulder bag over his shoulder and a Fast Delivery decal stitched on the bag. The messenger handed Teddy Dee a package and nodded as Teddy Dee handed back the notepad with a scrawl that looked like a plus sign and an empty bow minus the arrow.

The messenger turned and walked down the hall unconcerned if Teddy Dee had any questions. In less than ten seconds the messenger was gone and Teddy Dee was left standing with the door to his suite open. He closed the door and went to the balcony and opened the package. Inside were all the details of the trial including all the names of the jurors, the judge, the prosecutor and the defense team. Teddy Dee marveled at the resourcefulness of the corporations when executives were in jeopardy.

Teddy Dee sat in the oceanfront suite and tried to think of a way that he could fix this unfixable problem. Teddy Dee realized that he had come in after several failed attempts to stop the trial. The judge had been approached to no success. The prosecutor had refused to speak to anyone associated with the case without witnesses and taping of the entire meeting.

The work Teddy Dee was contracted for in Hawaii was just making sure the case never made it to trial. The job was simple enough. All Teddy Dee had to do was stop the trial in whatever way was possible from happening.

His instructions were clear. Teddy Dee was to insure that the client saw no prison time. Teddy Dee was to protect the client. The trial was already underway when Teddy Dee arrived. It seemed the only logical conclusion.

Teddy Dee poured over the papers and assessed the situation and figured that the easiest way to protect the client was to derail the whole system. Those that had come before him had thought too small. His focus switched from the client to figuring out a way to create a mistrial.

Of all the thousands of criminal and questionable jobs that Teddy Dee had participated in while trying to use the eight simple rules Teddy Dee didn't imagine that a corrupt and power hungry megalomaniac would be the catalyst of Teddy Dee's inevitable change.

The jury was made up of twelve members. Nine jurors were men. There was only three women on the jury.

Half of the jury were upright. The first half of the jury was squeaky clean. The worse that any of them had done, as far as Teddy Dee's research suggested, was speeding tickets, there was a driving under the influence violation, a shoplifting charge that was later dropped, and driving without a license. There was nothing significant enough to use as leverage against any of them.

Teddy Dee looked at Mary Flood with hopes that she had some darker side to her squeaky clean persona. Mary Flood had been a business major at Harvard University and was recruited to International Business Machines out of college. She had worked for International Business Machines for five years and left when Microsoft hired her as a Vice President of Information Technology. Flood had launched Vista. She was incredibly powerful and had landed in Hawaii only five years ago and was now running one of Hawaii's largest computer firms. She was the sole woman on the jury and a very focused and efficient individual.

Mary Flood was married to a doctor named: Lionel and the mother of two beautiful daughters: Heather and Danielle. The Floods and their wealth in

Hawaii had been compared to the likes of the lofty talents in the techno-geeks world.

Harold Bell was the oldest member of the jury. He was 65 years of age and an ex-Navy mechanic.

Stewart Black was the owner of a construction company and a local celebrity of sorts having done the Ironman Triathlon five times.

Jason Evans was the owner of several gas stations on the island and an avid fisherman. He owned a fishing fleet of six boats that took tourists out to fish for marlin and cod.

Kirk Neil was the son of a surfer who had found a way to make Teddy Dee's hobby into a career. He had been asked to be on the board to bring a different perspective to the energy company. It was Teddy Dee's ideas of an energy rebate that had made Hawaii Energy one of the most innovative energy companies in America.

Matthew Sutcliffe was an automobile dealer who had been ahead of the curve when the gas crisis hit everyone else. He had bought a dozen electric cars and rented them to local rental car locations and eventually selling them for a huge profit.

Those six were impervious to bribery or intimidation.

In 1856 Daiki Yuuta was visiting Okayama and fell ill.

Daiki Yuuta was one of the emperor's emissaries. He was sent to areas where the emperor preferred not to go unless absolutely necessary. As a result, Daiki Yuuta was a very important person for the emperor. He was the eyes and ears of the emperor in the outlying areas of the empire.

Yuuta traveled with a small entourage. He had his personal assistant; Engo. Yuuta also had a business assistant, Rishu, who made sure that the emissary addressed issues that the emperor required. He had his required bodyguards; Fuuto and Fukashi. Yuuta also brought with him Haruka, his cultural attaché. Haruka was responsible for knowing who was essential to talk to wherever they went.

The cultural attaché had arranged the Okayama visit. It had been planned for months. Being in Okayama was very special honor. The emperor's emissary's arrival set the small town on its ear.

The provincial leader, Makito, had made a special request and invited Daiki Yuuta to stay at his humble home; a 24-bedroom castle that overlooked the China Sea. The merchants' council had planned a lavish luncheon for Yuuta to display their wares and entertain the emperor's select messenger who had never been to Okayama. There was a parade scheduled to showcase Okayama's potential. Several schools were pressed into service to show off their brightest and most brilliant students in Okayama. Yuuta was to be in Okayama for five days. Each day was to begin with a brilliant display of Okayama and by lunch Yuuta was to marvel at the hidden gem that was the small fishing town on the border of the China Sea. At night, Yuuta, it was hoped, would be made aware of the cultural depth of Okayama. There were singers, dancers, entertainers, and musical events planned for every night that the emperor's emissary was to be in Okayama. Yet, it was not to be. Yuuta had fallen ill three days after his arrival in Okayama.

He had the night before the merchant's luncheon visited a cabinet maker and considered purchasing a dozen of his largest and best made storage cabinets. Yuuta had also gone and been impressed by the local delicacies at a local market. The emissary had lunch with, Masa Nakamura, the largest landholder in Okayama and discussed the future of Okayama with the elder Tanaka.

As evening approached Yuuta had returned to the humble home of the provincial leader and been invited to dine with the oldest and most influential family in Okayama. Yuuta and the provincial leader and their entourage had gone to the castle home of Sadao Dan. There they had a sumptuous meal of rice, fish, and vegetables. They were treated to an unexpected treat of rice ice cream. Afterwards, the emissary and the mayor had been entertained by a very talented group of dancers led by a hauntingly beautiful girl named: Sakura.

After a long night of drinking, dancing, and laughter Yuuta and the provincial leader returned to the provincial leader's humble home. Tired and slightly drunk Yuuta had fallen asleep with dreams of the beautiful and bewitching Sakura.

The next day Yuuta woke and found himself drained of all energy. He, literally, could not lift a finger. The emissary panicked. He called for help.

Instantly, his bedroom door slid open and Fuuto and Fukashi, his two guards, entered the bedroom with swords drawn. They, his personal guard, found that Yuuta was unable to summon enough strength to climb out of bed. Worse yet Yuuta was unable to do the business of the emperor. He sent for his assistant. Instantly, Engo, the assistant, was sent to find a remedy.

The assistant pressed Rishu and Haruka into service to help him find a remedy for his master's ailment. The trio sought out a number of doctors but no one could remedy their master's ailment.

By the end of the third day everyone in Okayama had heard of the ailment of Daiki Yuuta. Remedies were wide and varied. Some suggested teas. Others suggested leeches. Even others suggested acupuncture. Yet, no remedy brought back the emperor's emissary's strength.

Hiro Fujinaka had been in Okayama when he heard of the wealthy businessman in need of a remedy. Fujinaka had wanted to visit the businessman but was not allowed. The home where the wealthy businessman was staying was that of the provincial leader and no one was allowed to enter his gates without a letter of introduction. Yet, Fujinaka was not deterred. He went to the gate and spoke to one of the guards and told him that he was an herbalist.

"There have been many doctors, herbalists, and specialists who have come to see the emissary. They have all believed that they knew what the ailment was but have been incorrect in remedying his particular ailment."

Fujinaka listened to the guard.

"Our master, the provincial leader, wishes Yuuta a speedy recovery. He had only been here for three days and fallen ill. He is a powerfully built man, strong of mind and body. My master had invited him to the province numerous times but this was the first time that his schedule allowed him five days to visit. As a result, my master treated him to some local delicacies that were only found in this region. Our guest was particularly fascinated by the beets grown here. He could not get enough of them. It was a great thing and honor to have someone of such stature in our province. Now, we are dishonored."

"I think that I might be able to restore honor to your house," Fujinaka decided.

The guard looked at the little man curiously.

"When I return I will have in hand a solution."

With that, Fujinaka walked away from the provincial leader's house.

Hearing of the guest's activities and gastronomical tastes Fujinaka went out and found a particular root and herb to restore honor to the house of the provincial leader. He chopped up the herb and boiled the root that he had hunted for an hour in the cliffs near the coast of Hyogo. The ingredients were placed in a pot to brew for an hour.

Chapter Three.

While incarcerated Teddy Dee was mandated to twelve sessions of psychological observation by a Jacob Givorny, PhD. Givorny was a brilliant man. He was hired by the state of Hawaii to determine if inmates at Kulani Correctional Facility should be paroled or not.

The first session with Jacob Givorny PhD was an hour of introduction and box checking. He asked fact driven and open-ended questions in that first session. Teddy Dee listened and answered only the fact driven questions.

"You understand that I have to decide if you get paroled?"

Teddy Dee understood. He also understood that he was only sentenced to two years in Kulani Correctional and after a year he only had a year remaining. There was no real need to jump through hoops for a parole that would never come.

Givorny was not deterred. He continued his sessions with Teddy Dee and each session Teddy Dee stonewalled the prison psychologist.

There were moments, Teddy Dee had to admit, that he wanted to answer some of the psychologist's questions. They were tempting questions. They were ticklish questions. Givorny made Teddy Dee think.

One of the questions that got Teddy Dee thinking the most was: Has there ever been a time that you found your beliefs to be incorrect?

Teddy Dee had walked out of the psychologist's office and back to his cell thinking about that question.

He had never given the idea of his beliefs much thought. He worked for others. Teddy Dee was a tool used to the benefit of others.

He had done incredible things as that tool and simultaneously bad things. He was no boy scout by any stretch of the imagination. Teddy Dee was no monster either. In the near decade in the shadows he had done good things and bad. The bad outweighed the good by far. Yet, there was a few times that Teddy Dee had done good. It was one good thing that came to mind after the Givorny session; Albert Buck.

Albert Buck was a multi-millionaire who had a small construction and real estate development company that had through a bunch of unexpected developments found themselves working with Disneyland.

As Teddy Dee fell asleep the memories of happier times came to mind.

In front of him sat a balding man wearing a gray long sleeve shirt, Dodgers baseball cap, and reading glasses. The man was in his early forties but completely out of shape. Though he must weigh 150 pounds he had a visible beer belly. In front of him was a coffee cup, open book, and laptop.

Across from the Dodgers fan sat another dough boy of a man, 245-260 pounds, wearing gym shorts and a matching black and red Air Jordan outfit. The man had a zippered fronted jacket, socks, and basketball low top sneakers sporting the flying Michael Jordan logo. Air Jordan had a laptop in front of him. He was furiously typing the next great novel, recipe, or business report.

The thing was that the man was round faced, like a basketball and eating pastries from the coffee shop bakery. He looked like the anti-poster boy for Air Jordan and Nike.

Behind the Dodgers fan was a round faced Asian with short cropped hair wearing a running jacket and shorts. He was wearing Clark Kent like glasses and texting in between reading and writing notes. The Asian Clark Kent pouted as he read.

A beautiful Asian girl wearing a "Cal" hooded sweatshirt walked into the coffee shop wearing Ugg boots and tight black jeans. She had long, straight black hair and a curious Anime look about her. She sat down four tables away from Teddy Dee with her iced coffee and opened her binder.

Teddy Dee watched the beautiful stranger tilt her head to read. Instantly, the Asian beauty ran a pink acrylic painted handful of fingernails through her raven black hair to toss it from one side of her head to the other. Teddy Dee couldn't help but watch the young, beautiful woman reading.

Behind the beautiful Asian was a pair of boys dressed in T-shirts and faded jeans on laptops. The taller boy had one earphone hanging from his ear. The other boy was on his phone and texting.

Teddy Dee didn't know the man that he was going to meet in the next fifteen to twenty minutes, according to his Rolex Submariner. A drink order was called out and at that exact moment Teddy Dee's phone buzzed. He looked down and did not recognize the number. Teddy Dee tapped the phone and he could hear the faint sound of traffic in the background.

"Hello?"

"Go," Teddy Dee said watching the people in his view for anyone being on the phone.

"I'm running a little behind. Can you wait for another ten minutes?"

"Ten minutes. No problem," Teddy Dee said and rang off. Teddy Dee took a deep breath and looked around the coffee shop once again. He paid attention to changes.

The two boys on the laptops were packing up and getting ready to leave. The anti-poster for basketball was also packing up his laptop and heading for the rear exit of the shop. Teddy Dee watched the three people leave the coffee shop and slowly turned his attention to the Asian girl wearing the "Cal" sweatshirt.

"What are you studying?"

"Philosophy'"

"Interesting. How did you come to that particular subject?"

"I don't know. I just have always been fascinated by the whole idea of philosophy really," the beautiful Asian stranger smiled tossing her hair from one side of her head to the other. She had her noise canceling earphones around her neck to talk.

Teddy Dee nodded. "Sounds fascinating. Do you have a particular interest? Do you lean toward one philosopher above them all?"

The Asian narrowed her focus and wrinkling her brow for an instant, thinking.

"I would think that everyone loves Freud but the only thing I know about him is that he related everything to the penis and to our love and hate of our mothers."

The young beauty smiled and laughed awkwardly, suddenly embarrassed.

"Did I embarrass you? Sorry," Teddy Dee smiled.

"I'm not embarrassed," the philosophy student smiled. "I was just surprised that you knew that much about Freud. I would have imagined that you, like most, know of Spock the baby doctor."

Teddy Dee smiled. He liked this woman. She was opinionated. She was young, Teddy Dee calculated. Maybe she was 22 or 23. She was bright. Probably smarter than Teddy Dee by a mile. She would be a challenge.

"My name is Teddy," Teddy Dee smiled extending his hand. Instantly she reached out and took Teddy's hand. Her hand was so small in his.

"Helen," the beauty smiled. "Helen Park."

"Teddy Dee," Teddy lied. He couldn't tell complete strangers his real name. His name could get her or him killed. At least, that was how he justified lying to the young and beautiful Helen Park.

The pair talked and laughed and Teddy Dee concluded with an offer to do something when Helen Park wasn't studying.

"I have a boyfriend," Helen Park tried to deflect.

"Helen, did I ask you about your boyfriend? If you have a boyfriend, then he isn't holding up his part of the deal. No boyfriend I know, including me, would leave you alone at a coffee shop studying." Teddy Dee smiled. "Me, Helen, I would be sitting near you or out getting you lunch or whatever."

Helen Park didn't disagree.

"If you aren't studying and your slacking boyfriend ain't around and you want some attention give me a call. No strings attached. Just a chance to go out and enjoy Los Angeles with a new friend that's not your boyfriend."

Helen Park smiled and Teddy Dee slipped her his card with his phone number on it.

"I know you were studying. Don't let me disturb you," Teddy Dee smiled. "I have a meeting and it looks like he is just arriving." Teddy Dee paused. "Talk to you later, hopefully."

Teddy Dee concentrated on Albert Buck. Albert Buck walked into the coffee shop like he owned it. He was dressed in a dark blue Brooks Brothers hand tailored suit, with a starched white collared shirt and powder blue silk hand tie. Teddy Dee sat and watched as the CFO or CEO searched for him in the small shop.

Albert Buck was a crafty businessman who had acquired his first million before he turned 25 and become a billionaire a decade later. He was now the mind behind the music on the Internet. Teddy Dee knew that Finch had given him a thumbs up and that was good enough to have a fifteen-minute meeting.

Teddy Dee stood up when Albert Buck approached. Teddy Dee scanned the four tables and noticed that a small man wearing a gray T-shirt and blue jeans was sitting at one of the tables with a black Jan Sport backpack sitting in the seat next to him. The small man had a thin mustache and big ears. He had a small netbook in front of him and beside the netbook were several colored folders. Atop the colored folders sat a mechanical pencil and scientific calculator.

Back near the rear of the coffee shop sat three men dressed in loose fitting jeans sipping coffee. One man was white with a military feeling about him. He wore a gray striped collared shirt and had on leather Converse sneakers. He looked like Nick Fury from the comics. One man was black and had a mustache. He was a steely eyed man that looked used to violence. The third man was the older of the three and built like a bull, dressed in a Disneyland hooded sweatshirt. The third man had in earbuds. He was the obvious alpha dog of the three.

Teddy Dee assumed that these were Buck's personal security.

"Mister Buck, nice to finally be able to see you face-to-face," Teddy Dee smiled extending his hand to the gray haired, square shouldered, thin man. Albert Buck smiled broadly as if he had just been told that he had made a million dollars with the handshake.

"Have a seat," Teddy Dee said before Buck could speak. The two men sat at the coffee table. Teddy Dee studied Albert Buck intently. He was looking for bullshit. Everyone had a certain amount.

Albert Buck sat and twitched his nose and Teddy knew that Buck and he were not alone. He had brought protection. No biggie. Teddy Dee wasn't interested in harming Albert Buck, at least, not yet.

"So, can you tell me what brings you to talk to someone like me? Obviously, you have a bunch of people that work for you already."

Albert Buck nodded and stroked his goatee as he seemed to prepare to tell his story and explain the need for Teddy Dee's services. As the corporate bigwig sat in front of Teddy Dee he pulled at his ear lobe, scratched his nose, and rubbed his jacket sleeve like a baseball coach relaying signals to his third base coach. Teddy Dee was amused by the shenanigans for the moment. He would listen and if the story was interesting enough he would consider working for Albert Buck. If the story seemed too thin he would simply call bullshit and walk away from the baseball signaling Buck.

Buck began with the creation of his company. Most corporate bigwigs Teddy Dee knew and spent any amount of time with considered their businesses as a part of their family. Most considered their companies like children birthed from their heads like Zeus. Teddy Dee listened and tried to figure out who Buck was signaling as he spoke.

He had to assume that Albert Buck was signaling the bull in the Disneyland hoodie. As Buck's security was not Teddy Dee's concern at present Teddy Dee didn't care if Buck had brought a pit bull to the meeting. He simply wanted to judge the merit of working for Albert Buck.

"...after we brokered our deal with Disney everything started to fall apart. We were a small company that had figured out a way to improve the greatest place on Earth. Disney needed us. It was and is a great relationship that we at Small Planet have with Disney and most of our clients. When the idea of expanding the brand and establishing a resort in South America was proposed by the bigwigs in Anaheim we thought it seemed a logical development. We have assisted Disney in the creation of two of the three continental Disney parks in Europe, Japan, and hopefully South America." Albert Buck paused.

Teddy Dee looked up and watched as Buck lifted a finger and the crew cut white man wearing a loose fitting windbreaker stepped to the table and placed a drink on the table. Teddy Dee didn't react.

Buck looked at Teddy Dee.

"Continue," Teddy Dee said.

"Very well," Buck smiled and after sipping his drink continued. "So, we did our due diligence. We scouted locations. Deals were made. Contracts were signed. We chose three locations to consider. We were in negotiations for nearly a year before we made our decision. We knew that our decision would be an economic game changer on the continent. So, we chose wisely.

"There are a number of dangerous people in South America. We figured that those people would leave our development alone seeing the bigger picture. We were foolish sir. We were arrogant. And it is because of that ignorance and arrogance that I have need of your services today. The head of our research and development has been kidnapped and we want her brought back to the States unharmed. We are asking to enlist your services of problem solving. You were highly recommended for solving problems that most cannot solve. Andre told me that you are a very capable individual who knows how to be discreet. This is a very sensitive situation.

"Our security was breached and Jana Nichols and Eric Blanding were kidnapped two days ago on the border of Ecuador. We believe that the people responsible are members of one of the Colombian drug cartels. My security team has information that the men that kidnapped Jana and Eric are under the control of despicable man named: Gabriel Zamora. He also goes by the name of "El Gordo." So, that is the job. Can you assist me?"

Teddy Dee didn't react. Instead he thought. Albert Buck was a bull shitter. He had brought his personal security to a meeting about rescuing someone that his security was supposed to be able to protect. Teddy Dee stroked his upper lip and smiled at the question.

"I have a few questions," Teddy Dee smiled.

"Of course," Albert Buck nodded. "Proceed."

"What was your security doing when your two employees were kidnapped?"

Buck explained that the kidnappers had come at night, two days ago, into the compound and killed two guards during the kidnapping. Reports were varied but the gist of the attack was that a dozen interlopers had invaded the compound with high powered weapons. One security team member suggested that the kidnappers were well organized and ex-military. He suggested also that the attack was well coordinated.

Buck countered that report by pointing out that prior to the kidnapping the biggest occurrence had been theft of tools. Security had been adequate but the compound had not expected a concerted assault like the one the night of the kidnapping.

"Is the security team there, now, in Ecuador? If so, what have they found? Who is leading the search and rescue?"

Buck called over the Disneyland security member and allowed him to give a detailed report on what was going on in Ecuador. The man, Raleigh Stewart, was a retired Marine who had fought in several campaigns. He was a no-nonsense individual and straight and to the point.

"Security is still in place at the Ecuador compound. We have twenty men there at present. They are under the leadership of Tyler Getty. Getty is good people. From the last intel I received today Getty sent a search party out but when the trail headed into Colombia the team hesitated to enter into another countries border. So, all trails lead to Colombia."

"Do you think that your security has been compromised?"

"Hard to say," Stewart admitted. "Immediately that is what I'm smelling. The kidnappers knew too much. They attacked with a game plan. They didn't pick anyone else to kidnap. So, of course, we are thinking there is a rat in the kitchen."

Teddy Dee liked Raleigh Stewart. In a fight you needed someone like him.

"Anything else?"

Teddy Dee shook his head, no. Buck sent Stewart away to wait with his men.

"You stipulated that you want Jana back unharmed? Is there a relationship between you and this woman? I ask because kidnapping can quickly change to extortion if that is the case."

Buck was not surprised by the question. He seemed to anticipate it. Albert Buck smiled.

"You don't know me from Adam. I am a devoted husband. I have a loving wife and two children. Teddy, I have been in love with the same woman for nearly 28 years." He paused, closing his eyes and then focusing on Teddy Dee. Albert Buck continued, "No, there is no romantic relationship between Jana and myself, if that is what you're asking. She is my daughter." He quickly added, "Of course, the hope is that you bring everyone back unharmed. But the priority is Jana."

Teddy Dee nodded. He had one more question.

"Are you prepared for the unfortunate news that they might already be dead? If so, what is my job since I will not be able to bring them back unharmed?"

Buck swallowed. The idea of his daughter murdered in Columbia had to be a distasteful idea for the corporate bigwig. Buck took a deep breath and answered:

"I am hiring you to make sure that does not happen. If she is dead bring her back. Alive or dead bring her back. Now, my security team could go down and try and retrieve my daughter but I need someone that can be discreet. I need someone that has a history of extractions and safe returns. I need you to bring my daughter back."

Teddy Dee nodded. Buck was playing up the whole father-daughter angle. He was a businessman, Teddy Dee noted. Buck probably loved his daughter. Maybe, Teddy Dee thought more skeptically, Disney World Developments were breathing down his neck to stay on schedule and a kidnapping was not a way to stay on schedule. A Colombian drug lord trying to extort money or power was bad business no matter how you looked at it. So, if Albert Buck loved his daughter or not was irrelevant. The truth was that Buck's company SWWD a division of Disney International Development was losing money everyday that the two Americans were in the hands of El Gordo.

"I'll be in contact," Teddy Dee said and extended his hand to Albert Buck. Buck took his hand and studied the man in front of him. He shook hands with Teddy Dee and turned to leave the coffee shop.

The concoction that he had dreamed of the night before smelled unlike anything he had created before. It had a tart smell with hints of sweet and poignant flowers. Fujinaka poured the liquid with herbs only into a clay pot and took it back to the provincial leader's home. Hiro Fujinaka returned to the guard and presented him with his remedy.

"All he has do is drink this two times today and tomorrow he will be right as rain," Hiro Fujinaka explained to the guard and the guard not sure what to do had called the emissary's assistant.

The emissary's assistant was a sharp faced man with dark hair pulled into a ponytail and nearly snow white skin. Although he was not much taller than Fujinaka everyone scrambled to appease the second in command.

"I am Rishu, the second to the emissary," Rishu the business assistant had begun with his arms crossed in his kimono. He studied Fujinaka like he was about to eat him for dinner. Rishu had been summoned to determine if the remedy that a rice farmer had was worth trying.

"Where are you from, rice farmer?"

"Osa, sir," Fujinaka answered.

"How did you come to make this potion?"

Fujinaka paused and thought of the easiest answer. "I listened to the guard telling of the problems your master is suffering. It seemed that this potion would ease the discomfort of the emissary." Fujinaka paused and then added: "If he drinks this but two times before bed tomorrow he will be a new man."

Rishu asked Fujinaka a number of questions. Fujinaka answered every question honestly. The assistant then looked at the clay pot filled with a dark potion that smelled like sweat and roses. The assistant was skeptical.

"Drink some of it now," the assistant demanded. "If you want the emissary to drink this then you must be willing to drink it also."

"Of course," Hiro Fujinaka smiled and pulled a tea cup from his jacket and poured a cup of the liquid and drank it happily.

After he drained his cup Fujinaka smiled. Rishu nodded. Fujinaka nodded also.

"The drink is harmless if that was your concern," Hiro noted.

Rishu studied the small man with the round head and fisher's desperation.

"It is a combination of natural herbs directed at curing the sickness within your master," Fujinaka explained.

"I'll give it to him tonight." Rishu stated with finality.

"No," Fujinaka said to Rishu. "If you want him better he must take this drink twice tonight."

Rishu narrowed his eyes and for an instant no one spoke. He was unfamiliar with lesser people talking to him or for that matter correcting him. Rishu thought evilly for an instant to have Fujinaka beheaded. He did not have that power but he could threaten and make most afraid just by the suggestion of having their head removed from their shoulders.

"I will give my master two servings of this concoction tonight." Rishu paused. He continued glaring at Fujinaka. "If tomorrow he feels better then he will want to reward you."

Hiro Fujinaka smiled and shook off the idea of a reward. He had only intended to help someone with his herbs and nothing more. The idea of a reward was foreign to Hiro Fujinaka.

The gatekeeper gestured and suddenly two guards with pole arms stepped up and out into the courtyard. The two guards stood on either side of Hiro Fujinaka.

"What is this?"

Rishu looked back hearing Fujinaka and smiled. "This is just a normal precaution dear Fujinaka. You will stay close just in case we need you. If your remedy works my master will want to thank you personally. We prefer that you are close at hand when our master's health is at risk."

The powerful eyes and ears of the emperor were nothing more than a name to Hiro Fujinaka when he found himself sitting with Rishu and Engo, Daiki Yuuta's assistants. He was in a large room with a fireplace. There were tapestries on the castle walls that depicted the great war of 1547. Fujinaka had heard of the war and thought that it was truly an event that changed Japan forever. Yet, as he stared at the tapestry sandwiched in between the two assistants for the first time he was able to see the war in pictures before his eyes.

"How did you come to be here Hiro Fujinaka?"

Fujinaka snapped out of his reverie of the history of Okayama instantly.

He was an uneducated farmer from Osa. His knowledge had been handed down like everyone he knew. Fujinaka had seen writings on paper but was unable to read. He relied on his uncanny memory. If someone said something to him he could recall it as if it had been said only minutes ago. Time did not erode his memory. Fujinaka could recall almost every conversation he had since he could remember.

"Every year I come to Okayama to look at the things that Osa does not have," Hiro Fujinaka explained. "I came this year and everyone was talking about the emperor's emissary falling ill. I was curious being an herbalist."

"Isn't Osa a fishing town?"

Hiro Fujinaka smiled as an answer.

"Have you been an herbalist long," asked Rishu pointedly.

"I have been an herbalist for as long as I can recall," Fujinaka smiled.

"Yes, but you told the guard that you were a farmer," Rishu retorted as if looking for holes in Fujinaka's story.

Fujinaka laughed. He instantly lowered his head meaning no disrespect. Almost without thought Fujinaka said as respectfully as possible, "I am a farmer. I am an herbalist. My father is a farmer. His father was a farmer. His father before him was a farmer. So, I began as a farmer. I learned the secrets of the soil. The secrets of the soil made me respect the power of the various plants that so many overlook." He paused and dared look up and into the face of Rishu. Rishu seemed displeased.

"As a farmer I was born into that particular position. Yet, I was unaware that to be an herbalist and a great herbalist one needed to be able to respect the soil."

"We will see if you are a farmer or an herbalist soon enough," Rishu hissed.

The guards escorted Hiro Fujinaka to a bedchamber in the great house. Hiro Fujinaka prayed and fell asleep in the luxurious interior of the great house. He slept and had one of the greatest night's rest in his life.

The next morning Hiro Fujinaka had been awakened by one of the samurai guards. The guard kneeled before Hiro Fujinaka dressed in his ceremonial garb and holding the hilt of his sword.

"What is it?"

"Will you follow me," the guard asked and stood and moved to the door to wait for Hiro Fujinaka to dress.

Hiro Fujinaka dressed and tried to get answers from the guard but he did not answer any of the farmer turned herbalist's questions. Once dressed,

Hiro Fujinaka followed the guard through the halls to where the emperor's emissary had laid sick for three days.

"What has happened?"

The samurai guard had not responded. Instead he had led Hiro Fujinaka down a busy hallway.

The castle was a buzz of activity suddenly. People were running here and there. It was as if someone important had come to the castle. Or, Hiro Fujinaka thought for an instant, someone in the castle had died.

The samurai stopped in front of the door to an executive area, guarded by more samurai. The samurai studied Hiro as he and the nameless samurai moved to particular door.

"Rishu asked for the rice farmer, when he awoke," the samurai said to the man guarding the door. The samurai at the door nodded and moved aside.

The samurai that had brought Hiro Fujinaka to the door knocked and the door slid open a few seconds later. The samurai nodded and gestured for Hiro Fujinaka to enter. The rice farmer from Osa entered.

Standing in front of Hiro Fujinaka were two more samurai dressed in kimonos and samurai swords and katanas. Behind them two men, one dressed in a red kimono and the other in a black kimono, were in a deep conversation. The man in the black kimono was Rishu and in his hand was a parchment and pen. Two black haired women dressed in green and blue kimonos sat on the left side of the man dressed in a red kimono with golden designs.

The pair of men finished their conversation and Rishu turned and smiled. He excused himself and moved quickly to Hiro.

"I hope that you slept well last night," Rishu smiled.

"I did. Thank you for asking."

"The emissary would like to meet the man that remedied the problem that put him down for three days."

Hiro Fujinaka nodded.

Rishu led Hiro Fujinaka deeper into the executive suite where the emperor's emissary was residing.

"Are you the miracle worker," Daiki Yuuta asked with a smile.

Hiro Fujinaka lowered his head and bowed. He did not speak. His actions were his answer.

"Come in, my friend, you are more than welcome here," Yuuta said and instantly the two men were in motion. One man grabbed a low wooden table and slid it near Yuuta who took it and knelt down, using the table as a place to rest his arm. The other man moved quickly and quietly toward Fujinaka and guided him next to Yuuta. Without a word the serious man gestured to Fujinaka and then to the area near Yuuta. Fujinaka nodded and kneeled next to the powerful man.

Fujinaka had heard stories of the samurai when he was a child but had never believed them to exist until that day. The two men were trained and skilled warriors devoted to the protection of Daiki Yuuta. Even though they seemed like vassals, Fujinaka knew that at the first sign of danger or attack toward their master these two men would transform, like a caterpillar in a chrysalis, into fierce and dedicated warriors bent on protecting Daiki Yuuta from harm.

"You have done what no one else was able to do, Hiro Fujinaka," Daiki Yuuta smiled.

Fujinaka lowered his head in answer.

"What can I do to reward you?"

Fujinaka had thought to object and Yuuta saw his miracle worker begin to say something.

"What? You do not want a reward?" Daiki Yuuta smiled and Rishu made a movement just to the left that made Yuuta raise his hand. Fujinaka turned and saw that Rishu was frowning.

"Hiro Fujinaka you have brought me back from the brink of death. There was no one with a remedy. You had a remedy. For that you must be rewarded."

"As you wish my lord," Fujinaka said.

Daiki Yuuta had two trained bodyguards with him at all times. He was the assistant to the royal treasurer for the empire. As the emperor's treasurer he had incredible clout and power. His power was manifested in the signet ring on his right hand that was used to authorize any action detailed in letters or messages from Yuuta to provinces and province leaders.

So, that day Daiki Yuuta wrote a letter, a decree really, that made Hiro Fujinaka the owner of a business financed by the emperor and free from debt in the Okayama province, just a few miles from Osaka and less than one hundred miles from Tokyo. Suddenly there was a business named: Royal Family Remedy Company.

Chapter Four.

The Kulani guard's report read:

Prisoner was found on prison floor writhing. Checked vitals. Called for assistance. Was determined that prisoner was having a seizure of some sort. Suspected drug ingestion. Taken to infirmary. Restrained. Doctor Reynolds took over care.

Doctor Reynolds report was just as succinct.

Patient seems to have blacked out. Has no recollection of the cause? Has no recollection of symptoms? Last memory was sitting in office with prison psychologists and being released back to cell. Will keep under twenty-four-hour observation only.

There were all these layers to Teddy Dee. He had tried time and time again to hide parts of himself from others. So, few knew much about the elusive and quiet man. Even fewer could say that they knew what drove him.

"Everyday money is thrown at me, but not all money is good money," Teddy Dee reminded himself. When he began in this cloak and dagger world he was money hungry. Often he took jobs because of the money and didn't ask the right questions and nearly was killed more times than he liked to admit.

So, as he walked toward the Redondo Beach Performing Arts Center, hoping for a lunch on the beach, he weighed the money Buck was offering to the danger of going to Ecuador and eventually Colombia to recover two Americans working for Small Planet and Walt Disney International Development.

If it was just the money, then that was one thing. If it was just the thrill of going to Ecuador and outwitting a Colombian drug lord that would be another thing. Yet, the combination of the two was restrictive and filled with peril.

As Teddy Dee passed the Performing Arts Center and got close to the beachfront the whole cityscape transformed. He had walked from strip malls and businesses along the edge of residences and apartments and seen few homes so close to the main avenue into the beachfront community. Now, just a few minutes from the beach the familiar businesses popped up. 7-11 was replaced by Surf shops and Bikini salons. There were no fast food establishments any longer in the heart of Manhattan Beach. Everything was trendy and expensive. Suddenly, there were boys walking around in board shorts. At a stop sign was a new convertible VW Beetle with three blondes listening to some pop star singing about her love of her boyfriend.

Teddy Dee picked a restaurant that he had read about while in New York and always wanted to try when he was in Los Angeles. When he arrived at the quaint restaurant there were just about a dozen people in the eatery. The music was light and airy. It felt friendly and comfortable. The dinner crowd had yet to arrive and Teddy Dee asked to sit on the patio. He ordered and sipped a Spanish beer as he waited for his meal.

Teddy Dee recalled that he had toyed with the idea of working with Albert Buck and what he was asking Teddy Dee to accomplish three months before he had heard of Elliott Winslow and the Winslow Law Firm.

The whole Albert Buck mission had smelled like bullshit. As far as Teddy could tell Colombian drug cartels weren't in the business of crossing into Ecuador to kidnap people. Teddy Dee had expected Jana Nichols to be dead. Eric Blanding would be dead also, for whatever that was worth. The whole operation was a snark hunt that would put Teddy Dee in harm's way. It was interesting to note that Buck did not seem to care too much about Blanding.

Teddy Dee was not interested in going to South America to meet and kill people that he didn't know and bring back two body bags. He thought about the whole operation. It was all bullshit. Bullshit, he had believed.

The problem with bullshit was that there was this gradient to how bad the bullshit was. There was just a little bullshit that made the story or job acceptable. That was not too bad. Then there was the knee deep bullshit that got you dirty by association and that bullshit you could not wash off. Teddy Dee disliked that type of job most of all. It did not mean that he did not take those jobs, just that he disliked them.

Considering the levels of bullshit found Teddy Dee thinking about character flaws that he had seen in the corporate executives that played judge, jury and made him executioner. Teddy Dee tried not to think too much of the personality flaws of the men that he worked for. That was a slippery slope that he did not need to tackle.

If the Albert Buck mission was bullshit, then it was bullshit. Teddy Dee knew that most of the jobs that he was asked to get involved in were dressed up as corporate justice but they were all just rich kid bullshit. Teddy Dee understood that working with so much bullshit had to splash on him now and again. Again, bullshit by association.

He tried to keep a reasonable distance between himself and the bullshit of the corporations but it was easier said than done. Teddy Dee worked and made his work a shield against the bullshit that he did daily for the corporations.

Those that hired him did not know Teddy Dee. They did not want to know him. They just wanted to know that any job he was given would be accomplished as asked. Teddy Dee was result-driven. He turned himself inside out to accomplish the seemingly impossible.

"There is no problem that cannot be solved," Oscar Easton, his mentor had told him.

"How?"

"You have to sometimes look at it with new eyes."

Teddy Dee hid his feelings like buried treasure. He lived in hotels. His work was odious to most. He was not above violence to solve his and his client's problems. Daily he lied. Hourly he lived in a world of deception, double dealing, and at times he had to be judge, jury, and executioner.

Though Teddy Dee never admitted to anyone he liked the power of his weird and twisted job. He was god. He had the power of life and death in his hand when he showed up at someone's doorstep and Teddy Dee knew that. He tried to pretend that his job was horrible. Perhaps his job was horrible. Perhaps, the biggest bullshit about Teddy Dee was that he was a horrible individual pretending to be a decent individual. Teddy Dee had a bunch of bullshit around him. What was a little more bullshit in his life going to matter?

While he ate a twenty-dollar burrito he had considered the Buck mission. He liked Albert Buck. He seemed straight enough. He liked the ex-Marine that was in charge of security. Buck seemed legitimate enough. Albert Buck was not setting him up to fail. There was a clear objective; find Jana and Eric and bring them back to the States. Alive or dead Buck wanted the pair back. Buck knew that it was possible that his daughter was already dead. Buck just needed closure, Teddy Dee concluded.

So, after a late lunch or early dinner Teddy Dee thought about calling a cab and having the cab driver drive him to a local restaurant in Westchester for dinner. He had his rental; a new silver Jaguar XJ parked back by the coffee shop but had thought for a moment to catch a cab and be chauffeured to Westchester. He could pick up the Jaguar tomorrow. Sometimes, Teddy Dee had to admit, he liked to be driven around as a passenger. It gave him a different perspective and time to think.

While he had debated if he should call for the cab, he smiled at the fact that he was in Manhattan Beach. An old friend of his lived in Manhattan Beach. Amanda "Alabama" Fleming lived in Manhattan Beach. Teddy Dee had not seen “Alabama” in nearly a year. He had not ended his relationship with “Alabama” and though few things irked Teddy Dee not ending things got under Teddy Dee’s skin.

Teddy Dee had walked to the center of Manhattan Beach. He read a number of reviews of the suddenly trendy restaurant that sat on Manhattan Beach Boulevard named: Rock 'N Fish. Teddy Dee walked down Manhattan Beach Boulevard and found the quiet restaurant. He sat down at the bar and ordered a beer. He was escorted to his table and ordered his meal looking at the beach from the window.

Teddy Dee arrived in Manhattan Beach and snaked his way toward the beach. Teddy Dee stopped at a drugstore to get his bearings and then walked a block to the beach. He figured if he didn't see "Alabama" on the beach he would try and catch her after.

He checked his watch and hoped that "Alabama" would be out on the beach when he arrived. Teddy Dee loved to watch "Alabama" run. She had a fluidity about her when she ran. Teddy Dee tried to remember but was not sure if "Alabama" had ran track in college. She had run in high school. “Alabama” was a cheerleader and a track star in high school. Teddy Dee knew that. He could not recall where she went to high school but he knew that “Alabama” Fleming got her nickname while in high school because she wore a ‘Bama sweatshirt that was given to her by her uncle who lived in Birmingham, Alabama.

Before going to Ecuador Teddy Dee decided that he would try and see Alabama and end the on again and off again roller coaster ride with the smart and dangerous Alabama Fleming. Loose ends never were good in Teddy Dee’s mind.

Teddy Dee fished out his cell phone and made another phone call. He got the voicemail of "Alabama" Fleming. He considered hanging up. Instead of hanging up Teddy Dee left a brief message: “Hey, ‘Bama, in Manhattan Beach and thinking of having dinner at Rock ’N Fish. Should be there around seven and eating by eight, if interested.”

The sun was starting its descent into the Western sea and he figured that there was maybe about two hours of light left before sunset. As he watched the sun inching westward Teddy Dee found himself thinking of the first time that he had dinner with the most competitive woman he knew. The meeting had been arranged by Carl Ryle, Teddy Dee’s handler at the time.

"I'm Alabama," the curvaceous woman announced. The beautiful woman was dressed in a black pant suit with a blue jean jacket.

"Hi, Alabama," Teddy Dee said. He immediately placed his hand on his Walther PPQ 9mm pistol. They were in Hollywood and on Hollywood Boulevard.

"I didn't come to kill you," the green eyed woman smiled. "I came to compliment you on your escape. It was bold and daring. Most would have just given up the package."

Teddy Dee checked his surroundings. There were five men that he could see with the woman. Two were behind Teddy Dee. One man was just ahead of the woman. Two men were across the wide boulevard shadowing Teddy Dee and the woman.

"Thanks," Teddy Dee replied. He did not know how to take the woman.

"You have some powerful enemies Teddy Dee. Enemies that hold grudges. Enemies that have a bounty on your head."

"A bounty?"

"Yeah, a bounty. Me, I am a bounty hunter when the mood hits me. Most of the time I am just a suit's assistant," Alabama explained. "Just like you," she added with an evil smile.

Teddy Dee was puzzled.

"I see that this doesn't make much sense to you. So, let me boil it down to its essentials. The suits play this game and it's their version of a high priced hide the pickle. Whatever. They steal something and then hire us to steal it back. You know this game. The wrinkle is that after you retrieve the pickle they don't end the game. They keep the game going."

Teddy Dee wanted to ask a question.

"There is a window of opportunity opened after you take something from one of the privileged for them to retrieve it. It's anywhere from two to seven days before the fireworks end. It is all very high-tech. I think that there is a website that none of the norms understand. The privileged love hiding things in plain sight." She paused. "You have to have wondered why when you finish your ops why you don't get a call for two or three days." Alabama Fleming paused and studied Teddy Dee. He listened and did not seem to be too concerned. "You cannot be that dumb. Maybe you have been just plain lucky. You haven't noticed that there is more security needed after the op than before? Yes? No?"

Teddy Dee shook his head; no.

"Seriously?" Alabama smiled that bewitching smile that seemed all at once genuine, honest, and devilish and evil. "Chalk it up to dumb luck then. Just to make you aware there are usually bounty hunters, mercenaries, hatchets trying to cut off your water after every successful operation. If you were normal, then you would know that and load up and watch your back. During that time period you have to watch your back for at least five days because of the open bounty put on you after ops."

"What? How much?"

“It depends, of course. I have seen some bounties worth a mil. The lowest I have seen is one kay.”

“Are there a lot of bounty hunters?”

Alabama Fleming allowed a wicked grin to slide across her face.

“You’re a bounty hunter?”

"I said that already. Keep up," Alabama smiled. "Yeah, the people that recruited us don't like to start out with that in their recruitment pitch. Not many want to work, live, and continuously wonder when and if someone they don't know or might know is coming to cap them."

"So, why are you telling me this?"

"I suppose because it is rare to find someone nowadays that surprises me." Alabama paused. "In Clovis, the other night, you surprised me. That doesn’t happen too often. I figured that you were just another zipper head trying to act all tough. What you did took balls.” Alabama Fleming paused and smiled. Teddy Dee studied the small and beautiful woman who was so fluid in her movements. Teddy Dee figured that Alabama Fleming had been an athlete in another life and stayed in tip top shape.

Alabama Fleming smiled and said: “You looking at me like a dog with a bone Teddy. This ain’t that kind of meeting. I wanted to make you aware that not everyone in this fucked up topsy-turvy world is an enemy. Most are. Most you cannot trust further than you can throw them. But, there are a few that aren't that bad."

"You one of the not so bads?"

"No, I'm bad and I hold a grudge but right now I wanted you to know that I was impressed with your ballsy choice in Clovis. Not too many would have made that choice. But, the next time we cross paths, Teddy Dee, things may end a little differently."

"Thanks," Teddy Dee said as Alabama curtsied and spun on her heels and walked across Hollywood Boulevard to a waiting car. Her men simply evaporated in the California sun.

Teddy Dee liked "Alabama" Fleming. In another life he might have settled down with the beautiful and driven security consultant but that was not his life. He was a corporate blooder and she was a high powered security consultant.

Teddy Dee had dinner alone. After dinner he toyed with the idea of catching a cab back to Westchester. He opted out of the cab and walked back to the coffee shop. Teddy Dee retrieved his rental car and drove back to the airport watching planes taking off and landing as he made his way back to his hotel.

The rise of the Royal Family Remedy Company was slow and methodic. At the time of the company there was little competition. Japan was fighting for its own identity and trying to be a world power.

There was a world war. Japan had watched as the world fought against Germany and Italy and beat them soundly. Germany was kneecapped. The world returned to a semblance of normalcy.

Then there was a second world war. Japan decided not to sit on the sidelines. They attacked China. They attacked the Philippines. They attacked Pearl Harbor.

The United States stepped into the world war. Things changed drastically. Germans fled Germany. German scientists relocated to the United States.

There was Osaka and Nagasaki.

Royal Family Remedy Company offered those in Japan herbal solutions. Sanctions were levied against Japan. People died. People accused Royal Family Remedy Company of causing some deaths.

Royal Family Remedy Company was nearly shut down.

The company continued but only as a shadow of its operation prior to world war two.

Then the Olympics came a calling. Japan wanted an advantage for its athletes. The Royal Family Remedy Company was enlisted in the capacity of enhancing athletic performances through herbs and natural stimulants.

The Royal Family Remedy Company made leaps and bounds in terms of athletic performance. Japan and all those using the sports packets developed by Royal Family Remedy Company saw defined improvement. Some critics suggested that the Royal Family Remedy Company was performing some type of black magic on the Japanese athletes. Some suggested that the Royal Family Remedy Company were the masters of deception and that a majority of the packets were sweet smelling and equally sweet tasting placebos.

Asami Fujinaka knew the story of the Royal Family Remedy Company and the various ups and downs of the family business. Everyone that was born into the business had been taught of the illustrious Hiro Fujinaka. Everyone that was blood related to Hiro Fujinaka had been invited to be a part of the nascent company. There had only been seven members of the Fujinaka family to accept the opportunity to be a part of the Royal Family Remedy Company.

Few knew within and outside of the family that Royal Family Remedy Company would become one of the biggest herbal companies in Japan. Even fewer knew that because of athletic connections, the Olympics, and a renewed effort by the Japanese government to educate and move away from detrimental pharmaceuticals that Royal Family Remedy Company would become an herbal juggernaut and gobble up its competition. In half a century Royal Family Remedy Company was the most recognized herbal company in Japan.

Royal Family Remedy Company became Signet Industries after acquiring a gigantic manufacturing plant in Thailand. With the acquisition of the manufacturing plant Signet Industries was able to increase its footprint in Japan and most of the Pacific Rim. Signet Industries was suddenly an herbal giant and one of the top 500 companies in Japan when the great, great, great grandson of Hiro Fujinaka took over as the President.

Chapter Five.

Teddy Dee had driven down to Anaheim and met once again with Albert Buck before departing for Ecuador. Buck was seated at a corner office that overlooked the regal splendor of the greatest place on earth; Disneyland. The executive was dressed in a tailor made suit and reading the Investor's Business Daily news when Teddy Dee walked into the expansive office.

"Bring back my daughter," was all that Albert Buck said.

Teddy Dee had shaken hands with the powerbroker and left for the waiting shuttle. The shuttle took him to the private airport of Disney and the awaiting Gulf Stream of Andrew Buck.

Teddy Dee packed light. He didn't expect to be in Ecuador long. It was a smash and grab at best. Five days at the most. He had more guns than he had clothes for this trip.

The flight crew grabbed Teddy Dee's bags as he exited the shuttle and he noticed that there was more luggage on the Gulf Stream than just his. There were three duffle bags in the cargo area already. Add Teddy Dee's duffle and that meant at least three others were on this trip beside the pilot and co-pilot.

Teddy Dee closed his eyes for an instant and prepared to deal with corporate muscle. Unlike Teddy Dee corporate muscle thought that they were tough but rarely faced any real threat. Corporate muscle twisted the arms of other fat cat rich kids who thought that they were tough.

Of the corporate bad asses Raleigh Stewart, ex-marine, was possibly a real badass. Everyone else was just a bad ass in the boardroom. When the shit hit the fan he would make sure that Stewart was at his back.

"So, we can finally get underway," Stewart smiled and chuckled as Teddy Dee climbed aboard the G150.

"I didn't think that there was a time frame for private jets," Teddy Dee countered.

"There ain't, but we do want to get there the same day," Stewart joked.

Teddy Dee sat down and noticed that there were two others, beside Stewart, on board when Teddy Dee arrived.

Raleigh Stewart was a bull of a man and everything about him screamed Marine. He looked like a poster boy for the USMC. He was a chiseled man with thin eyes and a square chin that seemed always ready to engage in any action. Stewart was always aware of his surroundings. That awareness made Teddy Dee feel better about heading to Ecuador with people he didn't know.

As the G150 taxied onto the short runway Teddy Dee introduced himself to the other two men on the Gulf Stream; Franklin Johnson and Leland Edwards.

Johnson was sitting and sipping at a cup of tea when Teddy Dee sat down. Johnson didn't move. Teddy Dee reached out and introduced himself to Franklin Johnson again.

Johnson was a dark eyed, dark haired, average sized man with no visible chin, wearing a blue collared shirt, blue suit jacket, and khakis. He looked like he should be selling insurance. Though Johnson was only five foot eight inches tall and 170 pounds he was dangerous. He had a short man complex in the land of the giants. Johnson wore a Desert Eagle under his jacket.

"Damn, man, you hunting bear?"

"Never know what you might face in a third world country," Johnson returned.

"Leave him alone Teddy, Franklin is over cautious. He was a cop in another life," Stewart laughed.

Johnson was a retired cop from Oxnard. He had been a cop for nearly 13 years and seen his share of trouble. Franklin Johnson had only recently left the Oxnard Police Department and been hired as a corporate muscle for Andrew Buck. He was a quiet and mean cop and a quiet and mean man with a permanent scowl on his face.

Franklin Johnson smiled, a slight curling of his right lip and he nodded at Teddy Dee. Teddy Dee nodded also and turned his attention to Leland Edwards. Both men had been with Raleigh Stewart and Albert Buck at the coffee shop near Manhattan Beach that day he had met and discussed the trip to Ecuador.

"What up man?" Teddy Dee nodded nonplussed by the tense exchange between Johnson and himself. Teddy Dee extended his hand toward Leland Edwards.

Leland Edwards smiled and extended his hand to Teddy Dee.

"Hey, don't let Johnson get to you. He's wound up way too tight," Leland Edwards smiled cutting his eyes toward the brooding Franklin Johnson, who was quietly watching Teddy Dee and Leland Edwards meeting.

Leland Edwards was the only color in the Buck muscle. Leland Edwards was African-American but aware of the corporate world he was in. Thus, he didn't attempt to befriend Teddy Dee although they had much in common.

Teddy Dee too knew that Leland Edwards might be his harshest critic. In the corporate world that the two found themselves in there were few if any allies. Letting down your guard could make you vulnerable or worse.

Maybe, just maybe, on the other side of this operation Teddy Dee might meet up with Leland Edwards and talk to him one-on-one. Those were his thoughts as he shook hands with the only other black man on the Gulfstream G150 winging toward Ecuador.

"Nice to meet you," Teddy Dee said. Leland Edwards said the same. There was a pregnant pause and Raleigh Stewart leaned in and got Teddy Dee's attention.

"Buck sent us along to make sure that things go smoothly. He sent me along to smooth over any issues with you and Getty if there is anything that needs to be smoothed over."

Teddy Dee digested what Stewart said.

"I brought these two because in a firefight they are two people that I can trust when things get hot."

Teddy Dee listened silently. He had his reservations about corporate muscle. They usually wanted to shoot first and figure things out later. Or, they didn't want to pull their weapons when absolutely necessary.

Stewart and Teddy Dee sat near the front of the G150 eating snacks and sipping Cokes. Edwards and Johnson were playing dominoes near the middle of the private jet.

Teddy Dee liked Raleigh Stewart. To be a Marine and to come out alive you had to be a legitimate badass. If he questioned anyone's credentials it was Johnson and Edwards but they were the least of his concern. He had to figure out what he was facing.

"Teddy, you do a lot of extractions?"

"I do whatever the client needs to be done. If it is an extraction, then it's an extraction." Teddy Dee paused. "I have done my share of smash and grabs. This isn't my first rodeo. I know you were military but can you color in the gray spots a bit?"

Raleigh Stewart smiled. "I was a grunt when I joined the USMC, and was only 17 when I signed up. I have always loved hand-to-hand combat and guns and those skills helped me become noticed. I was asked to shoot for the USMC and in less than a year I became a marksman. I was recruited to Special Forces and there, once accepted, spent nearly ten years stopping the bad guys from winning."

Teddy Dee nodded.

"I retired and still wanted to kick some ass. So, I signed up as a security consultant, at first. Then Mister Buck called me and I have been with him ever since." Stewart paused, and added, "Four years of kicking ass in the corporate world. Nothing too spectacular. Barely have to work up a sweat."

"What about Edwards?"

"Leland? He is a good egg. He is still relatively young for this business. He's—" Stewart raised a finger and redirected his attention to Edwards. "Leland are you 40 yet?"

"No, sir," Leland Edwards smiled, looking up from a game of dominoes with Johnson. "I'm 36 next month."

"You see, young and still wet behind the ears."

"Full of jumping beans, eh," Teddy Dee asked.

"Now, Leland has a background in security. He didn't do military. Edwards was a part of private security. He cut his teeth with some big time hip hop artists. That guy's been through hell. He's seen his share of gun battles and car chases and evasions. He's the wheels of the team." Stewart pointed out. "If it has an engine and four wheels Edwards can drive it." The ex-Marine had told him about Johnson first.

"And Johnson?"

"Franklin? Ex-cop. Oxnard. Nothing new or spectacular. He was a kid without direction. He joined the Army and like me after his tour signed up to be a badge for Oxnard of all places."

Teddy Dee nodded.

"What about you?"

Teddy Dee smiled at Stewart.

"Just a knock around kid, I suppose," Teddy Dee began. "Graduated from high school. Went to the Army. Tried to figure out what I was going to do with my life. Left the service. Returned home. Once on the street and back in the old neighborhood I ran into a friend of a friend and he led me to my current position as a corporate blooder."

"We are very similar Teddy, you and I," Raleigh Stewart said.

"Perhaps," Teddy Dee lied with a smile. He was nothing like Raleigh Stewart who lived in a house somewhere in the valley. Stewart had a wife and possibly children. He smelled like a father of three. He had that tired look about him that only children can create.

Unlike Stewart, Teddy Dee didn't wake up and go to work at any specific time and have lunch and then clock out at five o'clock to go and watch little league games or pee wee football. Teddy Dee was nothing like Raleigh Stewart.

Stewart lived with the belief that he could create security. Teddy Dee on the other hand realized that security was a moving target. Security is man-made. Everyday, Teddy Dee was reassured that what he offered was not security but truth.

The truth for Teddy Dee was that the world was a dangerous place. There were dangerous people everywhere. There were people that didn't care one whit about anyone else and it was Teddy Dee that stood up to those dangerous people and made them aware that there was someone bigger and badder and meaner than themselves. Teddy Dee was willing to fight, protect, and if necessary kill those that threatened others. That was security. That was the truth. That was the ugly Teddy Dee truth.

In that truth, Teddy Dee also knew that some dangerous people changed and that caused things to change. Stewart and his men to a large part, as well as Buck, were change agents.

"Raleigh, it's cool to come down on the flight," Teddy Dee said. He added, "But I usually work alone. It don't mean that we can't work together but until I figure things out I will need to do what has worked for me on my own." Teddy Dee paused, gauging Stewart's reaction.

"Well, things change. Buck sent me to make sure that his daughter isn't dead. We are to do everything in our power to ensure her safe return."

"Yeah, yeah, yeah, I get it," Teddy Dee said raising his hands in surrender. Stewart was a juggernaut. He was a point and shoot kind of guy. Teddy Dee figured that he might be able to use him if things went terribly wrong.

"Well, we are in this together until we climb back on this plane and head back to Anaheim," Stewart pointed out.

"I understand. You can help me out by figuring out what Getty knows. Cut through the bullshit and get the real scoop. No chaser."

"I can do that."

"Might want to hit the ground running. When we land can you get four or five of the men together to take us in the direction the kidnappers took the hostages?" He added, "No disrespect. I have only a few hours to craft a plan that makes sense in Ecuador and eventually Colombia."'

"Understood," Stewart nodded.

Teddy Dee opened up his MacBook Air and pulled up the latest intel on the reported residence of El Gordo. He also mapped the distance between the Disney construction site and El Gordo's residence. Just a few hours on foot. Manageable.

Seven hours later, the Gulfstream G150 landed on the private runway of the unpublished and undisclosed Disney construction site in northern Ecuador. Raleigh Stewart was the first to exit the Gulf Stream followed closely behind by Teddy Dee.

The weather was hot and humid. Teddy Dee thought that he had prepared himself for the temperate nature of Ecuador but he was not prepared. A few steps from the Gulf Stream and he was sweating like a man about to go to the electric chair.

Four men stood at the plane steps dressed in camouflage fatigues. They had pistols on their hips. All had radios. Their names on their uniforms were: Gardner, Lively, Milton, and Stanley. The man with "Gardner" over his breast stepped forward as the men began to disembark.

"Welcome to Ecuador," Gardner smiled. "They are expecting you in the command center."

Teddy Dee followed Stewart and Gardner toward the command center. The command center was a big white tent in the center of the compound. The compound was made up of two dozen smaller tents of varying sizes. There was construction equipment in each of the four directions of the camp. As Teddy Dee followed he watched as a piece of heavy equipment moved a dozen steel beams from one point to another.

"Damn, man, can someone go and turn on the AC," Edwards joked as he wiped at his brow with the back of his brown hand.

Teddy Dee turned and noticed that Edwards and Johnson were following him and sweating like stuck pigs. The four walked to the biggest tent and entered. Inside, was a hive of action.

At a makeshift table with a topographical map spread out on it stood four men dressed in camouflage fatigues and snap brim caps. They had pistols on their hips. One had a shoulder holster. Their names on their uniforms were: Howard, McGregor, Clark, and Chavez. At the head of the table stood a dark eyed man with dark hair and a day's growth of facial hair. He was a tall, thin man surveying the table with the map on it. This was the man in charge.

"Sir, the people are here from Anaheim," the small man who had met them at the jet announced.

Tyler Getty looked up and his stern and concentrated expression that was aimed at the map on the table lifted and came to rest on the four newcomers. His dark eyes narrowed and his dark eyebrows wrinkled. Getty's pinched look took in the new faces. Tyler Getty wore a wedding ring on his right hand and was six foot five inches tall easily and slender. In his shoulder holster rested a Browning automatic pistol.

Upon seeing Raleigh Stewart Tyler Getty's expression softened slightly and what passed as a smile etched itself on his weather beaten face.

"Damn, man, what does a guy have to do to get a drink of water in this shit hole?"

"Don't start, you old rattlesnake, unless you want me to cut your head off," Getty spat, smiling broadly as he closed the distance to Raleigh Stewart. The two giants met and hugged in the middle of the tent. Everyone inside of the tent simply watched. Getty pushed Stewart back and Stewart threw a kick at Getty. Getty avoided the kick without much effort. They stood apart like two pit bulls deciding on the next attack.

"So, looks like you fucked up and I have to pull your ass out of the fire again Getty," Stewart joked, his hands up defensively.

"No, it looks like you wanted a vacation from married life and the corporate world and you came down to work on your tan, is more like it," Getty returned with a smile.

"Bullshit," Stewart growled.

"Double bullshit," Getty returned and the two began to laugh.

The men in the tent all relaxed once the two combat soldiers began to laugh. Laughter suggested that they weren't going to kill each other then and there.

Edwards shook his head.

Johnson leaned over to Teddy Dee and whispered the most obvious thing imaginable: "They are close."

Teddy Dee nodded at the comment despite not wanting to. It was humorous for all the wrong reasons.

Getty's tent was comfortable. It was bigger than most tents used only to store all the valuable equipment he had inside. He was the camp director of security. Tyler Getty monitored everyone and everything in the Disney construction site.

"Sit down," Getty said waving toward the camp chairs.

Stewart was already seated and sipping a beer. Edwards and Johnson sat down also. They took a beer each.

Teddy Dee dragged his chair to the side of Stewart and sat down. He was drinking water. He preferred water.

"So, let me bring you up to speed. Jana and Eric have been missing for less than 48 hours and we have gotten no notification from the kidnappers. That is a good sign. We sent Chavez and three of his men after the kidnappers but they were outgunned and outmanned when they got near Colombia." Getty was leafing through a folder with an embossed outline of Mickey Mouse on it with the four familiar letters: SPWD written in yellow across it.

He threw the report on the camp table and walked to his desk where there was a laptop. Getty tapped a few keys on the laptop and on a monitor flashed a frozen scene. Getty tapped a few more keys and the screen went black for a few moments.

"This is the security tape of the night raid. It is clear that the raiders knew what they wanted. They had to have inside help."

The camp site flashed on screen and one of the guards walked into the picture holding a M16 rifle. He was wearing the blue coveralls. On screen flashed the name of the employee and his vial details: Nguyen. Humboldt, California, USA. 12/03/89. Night patrol. 9P-2A.

Nguyen walked the perimeter of the compound and suddenly there were two intruders on the other side of the fence. Nguyen turned around but had little chance to shoot or protect himself. He crumbled to his knees and then pitched face first into the dirt. More intruders came over the fence.

The camera perspective shifted. Suddenly, the intruders were running through the compound in pairs searching for something. A pair stopped at a tent and entered. Another pair watched the exit.

Angelokas. Gary, Indiana, USA. 04/18/91. Welder. Off duty. Flashed on the screen. The welder from Indiana opened the door to his cabin and the camera took him in as he pushed open the door. He was wearing a Colts baseball cap. He was in shorts and a T-shirt. The welder stepped out of his tent and was hit in the head by one of the intruders.

The camera view switched again. Teddy Dee was impressed by the sophistication of Getty's motion sensor camera activation.

Suddenly, Jana Nichols and Eric Blanding flashed on screen. Two men with automatic weapons were threatening them. Jana Nichols tried to fight. The intruder reacted and Nichols went flying over a camp table. Blanding reacted and was clubbed by the other intruder. Nichols and Blanding were dragged to their feet and were being taken from their cabin. Two intruders were pushing them and moving them toward the fence. The camera followed them as far as the fence and lost them.

The camera view changed once again. The intruders were retreating.

Thomas flashed on the screen. The kid was from Atlanta, Georgia, USA. He was born: 08/27/93. Thomas was a part of the Night patrol. He ran forward firing his M16. One of the raiders was hit and fell to the ground.

Then Thomas was shot. He fell as if he were sliding into home plate. The M16 fell from his hands. He was dead.

As Jana Nichols and Eric Blanding were led out of the compound one of the raiders fired off easily thirty rounds into the air and then slipped into the Ecuador night.

The screen froze.

"Wow," was the first words out of Edwards' mouth after watching the video of the night raid.

"Who was in charge of the night patrol that night?"

"Howard," Getty announced and added, "I already braced him. He lost two men that night. Howard wasn't in on it."

Teddy Dee listened and immediately put Howard at the top of the list of possible rats.

"You said that Chavez and three of his men went searching for Nichols and Blanding?"

"Yeah, I sent Chavez because I suspected Howard." Getty explained. "They went out less than twenty minutes after the attack and discovery that Jana and Eric were missing."

Teddy Dee leaned forward and grabbed the report and leafed through it as Stewart asked questions. He read the various reports compiled in the folder. There was an initial report from Michael Howard. He detailed the typical night on night patrol securing the primary compound where everyone slept and the construction site where the equipment was housed. There were always three night patrols circulating on four hour shifts 24-hours a day. Two were on the two main areas; compound and construction site. The third night patrol was a rover moving between the compound and construction site. The third night patrol was on three hour shifts.

Howard pointed out that the third night patrol had just left the compound when the raid began. It was beyond strange for the raiders to attack when the third night patrol had left for the construction site.

Teddy Dee read the report from Hector Chavez. He had gotten four of his men together including: Gerardo Ayala, Daniel Baracas, Cesar Diego, and Fidel Limon. Those were Chavez's men. He had also had to enlist the service of Herbert Galindo and Jesus Lopez. Galindo knew the jungle well. Yet, it was Lopez who had a skill for tracking.

The report was pretty much as Getty explained. Galindo and Lopez tracked the raiders to the border of Ecuador and at a river were fired upon. Chavez and Baracas crossed the river but they were outnumbered and had to retreat. Chavez also hesitated because Galindo and Lopez were afraid and coupled with the fact that he realized that they were in Colombia they retreated. He radioed in the situation and Getty had told them to return to base since they had not set off to engage in a firefight.

"We'll leave in the morning. Can we borrow Chavez and those two trackers?"

"Of course," Getty said. He picked up his phone and tapped in a brief message.

Bright and early Teddy Dee, Raleigh Stewart, Franklin Johnson, and Leland Edwards headed into the Ecuadorian jungle led by Hector Chavez and the two trackers Galindo and Lopez.

Galindo and Lopez were dressed in the SPWD uniform including the Disney embossed outline of the most popular mouse on earth. They carried a SPWD backpack and were outfitted with a standard issue silver Beretta M9 and a M16.

Teddy Dee liked Chavez almost immediately. There was a confidence in the security advisor. He was a clear eyed man with a pointy chin and broad smile. He was not six feet tall but built for combat. Dressed in the dark blue of the SPWD that morning Chavez had a M9 strapped to his right leg. He carried a backpack and an assault rifle and nothing else. Chavez also carried the satellite phone.

"You are dressing light?"

"Well, we aren't going to climb Mount Kilimanjaro today. We are going from Ecuador to Colombia. The worst thing we'll see might be monkeys and mosquitoes."

Despite Chavez and Galindo and Lopez light preparation Stewart and his team were packing for bear. Everyone on the Anaheim team was armed for any circumstance.

Raleigh Stewart was a cowboy and carrying a backpack that held two hundred shotgun shells for his SPAS-12 shotgun. On his hip was a gun belt that held twenty-five of the one hundred rounds for his .357 Magnum. Stewart was a mountain of a man and refused to simply hike through the jungle on the jungle's terms. He wanted everyone to know that Raleigh Stewart had been there.

Franklin Johnson was carrying his Desert Eagle, as well as an Uzi.

Leland Edwards was carrying a Beretta M9 and a M16.

Teddy Dee was packing light or as light as he could. He had packed his backpack with his essentials and one hundred rounds of ammunition for his reliable Walther PPQ 9mm and battle tested AR-15.

The team moved out and after about two hours they were in the thick of the Ecuadorian jungle. Teddy Dee marveled at the heights of the trees in the jungle. He was a city kid. He had grown up in Chicago and only once or twice been in a forest but nothing like the jungles on the border of Ecuador.

As the party snaked its way through the jungle canopy Teddy Dee had to stop and take in the beauty all around him despite the circumstance. He was shocked and unable to move when he witnessed the most unrehearsed act of nature under the watchful eyes of only him and a handful of others.

Galindo and Lopez were in the lead with Chavez and Edwards right behind them. Stewart and Johnson were the third rank and Teddy Dee was watching the rear when the whole train paused.

They had turned a bend and run into the aerial play of thousands of nameless small blue birds and hundreds of parrots. The smaller blue birds circled the bigger parrots as the parrots spun and banked in the suddenly open greenery. The brightly colored parrots would whoop and call as they followed the fearless parrots from the heights of the trees to the floor of the jungle below. What was unimaginable was the precision performed by the smaller unidentified blue birds. No parrot flew in that jungle opening alone. Every parrot that dared leave the safety of the canopy was circled by no less than five small blue birds.

At first, it seemed that the parrots had invaded the sanctity of the unknown blue birds but with a closer look it was evident that the smaller birds were not attacking the parrots or the parrots the blue birds. The birds seemed to be playing if that was possible. Teddy Dee searched his memory and tried to recall if parrots and macaws played. He was not sure.

The play between the two distinctly different avian species was a wonder, to say the least. The play was very regimented. There were one or two parrots that launched into the opening high in the treetops and that action was immediately responded to by the smaller blue birds. As many as ten birds would circle the parrot that left the branches high in the jungle canopy. Then as the parrot picked up the blue daredevils it would begin its breakneck plummet toward the jungle floor, all the while the blue birds were circling the parrot like an avian made merry-go-round.

Perhaps fifty feet from the jungle floor the parrot would increase speed and the blue birds, nonplussed by the action continued circling the parrot. Only inches from the jungle floor would the parrot pull up and the blue birds disperse.

It was a truly fascinating experience. The tracking party watched as the parrots and blue birds continued their swooping down unsure what to do next. Often as the parrot got close to the jungle floor one of the men recoiled thinking that the parrot or the bluebirds were going to be killed.

Thankfully, in the time that the tracking party stood there only one parrot misjudged the distance toward the forest floor and crashed. The bird bounced off the floor and the blue birds that had followed it circled it like a cartoon character who had hit his head.

The parrot tried to take wing but the crash had made flight impossible.

"He's a goner," Johnson said under his breath.

Teddy Dee had watched the injured parrot hoping that it would be able to fly away. Of course, after five minutes, he agreed with Johnson.

It was a remarkable thing to witness.

The avian display stretched out for nearly thirty minutes and no one seemed to care. It was not often that anyone had witnessed a sight such as this. Even Stewart, the battle hardened ex-Marine watched the avian acrobatics with awe.

The arrival of several Capuchin monkeys ended the aerial display.

The tracking continued.

Thirty minutes later Galindo stopped. He spoke briefly to Lopez. Chavez and Stewart walked forward to see what was the problem.

"It's getting dark," Edwards pointed out.

"Yeah, man, I don't want to keep walking through the jungle at night. The worst thing that could happen is running into a jaguar or a panther or worse," Galindo suggested.

"Besides, we can't see the trail." Lopez added.

"Bullshit," Stewart growled. "We still got daylight. I say, we keep going."

"In the rain forest the sun is not always the guide for a day's work," Chavez responded. "We need to rest and then figure out our next steps."

Teddy Dee was still in the rear and the trail was leading into a denser part of the jungle.

Chavez slipped off his backpack and sat down on a fallen tree. He opened the backpack and fished inside of it for his canteen. He sipped at his canteen and ate an energy bar.

Galindo and Lopez were seated on a flat rock outcropping. They had their M16 rifles slung over their backs like an archer might place their strung bow across their chest.

Although they had only traveled a few miles in the dense forest the effort was tiring.

Stewart reluctantly took off his backpack and rested his SPAS-12 by his side. He leaned against a tree and then sat down, physically tired. Next to him was Johnson and Edwards. The pair looked as tired as Stewart if that was possible.

Teddy Dee was the last to sit down with his back to the group. He was still watching the rear. He slipped off his backpack and instantly his muscles relaxed shedding thirty pounds from his shoulders. Teddy Dee found his canteen and unscrewed the top. He cherished the splash of water against his throat.

The taste of water was so refreshing. It, the water, in its simplest form was a part of Teddy Dee as well as any living creature on earth. Thus, sweating removed what was a part of everyone. Drinking the water then replaced and re-introduced the world and all those connected to Teddy Dee to him again in its own small way.

"Okay, we'll camp here. Let's make camp," Stewart said reluctantly.

The two compound security guards were: Herbert Galindo and Jesus Lopez. The two were interchangeable to Teddy Dee. They were small men compared to him or Stewart.

Galindo was an odd duck in the field. He was a handsome young man with dark eyes and small mustache who looked more like he should be playing in a band in some tourist town than in the jungles trying to find a kidnapped daughter of some executive. Galindo had a dreamer's feeling about him. Looking at the slender security guard Teddy Dee could not shake the image that came to mind of Galindo playing the guitar and singing in a bar. He seemed so unsuited for traipsing through the jungles of Ecuador.

Galindo wore all the appropriate clothing but things seemed too new and too crisp for some reason. His pants were still holding their creases in the sweltering heat. His hair seemed an unmovable helmet. Teddy Dee noted that his combat boots looked still relatively new despite the fact that Galindo carried a near spotless standard issue M16 rifle over his shoulder unprepared to fight. On his hip was a nine-millimeter pistol. In his hand was a machete.

Next to Galindo as the team set up the area for the night was Jesus Lopez. Lopez, the more confident of the two had shaved his hair into a faux Mohawk. He too had a well-trimmed mustache and the dark and shifting eyes of a man looking for an angle. He was the schemer. Lopez was as old as Galindo, maybe. They were close friends it seemed. Dressed in the uniform of the compound, his outfit was as clean as Galindo's and like Galindo Lopez had his M16 slung over his shoulder. Neither seemed ready for fighting or ambush, which threw up a flag of concern for Teddy Dee.

The unknown was Chavez. Unlike Galindo or Lopez, Chavez seemed a steady and reliable individual. He was a thin faced olive skinned man in his early thirties with dark features and a thin mustache. He wore the jungle hats that were made popular by the incredible humidity and dampness of the Ecuadorian rain forest. Unlike Galindo or Lopez, Armando Chavez held his M16 like a soldier.

"What do you know about the three stooges," Teddy Dee asked Stewart as the camp quieted and he and Stewart prepared to set watches of two hours.

"Don't know much," Stewart noted. "Getty told me to watch out for Lopez. He's the type that thinks he's smarter than he is and that is a recipe for disaster."

Teddy Dee nodded. He understood. Lopez was a boaster who thought that he was smarter than everyone around him. Stewart noted that Getty didn't think that Lopez was smart at all. Teddy Dee had been around people who thought like Lopez. They always ended up beaten up or dead. Beaten up usually was the symptom of the terminal stupidity that was only a smart alecky remark away.

"So, what you feeling?"

"I feel that I would sleep a lot easier if Lopez and Galindo weren't watching over us together. Maybe, put Lopez with Johnson or Edwards. Then we can be assured that no funny business will happen tonight."

"I'm of the same mind,"' Stewart agreed.

So, that night the first watch was Lopez, Teddy Dee, and Johnson. The second watch was Galindo and Stewart. The third watch was Chavez and Edwards.

Teddy Dee and Stewart slept lightly.

The night went by without incident.

The next morning after breakfast and cleaning up the camp the search party followed the trail across the rough terrain of Ecuador and after an hour they came across a brook and 70-85 minutes later they crossed a shallow river.

“Is this the river where you guys took fire?”

Galindo and Lopez nodded.

On the other side of the river it was Lopez that pointed out where the trail ended and Colombia began.

"We keep going," Stewart growled.

"But we were only asked to take you to Colombia," Lopez smiled. "We did all that was asked of us. We weren't told to do anything else but take you as far as the river and we have done that."

Galindo nodded silently. Chavez looked irritated at the discussion. Edwards and Johnson looked ready to beat Lopez's brains out. They simply were waiting for Stewart to signal them.

"Lopez, you aren't going to desert us now that we are in Colombia are you?"

"Maybe Lopez is scared of the Colombians," Johnson grinned. He had his combat knife in his hand and pressed against his thigh out of sight of everyone except Teddy Dee.

"Scared? We aren't scared. What are we scared of," Lopez asked no one in particular.

"So, since you ain't scared then you and Galindo will keep following the trail and lead us into Colombia?" Raleigh Stewart suggested.

Lopez hesitated, reveling in the moment. He was thinking. The dark eyed worker smiled.

"We are in Colombia."

"So, lead us to the closest town," Stewart said.

According to his intel El Gordo was in a border town near the Ecuador border but he did not know if the town had a real name. Teddy Dee had read that El Gordo was in a border town called: Empanada.

"Sure, I can do that," Lopez agreed.

Lopez and Galindo shared a silent moment and Stewart and Teddy Dee watched the silent exchange like two snakes kissing.

Galindo and Lopez walked ahead of everyone talking. Chavez and Johnson were the second wave. Stewart and Teddy Dee were the third wave. Edwards was guarding the rear.

"My Spanish is none too good," Johnson admitted switching with Stewart after a short stay next to Chavez. "It is better that someone that can kind of understand what the two chuckle heads are saying is closer to them."

"Well, the game is at hand," Teddy Dee said snapping off his holster guard over his 9mm pistol.

"What does that mean?"

"It means keep your eyes and ears open. We are walking into the lion's den dressed in a meat suit with two of the jackals leading the way."

"Damn," Johnson breathed.

"Damn is right," Teddy Dee agreed.

Teddy Dee blinked and found himself suddenly back in Kulani sitting on the examine table with the prison doctor in front of him. The doctor, pot bellied, smiling slightly, and trying to figure out a delicate way to deliver the news that he had only recently found out nearly a month after the tests had been sent to Honolulu General. The doctor seemed to be psyching himself up for the delivery of bad news.

"I'm not going to be delicate about this," the doctor said. He pursed his lips, preparing himself for the words. "I give you maybe a year. That's being generous."

A year? Less than 400 days? If he were released that moment, he would have 365 days? If he was released, when he was expected to be released, he would have 175 days.

Teddy Dee after the mental calculation allowed himself to feel mortal. He felt gut punched. He had received bad news throughout his life. He had been devastated when he learned that his aunt Dorothy had died in Chicago while he was in Croatia. He had cried when Katherine Rogers had died in Boston. He had wept when his mother died. Yet, the feeling that came from the doctor's diagnosis had frozen Teddy Dee. He was paralyzed. He did not know how to absorb the words or anything suddenly. The doctor had suggested things and said things but Teddy Dee had not been able to comprehend any of it. All he heard was that he was suddenly on a clock.

His mind considered the time frame and suddenly that meant that by October of next year he would be dead.

Hiro Fujinaka was the fourth Hiro Fujinaka in the Fujinaka clan when he took over the Royal Family Remedy Company. He had gone to Haas Business School in the United States and come back with innovative ideas. While in the United States he had met his future wife, Keiko. After graduating, he and Keiko had returned to Japan and started a family. Hiro Fujinaka was made a VP of Finance at a competitor company and given a five-million-yen budget to balance.

His success at the competitive company made the Fujinaka family look at their own family to run the Royal Family Remedy Company and then Signet Industries. The selection of Hiro Fujinaka as President and CEO of Royal Family Remedy Company and Signet Industries was unanimously approved by the board of directors. The board of directors were all family members.

The position, though lofty in title, was not a position that anyone coveted in the family. The company had been an albatross around the neck of many and a lodestone to most. It was a wieldy thing. The main offices were in Tokyo. The manufacturing was in Thailand. The CEO had to be willing to travel at least half the year to insure that manufacture was smooth.

There was a monthly board meeting in Tokyo that was contentious at times. The family did not all play nicely. There were continual attempts at chair shifting.

It was not a good job. It was not a bad job. The company was rising as an herbal innovator as a result of the leadership of the biggest family owned business in Japan.

Hiro Fujinaka IV and Keiko had Tanaka, their first child and son, and almost immediately began to groom him for a position at the Royal Family Remedy Company. His son was bright and impetuous. He was calculating and somewhat of a bully. If there had been gangs where he went to school little Tanaka Fujinaka might have been the gang leader. Tanaka Fujinaka liked to cut corners. He was smart but lazy.

When Tanaka turned seven Keiko delivered Asami Fujinaka, Hiro Fujinaka's daughter was exceptional from birth. She had these large brown Anime eyes, an oval face, and gentle spirit. Her mother could not recall a time when Asami just cried to cry. By two, she was walking and talking. She was bright and curious about everything. By the age of five she was the star of her school. Asami Fujinaka was gifted and sensitive.

Yet, she was not groomed to take part of the Royal Family Remedy Company. Her role was, it was believed, to be like all the Fujinaka women, an obedient child, loving daughter, and devoted wife and nothing more.

Royal Family Remedy Company had been handed down from generation to generation. The company business had been handed down to the first male heir of Hiro Fujinaka.

Chapter Six.

"Find my daughter," Albert Buck said in Teddy Dee's memory. He had awakened still in Kulani. Teddy Dee was still nursing a headache that he could not shake. Teddy Dee recalled the memory of Ecuador.

"How much farther," Teddy Dee asked and the message was relayed to Lopez and Galindo.

"We are nearly there," Galindo smiled.

"Five minutes maybe ten," Lopez corrected.

The team climbed over a hill and there it was the first sign of human development in the Colombian jungle. The development was a small town near the border of Colombia.

"This is El Gordo's town," Lopez pointed out at the edge of the small town.

The team walked into the small town and took in the dull faces of farmers used to hard work dressed in the traditional garb of the region. There were several women near a well when Galindo and Lopez strode through the streets like conquering warriors. Chavez and Stewart were warier.

Teddy Dee and Johnson saw four or five boys playing soccer in the dirt as they walked toward the center of the town. Teddy Dee noted the biggest building in the town was a church with a small fountain in front of it.

"Let's go to the church and regroup," called Stewart. Lopez and Galindo nodded. Everyone headed to the front of the two story church with a bell tower.

In the shade of the church Edwards put his hand in the fountain and poured cool water over his head. Lopez and Galindo leaned against the wall patiently waiting for instructions. Chavez pushed against the church's double doors but the church doors were secure. He hunkered down and studied the rooftops for any snipers. Johnson took up a position on the far side of the church making sure that they were not surprised by someone appearing without notice.

Stewart and Teddy Dee walked to Lopez and Galindo. Lopez was drinking water from his canteen. Galindo was dabbing at the back of his neck with a wet handkerchief.

"So, what now?"

Stewart smiled at the smiling Lopez. He placed a hand on the man's shoulder. Stewart smiled and Teddy Dee figured that was the smile that most people that got on Stewart's bad side saw just before he killed them.

"Now, what do you say, Jose? Take us to El Gordo?"

"What?"

"It's obvious that you know where you are. So, where is his headquarters?"

"I'm not sure," Lopez lied.

"Bullshit," Stewart growled. "You know Lopez you smell like a rat."

"What?"

"Where is El Gordo? How much did he pay you to rat us out?"

Lopez was a horrible actor. His lying was unbelievable. He protested but nothing he did seemed to have any truth in it.

"I have done everything you asked of me. You wanted me to track the trail. I tracked the trail. You wanted me to take you to Colombia. I took you to Colombia. You asked me to take you to the closest town. I did that. Now, you want to accuse me of kidnapping? I don't know El Gordo. I have family that lives in a town a few miles from here. Getting here from Ecuador isn't that hard if you grew up here."

"So, you grew up here?"

"No, I have family that live near here. I grew up in Mexico," Lopez backpedaled.

"Then you know El Gordo, right?"

"Everyone knows El Gordo if you live or have family that live near the border," Lopez pointed out. "He is a very powerful man on the border."

At that moment Johnson pulled his pistol out and aimed it at Lopez.

"Whoa," Lopez said raising his hands in surrender.

"Don't move," Johnson growled.

"Easy man," Lopez suggested.

"What do we do with him cap," Johnson asked holding his pistol down and away from Lopez.

"Well, let's wait and see," Stewart decided. He turned to Edwards suddenly thinking out a plan that came to mind. "We are going to need a place to stay for the night. Edwards find us a secure location. Chavez you are standing over watch. Teddy can you get us in this church?"

Teddy Dee nodded and walked the perimeter of the church and was not surprised to see that the whole structure was made of brick and mortar. It was a sturdy building but a building that was built to house not to deter. The church was not Fort Knox. It was a place of worship. There would be a door or window that would give with the slightest effort. Teddy Dee knew that as he moved around the building in the shade of the church. In the rear of the building Teddy Dee found an open window.

He climbed in through the open window and into a gray darkness of the rear of a church that probably didn't have running water or an indoor toilet. Teddy Dee paused and allowed his eyes to adjust to the dimness. He was in what had to act as the storage area of the church. There were several boxes labeled: Nina 9-12. A few boxes had penned on their sides: Zapata's. Piled near Teddy Dee were a short stack of smaller boxes labeled: wafers. To the left of Teddy Dee sat a dusty cabinet.

Teddy Dee moved silently through the darkness like a ninja. He didn't expect to run into anyone. If there was anyone in the quiet church it might be the priest or a caretaker.

He moved from the back of the church into the sanctuary. Once inside the tall and spacious interior Teddy Dee noted that there was only the door he had snuck in and the front double doors. There were several windows and no ceiling fans. As far as Teddy Dee could tell there was no electricity in the whole building.

There were a dozen windows that were ten to twelve feet off the ground. There were two smaller windows that stood over the altar and allowed the sun to play and create a myriad of colors inside the cool of the sanctuary.

Teddy Dee opened the double doors of the church and let Stewart, Lopez, Galindo, and Johnson inside. Suddenly, Teddy Dee thought that staying in the church was a bad idea. They had gone from gringos to blaspheming gringos. Not a good situation.

Stewart was in charge with Johnson and Edwards as his faithful lapdogs. Teddy Dee thought to voice his concern but knew almost immediately that the concerns would fall on deaf ears. So, he held his tongue and waited for the opportunity to close the account that Raleigh Stewart, the cowboy, had opened. At that moment Johnson shoved Lopez into the church at gunpoint. Galindo followed quietly.

"We haven't done anything,"' Lopez pointed out.

"Shut up," Johnson spat having taken their rifles from them and their pistols. "Sit down and don't make me shoot you."

Teddy Dee allowed Stewart to play out his best cowboy movie before approaching him. Lopez and Galindo were disarmed. Johnson was watching them like a hawk. Edwards had come back and told him that the town only had four buildings beside the small houses that fought the jungle everyday. Chavez had been relieved and Edwards and Chavez and Johnson were in over watch using the church's bell tower as the crow tower.

"So, what now?"

Raleigh Stewart was a bull of a man and one that you didn't want on your bad side. So, as he narrowed his eyes at Teddy Dee trying to figure out if Teddy Dee was becoming an annoyance Stewart continued strategizing.

"Well, the way I see it we hunker down and rest up and then we go and ask some of the locals where El Gordo is. We haven't blown this yet. It is balled up pretty badly but it is still manageable."

Teddy Dee nodded. He didn't have much confidence in Stewart's plan. For an instant he thought to remain quiet and allow the situation to become unmanageable. Then, he thought better of it and spoke.

"Listen, Raleigh, you may have this whole thing wired and if you do that is Kool and the Gang. So, if you don't, let me offer this idea to chew on. Again, it's all Kool and the Gang if you listen and think that my idea is a little far-fetched."

Raleigh Stewart nodded.

"Okay, this is what I am thinking." Teddy Dee laid out an elaborate plan that was a high-stakes gamble. It involved Stewart's trust despite the present situation. It also meant that one of the rats had to be allowed to escape.

"The way I see it we can wait for things to happen and play it all defensively. Or, we can go on the attack. I am more comfortable when I have the perceived advantage." Teddy Dee paused waiting for Stewart's objections. The ex-Marine offered no objections. "Go big or go home is my motto."

"Agreed."

"For this to work you have to do your damnedest to show that your pride is more important than the outcome."

"I get it," Stewart smiled. "I am the asshole here."

"You got it."

"I got it."

"Holler, if you need me." Teddy Dee said as he went to the far side of the church and disappeared into the shadows.

In the exchange of duties handled by Stewart a few hours later Lopez asked if he could go and pee.

Edwards had been given the responsibility of watching over the mouthy Lopez.

Lopez and Edwards returned from the toilet and for one reason or another Edwards got distracted and dropped his handcuffs and Lopez found himself loose and near the open door of the church. Lopez paused only long enough to check that no one was aiming a weapon at him while Edwards fumbled with his handcuffs before Lopez escaped.

It was almost comical. Galindo and Lopez had exchanged glances seconds before Lopez made for the door. Galindo could only watch.

Leland Edwards surprised by the brazen nature of Lopez uttered one word and then chased his prisoner out of the church door but Lopez was a jack rabbit and heading for the high grass.

"Leland come back. Come back man," Stewart screamed.

"Let me go get him Sarge," Johnson pleaded.

"No, we have to stay together. We cannot let this shit get anymore fucked up than it already is now," Stewart growled.

Teddy Dee simply watched silently.

Galindo smiled at the successful escape of Lopez.

"Where is he going'" Johnson asked Galindo just inches from the other man.

Galindo shrunk back from Johnson instinctively. Johnson took that as an opportunity to grab a handful of Galindo's uniform and threaten to beat the hell out of him.

Stewart, cool headed and a battle weary soldier called out over Johnson, "Chavez, follow Edwards and bring him back here. You got a radio?"

"Yeah," Chavez said as he climbed to his feet and began running out the church door s fast as he could. Instantly, he was gone once he reached the threshold.

"Johnson, keep it in your pants," Stewart growled at his man and Johnson's fuming seemed to back off.

Ten minutes passed.

Chavez returned. "They are in the brush. They seem to be headed north as best as I can tell. Sadly, it is getting dark and I need more equipment and time."

"Okay," Stewart said, rubbing his chin.

In the silence that followed, Chavez continued.

"They are in the wind, my friend," Chavez admitted.

Stewart nodded, dejectedly. He glowered at those that dared to catch his eye. The last one that looked in his direction was Teddy Dee. Stewart paused and then narrowed his eyes before responding to the silent reproach.

"Don't say shit man," Stewart growled.

"My lips are sealed."

After the dust settled and Edwards and Lopez did not return, Chavez offered another solution.

"What say we go to the cantina and figure out where El Gordo is? He probably knows we are here already."

No one objected. So, Johnson stayed at the church with Galindo and a radio.

"If things get hinky take Galindo into the brush and wait for us. We'll ping you when we are clear. Worst comes to worse head back to HQ."

Johnson smiled at the solution.

"Are you sure that leaving Johnson with Galindo is such a good idea?"

"What do you mean?"

"I mean that Johnson seems a bit of a hot head. He nearly tore off Galindo's head when Edwards didn't return from chasing Lopez."

Stewart looked as if Chavez was speaking Greek. The big man tilted his nearly square head trying to understand what Chavez was trying to say.

"Galindo is no good to us if Johnson beats him to a pulp."

"I'm well aware of that Chavez," Stewart hissed suddenly annoyed with the SPWD man trying to second guess him. They were near a building that passed for a feed store. Stewart stopped and stretched out his hand to stop Chavez. Chavez stopped and stared evenly at Stewart.

"Let me make this clear, Chavez. We aren't rookies here. We ain't wet behind the ear pups that don't know our asses from a hole in the ground. My men are highly qualified and trained. If I tell Johnson to watch Galindo, then that's what he will do. He knows the value of Galindo in this operation. He and Lopez are our connection to El Gordo and Buck's daughter. We aren't going to allow this to get out of hand. You can damn well believe that."

"But it is already out of hand," Chavez pointed out.

"Chavez, I'm going to let you have that one but know this," Stewart paused, looking at the audience he had. He was wound up. He couldn't stop if he wanted to. "We came down here to find and retrieve Buck's daughter. You can book it that we will find and retrieve her come hell or high water."

Stewart turned and stormed forward and in the direction of the closest watering hole; El Rojo Gecko.

After a moment everyone followed.

The closest cantina was just a few minutes walk from the storefront the group had stopped in front of for Stewart's diatribe. The quartet of Stewart, Teddy Dee, Chavez, and walked in the quiet place and the cantina owner smiled a toothy grin.

"Hey, gringos, what will it be?"

"Beer, cold?"

"Si," the toothy cantina owner smiled. He was square headed man with a Billy goat gruff strip of beard on his long chin. The cantina owner was easily forty and overweight.

"Let's start with six."

They sat down at a table and looked around the cantina.

Chavez sat uncomfortably with his back to the open the door. Teddy Dee sipped at a warm beer and tried to figure out the play of the game afoot. There were limited choices in his mind. El Gordo was not going to be sitting in this cantina any time soon. If El Gordo did appear at this cantina, then there would be a whole lot of shooting and guns. In a shootout against a drug lord and four or five company employees the odds were always stacked against the smaller force.

Stewart sat sweating in the heat of the South American day leaning back and drinking a warm beer.

"This is lukewarm, at best," Stewart complained to no one in particular. The bartender, a round faced Latino smiled and wiped down the makeshift bar. Beside the bartender there were four people that were not with Stewart; sitting near the window reading a newspaper was an old man, in his sixties, with a slightly round face, similar to the bartender, with a ponytail and wearing light and blousy shirt and loose fitting jeans, on his head was a Cincinnati Reds baseball cap, another man, younger, maybe in his forties, passed out on a table in the corner of the bar room.

They drank beers and waited for El Gordo or one of his cronies to come into the hole in the wall bar. After about an hour Stewart rethought his plan.

"Okay, let's get back to the church. We'll rest and regroup."

After an hour Leland Edwards walked back in the church. He looked a mess. He was dirty and scraped up on his arms.

"I have some good news and some bad news," Edwards was seated and resting. He smiled as he sipped on a lukewarm beer.

"Good news first," Stewart said.

"Found El Gordo's compound. It's not that far away either," Edwards said.

"The compound is maybe ten clicks away."

"Ten clicks?"

"Hell, man, that ain't that far," Stewart announced.

"Yeah, maybe two hours away," Edwards said.

"What's the bad news?"

"Think that Lopez was working for El Gordo," Edwards said.

"What happened?"

"Don't really know. I nearly caught him but when he got to the gates he started talking about gringos and pointing back to where I had been chasing him. I didn't stay for the translation. Figured that I got the highs and lows of the show."

"Okay, then we are saddling up and heading for El Gordo's lair," Stewart announced all John Wayne reincarnated. "Find us some transportation. Someone in this backwater hole has to have a working vehicle that we can borrow." Stewart was talking to his faithful lapdog, Edwards.

Teddy Dee listened and as he had before felt that Stewart was moving in the wrong direction. This time, he held his tongue. In his mind, Teddy Dee figured, that if Jana Nichols was anywhere it would be at El Gordo's compound. So, good or bad his mission was taking him inevitably to El Gordo. Of course, Teddy Dee wanted to plan the attack a little better but sometimes a plan was simply just a plan when there were so many moving parts in action.

Thirty minutes later Edwards skidded to a stop in front of the church in a battered van that had seen better days. Edwards was smiling from ear-to-ear. The rag tag group of soldiers climbed aboard the grayer primer van than van.

"Be careful," Edwards advised as everyone climbed aboard. The floor of the van was paper thin in areas and in some places there was a clear view of the ground below. There were only two working doors in the barren van. It had no creature comforts and barely was able to stay above thirty miles per hour but it was better than walking.

At 12, Asami Fujinaka loved getting up early and going and sitting near the koi pond. There was a peacefulness that the beautiful and graceful fish exuded. As Asami sat silently on the wooden bench that surrounded the pond the teen felt her worries diminish. The koi moved gracefully around the enormous koi pond on the western side of the complex.

The koi caretaker arrived as he usually did in his small Mitsubishi Minicab. He unloaded his carrier and headed for the pond. The caretaker never had been inside the main complex of the Fujinaka compound. He had only once been to the Fujinaka kitchen. A shapely woman named: Chiharu had invited the caretaker to the Fujinaka kitchen. Chiharu had fed the caretaker. The koi caretaker later married Chiharu.

The caretaker had been working at the Fujinaka complex five years after they introduced the koi to the pond nearly a quarter of a century ago. The caretaker he had taken over for nearly six years ago was a legend in the koi fishing industry. The caretaker had watched the powerful Fujinaka family prosper. The President of Signet Industries had hired him personally: Hiro Fujinaka. Fujinaka fashioned himself as a bit of a koi expert and was very hands-on with his koi.

He had also seen many things in his twice-weekly visit to the Fujinaka compound. As the family and business grew so did the security and personnel. When the caretaker first began working there were already two layers of security to pass through before his arrival to the koi pond. In the last two years another layer of security had been introduced and the company brand had expanded. It was something that had to occur if the business was to grow. The quiet and older caretaker understood the ebb and flow of business, as it was very similar to the care and feeding of the hundred plus koi in the 2,500-gallon pond.

Yet, as he prepared to work the caretaker knew few in the compound even knew him or his name. Of course, Hiro Fujinaka IV knew his name. Chiharu knew his name but she was no longer working in the kitchen. She had retired and was now at home doting over her 34-year old daughter. Tanaka might know his name. Keiko, the wife of Hiro might know his name.

"Good morning Mister Masamoto," Asami said from the bench. She was dressed in a gold colored silk kimono with an intricate koi design on the back and sleeves. Her hair was pulled up and away from her flat diamond-shaped face to show off her small ears and long, delicate neck. Asami possessed lineless skin, a thin nose, and thin lips. She was thirteen and had the physical shape of a twelve-year old boy.

The caretaker nodded to the daughter of Hiro Fujinaka IV pulling out a fishing net that looked more like a sports fisherman's net than a tool used for koi ponds.

The caretaker had few tools. He had his trusty carpetbag by his side. In his hand was an eight-foot length of bamboo pole. He was dressed in dark blue coveralls, sturdy shoes, and a light blue collarless shirt. On his head was a straw hat. Around his neck was a thin chain with a locket hanging from it. By his feet was a small plastic wading pool that he used to collect and check the koi when needed. The only other tool beside the deep sports fishing net was a shallow net.

He kneeled down at the far end of the Fujinaka koi pond and studied the koi that swam to the surface of the pond. The pond was 2,500 gallons and actually five 500-gallon ponds on three different levels combined to create the illusion of one pond. The caretaker had helped in setting up the pond's filtration and cleaning system. In the midst of the pond were five giant structures used to conceal the motors that maintained the temperature and filtration of the pond. The structures looked like little islands.

The caretaker was on the northern edge of the pond and studied the 20 or so koi that gathered in front of him. He looked up and noticed that Asami was near. The caretaker could not help but smile at Asami and her interest in koi. She was very similar to her father in some of the most unexpected ways.

He smiled at the fish and their docile behavior. There were over one hundred koi fish swimming in the pond and every time he appeared the koi would approach like faithful puppies. He studied the red, white, orange, silver, gold, and black of the koi that were crowding the shore closest to him looking for his newest koi introductions: Aramis, Athos, and Porthos.

"Today, while I am here I want to check on the three newest introductions that you named: Aramis, Athos, and Porthos."

Aramis was a white and black koi that seemed to love to circle other koi for some reason. Aramis was a young Kumonryu. There were only five in the Fujinaka koi pond.

Athos was a golden metallic koi with a black freckled tail fin. He had been given the name because he was so unusual. Athos was young and a big personality. Athos loved to be touched and was very friendly. Athos was one of now ten Ogon in the Fujinaka pond.

Porthos was an orange and black koi with a very friendly nature. There were more Kawarimono than any other koi in the Fujinaka pond. Porthos though had a "third" eye on its forehead that no other koi exhibited.

Only Aramis seemed to be on the northern side of the koi pond at the moment.

"Is that Aramis," Asami said pointing toward the white and black koi pushing toward the shore.

"Yes, I believe that is Aramis," the caretaker smiled.

Chapter Seven.

Teddy Dee was just a month away from his release and counting down the days to his imminent return to the shadows. It was December. It was December in Hawaii.

Thirty days before release was always interesting. Teddy Dee had watched as other minimal threats had been released from Kulani before. There was a whole process. Teddy Dee dreaded the process but knew that he had to suffer through it, nonetheless.

In the month leading up to his release Teddy Dee found himself under more scrutiny than he preferred. He had blacked out three days before. He had, in two years, blacked out twice. So, with less than a month to his release Teddy Dee had been released from the infirmary.

He was bandaged and bruised but recovering. Teddy Dee returned to his cell and was given light exercise and guards were asked to monitor him just in case he blacked out again. Teddy Dee thought the precautions were alarmist. He blacked out, in his memory, maybe a handful of times but the black outs were not serious or frequent, at least not in Teddy Dee's memory.

Thinking about black outs made Teddy Dee also think of the last good memory of being in the shadows of the corporations was doing a suit a good turn returning his abducted daughter from Ecuador. Tracking. Fighting. Betrayal. Everything going to shit. Recovery. Return. Reward.

"We get there and try and talk with El Gordo about his demands," Stewart explained as the van weaved through the dirt trail that was the road from the small town to the gravel road that was the more developed road in this part of Colombia.

Teddy Dee did not listen to Raleigh Stewart. He had decided once he was close to the compound he would have to go rogue if he was going to extract Jana Nichols from El Gordo.

Edwards listened and in about twenty minutes the black lapdog had driven through the countryside to the edge of El Gordo's compound.

“Okay, so this is the plan,” Edwards explained. “We are going to blow up the van near the compound and cause a distraction. When they come to investigate we rush in and get Jana and Eric. Easy,” Edwards smiled.

“So, this is where you and I part company,” Teddy Dee said as the van slowed to a stop on the country road. Teddy Dee opened the van’s door and stepped out of the van.

“You sure you want to go all Rambo now,” Raleigh Stewart asked.

Teddy Dee nodded and walked toward the side of the road and into the tree line.

"This is some real "A Team" shit," Edwards announced as the van drove away from Teddy Dee and toward El Gordo’s compound without a plan.

Teddy Dee cut through the countryside and came upon the compound of El Gordo. It was not hard to find. It was the only walled compound in the small city.

"Whatever works," Teddy Dee said watching from a hill that overlooked the compound. He was hidden behind a rock outcropping. He planned to traverse the 30º slope as soon as Stewart and Johnson blew up the van at the gates of El Gordo's compound. Teddy Dee hoped that with enough distraction he could scale the eight foot wall and find Jana Nichols and Eric Blanding without much blood shed. He had one problem of course, Jose Lopez. If that rat had given them up, then El Gordo would be waiting for Stewart and Teddy Dee and their gooses were cooked.

The explosion shook the earth. Teddy Dee had his AR-15 slung across his back. He had his two Walther PPQ 9mm pistols under his armpits when he took off down the 30º slope. Teddy Dee tore down the rocky terrain like a mountain goat and hit the eight foot wall in one single bound. He felt like Superman as he scrambled up and over the wall and fell like a rock into the compound.

As Teddy Dee hit the dirt of the compound he heard Spanish epithets thrown in his direction and came under fire from his right. Teddy Dee used the momentum to tumble forward and behind a patio set of furniture. The furniture offered little cover but it gave him a moment to see who was shooting at him. Two Colombian shooters were hunkered down in a corner bunker that served a double purpose of cabana and shooting gallery.

Teddy Dee scrambled for protection and found a watering trough where he could get his bearings. Gunfire peppered the ground on either side of the watering trough. Bullets burrowed into the dry ground sending plumes of dirt into the air.

Teddy Dee thought about the AR15 on his back and then pulled his Walther PPQ 9mm pistol and snapped off the safety and stood up. He expected to be fired on but for that moment he was unmolested.

"Might as well push my luck," Teddy Dee mused standing in the rear of the compound he had just entered. So, Teddy Dee ran headlong toward the cabana/shooting gallery. His pistol leveled and ready as he ran forward.

The first to be shot was the baby faced killer dressed in a striped hooded shirt and blue jeans. Teddy Dee fired three times from each pistol and the baby faced killer jerked left and crashed into the wall: dead. His shotgun fell out of his hands useless.

The second killer fired an unplanned shotgun blast from inside of the cantina but missed. The shot from the shotgun was loud but inaccurate. Teddy Dee knew that unless the shooter was close the shotgun was useless.

Teddy Dee slammed against the wall of the cantina and after half a moment crouched and entered the dark one room cabana. The killer fired again but too high and Teddy Dee returned fire hitting him in his shoulder and arm forcing him to drop the shotgun. Teddy Dee moved fearlessly forward in the dark room checking corners as he moved deeper into the cabana. There was no one else in the cabana but Teddy Dee and the moaning, would be killer.

"Damn it. Damn it," the wounded man growled, holding his left shoulder, having been shot but not killed.

Instantly Teddy Dee kicked the shotgun away from the wounded killer. The shotgun rattled and banged against the wall. Then there was silence. In the dark room he saw that the killer had a chain around his neck that had a gold "J" on it. Juan.

"El Gordo will kill me for allowing you, black panther, to enter his compound. If I had that pistol I would kill you now. You have wounded me, black panther. Perhaps, I can make you make a mistake and kill you when you let your guard down," Juan babbled.

Teddy Dee patted Juan looking to see if he had any other weapons.

"This is my chance. I am wounded and the black panther is bigger and stronger but he is overconfident. This is my chance. I will poke out his eyes. The blind black panther will not be any match for me," Juan decided. Juan looked up and into Teddy Dee's eyes. Teddy Dee narrowed his dark eyes.

Juan didn't see the sledgehammer of a punch coming. He didn't try to block it. He didn't try to avoid it. One punch and all the talk in the cabana ended.

"You know that you shouldn't talk about what you are going to do in a tense situation. You give yourself away," Teddy Dee said to no one in particular realizing that no one in particular in the cabana cared about what he was saying.

Teddy Dee ran from the cabana toward the back of the mansion of El Gordo. Surprisingly, there was no one guarding the back of the villa except the two babbling bandits in the cabana.

Teddy Dee believed that most of El Gordo's men had to be in the front trying to stop the attack being launched by Stewart and his men.

Teddy Dee ran up the stairs and to the patio door. He looked inside. No one was in the room. So, Teddy Dee entered. He crossed the room and halfway across the room in ran two men carrying submachine guns.

The men had come from a hallway off to the right of Teddy Dee. They were dressed in collared shirts and slacks. One was wearing sunglasses. The other looked a little like a Mexican bodybuilder with a thick chest and gigantic arms.

Teddy Dee crouched down and fired at the first gunman wearing sunglasses. The gunmen froze as they were fired upon. In that moment, Teddy Dee expertly shot the sunglass wearing gunman in the chest driving him back and to the left. Instantly, the body builder leveled his machine gun but never had a chance to fire.

Teddy Dee climbed to his feet and moved quickly to the dead men. He grabbed the radio and sub-machine gun of the body builder and moved deeper into the mansion of El Gordo.

The mansion was a three story Spanish Ranch house that sat on twenty-two acres of land bordering a river. There was a small water tower and winepress on the grounds. Beside the mansion was a guest house, pool and pool house. There was a barn and Teddy Dee presumed that there had to be horses here, somewhere. But, the horses were the least of his concern. All that Teddy Dee wanted to find was where El Gordo or his men were hiding Jana Nichols and Eric Blanding if they were not already dead.

"Ernesto, get the scientist and the woman," announced a voice on the radio. Wherever Ernesto was Teddy Dee wanted to be suddenly. If the scientist was Eric Blanding, then the woman had to be Jana Nichols.

Teddy Dee stopped and listened.

Somewhere far from him he could hear the fight taking place. There was an explosion. There were the sounds of automatic gunfire. People were screaming.

Then, Teddy Dee heard the sound of someone upstairs moving quickly toward him. He also heard a bolt unlatch somewhere closer to him. A woman screamed. Then there was a shuffling moving away from him.

Teddy Dee reacted and moved toward the sound where he had heard the woman scream. He hoped that the woman was Jana Nichols.

Teddy Dee climbed up a short flight of stairs and down another set of stairs to find himself still in the rear of the mansion. Through an open door he had saw, in passing, a library. There was also a spacious entertainment room. Yet, Teddy Dee had no time to investigate those rooms. He was hunting Jana Nichols and Eric Blanding and if he found Ernesto he might find them alive.

Through a hallway and down a short flight of steps Teddy Dee stepped into the kitchen and studied the restaurant like space. There was a restaurant sized freezer. There was a double refrigerator. A gigantic restaurant stove sat against the wall next to the double sink. In the center of the kitchen was a marble island which had hanging above it an array of pots and pans.

No one was in the kitchen. Teddy Dee took a moment to think and as he did he heard the basement door beside the restaurant freezer open. Teddy Dee narrowed his dark eyes. He smiled for all the wrong reasons. He smiled because in a moment two Colombians had come out of the door carrying a white woman with blonde streaked hair and wearing thin glasses on her nose. The woman looked like she should have been still in high school. She was petite and dressed in dirty blue jeans and a thin T-shirt with a cartoon character on it. Beside the bedraggled woman was a square-faced man with a slight beard and mustache. He was dressed in dirty jeans like the woman. Unlike the woman he was wearing a hooded Mickey Mouse sweatshirt and had a split lip. He was a thin man that looked more inclined to giving orders than working with his hands.

The Colombians were in mid-speech when Teddy Dee casually walked up and shot one of the two in the head. As the first Colombian fell to his knees, dead, the woman began to scream and the man reached out to protect her. Teddy Dee spun and shot the other Colombian in the heart twice and pushed the couple away from the recent death and destruction.

"Are you Jana Nichols and Eric Blanding?"

The man was holding the woman and trying to shield her from the violence that was only inches away.

"Are you Jana Nichols and Eric Blanding?"

"Yes," the man said. The woman sobbed against the man's chest.

"Okay, I'm here to get you back to Ecuador and then to Anaheim. I don't have too much time to explain. So, let me say a few things and then you have to trust me." He paused and said: "Albert Buck. Small Planet. Your mother and sister miss you incredibly."

Teddy Dee ushered the pair from the kitchen and toward the rear of the mansion. Then they were on the move.

"Where are we going?"

"Well, our choices are limited," Teddy Dee began explaining that they would have to scale a wall and then climb a 30º slope to freedom.

Eric Blanding paused and said before leaving the kitchen that the garage was only a few feet from them.

"We can drive away," Blanding concluded.

Teddy Dee narrowed his dark eyes at the idea.

Teddy Dee was the first to enter the five car garage. There was a fire engine red Ford F-150 sitting in the garage. The trio moved past the black F-150 looking for something that had a little more horsepower. There was a silver Porsche 911 but that was a two-seater. There was a new blue BMW X5 in one of the garages. There was an olive green Hummer. Instantly, Teddy Dee figured that they had found their transport out of El Gordo's compound.

"Wait, what if there is a better choice in the next garage?"

"Doesn't matter. I decide."

Jana Nichols and Eric Blanding climbed into the Hummer and Teddy Dee got behind the steering wheel and smiled. He looked back and started the Hummer. Once inside the cramped interior of the Hummer Teddy Dee signaled Stewart and told them to head back to the town. Teddy Dee floored the Hummer as the garage door lifted up and away and drove into the middle of the courtyard surprising several men near the garage.

The men scrambled to the left and right as Teddy Dee drove the Hummer forward as if the over sized vehicle was on rails.

"First test passed," Teddy Dee said to himself as he crossed the courtyard and then reached the edge of the mansion and began to hear gunfire.

"So, this should be really easy or all sorts of hard," Teddy Dee said to the passengers in the back of the Hummer. "Until we get out of this stay down and out of sight."

Instantly, the two bedraggled SPWD employees sunk lower in the back of the Hummer. They had been hidden before the advice. Now, they were imperceptible.

As the Hummer turned around the corner of the mansion there was the sound of sporadic gun fire punctuating the air. There had been a gun battle near the front of El Gordo's mansion. Busted pots and bullet casings were evidence of the pitched battle. Yet, as Teddy Dee navigated the Hummer through the remnants of the last battle he noted that there were few dead bodies. There were instead several people scrambling in front of the Hummer and headed toward the front gate.

Teddy Dee drove slowly through the courtyard and El Gordo's men stopped and were not sure if they should shoot. El Gordo was nowhere to be seen. Teddy Dee thought to himself at the fact that he had been to El Gordo's mansion and never even met the man. Instead, Teddy Dee watched as Stewart and his men retreated into the woods having received Teddy Dee's signal.

Teddy Dee drove the Hummer out of the front of El Gordo's compound and onto the short paved road that gave way to the dirt of Colombia. For the next five minutes Teddy Dee drove over the roughest dirt packed roads imaginable.

As he drove he fiddled with the radio and found that El Gordo had a particular inclination for Classic Soul and R&B. On disc number four Teddy Dee let the soothing sounds of Aretha Franklin fill the Hummer.

"Can we hear: "Do Right Woman," I love that song," Jana Nichols asked. She had been through hell but in that moment she had shown the pluck of a child raised by the indomitable Albert Buck.

Teddy Dee nodded at the daughter of Albert Buck. Teddy Dee prided himself in his inner fortitude. He was not swayed usually by women or their female wiles. Yet, as he looked back at Jana Nichols crouched down in the back of the Hummer he could not help but try to find the Aretha Franklin song. He punched the disc select and searched for Jana Nichols request.

"Do Right Woman-Do Right Man" filled the Hummer as Teddy Dee maneuvered the gigantic vehicle through unfinished roads that were not designed for its width or weight. In less than ten minutes Teddy Dee was on a broken paved road that led into the small town where he had first started this odyssey. Parking the Hummer in front of the small fountain in the center of town Teddy Dee took a beat before moving.

"Listen up, we are leaving here in the next five or ten minutes," Teddy Dee said as he muted Aretha Franklin. "We only stopped for Stewart and his men. No one gets out of the Hummer. If you need some thing, then I decide if you get it or not."

Nine minutes later Stewart, Chavez, and Edwards arrived in the small town. They were sweating and tired and armed to the teeth as they clambered into the Hummer. Stewart climbed into the front passenger seat next to Teddy Dee.

"What's the break down?"

"We had to punch Lopez and Galindo's tickets. They were dirty." He paused and added, "Only people I trust are in the Humvee." Stewart responded as the men climbed into the Hummer and stowed their weaponry.

"Good to know," Teddy Dee responded as he drove the Hummer away from the village and toward the dirt road that cut through the jungle and to the edge of Ecuador. Teddy Dee drove away from the town of the now dead El Gordo and back to Ecuador without incident.

Aretha Franklin and Teddy Dee sang as the Humvee bounced along the makeshift roads and mere dirt roads toward the SPWD compound. The Hummer chopped through the jungle like a machete. Nothing slowed the Hummer as it hurtled toward the Small Planet compound.

The two guards at the compound gates were surprised upon seeing the Hummer skid to a stop at the gates of the SPWD compound. Chavez stuck his head out of the rear of the Hummer and waved to the guards at the gates.

"Can you open the gates," Chavez asked.

Tyler Getty had smiled so broadly that he looked as if his head might crack like an egg. The entire compound roared upon hearing the news that Jana and Eric had been found and returned alive.

"Is the G150 fueled and ready to go?"

"Yes," Getty admitted.

Teddy Dee had a headache that got worse and did not go away. He was suddenly back in his hotel room but unclear how he had gotten there. Teddy Dee was dressed in shorts and T-shirt. He had no socks or shoes on.

Teddy Dee leaned forward on the edge of his hotel bed and tried to recall what had happened. Had he blacked out? Had he blacked out and while unconscious replayed the whole Albert Buck episode in his mind?

He tried to stand up but he did not have the strength. So, he sat on the edge of his bed and noticed that his hands were shaking just a little. Was he dying?

The doctor who had told him he was living on borrowed time that he would not die like he had a heart attack but more like a wind-up toy soldier.

"Teddy, be brave," the doctor advised.

Teddy Dee smiled at the doctor's advice.

"Thankfully, what you can expect before the end is nothing painful. It will just become more chronic." He studied his chart. "You will continue to get headaches. You may experience more black outs. There will be vomiting. As you progress you will have problems sleeping. Your memory will not be great because your brain will be fighting you. You may experience blindness. In the end you will go to sleep and just never wake up."

"Not so bad," Teddy Dee said absently. "There are worse ways of cashing in the chips I suppose."

The doctor did not respond.

"Well, I cannot say that I want to do this again because I don't. Been a pleasure but thankful to be leaving you and this heat," Stewart laughed. The two men hugged and slapped each other on the back. Raleigh Stewart climbed aboard the G150 ahead of Teddy Dee and behind them Jana and Eric. Bringing up the rear was Leland Edwards.

The crew climbed on the G150.

"Back to Anaheim."

"You figure that we won, right?"

Teddy Dee nodded.

"We lost a man," Edwards nodded.

"We did lose a man. A good man."

"Are any of us good in this business?"

"We were the good guys today," Stewart stated.

Teddy Dee did not speak.

"You don't think that we were the good guys," Stewart asked.

Teddy Dee shrugged.

Raleigh Stewart stared at Teddy Dee, waiting for a response that was not coming.

"Do you think that Howard was involved?"

"I don't," Stewart stated.

Teddy Dee did not comment.

"Think that this is over?"

Teddy Dee did not answer.

"Say something."

"This type of thing seems to happen again and again because they don't see the problem." Teddy Dee stated.

"The problem?"

"Suits and their family are always in the crosshairs. They are easy touches." Teddy Dee concluded.

"Yeah, I see that," Stewart noted.

"It's over, for now," Teddy Dee reassured. "I mean, we're on a plane and heading back to Anaheim."

"Yeah, we got that going for us," Stewart noted. "Well, for now, at least, it is over."

Teddy Dee smiled, but kept his thoughts to himself.

"What are your plans, after this?"

Teddy Dee did not answer.

"Me, I am going on vacation after this," Stewart laughed. "I'm sure the boss will be pleased. He will probably give me a bonus."

Teddy Dee smiled. After the job he was heading back to Atlanta. He was based in Atlanta at the time. He was staying in a four-bedroom condominium near Buckhead. Teddy Dee had purchased and owned the condominium for nearly a year and had just furnished one of the three bedrooms and part of the living room.

Six hours later, Albert Buck was waiting at the airport with a petite blonde beauty dressed in something too small and too young for her age. Buck was wearing a hand tailored suit with a lavender collared shirt and matching silk tie. He looked as crisp as a hundred-dollar bill when the G-150 landed.

Teddy Dee was pleasantly surprised to see the head of corporation of SPWD greet his daughter warmly and genuinely after the doors of the Cessna were opened and the flight crew allowed the passengers to exit.

"Looks like Buck has a heart anyway," Edwards said to Teddy Dee with a smile.

Teddy Dee nodded, thinking of the Tin Man from the Wizard of Oz. Teddy Dee could not help but look from Albert Buck to Raleigh Stewart. Stewart smiled nervously and in that tenuous smile Teddy Dee thought of the Scarecrow from the Wizard of Oz suddenly.

That nervous smile said so much. Stewart had said that Buck was all about his business. So, Teddy Dee read that nervous smile as: If you think that he has a heart you have another think coming. This guy, Albert Buck, will eat you for lunch.

Albert Buck was a businessman. He just happened to have a wife and a child. His love, as far as Teddy Dee could tell, was his business and the obscene amounts of money that his business generated. He loved his wife and his daughter, certainly but his love of them paled in comparison to the creation of SPWD and the pursuit of more money. That was the way of the world in corporations and the shadow world.

Money and the stockpiling of that money superseded everything. In the seven years Teddy Dee had first twisted an arm, then broken a finger, arm or leg everything, in the high stakes world of corporations, revolved around the pursuit of the seemingly endless Monopoly game like money. Corporations rose and fell based on money and lack thereof. People lived and died based on that simple commodity. There were no philanthropists in the ruthless world of corporations. No one gave anything away for free. There was always a cost. There was always a price in the world that Teddy Dee worked.

The Fujinaka family had asked for every variety of koi to be represented in the koi pond. The caretaker thought about the absence of the black, blue, and green koi that were introduced a few months ago.

As the caretaker thought about a way to check on the missing koi he found himself struck by the sight of Coco popping up twenty feet from the shore. The caretaker smiled and watched as the biggest koi in the Fujinaka pond bulled her way toward him. She was a three-foot long beautiful black Utsurimono koi with red markings in a distinctive zebra pattern. There were other Utsurimono koi in the pond but none as big as Coco. Coco pushed through the other koi and the caretaker could only smile at her desire to be noticed.

"Why are you smiling," Asami Fujinaka, 13, asked, suddenly at the koi caretaker's side.

"Coco," the wrinkled old man said, pointing toward the big koi now at the shore and opening and closing its mouth in a silent cry for food.

"She is greedy," Asami Fujinaka replied.

"No, she is just displaying her koi nature," the caretaker retorted.

"What is the difference?"

"Greed has to do with intention. Nature has to do with breeding."

Asami Fujinaka paused and thought about what the koi caretaker had said. Her smugness fell away in that instance. The caretaker pulled a small pouch of fish food from his belt and handed it to Asami Fujinaka.

"Can you feed the koi on the east side of the pond?"

The little girl took the pouch of fish food and moved toward the east side of the koi pond and the bench that bordered it. Asami watched as the caretaker studied the koi that were gathering near the edge of the pond. Asami smiled at the caretaker's care for the koi. At her feet, on the edge of the pond thirty koi pushed forward for their fish food.

Asami kneeled down and fed the handful of koi closest to the edge of the pond. There were Taisho Sankei, Tancho, Shusui, Ogon, and Bekko fighting for attention and food. There was a golden metallic koi that was at the front and closest to Asami that was pushed to the side by another koi. The other koi was a white skinned koi with black markings. The tortoise shell koi was aggressive. The koi near the tortoise shell koi gave it room. The golden metallic koi pushed the tortoise shell koi out of the way.

It was strange to watch the two koi finning each other for room. The tortoise shell koi splashed on the edge of the pond and caused a little koi drama. The metallic gold koi pushed against the tortoise shell koi unmoved.

"Do the koi ever fight?"

"Of course," the caretaker said. "They fight everyday."

"What do they fight for?"

"What does anyone fight for? Food? Attention? Superiority? You name it."

"But they all get fed. They all get attention."

"Some need more than the others and that is the cause of friction."

Asami listened to the caretaker who came to her home twice a week to care for the koi. He was so knowledgeable. Asami always found herself asking Mister Masamoto things that she could not ask her father.

The caretaker was feeding the koi and netting koi to check their health.

Asami enjoyed feeding the koi. They were puppies in fish form. The koi wanted attention. They were so docile that they would almost climb out of the pond for food and attention knowing that the humans would return them safely back to the pond.

"You see, Coco thinks that just because she is bigger than the others she can bull her way to the front," the caretaker opined.

"But the koi aren't aggressive and just allow the black zebra to do what she wants. It's not fair," Asami pointed out.

"The koi pond is a microcosm of our world really," the caretaker said reaching into his handy pouch and feeding the koi that had moved to the edge of the pond by hand. Feeding one koi caused all the koi near to press forward. Of course, Coco, was the first to be fed.

"There are bullies everywhere," Asami noted.

"There are bullies and those that stand up to bullies," the caretaker replied. "Even in the koi pond there are koi that refuse to be bullied."

"What happens if no one stands up to the bullies," Asami asked watching the metallic gold koi mouthing the air and waiting for food. Beside the metallic gold koi was the tortoise shell koi but not against the other koi as it had been before.

"Even if there seems to be no one to stand up to the bullies there will always be someone that will eventually stand up to the bully," the caretaker pointed out.

"Why is it so hard to stand up to bullies?"

"Nothing worth anything is easy," the caretaker laughed. "The way life works is that most people run from things they are afraid of. That fear makes people back down to bullies. Fear makes us cowards." The caretaker continued to feed the koi. "Everything you want is on the other side of fear."

Asami Fujinaka smiled at what the caretaker said. She nodded despite being afraid.

"Everything I want is on the other side of fear," Asami said to herself.

"Why are you worrying about bullies and koi, Asami," the caretaker asked.

Asami lowered her eyes and studied the koi gathering at the edge of the pond.

Not a teen, Asami Fujinaka could not express clearly why she felt the need to question Mister Masamoto. She wanted to mention her father and his direct and sometimes unfeeling messages to her. Asami wanted her father to be proud of her. She did not feel that he was. Then, she did not know how to tell Mister Masamoto about her big brother Tanaka. Tanaka was seven years older than her and treated her like a stranger. That was hard.

But Asami Fujinaka did not say anything. She simply thought about her family and their lack of ability to talk about things.

Chapter Eight.

After Anaheim, Teddy Dee returned to Atlanta for three days. Three days in Atlanta was different. Teddy Dee did not do much in those three days. He rested and recovered.

Teddy Dee liked that there was a concierge. Teddy Dee liked that there were protocols in place. He knew that if he wanted to enter the Viewpoint there were few people that could stop him. Yet, as he entered the condominium it was nice to see a guard in the lobby. He did not talk to the concierge. Teddy Dee rose to the twenty-fifth floor and exited the elevator.

He walked to his condominium. It was an unusual trip for Teddy Dee. He rarely came to Atlanta and more rarely came to the exclusive Viewpoint Condominium on Peachtree Street.

He did not have a conventional home or home address but when he had started to amass a significant amount of cash he invested some of his capital in a condominium in one of the exclusive developments that overlooked and was a part of the cityscape. Teddy Dee lived in the iconic building that was always featured in every movie that was filmed in Atlanta.

The view from the condominium penthouse that Teddy Dee purchased over five years ago was still breath taking. The condominium was still one of the tallest buildings in Atlanta and offered a view that was worth the cost. Teddy Dee sat on the one piece of furniture that he had in the living room of the four-bedroom condominium that had once been owned by a baseball player or rapper long ago.

Teddy Dee did not care about the lineage of those that had come before him in the condominium. All he cared about was that in the four-bedroom space of 2,750 square feet that no one knew or cared who he was. The penthouse had a private elevator. The penthouse had an infinity pool that Teddy Dee had used half a dozen times, if that. There were two beds in the condominium. Teddy Dee, when he was there, slept in the master bedroom that had yet another balcony that looked out and over Atlanta.

In five years, Teddy Dee smiled at the intentional sparseness of the condominium. He could have adorned the four-bedroom space exquisitely. Instead, he chose not to spend too much energy worrying about inconsequential matters. All he worried about was the kitchen and a stocked refrigerator. Well, the refrigerator was stocked with essentials. Teddy Dee did not believe in keeping food that might spoil. Eat and finish. Leftovers were eaten the next day or disposed of, simply.

Sitting in his living room and watching the sun slowly descend from the skies his phone rang. Teddy Dee checked his phone. He was slow to answer the phone when not working.

He studied the phone and checked to see who was calling. It was Roberta, his handler. He smiled. She was the fourth handler he had in seven years in the shadows.

His first year in the shadows was a mess. Teddy Dee had thought that he could manage all the particulars. That first year was horrible. After getting a handler to deal with requests, money, payments and the like things improved significantly. Teddy Dee did the work, got paid and never worried about money or finances again.

The first handler was recommended by Oscar Easton, the man that had brought Teddy Dee into the world of shadows. Tyler Cobb was the best handler Teddy Dee had and a pro. Unfortunately, Tyler Cobb died and forced Teddy Dee to find another handler. After Tyler Cobb Teddy Dee had hired Aaron Thomas. He was good but not great. So, Teddy Dee had fired Thomas and hired Izabella Bloom. Izabella Bloom was this overly energetic, fast talking bright woman who was recommended by someone that knew Easton. Teddy Dee liked Izzy but she was like one of those annoyingly hyper lap dogs that only some liked. Teddy Dee did not need an over active handler. That left Teddy Dee with Roberta Jackson. She had been Teddy Dee's handler for nearly three years.

"Are you up for a flight to Frankfurt?"

"Always."

"Well, I just got this request a few hours ago. It is a fixer job in Frankfurt. One of the security staff has derailed a bit. Hans H., a security staff member, was found in a hotel room with an underage girl. The hotel security detained him until the Frankfurt police arrived and arrested him. H, is in jail in Frankfurt awaiting trial. The twist is that H. says that he was not in the hotel room alone. He is making noise like he was in the hotel room with an executive of Audi."

Teddy Dee listened. He knew the drill. He was a fixer. Teddy Dee was a corporate blooder. He would be hired because he could get into any country and out of any country without much ado to protect the interests of any corporation given the right incentive. If he was going to punch Hans Heinrich's ticket, then he would have to be a ninja and no one in Germany had to know that he was there.

"The goal," Roberta Jackson explained in her slightly Southern accent, "was to make Aich aware of the error of his course of thinking. Worse case scenario punch his ticket and figure out a way to make it look like H. accidentally stopped breathing."

"What is the timeframe?"

"Today," Roberta said. "He is supposed to go to trial sometime next week; Wednesday."

Teddy Dee pursed his lips, thinking. It was Tuesday, Teddy Dee noted looking at his Rolex Submariner watch and smiling at the memory of the extravagant gift. Twelve to fourteen hours to get to Germany. Two hours to get situated. Roberta would arrange for everything on the ground. Teddy Dee would check in with the client. He would visit the target and determine how to convince him not to implicate any big wigs at Audi. Five days to flip this possible corporate bad decision from a night of stupidity into a meaningless and understandable mistake during consensual sex. Small window of opportunity, Teddy Dee thought as Roberta spoke in the background.

"I'll do it. Get a bump on the rate and have a flight for me from Germany to Russia Sunday. Remember, that this trip should find me back in States before next week. I'll call you from Russia. Think that I'll go through Thailand to throw off the scent. I haven't been in Bangkok in a while." Teddy Dee paused. "I'll contact you when I am in Bangkok." He added, "By then, I hope you have news."

Teddy Dee packed for Frankfurt. Two hours later he was on a United flight headed to Frankfurt International Airport. On the flight he read the dossier on Hans Heinrich from Audi that Roberta had e-mailed him.

Heinrich was a low level manager with Audi's E-mobility division. He was a high classed supervisor of a division of the E-mobility division. As Audi was in development of their first production hybrid Hans Heinrich could potentially cause a problem for Audi and their soon to be released hybrid.

Teddy Dee read the personal file and noted that Heinrich was married. He had been married for nearly 16 years to a woman named: Anna. Hans and Anna had two children. Gunther was 14 years old. Katherine was 12 years old.

The kid angle was an easy way to go, Teddy Dee thought. Yet, it was too easy. It lacked sophistication.

If Heinrich was willing to sell out Audi, then threatening his kids wasn't going to shut him up. Double-crossing Audi meant that Heinrich was already ready to die. Crossing a corporation like Audi or any multi-national and threatening them with the loss of significant money usually meant that someone had to come and identify the body. Teddy Dee thought about the way he would have to handle this delicate matter.

Once in Frankfurt, Teddy Dee wanted to concentrate on Hans Heinrich. He had to see him. He had to figure out where Heinrich stood.

Teddy Dee contacted Audi and spoke directly to the corporate executive in charge and asked when the lawyer was going to see Heinrich.

"Mister Dandridge, we appreciate your concern. We at Audi are not at liberty to discuss this matter at this time," the executive said over the phone.

"Klar,"' Teddy Dee responded. He had responded clearly and rung off. "Understood."

Fifteen minutes later Teddy Dee was in the office of Claus Oster, the executive in charge. In the office was a thick-necked German named: Lars Schultz. Schultz was one of the attorneys at Audi assigned to the Heinrich case. Also sitting in a chair was the Vice President of something important. He had come to make sure that things were handled delicately.

"Mister Dandridge, thank you for your quick response. We are in a particular bind," Claus Oster smiled, shaking Teddy Dee's hand firmly. "We need this matter handled quickly and quietly." Oster had the bluest eyes Teddy Dee had ever seen on a person. It was like looking into a swimming pool when looking into Oster's eyes. He had the crew cut and blonde hair like most Arians that Teddy Dee dealt with. Oster was clean cut and possessed a classic square jaw. When looking at Claus Oster Teddy Dee could not shake the idea of a Nazi poster of the Gestapo he had seen once.

"We are not prepared to expose Audi or any of our board members to possible scrutiny or worse," Oster explained. "So, we need Heinrich to have an accident."

Teddy Dee listened to Oster and narrowed his eyes.

"Accident," Teddy Dee repeated, nodding his head.

"You have a question," Claus Oster asked tilting his head.

Teddy Dee had learned long ago that there were no questions to be asked of a big wig in the corporation. They were juggernauts. They bulled ahead. They directed people. They managed people. They did not answer questions.

Questions were asked earlier. When face-to-face Teddy Dee listened to the particulars. He felt the big wigs out and then acted.

Teddy Dee looked up and saw Claus Oster staring at him.

“So, we are moving forward,” Oster asked.

Teddy Dee nodded. Immediately he felt the bad taste of a bad job in his mouth.

“I look forward to hearing a good outcome,” Oster smiled.

Teddy Dee closed his eyes and thought. He looked back into the swimming pool blue eyes of Claus Oster.

"Okay," Teddy Dee swallowed. “What if Heinrich says he has had a change of heart?”

“Mister Dandridge that is not going to happen but if it does then contact me and we will advise based on the reassurances we can secure.”

Teddy Dee nodded. He raised his hand once again, “Can you get me in and out of the jail? Need a throw away passport. Need a car. Will probably need about $25,000 euros’ cash since I have to get out of Germany immediately."

"Lars can get you in and out of the jail. The ID will be ready in the next hour. A passport is already ready. Do you have a preference of the car?"

Teddy Dee shook his head; no.

Oster removed an envelope from his inside jacket pocket. He tossed it to Teddy Dee. Teddy Dee caught the envelope in midair and opened it. There was, by his count $25,000 euros inside and a signed cashier voucher from Claus Oster in the amount of $450,000 euros. It was the payoff. He looked at Oster who was studying him like a scientist might an unidentified bug.

"You aren’t moving, Mister Dandridge. Is there a problem,” Claus Oster asked with a thin smile that showed off his perfect white teeth. “You come highly recommended. We are not going to be disappointed are we?"

Teddy Dee shook his head; no. Teddy Dee knew that his job was doing what no one else was willing to do. It was not a glamorous job. Quite the opposite, Teddy Dee realized, this job was odious and brutal.

"You were hired Mister Dandridge because you solve problems. Your talents are notable. When you were mentioned we all knew that if an extreme measure was needed we could count on you." Oster paused. "You are still the right person for this job?"

Teddy Dee didn't smile. He had heard this speech from a dozen Claus Osters. Rich kids trying to be tough. Teddy Dee thought, for an instant, of back slapping Claus Oster the way that the pimps in his neighborhood had slapped whores that dared backtalk them. He wondered if Claus Oster would be so tough once Teddy Dee laid hands on him the way he had observed pimps do when he grew up.

Instantly, in his mind, Teddy Dee went back to Chicago and the West Side, where he had grown up struggling and being stopped by Miles, a pimp that drove a Cadillac, as Claus Oster smiled at him with his perfect white teeth.

Teddy Dee thought about Miles, the pimp, for a long moment, as he stood in the offices of Claus Oster and Audi. Oster had the audacity to think that Teddy Dee didn't know his job. In the back of his mind, Teddy Dee asked himself a question: What would Miles do?

He imagined that Miles would reach out and grab a handful of that thin blue striped shirt and smile at the blue eyes of Claus Oster. He would slap Oster three times increasing the intensity until the last smack dropped him like a sack of nickels.

Of course, Teddy Dee imagined if he started with Oster he would have to bitch slap the blonde crew cut Nazi standing next to him too. He deserved it for his silent approval of Oster.

Lastly, Teddy Dee would have to slap the smugness off the face of the smug German Vice President on the couch.

Teddy Dee smiled at the idea of slapping some sense in this group of Germans. He found the Germans looking at him as if he were some German bratwurst, suddenly.

"You Americans love movies. Is that right?"

Oster looked directly at Teddy Dee as if he were sizing him up for a fight. The stare snapped Teddy Dee out of his slapping fantasy and he registered what Claus Oster had just said and nodded in reply, not sure where Oster was going with his train of thought.

"Well, you are familiar with "Mission Impossible?"

Teddy Dee nodded beginning to become annoyed with the smug German in his tailored suit.

"Like "Mission Impossible" Mister Dandridge, if you are caught we will deny any association with you. There is no connection to Audi once you accept this payment. We will not protect you. We will not acknowledge any past relations." Oster stated as if he read something. "Is this clear?"

Teddy Dee nodded. This was nothing new to Teddy Dee. Corporations had been trying to cover their asses for as long as they had been doing this under handed, under the table deals and double crossing employees.

Teddy Dee had thought that the corporations were smart and powerful until he talked to his mentor; Oscar Easton.

The two blooders were sitting at a cafe looking at the Public Market in Seattle, Washington.

"Corporate lawyers are always trying to figure out a way to bottle the air. It's a fool's gambit. They can say all the college words they want but if we want to tear down the palaces it is quite simple. We know where the bodies are buried."

"But wouldn't they kill us to keep us quiet?"

"Yeah, of course. It's a catch-22. It's like owning a dog and training him to kill and knowing that he is a trained killer sleeping in your house. All you have to do is make a wrong step and all of a sudden you are in a shit storm. It's a fucked up situation, any way you cut it. They need us and simultaneously hate that they need us. We possess secrets that they cannot allow any of us to divulge. They have built their empires on lies and secrets that we know. It is a vicious circle."

Teddy Dee understood the viciousness of the circle better than most. He had voluntarily entered the seven rings of hell, that was the amorphous shadow world. Everyone that worked in the shadows called it something else. Easton liked to equate the world of shadows to the feudal world of kings and queens. Oscar Easton saw himself as a paladin. Teddy Dee thought that he and Easton were more anti-paladin than paladin than anything else.

Yet, for Teddy Dee when he tried to describe the world of shadows it always seemed like the seven rings of hell. At the lowest and deadliest level was the day-to-day workers fighting for scraps in the shit of the world that most called: daily life.

Above them, but barely, was the sixth ring where managers of the day-to-day workers dwelled. They thought that they had power but it was only power in word alone. The managers fought to meet deadlines that if they could not meet would send them down to the shit ring of hell.

The fifth ring of hell, in the shadow world, was filled with the men and women that were not the elite or exceptional but over the sixth ring managers. They were glorified managers, maybe assistants to the Vice President but not the Vice President. They struggled to maintain their place on the fourth ring fighting an endless fight for status and recognition by those above them.

One ring above the assistants, was the fourth ring of hell, where Teddy Dee rarely dwelt. This ring was where the Vice Presidents dwelt. On the fourth ring Vice Presidents found themselves fighting with other Vice Presidents in a continual teeter-totter of endless wars attempting to topple others from the fourth ring.

Above that, on the third ring of hell, there were the Vice Presidents and Board of Directors and board members that continually found themselves under attack by all those below and occasionally above. They were the money men and women. They were pulled in various directions by the money and the pressure of status. Too often, Teddy Dee had noticed that the third ring of hell in the shadows was driven by the merciless grip of cancer for those on that ring.

The second ring of hell was where the Presidents and CEOs resided. The second ring was high pressure. Any mistake on that ring of hell spelled disaster for all those below that had put trust in the President or CEO.

The first ring of hell in the world of shadows was where the founders, Presidents, modern day kings and queens of industry resided. These were the faces of corporations. These faces of corporations found their lives magnified and exaggerated under the microscope of media and paparazzi. Teddy Dee had, in his life in the shadows, only been close to the first ring of hell once and that had been accidentally. The first ring of hell seemed on its face as if it would have been a joyous place but there most feared losing their place on the ring. Stress, pressures, jealousy, sleepless nights, inability to eat or enjoy all they had acquired plagued those in the first ring.

He, in his mind and dealings, rarely got above the third ring of the back stabbing and ruthless circle dealing with the corporate managers and lower level executives who were usually just below the Vice Presidents. In his entire career Teddy Dee had met three heads of corporations and they had all been different and unique in their own ways.

At the highest ring of power, the heads of corporations wielded incredible power without much oversight.

"Are all the heads men?"

"Mostly," Easton said and added: "Well, the ones that matter."

"What's that mean?"

"It's a pecking order, right. They are the bigger fish and everyone else."

Teddy Dee nodded.

"So, who watches the heads of corporations?"

Easton looked at Teddy Dee as if he had grown another head.

"Is there anyone that—" Teddy Dee trailed off.

Teddy Dee understood his role. He worked for others. He was the employee of the head of corporations by proxy. All that he did, in the shadows, had been green lighted by the head of corporation and if anything went wrong Teddy Dee knew the corporations would protect him as they protected the corporations.

It was the knowledge that the corporations protected Teddy Dee's actions that gave him confidence to do what he did. Corporations had incredible power. They were small nations onto themselves and had all the legal and financial power needed to drive that small nation. In every corporation there was security but Teddy Dee never had to address the paid enforcers. His work was shadow work. By the very nature Teddy Dee worked outside of the corporations.

So, Teddy Dee walked out of the offices of Audi and went to the hotel closest to the jail. Audi delivered an A8 Audi there an hour after he checked in. 30 minutes later he received a text message from Lars Schultz.

"You have been added to visitors allowed to see Heinrich. Visiting hours' end at 20:00, eight o'clock."

It was 19:00, seven o'clock, when Teddy Dee received the text message. He walked the seven blocks to the jail and signed in to see Hans Heinrich. It was 19:15 when Teddy Dee was allowed to see Hans Heinrich. The police officer escorted Teddy Dee to the visitor's room and ten minutes later, 19:25, Hans Heinrich appeared.

Hans Heinrich was easily 6'4" tall but weighed less than 180 pounds. He had a crew cut hairstyle like Oster and Schultz. Heinrich was tall and wiry. Heinrich possessed gentle blue eyes that were in a perpetual squint. His wedding ring was confiscated, Teddy Dee noted as well as his watch. He was dressed in jailhouse coveralls and house shoes.

"Who are you, soul man?" Heinrich smiled, surprised to see Teddy Dee in the waiting room.

Teddy Dee smirked. Hans Heinrich was trying to be tough. He looked at Teddy Dee more curious than a neo-Nazi. Teddy Dee having dealt with so many people in so many stressful situations depended on his years of reading people to determine if this was going to go well or bat shit crazy.

Teddy Dee sat at the table and waited for Heinrich to sit. Heinrich studied Teddy Dee and slowly sat at the table. He was not a racist, Teddy Dee decided. Racists did not sit at a table with dirt people or degenerates.

Heinrich was tired. He looked as if he had not been sleeping too well in the German jail house. Teddy Dee sat and studied Heinrich silently.

"I don't have time for this," Heinrich said, resting his elbow on the tabletop. "I told the last reporter that I don't have anything to say," Heinrich said.

Teddy Dee liked that. Heinrich was a straight shooter. He had his back up against the wall and knew that he was not long for this world. Heinrich didn't have time to bullshit. Teddy Dee liked that about Heinrich.

"You asked me, who I was?" Teddy Dee said holding Heinrich's tired blue eyes as he spoke. Heinrich listened. "I am your Gabriel or Michael based on your next answer," Teddy Dee said at the round metal table in the visitor's room.

"A black Gabriel or Michael? Interesting," Heinrich mused. He paused. "Didn't know there was a black Gabriel. Only black Michael I know is Michael Jackson."

Teddy Dee did not smile at Heinrich's attempt at a joke.

"What is your question?"

"Are you prepared to leave all you love behind, including Ana and Gunther and Stephanie?"

Hans Heinrich smiled at the question. He didn't answer immediately. Teddy Dee had his answer.

"Okay, Hans, this is how this is going to happen. You will wake up tomorrow and go through your normal day and I'll show up and you will forget all the things that happened in that hotel room."

"But—"

"No, Hans, if you care about your family you will get a quick case of amnesia and forget everything that happened in that hotel."

Hans Heinrich opened his mouth only to close it, silently.

"If you want to make Anna a widow and Gunther and Stephanie fatherless keep talking," Teddy Dee said sternly.

Hans Heinrich twisted his lips, struggling not to speak.

"You stay above ground as long as you don't step on anyone's toes. I have to talk to a few high placed people and make them aware that I don't have to stamp your ticket. They think that you want your fifteen minutes of fame." He paused. "You looking for fifteen minutes of fame?"

Heinrich's eyes widened. He was feeling the weight of the situation suddenly. Heinrich was face-to-face with the man sent to kill him.

"I don't want my—"

"Everything goes right tomorrow and you step into court and tell the magistrates that you cannot recall what happened in the hotel room. You cannot remember anything. You just forget everything. Do that and you walk out a free man. You have Anna, Gunther, and Stephanie." Teddy Dee narrowed his eyes and added, "If you try and get cute and pull a double cross I show up or someone like me and things go to shit pretty quickly for Ana and the kids."

Hans Heinrich nodded. He was not a dumb man. Hans Heinrich understood what was at stake.

Teddy Dee had returned to his hotel in Germany and thought that he had solved the Audi problem. He ate dinner. Teddy Dee went to sleep with dreams of a solution.

The next day Teddy Dee was at the Audi offices. He was sitting in the office of Claus Oster. Lars Schultz was there as was the anonymous Vice President.

"What have you to report?"

"Well, did my scan of the facility and got a chance to talk to Hans and he said that he was never given a real chance to tell your people what he was going to do." Teddy Dee stated, looking for a reaction but not really expecting one. He continued, "Heinrich has had a change of heart. He is planning on forgetting everything he saw in the hotel. He just wants to know if there is any bad blood between you and him. Oh, yeah does he still have a job at Audi after all of this."

"Mister Dandridge, we have no intention of hiring Heinrich back in any position at our company. He is a liability."

"Does he get a severance package? A golden parachute or umbrella?"

Claus Oster shook his head; no.

"Really," Teddy Dee thought. That dismissal of Teddy Dee's question rankled Teddy Dee a little bit more than he cared to admit. Here was this schlub, Hans Heinrich, who could have played hardball with the corporation and put them over a barrel but he was willing to roll over so that this multinational kept its reputation despite hiring scum that took advantage of drunk and defenseless women in hotel rooms. The rub here, as far as Teddy Dee saw it, was that Audi could make Hans Heinrich disappear and no one in Germany would care. Well, few would care.

Rich kids playing in their ice cream castles floating above everyone else, Teddy Dee thought bitterly. They thought that they were above it all. Rules, laws, civility was beneath them. These simple things did not matter to them or affect them. That truth infuriated Teddy Dee, for some reason. Teddy Dee figured that one of the rich kids had to have some compassion for someone other than themselves. But he was wrong, at least here, at Audi.

Teddy Dee decided that giving Hans Heinrich a severance package was not too much to ask from the coffers of the multinational. It was a drop in the bucket. So, Teddy Dee decided then and there to make sure that Hans Heinrich and his family were taken care of, temporarily, for his hard work and not ratting out Audi. That didn't seem too big of a deal to Teddy Dee.

"Mister Dandridge, you have a job to do. We do not care if Hans Heinrich decides to get religion now that he is facing heaven or hell," Oster hissed behind his ocean blue eyes. "Just make him no longer a liability." Claus Oster rose up from behind his desk and placed his hands on the desktop. “Erase him. Zap him. Bump him. Whatever it is that you hatchet men say. We do not want any loose ends with this whole ugly business.”

Teddy Dee was not a hatchet man. He was a blooder. Worse yet, Teddy Dee didn't like when the rich kids acted like snots. It, their behavior, irked Teddy Dee. So, to balance the scales, in some way, he decided to teach Oster a lesson in humanity and humility. Teddy Dee knew that multinationals did not appreciate or desire correction. The worst part of what Teddy Dee planned would make Audi an enemy of Teddy Dee for as long as he lived.

He weighed the pros and cons of the action that he was considering. Doing it, exacting revenge, put him on the bad side of big money and endless power. When Oster and Audi learned that Teddy Dee was behind, what he was planning, they would unleash the dogs of war; hatchet men and women, to erase him from the face of the earth. There was no advantage to what Teddy Dee was imagining but he wanted to do it nonetheless.

Teddy Dee left the offices of Claus Oster. He took the elevator down a few floors and before leaving Audi made his way to another department. He pulled out a payment slip in the amount of $450,000 euros and submitted it to the cashier on duty. He waited while the cashier checked the cashier slip signed by Claus Oster. Everything seemed to be in order. So, ten minutes later Teddy Dee walked out of Audi with $450,000 euros in a large padded portfolio.

Hans Heinrich was released. He had recanted his statement. Heinrich told everyone that would listen that he didn't recall anything that had happened that night in the hotel room. He said that he was drunk and confused. The prosecution released Hans Heinrich.

An hour later Anna, Gunther, and Stephanie met Hans Heinrich and took an unscheduled vacation to Argentina $450,000 euros richer.

Teddy Dee had taken the Audi A8 that Audi had loaned him and hit the Autobahn. While on the Autobahn Teddy Dee put in a call to Roberta.

“Roberta, I have a situation. Decided to be Mother Teresa and help out the target over the client. Figure that the client is not going to be all that happy but there is no trial. The target is gone and alive. Everyone wins. Well, I am in one of the A8s that I was supposed to be borrowing. Maybe I'm being tracked. Doubt that. I am headed to Switzerland. Figure that Switzerland is a good place to drop off the car and catch a plane to Russia. So, need you to make arrangements for that plane ticket to be ready to go in Switzerland. Contact the client and tell them that the A8 is parked in the rental car return with the keys in it. Want to spend the night in Russia. Make that two nights. Then, onto Bangkok." Teddy Dee paused. "What a rush."

"Got it," Roberta sang. "Give me ten minutes."

"Take your time," Teddy Dee laughed as he drove the A8 on the Autobahn headed for Switzerland. "I should be in Switzerland in four hours. Can you book me a hotel by the airport?"

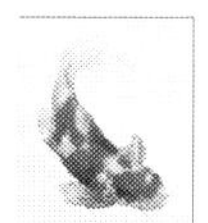  

By 2001, Signet Industries was one of Japan's biggest employers. It had two offices in Tokyo and Kyoto and three plants in each region of the island nation producing everything from hair darkening dyes to sleep inducers. It's CEO and president, Akira Fujinaka, was unquestionably one of the richest and most powerful individuals in Japan.

There had been rumors that Bayer and another global pharmaceutical corporation had attempted to take over Signet Industries. Signet Industries was a billion-dollar business, but small compared to Bayer Industries and others and seemingly easy pickings. The businessmen didn't understand that Signet Industries was a family business and that all the Fujinaka family would fight to the death to protect their heritage.

Needless to say, Bayer and then the next hostile takeover contestant withdrew its bid to buy Signet Industries for no apparent reason. Everyone in Signet Industries knew the reasons.

In 2008 Hiro Fujinaka IV took over the duties of CEO of Signet Industries against the protests of his faithful wife Keiko. His uncle Akira Fujinaka had an unexpected heart attack and Hiro Fujinaka IV, the eldest Fujinaka, took over, despite the board's seeming negative reception to the election of Hiro Fujinaka IV.

Hiro Fujinaka did not take on the responsibilities as president for the significant money or attention or influence. His decision was purely for his family, the Fujinaka family. As a result, Hiro Fujinaka IV became the new CEO of Signet Industries.

His immediate family, like most of the Fujinaka members, was business savvy but the board of directors was lukewarm toward Hiro Fujinaka IV. They, the board, were considering an outsider from the family and even a female to lead the Signet herbal venture when Hiro Fujinaka IV took the helm of one of Japan's most powerful herbal companies.

Chapter Nine.

"I love this bar," Elliott Winslow tanned and blonde dickhead who seemed more evil than good remarked sipping a martini, in Teddy Dee's memories. He was dressed in a Tommy Bahama Hawaiian print shirt, khaki trousers, and casual brown dress shoes. On his wrist was a Rolex Yachtmaster, the only thing that stated that Winslow had money. He might have been another tourist come to the Royal Hawaiian Hotel from the mainland except for his tan and Rolex. "I don't know if you know this or not but they say that numerous heads of state, Hollywood stars and international jet-setters have mingled with kama'aina (island residents) to sip exotic handcrafted cocktails while soaking in the breathtaking panorama of Diamond Head, Waikiki Beach and the sparkling Pacific Ocean," the brown haired man that smelled of wood and lavender smiled waving his hand to take in the seaside bar.

Teddy Dee did not know anything about the Royal Hawaiian Hotel. It was a hotel. Hotels were places to rest your head, nothing more to Teddy Dee. There were hotels that cost more than others and had more amenities but they were lost on Teddy Dee. What did it matter to Teddy Dee that the Royal Hawaiian Hotel was a 1927 landmark? He was not born during that time.

Yet, Teddy Dee had listened attentively studying the two men that Elliott Winslow had brought with him that night to discuss a delicate situation.

The two men, both younger than Winslow, were dressed in Hawaiian print shirts, like Winslow. One was wearing a print shirt that had sea turtles swimming across the front and to the back. The other was wearing a pineapple and coconut dominated print. The sea turtle junior had a square chin and ice blue eyes. He looked as if he had played some type of sports. The sea turtle sat and sipped on a Belgian beer. The pineapple and coconut junior was taller than Winslow and the sea turtle and carried himself like he was a construction worker. So, Teddy Dee calculated that of the two pineapple and coconut would be the tougher opponent, if it came to a fight.

"There is a little bit of a sticky situation that you were asked to assist in," Winslow smiled as the sea turtle and pineapple and coconut juniors watched the beautiful people sitting in the bar with their toes in the sand.

Teddy Dee did not like that Winslow wanted to discuss the matter in the open. Then again Teddy Dee thought that there was less of a chance that the Mai Tai Bar would be bugged by anyone that could use the conversation against Winslow or Teddy Dee. So, he listened.

"There is a court trial that is imminent and we cannot win. So, we have to figure out a way to make sure that I do not walk into that courtroom or that there is not a trial."

Teddy Dee nodded, thinking.

"Any questions?"

"I know that I am walking into this behind some others. Can you give me a list of everyone you have already used?" Teddy Dee asked. He thought and added: "Is there anyone still working to resolve this?"

"We cannot put all our eggs in one basket," Winslow smiled. "So, we are attempting a number of avenues to stop this trial from happening. My assistant will get you your list and anything else you need." Winslow paused. He was looking at a table with three women that looked as if they were in Hawaii to celebrate someone's birthday or wedding engagement. Winslow turned back to Teddy Dee. "Is there anything else?" Winslow was suddenly bored and annoyed to be still sitting at the table with Teddy Dee it seemed. Teddy Dee had worked with belligerent and irrational rich kids a number of times and understood that their moodiness came and went for no reason. The behavior was a red flag but not a deal breaker for Teddy Dee.

Teddy Dee nodded and climbed to his feet signaling that the brief meeting that had revealed a bigger problem was over. Winslow smiled and turned to his two flunkies and began to talk about something as Teddy Dee walked away from the trio of rich kids. The scarred giant moved through the luxurious interior of the legendary Hawaiian hotel and out of the Mai Tai Bar. Teddy Dee made his way through the interior and to the valet who went to retrieve his rental car. While Teddy Dee waited for his rental car to pull up he reflected on the meeting with Elliott Winslow.

Elliott Winslow was a big fish on Hawaii and knew it. He was cocky. He liked playing games. There was a kind of entitled brat feel about Elliott Winslow that Teddy Dee disliked. Perhaps, it was that brattiness that Teddy Dee disliked. Brats were unpredictable. He should have known then and there that Elliott Winslow was toxic. That was a red flag that Teddy Dee ignored. Teddy Dee knew that toxic relationships, in the shadow of the corporation, usually ended badly. Toxic clients were jumpy. They were usually high maintenance and could not be pleased even with a successful effort.

Teddy Dee did not sweat the personalities. His job in Hawaii was a cleanup. There was a team there already. Teddy Dee was simply supposed to make sure that the client never was convicted. The case was on the docket. Teddy Dee had to figure out a way to make sure that the client never saw prison.

Teddy Dee arrived in Hawaii and rented a car and instead of checking into a five-star hotel near the airport Teddy Dee decided to zig rather than zag. Teddy Dee didn't want to be too predictable.

To change Teddy Dee's footprint, just a little, while he was in Hawaii trying to figure out a way to make sure that the client never was convicted on an ironclad case Teddy Dee rented a beachfront house near the Pacific. The cost was meaningless. Teddy Dee simply billed the cost to the corporation.

So, suddenly Teddy Dee was in one of the hottest areas in Hawaii and next-door neighbors with flash in the pan celebrities and starlets. Teddy Dee had come upon the location quite by accident. When Teddy Dee had been asked to come to Hawaii he had done a quick Internet search of rental properties that were in Teddy Dee's agreed upon price range and came upon the beachfront house.

Teddy Dee usually stayed in hotels close to the airport for convenience. Teddy Dee preferred high-end hotels because he could do anything there and not have to worry about police showing up unannounced. High end also meant that there was security and security made most rethink the idea of doing anything stupid.

So, while the waves crashed on the beach Teddy Dee tried to figure out who would be the easiest juror to bribe.

Teddy Dee had contacted the courthouse and gotten the jury list. Teddy Dee did a little research and made a few phone calls.

Teddy Dee had come in after several failed attempts to stop the trial. Teddy Dee assessed the situation and figured that the easiest way to protect the client was to derail the whole system. His focus switched from the client to figuring out a way to create a mistrial.

His job, simply was to make sure to derail the trial of a high level jack weasel of an executive who had decided to stick his dick in the wrong place. Teddy Dee did not really care if the big wig was guilty or not. That was not his job. His job was to make sure that the jack weasel never had to stand trial in a statutory rape case.

His instructions were clear. Teddy Dee was to insure that the client saw no prison time. Teddy Dee was to protect the client. The trial was already underway when Teddy Dee arrived. It seemed the only logical conclusion.

Teddy Dee had contacted the courthouse informant and gotten the jury list. Teddy Dee did a little research and made a few phone calls. A few well placed phone calls to the family of a third of the jury and suddenly the trial looked like it was going to go the way that the Winslow Law Firm desired.

The jury was made up of twelve members. Nine were men. There was only three women on the jury.

Half of the jury was upright. The first half of the jury was squeaky clean. The worse that any of them had done, as far as Teddy Dee's research suggested, was speeding tickets, there was a driving under the influence violation, a shoplifting charge that was later dropped, and driving without a license. There was nothing significant enough to use as leverage against any of them.

So, Teddy Dee concentrated on the lower half of the jury. The "everymen" were more corruptible. Teddy Dee began with Amos Hutchinson.

Amos Hutchinson was a plumber. It seemed that everyone had a price. It wasn't Teddy Dee's money. Teddy Dee simply offered what they thought would help them.

Vincent Buchanan was a soldier. Buchanan was the easiest. He simply wanted to insure that his family had a home. The corporation had homes a plenty. Buchanan got a deed for next to nothing and we got his vote whatever it needed to be to make sure that our client didn't go to prison.

Darren Gonzales was a retired teacher. Gonzales asked for a small sum of money to get him through a rough patch. It was so surprisingly small that we doubled it to insure White's loyalty.

Gladys Potter was a nurse. Potter asked for the return of her wayward son who had been lost on the streets. She had asked for a sum of money to assist her to find and return her son but changed the request in negotiations. We had a sizeable force to find Gladys Potter's son and return him for next to nothing.

Christine Nichols worked at a grocery store. She asked for a small sum of money to get her through the year. The amount was her yearly salary. Her salary was a pittance to the corporation.

Teddy Dee recorded the conversation between the jurors and his disguised and garbled voice and made it explicit that he was bribing and buying the juror's vote. After the bribes were recorded he had the recordings anonymously leaked to the news, the prosecutor, the defense team, and finally the judge.

Then one juror told the bailiff that someone had threatened her family over the phone. The judge called for a mistrial that led to the lead attorneys on the case being put on probation and Teddy Dee and five others being arrested.

Once the news reporters got the recordings they began to air the grainy recordings. They confronted the prosecutors on the courtroom steps. The news reporters surrounded the defense team and peppered them with questions about the issue of jury tampering.

It was a simple job of muddying the waters and throwing a monkey wrench into a process that most trusted that had gone by the books but had led to Teddy Dee and six others waking up in three of the five prisons in Hawaii.

It was ugly business. Teddy Dee knew that he was walking in shit from the moment that he had been hired. Yet he was too stubborn to refuse the job. He had not refused any job offered him in the shadows of corporations since his first job. Teddy Dee believed that it was his responsibility to see to it that the client and the corporation was protected. In this case, he was to make sure that the client didn't go to jail at all costs.

Jury tampering had ended Teddy Dee's spotless career as a corporate button man, a title that Mister Robert Winslow, the grandson of the founder of the law firm, and grandfather of Elliott Winslow, had given him three years' prior after Teddy Dee had been hired to solve a particularly ticklish situation of a client the firm was defending.

"You know that you can make this easier on yourself by cooperating. You are already caught. It's up to you how this goes. Make it easier on yourself and tell us the name of the man behind the operation."

Teddy Dee listened to the policeman trying to play good cop or bad cop but was mute until his corporate lawyer showed up.

"This guy ain't talking. Put him back in holding. Let him stew there a bit. Maybe then he will loosen his tongue," one of the cops said.

Teddy Dee was escorted back to holding. He sat in his jail cell and after an hour Teddy Dee's corporate lawyer arrived.

Teddy Dee let his lawyer, a dark haired Latina named: Gabriella Cabrera, do her job. All the while Teddy Dee figured that Gabriella Cabrera was going to say the magic words and Teddy Dee would walk out of the Honolulu Correctional facility and onto a plane.

Instead Cabrera explained: "Mister Dandridge I am not going to be able to get you a bail hearing. The Feds have locked you and your co-conspirators down." The Latina corporate lawyer whispered, "Elliott Winslow has given you and the others up for a deal."

Up until that moment Teddy Dee thought that he would get bail and then jump bail and get out of Hawaii. After Cabrera spoke Teddy Dee made it up in his mind that he would have to do some time. Teddy Dee was the fall guy.

"I am here to make sure that you get the best deal possible. Of course, the Feds want you to give up someone else for a better deal. They have offered you one year if you roll over on someone else other than Elliott Winslow. They know that Winslow was not the mastermind," Cabrera paused. "What do you have to say to the offer?"

Teddy Dee listened to the lawyer knowing that the Feds offer didn't apply to him. It only was offered to "normals." More importantly, Teddy Dee knew that what he said or didn't say to Cabrera was going to be passed on to the men that hired him to manage chaos in the shadows of the corporate world.

So, when the judge sentenced him to three years Cabrera told him, with good behavior, that he would be out in 18 months if not sooner. Teddy Dee didn't blink. Teddy Dee looked at the beautiful Latina and smiled. He smiled and thought that this situation had changed for him. He was no longer outside the "normal" life. He was a statistic suddenly.

Yet, Teddy Dee knew things about Elliott Winslow that he had gleaned in Teddy Dee's preparation for the trip to Hawaii. There were numerous rumors about Winslow's proclivity for transgender trysts. There had been an attempt to hide the perversion though with the Internet and social media all of Winslow's skeletons were laid bare.

Even though the prosecution never was able to prove that he had been involved in the crime Teddy Dee was still charged with jury tampering and woke up in the minimum security prison in Hawaii named: Kulani. Teddy Dee was sentenced to two years for conspiracy to commit a crime on purely circumstantial evidence. Teddy Dee was suddenly a humdrum criminal.

Everyday, for a year, Teddy Dee thought that the corporate executives would decide to flex a little muscle and twist some arms to free him from Kulani. Everyday, for a year, 365 days, Teddy Dee waited. It was the beginning of the second year that Teddy Dee began to realize that the old saw: Out of sight and out of mind was truly the way of all humans.

At thirteen Asami Fujinaka was sent to Somerset, England to one of the best schools in England to learn English, the language of business. She had been sent to the all girls boarding school just two hours from London. Asami Fujinaka learned that all her learning was not found in classrooms and books. While in the exclusive private boarding school in England Asami Fujinaka ran into racism, bigotry, and prejudice.

She ran into Fiona Easterbrook and her five friends, the K-Cups. Asami Fujinaka had heard whispers about the K-Cups and Fiona Easterbrook before running into them during a class visit to the Nature Reserve. Everyone was dressed in rubber boots. The science class was exploring and seeking specific life forms to highlight the invertebrate lessons learned. Asami's partner, Sarah Breckerfeld, from Germany, and she were searching for tadpoles when Fiona Easterbrook appeared.

"There's trouble," Sarah Breckerfeld had whispered upon seeing Fiona Easterbrook dressed in her rubber boots, riding pants, argyle sweater, and pigtails and attitude.

"Who is she?"

"Fiona Easterbrook. Her father owns a bus company," Sarah Breckerfeld explained. "She is really mean. She likes to hurt people and so do her friends."

"No one at school stops her?"

"No one yet," Sarah Breckerfeld admitted.

The pair watched as Fiona Easterbrook and her friends trampled through the Nature Reserve on their way to some other part of the campus.

"Who are the others?"

"The K-Cups? There is Jade Parker a rich kid from America," Sarah Breckerfeld continued as she and Asami hunkered down and watched the girls pass at a safe distance. "That is Vanessa Mackenzie she is a snotty girl from Essex. Behind her is Starla Leontine a high society darling that modeled and occasionally stole things. Her family is from France." Sarah pointed to the blonde wearing oversized sunglasses on a gray day. "Rebecca North was a hotel heiress who believed she was going to be famous just because her great grandfather had started a hotel chain in Yorkshire and was now worth $45 million euros."

"We all come from money," Asami pointed out.

"Yeah," Sarah Breckerfeld agreed. "That's true but because we all come from money or have money to be here we should all understand that the money isn't the thing that makes us important or better but our character."

Asami nodded. Asami Fujinaka liked Sarah Breckerfeld. Her family was somehow involved with BMW and her family had incredible amounts of money. Yet, the money had not spoiled or influenced the thin and brown haired Sarah Breckerfeld.

Sarah Breckerfeld, with her brown arched eyebrows, pointed to the last K-Cup who was walking gingerly through the rough that the other K-Cups had trampled. The last K-Cup seemed a little different than the others that seemed to orbit Fiona Easterbrook. She was dressed in a brown jacket, khaki trousers, and pink rubber boots. On her face were oversized glasses.

"That is Paris Benson she's the athletic one of the group. She is tall and lean and strongly built. The story goes that Benson became fast friends with Fiona Easterbrook because Paris would not back down from a fight."

"Keep your distance," Sarah Breckerfeld advised. "Sometimes it's better not to get in the way of a crazy person."

Asami Fujinaka had considered what Sarah Breckerfeld had said to heart. For the next few days she avoided Fiona Easterbrook and the K-Cups.

Then, one day, during a grade assembly Fiona Easterbrook and Jade Parker, Vanessa Mackenzie, Starla Leontine had left the assembly and run into Asami and Sarah.

"Don't stop," Sarah Breckerfeld said and when Fiona Easterbrook and Jade Parker barred their way the thin brown haired German tried to push past the stocky bully Jade Parker.

Jade Parker reached out and shoved the thin-framed Sarah Breckerfeld back and against the wall of the assembly. The bigger girl held the squirming Sarah pinned against the wall with one outstretched arm.

Vanessa Mackenzie walked past Jade and into the assembly and said: “This exit is closed. Please go to the other exits. Thank you.”

Starla Leontine stepped around Jade and behind Asami into the pathway that allowed people to leave and suddenly Asami was standing facing Fiona Easterbrook.

“What do you think,” Fiona Easterbrook hissed. “Just because you miniaturize things that you deserve to be rubbing elbows with us, Tojo?” She didn’t wait for a response before turning to Sarah Breckerfeld. “It makes sense that you would be friends with her. Old ties run deep, it seems.”

It all came to a head when Fiona Easterbrook and the K-Cups knocked Asami's books from her arms in the hallway. Instantly, the K-Cups circled the smaller Asami Fujinaka with Fiona Easterbrook at the top of the circle.

"What was all that for?""

The K-Cups only smiled and giggled. Fiona Easterbrook, the leader, stepped forward threateningly, with her hand balled into a fist.

"I ain't David Bowie and you ain't no China Girl."

"What does that mean?"

"It means stay away from me unless you want trouble."

"What have I done to you?"

Fiona Easterbrook growled. She gritted her teeth. She rolled her green eyes and then shot Asami a stare and spat, "You were born with that ugly face of yours."

Chapter Ten.

Teddy Dee had been released from Kulani Correctional Facility in January. The warden, guards and psychologist knew even less about the cagey Teddy Dandridge than they did when he first arrived.

The one person that knew anything of significance was the prison doctor. The prison doctor had been called into the emergency infirmary only to find an unconscious Teddy Dee. The two prison guards, who had brought in Teddy Dee, explained where they found him and the circumstances.

The doctor, Michael Burnside, had done the mandatory examination and discovered that Teddy Dee had a terminal condition.

"You may want a second opinion," Burnside explained. "I am just a prison doctor. The information that I got came through Hawaiian General. The information is not final but I would suggest that you consult with your own physician."

Teddy Dee had left Kulani and went to Hawaiian General for a consultation. He chose not to wait in the emergency room. Instead, he went to his airport hotel. The first night out of Kulani Teddy Dee had sat in the hotel restaurant and ordered a steak. He ate his steak dinner and washed it down with a Belgian beer.

That night, in the hotel room, Teddy Dee thought that he might stay in Hawaii to regroup. He stayed in Hawaii for a day and tried to decide what to do next. By lunch, Teddy Dee had decided to leave the island and relocate to the states.

He had a short meeting with his Hawaiian Parole Officer who arranged for Teddy Dee to return stateside and by the late afternoon Teddy Dee was suddenly on a short flight to Los Angeles.

Once in Los Angeles, Teddy Dee learned that twenty-four months in Kulani had not rehabilitated or made him invisible. The first indication that he was vulnerable was the second day Teddy Dee was in Los Angeles and had gone to the closest mall to purchase some essentials. He was in Los Angeles less than 48 hours and Teddy Dee noted that there were two men ghosting him. They remained in his periphery for nearly ten minutes. Teddy Dee, being six foot two inches tall and 225, did not seem an easy push over by any stretch of the imagination. He was also a seasoned professional. Teddy Dee wasn't prone to pulling his gun on a man who might be panhandling an executive, like so many young Turks.

Teddy Dee smiled to his paranoid self as he unconsciously counted the people on the street as he turned off the main street and began his slow walk toward the hotel looking for anomalies. In his nine years in the business Teddy Dee knew that his "Spidey" sense was almost always better than any early warning system.

A late model American made car slid down the long palm tree shaded street all shiny blue and chrome and at the far end of the street sat a Ready Rooter van. Six people were on the street and methodically Teddy Dee cataloged them and their threat level. A woman wearing a Nike T-shirt and raspberry colored tights was bending down to pick up after her labradoodle. She had a flat bottom and it was unappetizing to Teddy Dee. There was no threat there as far as Teddy Dee could tell.

A few feet away Teddy Dee noted that there was a couple holding hands moving down the sidewalk. They were not a threat either. They couldn't be a threat since they were too far away to do anything, Teddy Dee figured.

Crossing the four-lane street in a hurry was a dark haired man with horn-rimmed glasses dressed in a suit and carrying a briefcase. The man was in his forties with salt and pepper hair. He seemed to be a strange bird on the sidewalk near the airport.

Teddy Dee couldn't help but wonder, "Where was he coming from? What is in the briefcase? Why was he crossing the street?"

Too many questions put Teddy Dee instantly into a defensive mode. Teddy Dee turned his head and smiled as his hand moved nearly imperceptibly under his jacket to unlatch the Walther PPQ 9MM Semi Automatic pistol. Instantly, Teddy Dee stepped out and onto the sidewalk thinking of defensible areas and exit strategies that led to his car two blocks away.

If this was an ambush Teddy Dee knew his rental car's tires would have been slashed when he finally got to it, to thwart his escape.

A buxom blonde dressed in a red dress sashayed down the street wearing sunglasses and a smile. She was the distraction. Teddy Dee focused.

Behind the buxom blonde, dressed in a sweat suit, was a thin man wearing dark sunglasses.

Teddy Dee studied the people on the streets, like a butcher or a diamond cutter must before slicing the exact piece of meat or making a cut on a diamond. To the right were the work-a-day people. That translated into no threat. To the left was the imminent threat. So, Teddy Dee narrowed his focus.

The man with the briefcase made a move and suddenly Teddy Dee was moving quickly and in a crouch as he heard the mechanical burp of a semi-automatic weapon and saw the trail of bullet holes carve a connect the dot line up the wall of the building behind him. The briefcase skittered on the ground and the businessman was suddenly wielding a MP-5 sub machine gun.

The man that looked more like a barber than a killer fired again. The blurp of the sub machine gun stitched eight bullet holes about chest height where Teddy Dee had just been standing. Instantly, the labradoodle jumped and started running in the opposite direction. The woman in the Nike T-shirt stood stock-still and began to scream at the top of her lungs.

The couple disappeared behind a car. The man that had been behind the woman in red dived for safety in the thin space between the hotel and the next building. The only other person that was unaccounted for was the buxom blonde in the red dress. Looking to the left Teddy Dee saw the woman in red. She was crouched down beside a car with her hands over her ears, trying to protect her hearing for some reason. There was mayhem suddenly in Los Angeles.

Teddy Dee slammed against the closest car for protection with his pistol out and ready to use. Teddy Dee scanned the area. He didn't want to be ambushed from behind.

Teddy Dee looked down at his pistol and took a deep breath. He tried to remain calm. It was nothing new to have people shooting at Teddy Dee. It just happened to be that the shooters were shooting at him in a relatively busy part of Los Angeles. There should be police on their way Teddy Dee imagined in the next five minutes, at the most.

Teddy Dee peeked over the car door and suddenly the window shattered and spilled over him. Drat. The killer was in the middle of the street and moving toward Teddy Dee.

Teddy Dee had to play it all Afro cowboy or die there on the street. Teddy Dee was turning 43 in fifteen days he figured as he took a deep breath and stood up. The corporate blooder aimed his hand cannon at the man that had been carrying the briefcase and was now holding an MP-5 sub machine gun in his hands. As the MP-5 wielding man lifted the automatic machine gun Teddy Dee fired twice and then fired again before he ducked and listened as the killer on the street released another burst of lead.

The MP-5 peppered the pearl Lincoln Thunderbird that Teddy Dee had taken cover behind and then there was silence. Teddy Dee peeked over the car and watched as the dark suited man wobbled for a second in the middle of the two-lanes closest to him. The MP-5 dangled from his limp hand. The killer looked drunk suddenly. The MP-5 clattered to the street and seconds later the man fell forward and lay on the street unmoving.

Teddy Dee didn't have time to celebrate because almost immediately he heard and then saw someone fire from across the street as he dove from the gunfire. There were two shooters?

Teddy Dee rolled to the next parked car on the street for cover, a Honda, and tried to compose himself. Teddy Dee looked left and made sure the gunman was dead. Well, Teddy Dee saw the killer's MP-5 lying inert on the street and the gunman laying face down in the middle of the street. If he wasn't dead, he was pretty close.

Now, Teddy Dee had to deal with the second gunman. Teddy Dee looked under the car trying to see the other gunman who had to be across the street. The slope of the street did not allow Teddy Dee to get a good view of the entire street. There was a slight crown to the street.

Whoever was shooting at Teddy Dee was not the greatest shot. So, Teddy Dee climbed again to his feet and ran headlong across the street with his pistol at the ready. The shooter was to the left as Teddy Dee thought that the gunman would cut him down before he crossed the street and cut the distance to his opponent. Teddy Dee was wrong.

His unexpected attack had surprised the shooter it seemed. As the shooter looked up ready to shoot Teddy Dee was already at the car and passing the protection of the metal of the car and firing three shots neatly into the man that looked more like an accountant than an assassin.

Teddy Dee kept running avoiding the killer's expected return fire. There was no return fire. Teddy Dee stopped, his gun aimed at the unmoving killer. The three shots had killed the accountant/assassin. Teddy Dee closed in on the killer and braced the assassin not expecting to find anything of value. Teddy Dee grabbed his wallet, cell phone, and keys. Teddy Dee threw the assassin's gun into the gutter and down a storm drain.

In his head, Teddy Dee knew that he had only two or three minutes to leave the shooting before Los Angeles' finest arrived. Teddy Dee headed to the first killer he had killed, in the middle of the street, and braced him, tapping his pants pockets for a wallet or cell phone and looking for anything that would connect the dots to whoever was behind this assassination attempt. He found a wallet and cellphone. Teddy Dee took the wallet and cellphone knowing that if the assassin was a professional the phone was a burner and the ID was fake. He took the information to try and reverse engineer the hit.

There was always one man behind any big event, Teddy Dee knew. This street shooting was a big event and someone, one person had green lighted it, given it funds, decided that it was needed and was behind it. Teddy Dee just needed to figure out who that one person was.

Checking the killer lying in the street, the only things that Teddy Dee found was a Velcro skateboard wallet, a cell phone, and keys. He pocketed the wallet and cellphone. It was a standard practice. Teddy Dee looked at the MP-5 sitting in the middle of the street and thought for a moment that he should do something with that lethal weapon. It shouldn't be left for some gang-banger to find and use. Teddy Dee grabbed the weapon and pushed a few buttons on it and field stripped it into five parts. Teddy Dee slipped the two smaller pieces in the trash and another larger piece he threw into the storm drain.

Teddy Dee was about to leave when he happened to look left and see the blonde in the red dress lying on the sidewalk in a puddle of blood. She was holding her right side. It looked as if she had been hit by gunfire.

Teddy Dee closed his eyes to the blonde. He did not have time for saving someone. The LAPD were on their way. They might be blocks away. Teddy Dee could hear the wail of a siren but could not decide how far they were away because of the sound bouncing off the buildings around him. Teddy Dee shook his head. He had to leave or be caught by the Los Angeles Police Department. Teddy Dee didn't have many options. Teddy Dee had to leave.

The couple hiding behind the car poked their heads out.

"Is it over dude," the tan man that had a long face and a pseudo-Mohawk asked.

"No, don't think so," Teddy Dee said. Teddy Dee had slipped his pistol back in his holster beneath his jacket. "Do you have a cell phone?"

"Yeah, dude," the pseudo-Mohawk, said pulling out his cell phone.

"Can you call 9-1-1? This lady looks like she needs some medical attention."

The woman, dressed in a black and white striped top looked concerned.

"Can you come here," Teddy Dee asked the concerned woman. The woman moved slowly toward me and past her boyfriend. When she was close enough Teddy Dee pulled her down and next to the bleeding woman. "I need you to apply pressure here until the police or ambulance arrives."

"What?"

Teddy Dee directed her expertly. The woman pressed down on the side of the woman that had been hit by a bullet. She closed her eyes.

"You are doing good," Teddy Dee reassured the woman. "Just hold that there until the police arrive."

"Where are you going?" the woman opened her eyes with the question.

"I'm going for help," Teddy Dee lied. Old habits were hard to break even when he was doing something good.

Teddy Dee moved quickly away from the shooting, hearing the wail of sirens in the distance. He moved toward his rental car two blocks away. Teddy Dee would cancel his reservations in the present hotel and relocate to a more secure location where there were no eyes on him, in a few hours.

Teddy Dee had contacted his handler: Roberta and inquired.

Two hours later he got a call from Roberta.

"As you know that you do not disappear. Your actions do not disappear. Grudges do not end," Roberta said over the phone.

"Yeah, I get it but my question isn't: Have I stepped on toes. The question is: Who is coming for me?"

"That list is long," Roberta laughed.

"Give me the most likely list."

There was a pause. Roberta breathed on the other end of the phone. "There are a number of people that want you ghosted but from my research there are just three hitters that have movement right now. So, I would think it's one of the three on your trail," Roberta explained. "There is one from Audi."

"Yeah, I know the Audi connection. At some point I figured that I would have to deal with them."

"There is another from Boston."

"Boston? Who have I pissed off in Boston?"

"Question is: who haven't you pissed off in Boston?"

"Yeah, I suppose."

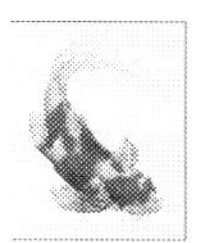 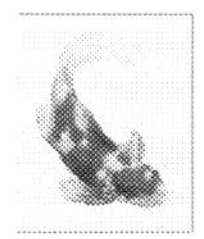 

At thirteen Asami Fujinaka was sent to Somerset, England to one of the best schools in England to learn English, the language of business. She had been sent to the all girls boarding school just two hours from London. Asami Fujinaka learned that all her learning was not found in classrooms and books. While in the exclusive private boarding school in England Asami Fujinaka ran into racism, bigotry, and prejudice.

Facing those big concepts Asami Fujinaka found herself recalling the sage words of Mister Masamoto, a year prior, at the edge of her family's koi pond. While in England fear seemed to be everywhere. It was palpable. It seemed to be in the very air of Somerset when Asami arrived. It threatened to suffocate her daily. Yet, she persevered.

Then she ran into Fiona Easterbrook and her five friends, the K-Cups. Asami Fujinaka had heard whispers about the K-Cups and Fiona Easterbrook before running into them during a class visit to the Nature Reserve. Everyone was dressed in rubber boots. The science class was exploring and seeking specific life forms to highlight the invertebrate lessons learned. Asami's partner, Wendy Breckerfeld, from Germany, and she were searching for tadpoles when Fiona Easterbrook appeared.

"There's trouble," Wendy Breckerfeld had whispered upon seeing Fiona Easterbrook dressed in her rubber boots, riding pants, argyle sweater, and pigtails and attitude.

"Who is she?"

"Fiona Easterbrook. Her father owns a bus company," Wendy Breckerfeld explained. "She is really mean. She likes to hurt people and so do her friends."

"No one at school stops her?"

"No one yet," Wendy Breckerfeld admitted.

The pair watched as Fiona Easterbrook and her friends trampled through the Nature Reserve on their way to some other part of the campus.

"Who are the others?"

"The K-Cups? There is Jade Parker a rich kid from America," Wendy Breckerfeld continued as she and Asami hunkered down and watched the girls pass at a safe distance. "That is Vanessa Mackenzie she is a snotty girl from Essex. Behind her is Starla Leontine a high society darling that modeled and occasionally stole things. Her family is from France." Wendy pointed to the blonde wearing oversized sunglasses on a gray day. "Rebecca North was a hotel heiress who believed she was going to be famous just because her great grandfather had started a hotel chain in Yorkshire and was now worth $45 million euros."

"We all come from money," Asami pointed out.

"Yeah," Wendy Breckerfeld agreed. "That's true but because we all come from money or have money to be here we should all understand that the money isn't the thing that makes us important or better but our character."

Asami nodded. Asami Fujinaka liked Wendy Breckerfeld. Her family was somehow involved with BMW and her family had incredible amounts of money. Yet, the money had not spoiled or influenced the thin and brown haired Wendy Breckerfeld.

Wendy Breckerfeld, with her brown arched eyebrows, pointed to the last K-Cup who was walking gingerly through the rough that the other K-Cups had trampled. The last K-Cup seemed a little different than the others that seemed to orbit Fiona Easterbrook. She was dressed in a brown jacket, khaki trousers, and pink rubber boots. On her face were oversized glasses.

"That is Olivia Benson she's the athletic one of the group. She is tall and lean and strong. The story goes that Benson became fast friends with Fiona Easterbrook because Samantha would not back down from a fight."

"Keep your distance," Sarah Breckerfeld advised. "Sometimes it's better not to get in the way of a crazy person."

Asami Fujinaka had considered what Sarah Breckerfeld had said to heart. For the next few days she avoided Fiona Easterbrook and the K-Cups.

Then, one day, during a grade assembly Fiona Easterbrook and Jade Parker, Vanessa Mackenzie, Starla Leontine had left the assembly and run into Asami and Sarah.

"Don't stop," Sarah Breckerfeld said and when Fiona Easterbrook and Jade Parker barred their way the thin brown haired German tried to push past the stocky bully Jade Parker.

Jade Parker reached out and shoved the thin-framed Sarah Breckerfeld back and against the wall of the assembly. The bigger girl held the squirming Sarah pinned against the wall with one outstretched arm.

Vanessa Mackenzie walked past Jade and into the assembly and said: "This exit is closed. Please go to the other exits. Thank you."

Starla Leontine stepped around Jade and behind Asami into the pathway that allowed people to leave and suddenly Asami was standing facing Fiona Easterbrook.

"What do you think," Fiona Easterbrook hissed. "Just because you miniaturize things that you deserve to be rubbing elbows with us, Tojo?" She didn't wait for a response before turning to Sarah Breckerfeld. "It makes sense that you would be friends with her. Old ties run deep, it seems."

It all came to a head when Fiona Easterbrook and the K-Cups knocked Asami's books from her arms in the hallway. Instantly, the K-Cups circled the smaller Asami Fujinaka with Fiona Easterbrook at the top of the circle.

"What was all that for?""

The K-Cups only smiled and giggled. Fiona Easterbrook, the leader, stepped forward threateningly, with her hand balled into a fist.

"I ain't David Bowie and you ain't no China Girl."

"What does that mean?"

"It means stay away from me unless you want trouble."

"What have I done to you?"

Fiona Easterbrook growled. She gritted her teeth. She rolled her green eyes and then shot Asami a stare and spat, "You were born with that ugly face of yours."

Act Two.

The second woman that Teddy Dee loved was the brilliant and powerful Jessica Lafayette, who lived in Vancouver. Jessica Lafayette was this curly haired redhead woman the color of caramel. She had bought him his one and only Rolex watch. Teddy Dee did not feel comfortable with the Rolex but wore it every once in awhile to remind himself of Jessica Lafayette.

He woke up naked. Murphy, what Teddy Dee called people, man or woman, that he did not know by name, was naked next to him in bed. Teddy Dee took in her short, black Prince Valiant hair and freckled shoulders. She had red streaks in her lustrous hair. She was the color of milk chocolate.

On the nightstand, just visible over Murphy's shoulder, sat a silver handgun. Next to the handgun was his distinctive tire tread cellphone case and tire tread wallet. On top of the wallet was a brand new golden Rolex Submariner watch. They all belonged to Teddy Dee, except for the handgun.

The handgun looked like his gun but he had not brought it with him. His handgun was safely locked in the hotel safe in his room. Whose handgun was on the nightstand? For the moment, it did not matter. Teddy Dee was in bed with Murphy and Jessica Lafayette.

Teddy Dee had rubbed at his dark eyes trying to figure out how he had come to be in bed with two women in this strange plush bedroom with its pillow top mattress and Egyptian sheets and down comforter. His head was throbbing. That was a sign. He had gone out the night before and somewhere and sometime he had drank too much. Teddy Dee had a vague memory of things but he could not actually recall the whole night.

There was a painting on the wall that looked incredibly familiar. It was, if he was not incorrect, an original Surat. That framed Surat jogged his memory just a little.

He had spent the night with Jessica Lafayette and Murphy. To the right, lying on her stomach, was the caramel beauty with loosely curled red hair. Jessica Lafayette had one arm hanging out of the bed. One arm was across Teddy Dee's chest.

Somewhere, somehow he had ended up with a brand new Rolex Submariner watch. Even though it seemed far fetched Teddy Dee believed it to be true. The watch screamed all sorts of attention that Teddy Dee usually avoided. The warm caramel brown body next to him and the original Surat said more than Teddy Dee's state of undress. This was Jessica Lafayette's home.

He pushed himself up to get a better vantage point of the bedroom he was in and the women around him. He looked around the well-appointed bedroom and noticed that his dark blue two-piece suit was strewn in a ball in a Louis XIVth armchair near a makeup table. A solitary black leather shoe was sitting on the table with a couple of bottles of champagne and three glasses.

Teddy Dee sat up and studied the two sleeping women he was in bed with and listened to the early morning quiet of the room. Murphy with her freckled shoulder, the color of chocolate milk lay with her arm over him. The other woman, golden brown, big breasts, and a heart shaped face that was framed by red curly hair lay with her ass pressed against Teddy Dee.

For the second time, Teddy Dee rubbed at his eyes trying to focus. His head felt several sizes too big. He closed his eyes and opened them trying to recall what he had done the night before.

He was in Vancouver. Teddy Dee knew that. Teddy Dee had been in Los Angeles on Monday. He remembered that. On Monday he had packed. The next day he was in Vancouver.

Teddy Dee narrowed his eyes and looked around the bedroom. There were the black jeans of Jessica Lafayette draped over a small settee. Her cheetah print high heels were near her jeans. A matching cheetah print bra was hanging on a doorknob of a room that Teddy Dee had never seen last night. Another bra in black lace was on one of the glasses on the table. There were handcuffs strewn without much attention on the carpeted floor.

Teddy Dee thought about getting out of bed but simultaneously felt the small hand brush and then grip the sleeping mayor. The grip and slight massaging of the mayor suddenly made all the things that concerned him, for the moment, became clear. He turned over and serviced the nameless girl next to Jessica Lafayette.

He was a big man and unafraid to use his weight and strength in pleasuring Murphy. Murphy writhed and tried to crawl away from the enraged mayor below Teddy Dee's waist. The connection was electric and Murphy bucked and trembled and after several thrusts fell into rhythm with Teddy Dee. They pushed and pulled and twisted and gyrated and after several minutes their morning tryst was over as quickly as it had begun.

Murphy smiled and lay next to Teddy Dee silently. Teddy Dee laid on the bed spent. He tried to keep his eyes open but it was a fight that he could not win.

Waking an hour later Teddy Dee found Jessica Lafayette still sleeping. Murphy was sleeping as well. He took a deep breath and climbed out of bed and went seeking the video room.

He slipped on his underwear and jeans. Teddy Dee could not find his T-shirt or shirt from the night before or his shoes. He would worry about those later. Instead, he went looking for the video room that he had been sent to find. He didn't have to go too far. In Jessica Lafayette's bedroom walk in closet was her secret video room.

Teddy Dee could not help but smile at the voyeur that he was suddenly smitten with. She was bad but that did not change his emotion about her. Jessica Lafayette, like Teddy Dee, was flawed. She had many flaws. So, did Teddy Dee. Yet, it was her flaws that attracted Teddy Dee to Jessica Lafayette.

He found himself wishing that Jessica Lafayette was not the bad guy in this drama that he had been sent to ferret out, but knowing that it only made sense for her to be the extortionist. Jessica Lafayette was ambitious. Jessica Lafayette was driven and for some reason needed the board to recognize her.

It was not Teddy Dee's responsibility to understand people's motivations. People did things for all sorts of reasons. Teddy Dee had seen good things done for the most selfish reasons. He had also seen the same good things twisted to be seen as something evil for the most benevolent of reasons as well. Teddy Dee did not dare to believe that he understood why people did things. He could only focus on his own motivations which were limited to fight, flight and survival.

In the walk in closet he found the Vancouver Bank video that Jessica Lafayette had labeled. Teddy Dee slipped the video into his jeans and erased all the others, including his recent performance. The bank video he took and slipped into his suit jacket pocket. He paused, now dressed in his jeans. All he had to do was leave the British Properties and deliver the package to his clients.

He hesitated. He hesitated. It was an unusual sensation for Teddy Dee. He was a man of action. He prided himself on his actions. When others hesitated when facing Teddy Dee, he usually attacked. Hesitation was a weakness that Teddy Dee fought off anytime he was uncertain. For Teddy Dee, hesitation happened because of lack of experience or information.

What was he lacking? He had the information. Jessica Lafayette was the extortionist. He had the evidence to prove that.

Teddy Dee wanted to pretend that he was an intellectual and he could compartmentalize his feelings like some higher thinking individual. He wanted to be like the people that he worked for; higher thinking individuals who looked at physical violence as something that was below them.

So, as he stood in the bedroom with the incriminating evidence that was going to destroy Jessica Lafayette he felt what he had not felt in years; regret. He had instant regret for what was going to happen once he got the video to the Vancouver Bank.

Teddy Dee wanted to believe that he hesitated because of love. It was not love that made him hesitate. It was the inevitable response from Jessica Lafayette that made him stand in the bedroom vacillating about if he should stay or go. Jessica Lafayette was someone that had jeopardized a client that Teddy Dee was hired to protect. He knew that. He understood that.

Yet, he hesitated. It was the belief that Jessica Lafayette and Teddy Dee might have that magical love experience that made Teddy Dee drag his feet. He had struggled with the idea of love. Had he loved anyone since Katherine Rogers? All the people he loved he had left. He had left his mother. He had left his aunt. He had left Katherine Rogers. Teddy Dee had experiences love but it had been so long ago that he had been stunned by the feeling.

The bigwigs, the corporates, the suits loved and that was seen as a weakness. Teddy Dee wanted to believe that he too loved, but knew that he was not cut from that cloth. If he was a romantic or a person inclined to love he would not take the video and leave Jessica and Murphy in the bed without a word.

Yet, Teddy Dee grabbed his clothes and headed for the front door. He was not meant for love. The love that Teddy Dee experienced was short-time. He had learned that long-term love was messy. In his world there was no time for messy situations. Teddy Dee was sent to deal with messy situations. So, as Oscar Easton had pointed out, he was not allowed to be the hero in his own story.

"We are all parts of the tragedy called: hard work," Easton had confessed.

"Is it worth it?"

"To many, it is more than worth it," Easton admitted. "To some, the cost is too much. You have to decide."

It took Teddy Dee two years, nearly 800 days to decide that working in the shadows was not an either/or but and/but. Working in the shadows was lucrative. Teddy Dee made more money than he had ever imagined possible. He made so much money that he never considered the expenses of anything. His money was spread out across four continents and 25 states in the USA.

Yet, at the same time it cost so much to make the money. The sacrifices were significant. Teddy Dee, in those early days of working in the shadows, often found himself questioning if breaking fingers, arms and legs was worth the guilt that followed.

Teddy Dee tried to rationalize it all as the cost of business. That was a lie. He tried to make himself believe that he was working for the greater good. That was a lie, as well. Teddy Dee knew that he was a bad guy working for bad men and women attempting to wrest power from the weak and vulnerable rich kids that played with businesses like Lincoln logs and Legos.

He had decided that he was the blunt object that the higher thinkers used when things went egg shaped. Teddy Dee had a job. He hammered in round pegs into square holes. He was Bam Bam from The Flintstones in a modern day world that attempted to move away from violence and physical interactions with his primitive negotiation tactics.

Jessica Lafayette was one of those rich kids. She was privileged. She believed that she deserved more than others. There was an entitlement and that entitlement irked Teddy Dee.

He crossed the bedroom and walked down the hall toward the front door. Teddy Dee tried not to think of the betrayal that Jessica Lafayette would feel. Her feelings were inconsequential.

His clients would be pleased. Jessica Lafayette would be barred from the boardroom and dealings with the bank as a result. They would pay Teddy Dee handsomely. Mission accomplished.

Leaving Vancouver, Teddy Dee toyed with the idea of returning and seeing Jessica Lafayette. The idea was just a fleeting thought, at first. Teddy Dee knew that going to Vancouver was a fool's play.

Jessica Lafayette would have Teddy Dee beaten within an inch of his life to teach him a lesson, if she was feeling nice. At worse, she might have her men beat, kill and bury Teddy Dee in the Vancouver swamps. Despite that possible reality Teddy Dee found himself thinking about Jessica Lafayette. His thoughts suddenly for a brief moment had Teddy Dee thinking that he wanted to be with Jessica Lafayette, even if she was someone that might kill him. So, though Teddy Dee believed that he had some measure of feelings for Jessica Lafayette he had burned the bridge, village and ground around the bridge back to Jessica Lafayette.

Chapter Eleven.

"You know that no matter how you look at it the black knight is all by himself," Eric Robinson stated.

"So?"

"Well, I think if the black knight had some support, any support he might do better. I mean, I don't know if he would win. The game seems stacked against him. But, at least with a little help he might not be ... all alone."

Teddy Dee nodded.

"Eric, I have a meeting this afternoon. So, I will leave you a little early. I hope that is not a problem."

"No, it's your dime," Eric Robinson smiled.

"It is my dime, indeed."

Eric Robinson smiled and nodded sitting at the table. The teenager studied Teddy Dee silently.

Teddy Dee climbed to his feet. The giant of a man paused, noting something.

"You have something else?"

"No, not exactly," Eric Robinson said, suddenly bashful.

"What is it?"

"Well, I was wondering how you got into the business you do?"

Teddy Dee smiled.

"That's a long story. Remind me, the next time we meet, I will tell that story. But, now, I have a meeting I have to get to."

Eric Robinson smiled and nodded his head.

Teddy Dee exited the conference room in the Beverly Hills Hotel and made his way to the lobby. The lobby was busy that Saturday morning. He weaved his way through the crowd of suntanned, well-dressed, beautiful people and to the main exit. He walked to the front and waited for his car to be retrieved by the blonde, blue-eyed valet.

Beverly Hills, Teddy Dee thought as he waited for his car to be brought to him, is just a picture postcard of 1960's Hollywood with all its racism and white privilege. Teddy Dee scanned the front of the hotel and looked for the stereotypical black jockey statue that had been in the front of every high-class establishment when Jim Crow laws were enacted. Of course, there was no black jockey with his hand holding a ring for horses in the front of the Beverly Hills Hotel but Teddy Dee could not think that years ago blacks would have been barred from entering the iconic hotel.

His rental car that day, a metallic blue Porsche Cayenne. Teddy Dee handed the valet a tip and climbed into the lush interior of the sports SUV. He put the Porsche in gear and slid effortlessly down the circular driveway and toward downtown for his first meeting with Rupert Williams.

Teddy Dee's first meeting with Rupert Williams was notable for all the wrong reasons. He parked the Porsche Cayenne in a lot and walked three blocks to the downtown office of his newest overseer. Teddy Dee tried to think of a positive way to see his meeting with Rupert Williams. Maybe, he was a decent and good guy. Maybe, he was a guy that wanted to help re-introduce convicts to the society and the workplace. Teddy Dee shook his head knowing that he was not delusional or demented. He was a pragmatist. He knew that nine times out of ten that the scum of the earth were always ready to pounce on the weakest and most vulnerable.

The office was a small dark hole with blinds over the two large windows. There were no plants in the office. The ceiling of the office had easily a dozen lights in the hanging ceiling but for whatever reason Rupert Williams chose not to turn any of them on. The office was a dark cave.

On one wall of the office was a floor to ceiling bookcase filled with various books. Teddy Dee noted that the books were mostly law books and books on parole or probation. There was: Prisoners in 2012, Re-entry in the United States, Probation and Parole, State of Recidivism, Drug Use and Dependence, and State and Federal Prisons. Teddy Dee wanted to laugh at the book choices. Rupert Williams was a hard-on. There was nothing that he would have read for an early release from Kulani Correctional Facility.

Yet, as he scanned the books waiting for Rupert Williams to finish a call he noticed a few books that made him do a double take. Domination and the Art of Resistance made him think that Teddy Dee's parole officer was going to be a real hard-on that he might have to snap in two. The other title that gave him pause was Weapons of the Weak. These books seemed unusual for a Parole Officer. Teddy Dee smiled. Rupert Williams was definitely not going to be a typical Parole Officer.

Rupert Williams was a thin-faced man in his forties who loved showing off his considerable power. His power came in comparison to the ex-cons that were his responsibility. He knew some heavy hitters, politically. There were pictures of Rupert Williams shaking hands with a couple of dark suited men smiling for the camera. Teddy Dee noted that the parole officer's office was above a 24-hour bail bonds office.

The first meeting with Rupert Williams was just like Teddy Dee had imagined a parole officer meeting would be. Innocuous. Rupert Williams wanted to exert his dominance. He wanted to prove that he was the alpha dog in the pack. Teddy Dee listened, unmoved.

"My name is Rupert Williams and you can call me Rupert or Mister Williams," Rupert Williams explained as he shook hands with him. His handshake was limp and non-committal. Teddy Dee noted that. Williams sat in a high backed leather chair that sat behind a heavy dark wooden desk. There were stacks of papers stacked neatly in various piles on the desktop.

Behind Rupert Williams were several pictures of the thin-faced Rupert Williams and smiling men shaking his hand. Teddy Dee noted that one of the pictures was of Rupert Williams and the actor turned governor of the state. Rupert Williams was connected, Teddy Dee noted. He studied the six photos behind Rupert Williams and tried to place the faces. There was an ex-governor, an ex-mayor, two basketball players, one of the two had recently retired, the second basketball player had tested positive for drug use and been suspended a year before Teddy Dee had been released from Kulani. The last two pictures were of a businessman dressed in suit and tie and smiling broadly with his hand across Rupert Williams shoulder and a photo of a dark skinned man wearing thick gold chains and a leather jacket. The last picture looked as if it had been on stage or backstage. Teddy Dee knew that he was supposed to know who the people were in the pictures but he did not. He simply did not pay too much attention to celebrity. Celebrity was fleeting. It was a fickle thing celebrity. People loved to help you up to these great heights only to tear you down in the same instance.

"Have a seat," Rupert Williams smiled, gesturing to the two overstuffed chairs in front of the desk. Williams had not climbed to his feet to greet Teddy Dee. He had barely looked up, at all.

Teddy Dee sat down in the overstuffed chair in front of the desk. Rupert Williams smiled and nodded. He had dark green eyes, thin lips and small teeth.

"My job as your Parole Officer is to help parolees, like yourself, find jobs, attend schools, or get into therapy programs. For instance, former drug addicts may have to enroll in programs that help them stay off drugs," Rupert Williams said in his singsong way. "If parolees have financial problems, then I am to direct them to community agencies that can provide welfare benefits and other financial support. Some officers supervise halfway houses where small groups of parolees live together to share experiences and lend each other support. I don't do that. I am specific in my duties. I make sure that my parolees stay clean and out of trouble. If you need help, Theodore, then you can talk to me. I have access to drug therapists, psychiatrists, and social workers who can help you if you have any situation that is outside of my particular expertise."

Rupert Williams seemed pretty confident. Teddy Dee listened and tried to figure out the well-connected Parole Officer. His name sounded familiar for some reason.

"We will meet once a week for the first few months to create a routine for you and to monitor your progress," Williams announced leafing through papers in front of him. He paused. His left eyebrow arched a bit. "I see you were in Hawaii."

Rupert Williams said the last phrase as if it was a question but Teddy Dee didn't respond. It seemed rhetorical.

Rupert Williams looked up and at Teddy Dee with his dark green eyes. The Parole Officer narrowed his eyes and studied Teddy Dee.

"I asked you a question, Theodore," Rupert Williams smiled behind clenched teeth.

Teddy Dee nodded.

"It is quite unusual to have a parolee leave the state of their incarceration," Williams said flipping the papers in front of him absently. "Who do you know Theodore? I should ask: What tricks do you have up your sleeve, Theodore?"

The conversation and Rupert Williams instantly bored Teddy Dee. Rupert Williams was a prick. He would be a problem. Immediately Teddy Dee began to imagine ways to no longer be under the supervision of Rupert Williams.

Williams was thinly built. Perhaps, Teddy Dee thought, he could have an undiagnosed heart condition? Everyone in Los Angeles drove. He could have a fatal car crash. There was always the randomness of gang activity in parts of Los Angeles. Williams was not immune to gang violence Teddy Dee mused.

"Do you have any job prospects?"

Teddy Dee thought of all the corporate connections he had built in the twenty plus years as a corporate crisis manager and the plethora of opportunities at hand. Roberta, Teddy Dee's handler, had been contacted and would inform him to opportunities once the execs knew he was available. But, in the office of his parole officer he shook his head, no.

Rupert Williams reached across his desk and handed him a business card. Teddy Dee took the card and glanced at it not paying any attention to the information on the card.

"Go by this business and tell them that you need work. They hire parolees."

"Thanks."

Teddy Dee climbed to his feet and prepared to leave.

"The meeting is not over Theodore," Rupert Williams pointed out from behind his desk. He gestured for him to sit back down. Teddy Dee reluctantly sat back down in the overstuffed chair.

"As you know, I am monitoring your re-entry into the society. If you mess up, then that reflects on me. I don't want any problems, Theodore. If you become a problem Theodore, then I will make your days on the outside a living hell."

Teddy Dee listened and tried to figure out the thin white man dressed in a V-neck sweater with a white collared shirt open at the throat. Rupert Williams was clean-shaven and smelled of lilacs. The Parole Officer had shifty eyes. He seemed unable to hold eye contact with Teddy Dee. From Teddy Dee's estimations Rupert Williams had to be in his forties, if not older. He had a receding hairline and no visible jewelry on his hands.

Teddy Dee calculated that his Parole Officer was unmarried, single, possibly a homosexual. He had control issues. Rupert Williams was an insecure man using his power and position, what he believed he had, to compensate for something. He seemed to be a man that cared about things intensely.

Rupert Williams played a role. He was an actor. At work, he was this buttoned up, by the rules, pain in the ass with unresolved needs for control over everyone and everything he came in contact with. At home, he probably was into S&M and being choked, Teddy Dee imagined. Immediately, Teddy Dee tried not to think about Rupert Williams' home life.

All Teddy Dee knew was that Rupert Williams was going to be a problem if he was going to be his Parole Officer. Rupert Williams believed that as a Parole Officer he had every right to intrude into Teddy Dee's life. Teddy Dee did not need Rupert Williams thinking that he could barge into Teddy Dee's life. He had to solve the problem of Rupert Williams quickly. Teddy Dee had too much to do and Rupert Williams was not a part of those things. Teddy Dee had his goals and Rupert Williams would be a problem that needed to be addressed.

Perhaps, Teddy Dee decided, he was overreacting. Perhaps, he had read Rupert Williams wrong. It had happened. No one was infallible.

The Parole Officer reached into a manila envelope. He looked it over and then looked at Teddy Dee. Rupert Williams slid a pamphlet across the desk to Teddy Dee.

“Should I worry about you Theodore? I was reading your file and it seems that I might need to worry about you.” Rupert Williams narrowed his eyes. He studied Teddy Dee like a bug. “You are not well, Theodore. Not well at all. I am not sure you are meant to be on this spinning blue marble too long.” He paused.

Teddy Dee did not respond. He watched Rupert Williams and thought about strangling him. Teddy Dee wanted to strangle him then and there in the office under the pictures of Rupert Williams and his celebrity friends and his degrees and books. He wanted to but he resisted. He just had to breathe and after Rupert Williams was done get up and leave. What could Rupert Williams do to Teddy Dee? What could the Parole Board do to Teddy Dee?

“I am trying to get a gauge on you, Theodore. I have been in this business for a long time. I have seen my fair share of hard cases. I have seen my share of psychos. But you, you are definitely different. You, Theodore Dandridge who was released from Hawaii and flew to Los Angeles to become my problem are definitely different.” Rupert Williams paused again. He rubbed the side of his face, thinking. “I may have to watch you a little more closely than my other cases. You think so?” Rupert Williams studied Teddy Dee with his dark green eyes. He continued, “I need you to read the conditions of your parole,” the parole officer hissed. “You have to be aware that failure to adhere to the conditions in anyway will land you back in prison.” Rupert Williams pulled out a clipboard with several signatures on it. “I need you to look over the conditions and then sign and date on the first available line.”

Teddy Dee skimmed the pamphlet and smiled at the fact that he had already broken the conditions of his parole twice on a cursory glance before looking up and meeting the cocky stare of Williams. Teddy Dee lowered his eyes, knowing that his Parole Officer was trying to establish himself as the alpha dog between them. Teddy Dee simply waited another beat and signed and dated the paper that a dozen other parolees had done before him.

Teddy Dee thought that then and there it might be better to just reach across the table and choke the life out of Rupert Williams and end the charade that the bureaucrat seemed to need like a junkie seeking a fix. He could end the endless frustration in less than one hundred and eighty seconds and make it look like an accident or botched robbery gone bad. Teddy Dee preferred botched robberies because the criminals always made such a mess of things and that hid so much of his handiwork.

“Theodore, I need you to check in with me in two weeks. Let’s go with two weeks from today. If you get a job in the meantime you can call me so that I can swing by and check it out. You are my responsibility. I have to sign off on your rehabilitation and re-entry into society," Rupert Williams announced climbing to his feet and gesturing for Teddy Dee to do the same. Teddy Dee reluctantly climbed out of his chair and studied Rupert Williams again.

Instantly, he imagined reaching across the table that divided them and wringing his scrawny neck like a chicken's until it snapped. Teddy Dee calculated that strangling the life out of Rupert Williams might be easier than breaking the neck of a chicken. He was a thin framed man.

Teddy Dee blinked and turned on his heels and left the offices of Rupert Williams. He did not speak as Williams continued to talk. Teddy Dee just walked out of the office and descended the flight of stairs back to the streets below.

Rupert Williams and the Rupert Williams' of the world were cruel and diabolical because they could be. If they were left to their own devices, they would continue to do evil things and get away with them without any concern. The only way to beat a bully was to stand up to a bully.

Teddy Dee did not really register bullies or bullying. He usually confronted anyone that dared to intimidate him.

Asami Fujinaka was a fighter. She had always been a fighter. She just rarely showed that side of herself to others.

The daughter of Hiro Fujinaka IV thought about the obstacles in her way and how she had overcome things before. She was not gifted with incredible beauty. She was not incredibly strong. She did not consider herself to be anything but above average in her intelligence.

Yet, she was focused and determined. Rarely, did she give up. When there was a problem in her way she ultimately found a way to overcome it. That was Asami Fujinaka.

In school, when she lived in England for a short period of time learning English and all the essentials for business she had come upon a group of stuck up girls that thought the sun rose and set on their arses.

Asami Fujinaka decided to teach them a lesson. It was a humbling lesson. It was a lesson that was a long time in coming.

The first girl Asami faced was blonde, freckled faced, and mildly attractive. She had a straight and unattractive nose that sat in the middle of a small oval face. The girl was smaller than Asami and had shoulder length hair that was tied back in a ponytail while she fenced with another taller girl.

She was talented, Asami could tell. The girl with the blue eyes loved to lunge and "riposte" and quick to rely on her aggression rather than talent while fencing. Asami sussed her out instantly as an athlete that had only recently decided to be a part of the witches in training club.

Asami hoped against all hopes that she would not be forced to fence with the K-Cup; Olivia Benson.

The K-Cup used her foil well. Asami had to admit that she had talent. She hadn't gotten this far on meanness alone.

The instructor called out the next matching and low and behold Asami found herself opposite the K-Cup.

"Engarde."

Instantly K-Cup lunged and tried to touch. Asami had expected the attack and instantly parried K-Cup's attack. K-Cup lunged again and Asami parried the second attack. Asami, behind the fencing mask smiled. All the other opponents had not been able to weather the continuous attacks of the blue-eyed K-Cup. Asami, having watched the K-Cup's relentless attacks had figured out a strategy; defend and let her wear herself out then attack.

While Asami was thinking of defending the next attack the K-Cup had attacked and Asami had nearly missed the parry. Instantly, as Asami parried she sidestepped and attacked for the first time in "riposte."

"Touch."

K-Cup stopped and stood rigidly as if someone had driven a pole through her and then lowered her head.

"Engarde."

Asami positioned herself on the mat and waited for the inevitable attack. The K-Cup lunged forward. Asami parried and instantly responded again hitting the K-Cup.

"Touch."

"No," the blonde haired K-Cup hissed. She lowered her head.

"Engarde."

The match was over if Asami or the opponent scored three touches before the other scored three touches. It was similar to the murder rule in little league baseball.

So, Asami, having rattled the K-Cup, lifted her foil and dug in her feet on the scoring mat as the once emboldened K-Cup hesitated. There was no attack coming it seemed. The K-Cup had to think of another way to win this match.

Asami used the moment of thought by the suddenly unsure K-Cup to launch her own attack. She feigned to the left and then moved rapidly forward and twirling the foil as she approached stopped as the K-Cup tried to parry the attack. The K-Cup swung her foil up and to the left and right. Asami had expected as much and aimed her point to the right and the left touching her twice in the final match points.

"Touch and touch. Fait compleat," The Director announced. "Four hits to none. Good effort Asami. Good effort Olivia."

Asami removed her fencing mask and bowed to Samantha and then to the Director. Samantha too removed her fencing mask and bowed to Asami and then the Director.

For an instance it looked as if Olivia, the K-Cup, had seemed a sportsman. There was no animosity in that moment when she had bowed and then turned her attention to the Director.

The Director discussed the match with Asami and Olivia.

"You both are very talented. Asami I know that you have studied fencing before but Olivia where did you learn to handle a foil?"

"Middle form," Olivia admitted.

"Well, here you will need to learn to change your strategy or you will be beaten by the best of them," the Director advised.

Asami Fujinaka listened but did not give away any thoughts about the talent of Olivia the K-Cup.

The Director smiled after his brief discussion with Olivia and turned his attention to Asami.

"Asami, you are a wonder," the Director beamed.

Asami Fujinaka lowered her eyes and watched, peripherally, Olivia's reaction. With the words of the Director Olivia almost imperceptibly smirked. There was contempt there. She disliked that Asami had bested her.

"We will do well this year if you can maintain that intensity and grace."

Asami nodded, secretly watching the K-Cup standing there impatiently.

The Director went over the match and then dismissed both of the duelists.

Olivia and Asami walked away from the Director and headed to the shower room.

"You did well out there," Olivia said through gritted teeth.

Asami nodded and remained silent for an instant trying to think if Olivia was being sincere.

"I am a bit of a bully on the mat. Not too many get the best of me when I am on a tear," Olivia said suddenly. She seemed genuine.

"You did well also," Asami Fujinaka finally said.

Olivia smiled and once the two had entered the locker room separated.

Asami Fujinaka watched as Olivia Benson walked away and paused only to turn around and smile when she saw Asami there. Asami smiled also.

A few days later, over the weekend, when the majority of Somerset had decided to go to London for a shopping trip Asami Fujinaka had been lured out of the safety of the dormitory and into the quiet of the courtyards. It had been Jade Parker who had invited Sarah and Asami to squash all the past hostilities between herself and the K-Cups and Sarah and Asami.

"I won't go," decided Sarah.

"Why not, they are reaching out to us. We would be stupid to not accept the peace offering."

"We would be stupid to believe that the K-Cups believe in peace," Sarah Breckerfeld pointed out.

Asami Fujinaka had decided to go and meet with Jade Parker and the K-Cups despite Sarah's reluctance.

The faces of Fiona Easterbrook and the K-Cups suddenly surrounded her. Standing there in the half circle that prevented Asami from easily returning to the dormitories were: Jade Parker, Vanessa Mackenzie, Starla Leontine, Rebecca North, and Olivia Benson. Asami's heart fell when she saw Olivia Benson there. She had believed that Olivia Benson was different than the other K-Cups or Fiona Easterbrook.

"So, since you don't seem to understand English we have decided to teach you a new language of kick-your-ass-until-you-stop-trying-to-fit-in-here." She paused and added. "I think you will become fluent in that in one ass kicking lesson."

Asami furrowed her brow as Fiona Easterbrook stepped forward with her second, Jade Parker.

Instantly, Fiona Easterbrook launched an attack that Asami avoided while retreating. She backed away from Easterbrook and nearly into the arms of Starla Leontine. Leontine tried to grab Asami but the daughter of Hiro Fujinaka IV avoided the claws of the square faced K-Cup and moved quickly to her right and close to Olivia Benson.

"Be careful, I think that Fee has a weapon. Don't turn your back on Jade. She is definitely crazy enough to injure you permanently," Olivia Benson whispered.

Asami did not say a word. Instead, Asami took a deep breath and focused on Fiona Easterbrook first and then Jade, her attack dog.

Jade Parker was the first to make a move. She came at Asami all screams and waving of her arms like she was a crazed windmill. For most that were unfamiliar with hand-to-hand combat Jade Parker's attack might have put them on their back foot immediately. Asami instead stood her ground and analyzed the attack as Jade Parker approached.

Her eyes were narrowed down to slits as she came screaming and wailing toward Asami Jade Parker's curly asymmetrically cut black hair swayed on her diamond-shaped head as she charged the smaller girl. Her fists were balled and ready to pound the first thing she made contact with.

Asami Fujinaka drew back her right hand in a fist and lowered her center of gravity. She took a deep breath. As soon as Jade Parker was close enough

Asami Fujinaka spun on her heels and lashed out with a heel kick that caught Jade Parker just under her armpit and drove her toward a bench near the fenced tennis court. Jade Parker's momentum didn't allow her enough time to stop or avoid the bench or fence. Instead, Jade Parker went crashing over the bench and into the fence.

Asami Fujinaka turned and studied Fiona Easterbrook evenly.

"Kill this bitch," Fiona Easterbrook spat as she watched Jade Parker kneeling, crumpled against the fence as if she were praying.

Vanessa Mackenzie was the second that day to attack Asami Fujinaka. She stepped forward and swung hard at Asami's head and missed. Asami punished Vanessa for her efforts. She ducked the punch and threw a dozen lightning strikes into Vanessa Mackenzie's unprotected side and back. Asami Fujinaka finished her attack with a kick to Vanessa's thigh that slammed her hard to the ground. Vanessa Mackenzie landed hard on the ground and expelled all the air in her body with the crash.

"Skank, Jackie Chan, Kung Fu Panda bitch," Fiona Easterbrook screamed and attacked. Asami jumped back and away from the fierce attack. She narrowed her eyes and noticed that Fiona was wearing brass knuckles on both of her hands. Just one hit by one of those deadly weapons and Asami Fujinaka would go from combatant to victim, instantly.

So, Asami decided then and there that Fiona Easterbrook would never hit her. Her plans were not perfect. 95% of the fight with the dangerous Fiona Easterbrook had worked to plan. Frustrated and unable to hit Asami Fiona Easterbrook took greater and greater chances. In trying foolhardier attacks Asami Fujinaka was able to take advantage of her quickness and lightning attacks.

Fiona Easterbrook was no pushover. She was a tough and cruel fighter who expected to win fights. She didn't fight and expect people to just give up. Fiona Easterbrook fought and expected to beat the shit out of whoever she fought.

Starla Leontine had a length of pipe in her hand. Asami Fujinaka feigned an attack and Starla took the bait. She swung where she thought Asami was headed only to see the quicker girl dodge the length of pipe and kick her hard in her stomach and punch her in the side of the face.

Starla, the bully, fell down crying like a baby. She held the side of her face and went into a fetal position.

Rebecca North was a small girl with shoulder length hair. She screamed and came at Asami all noise and nails. Asami crouched and kicked Rebecca as hard as she could in the hip. Rebecca North winced as if she had been shot and limped off the battlefield.

Asami Fujinaka blocked one of the punches from Fiona Easterbrook and launched a lightning attack that began with a punch to her sternum then two downward strikes to Fiona's shoulders, two knife hands just above her breasts, and a right-left-right-left combination in Fiona's tender mid-section. Asami finished the attack off with a backhand punch to Fiona Easterbrook's face that dropped the bully there near the tennis court entrance.

Vanessa Mackenzie had recovered enough to pick herself up off the ground. She was dirty and hurt. Vanessa picked up the length of pipe that Starla Leontine had dropped and began to move forward stalking Asami Fujinaka. Olivia Benson grabbed Vanessa Mackenzie's arm and stopped her. Asami Fujinaka turned to stare at Vanessa Mackenzie holding the pipe in her hand and Olivia Benson holding her arm.

"I think it's over, Vee," Olivia Benson said. Vanessa Mackenzie turned and looked around her. Fiona Easterbrook was moaning, crumpled by the tennis court. Jade Parker had stumbled off hurt. Rebecca North was nowhere to be seen.

Chapter Twelve.

"Do you think there is a limit?"

"What do you mean?"

"Is there an amount of money that you want to make before you step away from the life?"

"Fuck no," Frederick Ornstein laughed. Ornstein paused and got serious for an instant. "I suppose that when I began there was a number. I suppose. But I haven't been in the business as long as you. My first year, not being a freelancer that is, I used to think that when I got in and if I got in that if I made a million dollars I would be satisfied."

"Doing freelance is the shits," Gunther Elmshorn spat.

"Yeah, I hated being on call. I loved the work. I hated the uncertainty of if I'd get a call or not." Ornstein paused. "Everyone has bills to pay."

"Yeah, the goal is always to find a corporation or an executive to work for," Elmshorn noted.

"Shit yeah," Ornstein agreed. "So, once I was on retainer things changed. You know how it is. That first year, those first few jobs, are all jittery. Everything is new and there seems to be all these possibilities. But then I started working with the legal of the group and trying to deal with one situation or the other and flying from one part of Europe to the next and seeing all the money that was possible."

Gunther Elmshorn nodded.

"So, you see that after a dozen jobs of doing the most unimaginable things a million euros is chump change."

"Chump change," Elmshorn smiled. "If I make a million dollars in a year I might as well retire."

"Yeah, I agree," Ornstein admitted. "Things change. Your view of things changes."

Elmshorn nodded.

Ornstein sipped at a cup of coffee that he had.

"What do you know about Steiner?"

"Not much," Elmshorn said. "He is one of the upper level crisis managers. He came up through the ranks and is no-nonsense. I think that he has been with the group for nearly a decade."

"Shit," Ornstein breathed. "That is a long time."

"Yes and no. There are some crisis managers that have been around longer. Time is all relative in this life right? All that matters is that he produces. He has to be good. He has to be thorough. Never worked with him but the word is that he is ruthless. He completes all his contracts. Nothing new."

"What happens when a target or a contract isn't completed?"

Elmshorn looked at Ornstein curiously.

"Are you kidding?"

"No, I know what they say," Ornstein said, lifting his hands in surrender. He smiled and continued. "I just want to hear it from someone that is in the trenches with me."

"That contract is reassigned," Elmshorn said as a matter-of-fact.

"Have you ever had a contract reassigned?"

"A couple of times when I was freelance," Elmshorn admitted.

"What happens?"

"All I can say is that reassignment is not something that you want to do too often in this business," Elmshorn stated. "Too much at stake. Too much risk involved. The execs and the corporations don't like loose ends."

Gunther Elmshorn and Frederick Ornstein sat in the short term airport parking in Los Angeles International airport in a brand new Audi 8 waiting for Yohan Steiner to arrive.

Gunther Elmshorn, dressed in a tailor made gray suit, seemed a bit nervous despite all his bravado. He rubbed at the side of his thin nose over and over again. When he wasn't rubbing at his nose he seemed to fidget nervously with the endless dials on the driver's side of the Audi 8.

Frederick Ornstein, dressed in a blue collared shirt, seemed bored and excited simultaneously as he sat in the Audi in short-term parking at the Los Angeles International airport. He was German by birth but had never been out of the United States. This was the closest he had come to international travel. He tried to contain his excitement as he studied the parking lot for any movement. While looking out of the car windows Ornstein saw the silhouette of a jet cutting slowly across the sky. He smiled at the sight, absently pulling at his ear.

Neither man seemed to be looking forward to the eventual meeting with the crafty German.

"Do you think that this means that we are being reassigned?"

"I doubt it. Usually, you have to fuck up and fuck up hard to be reassigned," Elmshorn pointed out.

"Yeah, but here we are and the contract is still open," Ornstein noted.

"It's a little different with this contract," Elmshorn replied. "This fucker is making things incredibly hard to close."

"You don't need to tell me," Ornstein almost laughed. "I have been with you seven days."

"So, there are extenuating circumstances in this contract. The higher ups know what is going on here. I am not hiding anything," Elmshorn said dryly. "I think Steiner is coming to offer a way to accelerate the contract conclusion." Elmshorn added, "But you know the rules," Gunther Elmshorn concluded.

"Yeah, the rules are pretty simple," Ornstein nodded.

"No excuses. Produce or become refuse," Elmshorn intoned. He had wanted to sound light with the phrase that everyone knew working in the shadows of the corporate world yet the words sounded harsh and colder than he intended.

"Produce or be fed to a badger is more like it," Ornstein volleyed, shaking his head.

"Well, I know that our contracts are not over yet since we are still here," Elmshorn decided.

"Why do you say that?"

"Simple, if we were reassigned then we wouldn't see it coming," Elmshorn breathed. His gray eyes narrowed as a handful of people walked from the elevator and into the parking structure.

"Movement," Ornstein announced a second later.

Elmshorn and Ornstein studied the passengers moving toward them. There was a couple dressed as if they had just come back from Mexico or somewhere in South America. The man was wearing a short-sleeved T-shirt that showed off his man boobs and shorts that highlighted his overly developed calf muscles. The man was built like a fireplug. The woman next to him was wearing yoga pants and a gray T-shirt that had some Aztec symbol on it with some name beneath. They were rolling matching luggage and talking very loudly about the trip.

Behind them walked a tall man with dark hair and a day's growth of beard on his square chin. He was dressed in a bright blue T-shirt, blue jeans, and sneakers. He pulled a single roller cart. In his hand was a cell phone. He seemed oblivious to all around him as he walked and talked.

Two women, one dressed in a black pants, blue spaghetti string top, and slide sandals, and the other dressed in a striped skirt with a purple top, were the next to follow the man on the cell phone. They had two bags a piece plus a roller for their heavier luggage.

A solitary man dressed in a blue suit, blue shirt, and blue silk tie, stepped out of the elevator bay, behind the two women. The man was carrying a single bag, a little larger than a roller bag. He had ash blonde hair and a chiseled face. In one of his ears was a diamond earring. On his wrist was a very expensive wristwatch. On his feet were soft black leather boots.

Behind the man in the blue suit came a green haired girl that was giggling and holding the hand of a man wearing dark sunglasses, a black T-shirt, ripped designer blue jeans, and fashionable basketball sneakers. The man was rolling his luggage as was the girl.

"Looks like that is our guy," Elmshorn announced.

"Yeah, I think so," Ornstein agreed.

"So, get ready for a talking to," Elmshorn pointed out.

Ornstein nodded.

Gunther Elmshorn climbed out of the rental car and so did Frederick Ornstein. They didn't wave. They didn't signal. They simply stood on either side of the rental car and Yohan Steiner moved silently toward the pair.

Elmshorn was the taller of the two. On his feet were black leather dress shoes. Elmshorn was not yet thirty and a seasoned professional. On the side of his face was a bruise the size of a melon. Under his thick eyebrows was a visible whelp. His dark gray eyes sat at on either side of a narrow nose. His thin nose was perched above thin lips.

Ornstein was a stockier and younger man than Elmshorn. Frederick Ornstein was dressed in a blue collared shirt, blue jeans, and comfortable brown suede shoes. The 25-year old had dark black hair and dark eyes. Unlike Elmshorn Ornstein had a soul patch on his otherwise clean-shaven face.

The soul patch was his attempt to look older than he was. Ornstein seemed to agonize over the moments when people thought he was too young to do what he was doing. He had only been in the shadows for two years.

Yohan Steiner walked up to Elmshorn and Ornstein and smiled holding his carry on bag easily.

"Gentlemen," Yohan Steiner said and lowered his eyes for a second.

"Mister Steiner glad to be able to work with you," Elmshorn said lowering his eyes for a second as Steiner had done.

"It looks as if I have been sent to figure out what is going on here. There are some some questions as to what has happened to this simple bag and tag," Steiner said.

"The target is not a typical target," Elmshorn responded, involuntarily.

"We can talk about it as you bring me up to speed," Steiner said lifting a hand to signal there was no need to go into any detail in the parking structure.

Elmshorn nodded.

Ornstein opened the rear door of the four-door Audi and watched as Steiner folded himself into the back seat.

Elmshorn climbed into the front seat of the brand new car and started the engine. Ornstein was the last into the Audi 8.

"Where to?"

"I suggest that you take us to the last location of the target," Steiner said from the back seat. "You still have eyes on him?"

"Yes," Elmshorn said. Elmshorn started the Audi and put it into gear. In an instant they were headed for the exit of the parking structure. Elmshorn paid the ticket taker and exited short term parking and found his way onto the airport thoroughfare. Eventually, he exited the airport and drove past the iconic LAX neon sign that signaled the entrance and exit from the international airport.

"Have you been in Los Angeles before?"

"No," Steiner answered curtly. "It looks like the movies," Steiner added. The crisis manager checked his watch and as the early afternoon traffic streamed up and down the wide avenue Steiner asked a question. "So, what is the delay?"

"The target is supposed to be remanded to Los Angeles and on parole. We figured that we would have a number of chances to simply bag him in Los Angeles but he disappeared," Elmshorn pointed out as the trio drove away from the Los Angeles International airport.

"What do you mean "disappeared?" No one disappears unless we make them disappear," Steiner noted.

"Yeah, I know that, but he has left Los Angeles in the first three days but he was supposed to be in Los Angeles," Ornstein explained.

"How?"

"We assume that he booked a flight from Los Angeles somehow," Ornstein continued. "The problem is that no parolee is supposed to be able to board a flight without that being red flagged."

"So, we cannot say for certain how the target left Los Angeles," Elmshorn stated. "All we know is that he just got back last night."

"Are you sure that the target is in Los Angeles?"

"Yes," Elmshorn answered. "We have someone watching him now."

"Where is the target's primary residence?"

"Well," Elmshorn said tentatively as he slowed the rental car and turned on his turn signal to enter the Renaissance Hotel on Airport Boulevard.

"Why are we going here?"

"This is where the target is staying," Ornstein pointed out.

"What? How?"

"We don't know," Ornstein admitted. "I'm still relatively new to the job and I thought that most of the targets were executives and annoyances to executives but this target is a little trickier than either executives or executive annoyances," Ornstein finished.

Elmshorn parked the rental car in front of the Renaissance Hotel. Immediately, a valet ran out of the hotel and to the door where Ornstein was. The valet opened the door for Ornstein and Steiner and then moved deftly to the driver's side to open the door for Elmshorn.

"Welcome to the Renaissance Hotel. How can I be of assistance to you today?"

"We have a meeting here today," Elmshorn lied. The valet nodded and handed Elmshorn a ticket to retrieve his car when his meeting was finished. Elmshorn slipped a ten-dollar bill into the valet's hand and thanked him. "Can you keep the car close. We may leave in an hour or less."

"Yes, sir," the valet smiled and drove the rental car away from the front of the hotel leaving the three men in front of the Renaissance.

"See the problem?"

Steiner nodded.

The trio walked into the lobby of the Renaissance Hotel and took in the beauty and splendor of the space.

Instantly the trio noted the two security guards watching their entrance. At the check-in desk two more people dressed in the dark blue jackets of Marriott Hotels, light blue shirts, and red, white, and blue bows and ties smiled at Steiner, Elmshorn, and Ornstein.

A young blonde girl dressed in a dark blue shirt with a name tag on it that said: Gretchen walked up to Elmshorn and smiled. Elmshorn leaned forward and slipped a pair of hundred dollar bills in the girl's hand. The blonde girl walked away and deeper into the hotel.

"The target has holed up in the one place that the idea of bagging and tagging is nearly impossible to accomplish without collateral damage," Elmshorn pointed out.

"Yes," Steiner agreed with a nod. "But for every problem there is a solution." He paused and smiled. "Have you booked a room here?"

"No," Elmshorn said.

Steiner was already walking to the registration desk.

"I'd like to check in for a few days," Steiner smiled. "I do not have a reservation. I know. I know. I just need to lay my head down for a few days before my next flight at the end of the week."

With that Steiner registered at the Renaissance Hotel.

After checking in Steiner, Elmshorn, and Ornstein headed to the hotel bar.

"Let's have a drink," Steiner smiled. Elmshorn and Ornstein followed quietly behind the older man. They entered the quiet bar and sat at a booth. The hotel bar was empty except for a bartender who was stacking glasses behind the bar.

The bartender nodded and walked from around the bar and to Steiner, Elmshorn, and Ornstein. He was a tall and thin man in his twenties with thick eyebrows and a hooked nose. The bartender looked as if he could have been in a band. He was dressed in a starched white collared shirt, black tie, name tag over his heart that read: Jayce, and black cotton pants. The bartender looked like everyone that lived in Los Angeles trying to become famous.

"What can I get you gentlemen?"

"Well, this is my first time in Los Angeles," Steiner smiled. "Are there any particularly Los Angeles inspired drinks that you recommend?"

"Well, there is the Star Wars that is pretty popular right now but I don't really recommend it," the bartender admitted. "It is too trendy and isn't my favorite." The bartender paused thinking. "Me, I am an Absinthe man. I like that stuff for some reason. I just love the taste of it. So, I recommend the Absinthe Cocktail or Martini to anyone trying to be a little more adventurous than the norm."

"What is in the cocktail?"

"Well, Absinthe, Benedictine, Bitters and Water."

"Is it good?"

"I like it."

"What about the Martini?"

"Gin, Dry Vermouth and Absinthe."

"Thanks," Steiner smiled. "I think I'll try an Absinthe Martini."

Steiner looked at Ornstein and Elmshorn.

Elmshorn gestured to the bartender that he was not drinking.

Ornstein nodded and shrugged.

"Don't have me drink alone." Steiner studied Ornstein and Elmshorn.

Ornstein nodded and smiled. "I'll try that Absinthe Cocktail."

"Can I get a Screwdriver?"

"Sure," the bartender smiled and turned to leave. "Be right back."

In the quiet and closeness of the booth Steiner, Ornstein, and Elmshorn studied each other.

"I have to ask," Ornstein began uncertain. "Are you here to reassign us?"

Elmshorn's eyes widened and he shook his head at the brashness of Ornstein.

"I did not come here to do anything but get a report on the situation since you missed a number of deadlines."

"I was told not to report if there was nothing to report," Elmshorn explained.

"That maybe true," Steiner agreed. "But you and I know that we do not have choice. We report good or bad. We report to someone bigger and more powerful than ourselves and our beliefs. It is our responsibility to report good, bad, or otherwise."

"Reporting that the target is inaccessible or unavailable seems a needless report. It isn't as if I went off the grid. I reported that the target was underground and I reported when the target was on the move."

"But how could he be underground and on the move?"

"He is not one of the typical norms that we deal with," Elmshorn admitted. "He is well financed and knowledgeable. I think that the suits have forgotten that this target was one of us and not stupid or careless by any stretch of the imagination."

The bartender returned with the drinks. The bartender handed out the three drinks and left the table.

"Do you have a timeline?"

"We had a timeline initially but that timeline had to be adjusted," Elmshorn pointed out as he sipped his Screwdriver.

Steiner paused and sipped his drink.

Ornstein took a sip of his Absinthe Cocktail and closed his eyes to the taste. He squeezed his eyes tightly for a moment and then opened them.

"How is your drink?"

"It is definitely different," Ornstein admitted.

"Well, I am only here for five days," Steiner said. He sipped his drink and let that sink in. "In those five days I need to make a report."

"Five days? Hope that we can close this operation in that time."

Steiner sipped at his drink and studied the men across the table from him. He also studied the nearly empty bar room. There was a big screen television playing some basketball game. On another screen there was an interview going on silently between two men dressed in suits with a ticker tape of the latest scores from baseball.

"Excuse me gentlemen, I have to go to the ... restroom? I think that is what they call it here, correct?"

"Yes," Ornstein smiled.

Steiner climbed to his feet and after talking briefly with the bartender headed to the restroom.

"What do you think?"

"What do you mean?"

"I mean do you still think that we aren't about to be reassigned?"

"No, I don't see us getting reassigned. I think that Steiner is here to evaluate, just like he said."

"I don't know. It feels like a reassignment to me."

"There's no reason for us to be reassigned. I think Steiner sees that now that he's here."

"We'll see," was all that Ornstein said as Steiner returned.

"Sorry for that," Steiner smiled. "Long flight."

"No worries," Elmshorn smiled.

Ornstein nodded but did not speak.

Steiner sipped his drink silently. Elmshorn and Ornstein finished their drinks and Steiner was the last to finish his cocktail. He smiled amiably. The slender man checked his watch and stretched.

"Let's head to the room," Steiner concluded.

The trio went to the elevator and caught the elevator to the seventh floor. On the seventh floor they headed to the recently booked hotel room.

"Make yourselves at home," Steiner said putting his carry on in the closet.

"You don't get jetlag?"

"No, I have been flying for quite awhile. You learn all these tricks in air travel. The easiest lesson to defeat jetlag is not to go to sleep until it is night where you have landed. Your body clock syncs with that time and you are good to go after that."

Steiner was near the hotel door and Ornstein and Elmshorn were awkwardly standing in the room.

"Sit down, relax, we have to figure out some things."

There was a desk near the bed. There was a lamp and table near the window.

The room was spacious. Closest to the door was a dividing wall to the bathroom.

"So, what next?"

Steiner looked at Ornstein with a gentle smile.

"There isn't much to do other than figure out how to smoke the target out."

"You got any ideas?"

"I have a few." He paused. He scanned the room. "For every problem there is a solution I was told. I don't know if that is always true but someone smarter than me said that you have to look at problems with new eyes." Steiner smiled. He was an easy going type of guy.

Steiner sat on the edge of the bed.

Ornstein had found the remote to the television. He turned on the television. He was flicking through the channels aimlessly.

"We remove the problem," Steiner hissed.

Elmshorn sat in one of the two chairs in the hotel room.

"Are you armed," Steiner asked Elmshorn.

"Yes," Elmshorn responded.

"Let me see your weapon," Steiner asked reaching out his hand.

Elmshorn obliged. He reached inside his jacket and removed his Sig-Sauer P250 Compact Pistol.

Steiner lifted the pistol in his hand and felt the weight of the handgun. He smiled. Steiner looked at Elmshorn evenly.

"Nice weight," Steiner smiled.

"Thanks," Elmshorn smiled.

"What room is the target in?"

"He is on the fifth floor, I think. I'm not sure." Elmshorn said shrugging his shoulders.

Steiner nodded. Instantly, Steiner grabbed a decorative pillow from the chair he was sitting in and pressed it to Elmshorn's chest and fired twice into the pillow and into Elmshorn's chest. The two bullets killed Elmshorn and set the decorative pillow on fire. Steiner took his hands and squeezed the pillow to put out the slightly smoking pillow. In the aftermath of the shooting the sound was loud in the room for only a second and then there was only a mild ringing in Steiner and Ornstein's ears.

Ornstein reached for his pistol and before he could Steiner had the Sig Sauer P250 aimed at Ornstein's head.

"Don't do anything stupid, Frederick," Steiner said without much emotion. "You know the rules. We have to be effective or be let go. Elmshorn was not being effective. You, Frederick, you get one more chance before someone like me shows up and puts you on a lead diet."

"What?"

"You get another chance to finish this operation before I call it in and we both are reassigned."

"But," Ornstein said looking at Elmshorn sitting in the hotel chair dead. Steiner had killed Elmshorn in his hotel room that he had just checked in.

"Don't worry about this," Steiner announced. "This will disappear before dinner is served. Now, let's figure out a way to eliminate an executive annoyance."

Steiner picked up his phone and made a phone call. He said a few words in German and then hung up.

"You hungry?"

Ornstein nodded.

"Any recommendations?"

Someone knocked at the hotel room door.

Instantly Ornstein had his pistol out and aimed at the hotel door.

Steiner placed the Sig Sauer P250 on the hotel dresser and smiled.

"Answer the door," Steiner smiled.

Ornstein looked from Steiner to Elmshorn and back to the closed hotel door.

"Answer the door," Steiner nodded.

Ornstein walked to the door. He opened the door without asking who was at the door. Ornstein turned around and re-entered the hotel room with another man, who was wearing glasses.

The man was a thicker built man than either Ornstein or Steiner. He was just a few inches shorter than Steiner. The man was dressed in a brown suit and white collared shirt. He wore a red tie. The man had dark hair and a mustache.

"This is Peter Hamm, he was sent to assist us in this operation," Steiner stated.

Peter Hamm smiled. He was broad shouldered. He seemed carved from beechnut.

"You were saying," Steiner continued. "Where should we get something to eat?"

Ornstein was a little muddled. He regained his composure a bit. "We are close to Manhattan Beach. There is supposed to be some great food there," Ornstein said as Steiner braced Elmshorn and found the valet ticket. He handed the ticket to Ornstein.

"Okay, let's go," Steiner smiled. "By the way, incompetence at any level is a reason for removal. At the lowest level you have to know all that you can about the target. By the time we get to dinner Frederick you should be able to tell me what room the target is staying in at this hotel. Right?"

Ornstein nodded.

“Good,” Steiner smiled and ushered Ornstein and Hamm out of the hotel room.

Ornstein walked down the hallway of the Renaissance Hotel thinking how things had changed so drastically in such a short amount of time. Suddenly, his life was on the line based on his ability to retrieve information about a target that he had yet to see. Elmshorn had been given the contract. Ornstein had been assigned the contract and was just responsible for making sure that the target was bagged and tagged. All that Frederick Ornstein knew was that the target was named: Theodore Dandridge. Most, though that knew him, called him: Teddy Dee.

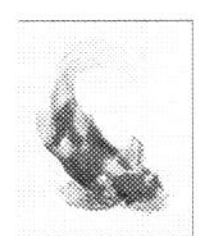  

Asami Fujinaka recalled England fondly. She had learned that having money did not make you better. Having money and power and brains made Asami Fujinaka better. At least, for the two years she studied there.

While in England Asami Fujinaka prided herself in being tougher than everyone she came in contact with. She did not have to be smarter. She did not have to be prettier. She just wanted to be tougher. She wanted to be fearless.

In her pre-teen mind she equated toughness with lack of fear. So, she worked hard to be fearless. For Asami Fujinaka fear signaled the boundary of where the better things resided.

Prior to England Asami had not really understood the concept of fear or want. Her life, prior to the perception of fear was a dream. The first signs of fear from her father and mother was with the appearance of Akio. When Asami turned ten she had been told by her father that Akio, one of the men that stood on the perimeter of the complex, was to take her to school and return her to the complex everyday.

Akio, was a tall and slightly handsome man with dark eyes, thin lips and a tenseness that suggested that he was always prepared for some disaster. Akio was very bright and had travelled across the country. He had been a teacher before becoming a bodyguard. Akio was nice and Asami's bodyguard for two years before he was called away because of a family issue. For a few months, after the departure of Akio, Asami Fujinaka went to school and was returned to the complex by various men that worked for her father.

When Asami Fujinaka was younger, before eighteen, she liked the attention. It was a way to avoid things that annoyed her. Unlike most pre-teens Asami Fujinaka only had to worry about school at school. There were no bullies bold enough to bother the girl with a bodyguard.

Then one day, before Asami Fujinaka turned fourteen, she had been called into her father's study and introduced to Daisuke, a grim looking man with a pointy chin and barely visible eyes that looked as if he were able to punch through steel walls with his gigantic hands and arms. Daisuke was not a talker. He was a strongly built man that had been in the military before being hired by Hiro Fujinaka IV and Signet Industries. Asami Fujinaka liked Daisuke because he was so serious. Daisuke was always dressed in a dark suit and collared shirt. He always had an earpiece sticking out of his ear when on duty.

When Asami turned sixteen she went to speak to her father about the men that watched over her.

"Father, can we talk," Asami asked in the spacious yet small confines of Hiro Fujinaka's study. Her father was just finishing a call with a banker when Asami entered. Seated in the corner nearest the door was Rin, the silent block of wood that protected her father. In the four or five years that Asami had known Rin, the bodyguard had said maybe one hundred words. Seated behind his desk Hiro Fujinaka, a small but powerful man nodded as he finished the phone call. He gestured for Asami to sit at one of the two seats in front of his desk. Asami could only smile, thinking of all the times as a girl she had run in her father's study and seen him talking with bankers, lawyers, realtors and scientists about the business of herbal products that he dwelled.

"How may I be of assistance to you," Hiro Fujinaka IV asked with a wry smile on his lineless face. He was dressed in shirt sleeves, tie and suit trousers. His suit jacket was hanging on the back of his chair.

"Can you tell me why I still need security?"

Hiro Fujinaka smiled and nodded. He was not one to rush his thoughts or his words. He had been in business and the CEO of Signet Industries for nearly two decades. Under his steady hand Signet Industries had become one of the biggest herbal companies in Japan. The company was expanding into international markets because of public demand.

"As you must know, when you were nine or ten a disgruntled employee nearly killed one of the board members," Hiro Fujinaka explained. "I implemented much needed security measures not just at our home but for all our board members." He paused, thinking how to address the next question delicately. "We are high profile individuals. Your name alone in the wrong areas is reason enough to kidnap you and demand a ransom. I am tasked with protecting you and this family. Thus the reason for your need of security."

"Are all the families protected?"

"I protect all the board members. The families are responsible for the protection of individuals. We have made the possibility of threats available to the others. Asami, is there anything else? I have a phone call I have to make—"

"Yes, one more question," Asami said, shaking her head and preparing for the question that needed to be asked. "Can I select the next person that I have to protect me?"

"I don't see why not. I will contact Eiichi and he will give you the opportunity to select your own personal bodyguard."

Sora was Hiro Fujinaka IV's personal assistant. He scheduled everything for the CEO. Anything dealing with business was sent to Sora first. Eiichi always redirected all the information to Hiro Fujinaka IV but the assistant was the first to review the items.

Two days later Sora Abe met Asami Fujinaka and discussed the possibility of her picking her bodyguard. Sora Abe dressed in his blue suit, white shirt and blue tie looked just like every forty something businessman in Japan. He had a wide thin smile. He also had long and thin fingers and seemed to be more bone than flesh.

"So, the idea of you selecting your personal security sounds very mature, Miss Fujinaka. Your father has always wanted you to be safe and secure and this is a step in the right direction. There are just a few elements of the security that you need to be aware of, as you look for a personal security guard. There are 24-hours in the day. You can only hire one personal security guard that has to be vetted by our security services. I will give you the name of our security consultant who will vet your candidate if we have not heard of this person or question their experience. We are still planning on protecting you the other twelve or fourteen hours when your security expert is unavailable. We are assuming that your personal guard will be with you during your waking hours."

Asami smiled at Sora Abe. She liked how thorough he was. He had to be a thorough individual as an assistant to one of the richest men in Japan. A small mistake could cost Signet Industries millions.

Three months later Tanisha Emerson was hired as Asami Fujinaka's personal bodyguard. Tanisha Emerson was hired because she was just like Asami Fujinaka. She was a petite firecracker. The black woman was twenty-seven and six years out of the Marines.

Tanisha Emerson was highly skilled and proficient with hand-to-hand combat, handgun and close combat. Before coming to Japan she had worked for several high profile clients including several female hip hop artists, a pop star and part of the team that retrieved a kidnapped child of a controversial religious leader.

Tanisha Emerson was given a room in the complex to sleep when Asami finally fell asleep. In the complex, there were no less than four outside security guards visible. Inside of the complex there were always at least three more security guards available.

"Why is there so much security," Tanisha Emerson asked Asami Fujinaka in the feeling out phase of the job.

"We are high profile. There has always been this political chess game in Japan where individuals attempt to gain more power. Even now, the politics and power plays are still going on. For us, the biggest threat to Japan is the Yakuza. They are everywhere. It is a real and present danger for us."

"The yakuza? The tattooed criminals," Tanisha smiled.

"Yes."

"Seriously?"

"It is serious, Tanisha. Ten years ago one of the families rubbed the yakuza the wrong way and one of my uncles was crippled and he lost his son. My father instituted the security protocol as a result. He said that he knew that it was inevitable with the yakuza as they continue to spread their fingers into everything eventually."

"Which uncle?"

Chapter Thirteen.

For nearly an hour Teddy Dee thought of ways that he could kill Rupert Williams. The thought began as he opened the ankle monitor and smiled silently at his newest pain in the ass; his new Parole Officer.

In the pre-arrested and now criminal Teddy Dee world Teddy Dee imagined that as soon as Rupert Williams had been bold enough to slide the ankle monitor over to him and smiled that Teddy Dee would have reached across the table and slammed Rupert Williams' head against the wooden desktop until he was dead or no longer smiling, whichever came first.

Instead, post-arrest and criminal record Teddy Dee, Teddy Dee had done as he was instructed and slipped the ankle monitor on his left ankle and had Rupert Williams activate it. Teddy Dee had left the offices of Rupert Williams and thought of one hundred ways to end the life of Rupert Williams. He toyed with the idea of storming back in and bashing Rupert Williams' head in under the watchful eyes of the celebrities and powerful men and women that the Parole Officer had taken pictures with. He considered simply setting the office on fire and when Williams exited killing him on the streets below. There were no limits to the ideas of ending Rupert Williams.

Yet, Teddy Dee chose another tact. He contacted one of his many contacts that knew how to circumvent state issued monitors. In an hour he had the ankle monitor off and sitting in the hotel he was currently staying in. Teddy Dee called Rupert Williams and told him that he was in his primary residence and they had a brief conversation that allowed Teddy Dee limited movement.

"You are required to remain in the restricted area that bound to the north, to the south, to the east and to the west on this map." Rupert Williams handed Teddy Dee a small map of Los Angeles. Teddy Dee scanned the map.

"This is only between the hours of seven in the evening until seven in the morning each day. Any movement outside of this restricted area will be seen as a violation of your parole and cause for your return to incarceration."

Teddy Dee left the offices of Rupert Williams and tried to imagine if Rupert Williams really could control his movements. Teddy Dee considered, not for the first time, of aerating Rupert Williams. The idea sprung into his mind fully formed and palpable. Teddy Dee could get a gun and return to the office of Rupert Williams and shoot him in the office. No one could pin it on Teddy Dee. There were possibly hundreds of potential suspects based on Teddy Dee's interaction with the preening Parole Officer.

Yet, Teddy Dee had left the offices of Rupert Williams and when he left the Parole Officer was still alive. On his right ankle was his new piece of state-issued monitoring property.

Teddy Dee smiled at the specificity of the Parole Officer and his limitations. Teddy Dee had been given instructions by the hacker that had freed him to use a proxy to fool the state issued monitor. The hacker he knew would show Teddy Dee how to remove the ankle monitor.

When Teddy Dee arrived at his hotel he called Eric Robinson. He asked Eric and his family to come over for a paid three-day vacation. For three-days Teddy Dee's proxy would be Eric Robinson.

He sent a limousine to pick up Eric and his family. Erica Robinson, her three daughters and her sixteen-year-old son walked into the hotel room. The hotel room was lavish. There was a forty-inch TV on the wall. There was a queen size bed and a pull out in the room. There was a connecting room that had two single beds inside.

Eric Robinson walked to the window and looked out. The view was of the Los Angeles airport.

"Eric, I should be back tomorrow or by the latest Sunday," Teddy Dee stated to Erica Robinson.

"We can't get in trouble?"

"No trouble for you," Teddy Dee explained. "This is just an inconvenience that will be corrected next week."

Erica Robinson nodded.

That afternoon Teddy Dee caught a ride to Los Angeles International airport. Span.Net had been the first to call Teddy Dee, once he reconnected with his handler and the shadow world of corporate dealings. Teddy Dee knew of the tech company, generally. They were in Silicon Valley somewhere and had gotten a goo gob of money very quickly creating some software that improved the Internet in some way. He caught a plane to San Jose.

Span.Net had flown Teddy Dee from Los Angeles to San Jose and picked him up in a limousine. He had been driven to the home of the president of the company to discuss the problem that Teddy Dee needed to address.

The home, was one of those Mac Mansions that new money and an inflated ego creates. The house was in a quiet neighborhood in Los Gatos, a suburb thirty minutes from San Jose Airport. The ten-foot-high gates swung open and allowed the limousine to enter the slightly uphill drive that led to the circular drive and fountain at the front of the house.

A pair of men stood dressed in suits watching the front of the home. Beside the pair of men were two women dressed in blue polo shirts with one three-inch-wide vertical white stripe that went down the right side of the shirt. One of the women was black. The other woman was white. They both wore blue and white ribbons in their hair.

As the limousine pulled to the front of the house the two women stepped to the car's door. The black woman opened the door with a smile. The white woman smiled and reached into the car to assist Teddy Dee out of the interior of the limousine.

"Good evening, Mister Dandridge," the woman smiled. "We are so very happy that you accepted our invitation to assist us in this delicate situation."

Teddy Dee stepped out of the limousine without the help of the woman. He reached back and grabbed his carry on bag. In it were his essentials.

"How was your trip Mister Dandridge," the black woman asked. "My name is Pepper. My partner is Marcia." Marcia smiled and tilted her diamond-shaped head at the sound of her name. Marcia's blonde hair shifted and fell effortlessly to the side of her lineless face in waves.

"Fine," Teddy Dee breathed trying to figure out the purpose of the tag team. More importantly, Teddy Dee was curious about the two men standing guard at the front of the house. They were obviously armed. From the look of it they might have handguns and maybe even submachine guns. As Teddy listened to Pepper his mind reeled at the reason that some corporate needed armed guards.

"Well, Mister Wayne is anxious to meet with you," Marcia announced. "Please follow us," Marcia continued.

Teddy Dee fell in line.

The trio walked past the two armed guards and into the foyer of the two story mansion. It was just as Teddy Dee imagined having seen so many of the Mac Mansions before. Everything was on a grand scale. From the marble floor that began inside of the house to the grand foyer that looked as if it could house a full grown elephant the Mac Mansion was immense. The imported tile of the entryway and the sweeping staircase that led to the second floor were straight out of a movie. Hanging overhead twenty feet in the air was a chandelier that probably cost several thousand dollars. There were numerous art pieces on the wall and expensive looking vases and sculptures that seemed as if they should be in a museum rather than in the foyer of Mitchell Wayne, the President of Span.Net.

The pair of identically clad women walked to the left and through an open doorway into a high ceiling library that had a rail and ladder attached to the wall to reach the higher books. In the center of the library was a lone wooden desk with a number of books on it and a laptop computer. Teddy Dee noted that there was a black and white movie playing on the laptop that he had seen along time ago about a boy and a dog in a post-Apocalyptic world.

"Mister Wayne is in his study," Pepper announced. The two women stepped through a doorway and into another room and seated in a leather, overstuffed chair was a man with a hooked nose, acne, and no visible chin, with brown hair pulled back into a loose ponytail. He was dressed in a brown checked collared shirt and blue jeans. On his feet were a pair of untied basketball sneakers. Mitchell Wayne looked like a normal 27-year-old, except he was the President of a tech company that was worth, at last reports, $2.3 billion dollars.

Pepper approached Mitchell Wayne while Marcia and Teddy Dee waited at the entrance to his study. Pepper leaned in close and whispered something to the President of Span.Net. Teddy Dee watched the pantomime and tried to read the lips of Pepper and the man that he was about to meet.

Pepper did not need to say much. Mitchell Wayne blinked, smiled and nodded and Pepper gestured Teddy Dee forward. Marcia followed close by Teddy Dee's side. As Marcia and Teddy Dee walked toward the man behind Span.Net he wondered suddenly if Pepper or Marcia was armed? Perhaps, he thought, idly, they were versed in some martial arts.

Teddy Dee dismissed the issue, as he was a guest of Mitchell Wayne, President of Span.Net. He was there to do Mitchell Wayne a service. It did not matter if Pepper or Marcia had Uzi machine guns secreted on them, then and there. They were not threats.

"Come in," Mitchell Wayne smiled. "Thank you for accepting my invitation."

Mitchell Wayne extended his hand and Teddy Dee shook it. He was a slender man of maybe thirty, Teddy Dee figured. Mitchell Wayne had a surfer's tan and a short mop of blonde hair on his round head. Instantly, Teddy Dee thought of Patrick Swayze.

Mitchell Wayne was bright. He was probably a genius, Teddy Dee estimated. Wayne was one of the many Silicon Valley wunderkinds who had figured out ways to make the Internet more accessible to people that were looking for entertainment or information. He had gone to Harvard, Teddy Dee recalled. Mitchell Wayne had dropped out of Harvard when he figured out his first big idea. That big idea had morphed into Span.Net.

Teddy Dee sat across from Mitchell Wayne in an overstuffed chair in the study of Mitchell Wayne and took in the spoils of technology that the President of Span.Net had acquired since starting his company. Teddy Dee was no techno-geek by any stretch of the imagination but he had seen some science-fiction movies. In a corner of the study was a life-sized statue of the Terminator. In another corner was a piano. There were two French doors that lead, Teddy Dee assumed to the backyard and whatever was out of doors.

Mitchell Wayne explained his situation. Teddy Dee knew immediately that he needed muscle, strange, untraceable muscle, to remedy a nagging problem that had cropped up at Span.Net. That was what Teddy Dee did; solve nagging problems.

"Paul Pritchard is the fly in my ointment, Mister...," Wayne was studying his notebook tablet and paused. He looked up with a smile. "Dandridge?"

Teddy Dee nodded.

"We believe that Paul Pritchard has been stealing information and selling, if not hoarding it to sell eventually, to one of our competitors."

Teddy Dee listened waiting for the job that Mitchell Wayne had paid Teddy Dee in advance to complete. Rich kids loved to appear tough but simultaneously they wanted to feel justified in their toughness. They did not want to be found to be heartless.

"I need you to simply go and check and see if Paul Pritchard has taken work from my company and if that work is in his home. If it is in his possession, then I need you to retrieve it without him connecting the dots back to me or Span.Net. Can you do that?"

Teddy Dee nodded.

So, Mitchell Wayne and Snap.Net had been the first job that Teddy Dee had taken after his release from Kulani. It was a low priority, off the books, start-up job. For Teddy Dee it was not an official operation. It was an everyday easy smash and grab affair.

That was Friday afternoon. Teddy Dee had been given the operation and it did not seem too difficult. Low risk. Soft target.

Paul Pritchard was the target. He was suspected of corporate stealing of sensitive documents. The corporation suspected that he had delicate information on one or more of his personal devices. They had checked his office computers and found nothing. So, they needed to check his personal data to be sure.

Of course, there was no law being broken in Pritchard taking information home, theoretically, but the idea that an employee might have sensitive information available and accessible outside of the corporation was frustrating and infuriating to the higher ups. Mitchell Wayne decided that Pritchard had the information and was selling it off or in the process of selling it off. Either way, that sensitive information was Sanp.Net property and Mitchell Wayne did not like the idea of it being on the open market, whatever it was.

Teddy Dee was simply called in to grab all the data that was on the devices of Paul Pritchard including his cell phone, home computer, and any other devices that might be able to store sensitive data.

"Okay there are some very specific details in this operation," Wayne had said with a slight smile. "I need you to make the personal assault look like a mugging."

That part of the smash and grab was nothing novel or new.

That was the last time that Teddy Dee spoke with Mitchell Wayne. Wayne liked to direct. He was a mastermind. Yet, he needed plausible deniability. It was nothing new to Teddy Dee. Rich kids and their desire to be seen as pure, perfect and innocent. It was all a façade.

He had been told where to find Paul Pritchard and Teddy Dee worked on a plan as he headed to find the corporate thief. Teddy Dee went to a local watering hole and instantly located Paul Pritchard. Paul Pritchard was a tall, thin dark haired white guy in his early thirties that could have been any other white guy that Teddy Dee might have run into on the street. He was dressed in slacks, dress shoes and collared shirt. Pritchard was not handsome but he was not ugly either. He had a pencil thin nose and thin lips.

Teddy Dee did not want to think too much about Pritchard or if he was a good or bad man. It did not matter. All that mattered was that Teddy Dee had been hired to toss Pritchard's home and grab all the computer storage media available and make it look like a burglary.

So, as Teddy Dee played out scenario after scenario of how he was going to do his job for Span.Net he watched Paul Pritchard nursing his drink. A couple of Pritchard's friends showed up at the local watering hole. They talked and drank. They drank and talked.

After a couple of hours Pritchard left the watering hole alone. Teddy Dee followed Paul Pritchard to his home and as he parked his car and was walking into his garage, rather than through the front door, Teddy Dee walked up behind him and put him to sleep. He fell like a fifty-pound bag of potatoes from a twelve-year olds arms.

Teddy Dee dragged the unconscious Paul Pritchard into the house and closed the garage door. He deposited Pritchard on the kitchen floor and walked through the three-bedroom home and grabbed everything that could store sensitive information.

Teddy Dee slipped two pillow cases off the beds and tossed the ill-gotten goods in them. He grabbed Pritchard's three-laptop computers. Teddy Dee also bagged the cable boxes and two tablet notebooks. There were a handful of cell phones that Teddy Dee took for good measure. Before leaving, Teddy Dee tossed the bedrooms to make the smash and grab look like a home burglary. He grabbed a few knick knacks and moved the TV monitors as if he was going to take them. Classic shadow signature. Teddy opened the back door and walked through the backyard and out of the back gate effortlessly, unrushed, to his car that he had parked three blocks away and drove into the night.

Teddy Dee dropped the technology off and by midnight a representative that sounded like Pepper had contacted Teddy Dee.

"Mister Wayne would like to send his sincere appreciation for your services. Thank you so much," and the caller rang off.

Teddy Dee caught the red eye back to Los Angeles. He was back and in the hotel by two o'clock. He was asleep and dreaming by three o'clock.

The next morning he had breakfast with Eric Robinson and his family at the hotel restaurant.

"What you do is illegal?"

"No," Teddy Dee lied.

"Then why did you ask Eric to wear your ankle monitor?"

"The monitor is a mistake that I am going to correct this week."

"A mistake?"

"Yes. A mistake. An error. Something that is not correct."

"I know what a mistake is," Erica Robinson said, narrowing her eyes.

"I didn't mean any harm," Teddy Dee said, with a slight smile.

"Now, I have one more ask," Teddy Dee admitted. "I will need to ask Eric to do the monitor one more time and that will be the last time, I promise."

"My boy isn't going to get into any trouble?"

"Of course not."

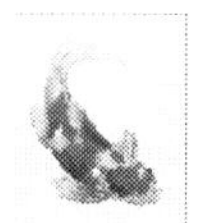  

Before Asami turned twenty-one she had been a part of the last Seijin no Hi, a celebration of people turning twenty in Japan. Asami Fujinaka and thousands of people who had reached adulthood went to shrines and a municipal ceremony that was marred by the appearance of a group of rowdy people who fought and seemed to lack the respect of the ceremony. Obon, New Years day, was another event that Asami Fujinaka dressed in traditional attire and went to a shrine in Tokyo to listen to the ringing of the bells. Yet, it was the Doll Festival that Asami Fujinaka looked forward to each year. It was a miraculous time the Doll Festival. It made Asami feel as if all the cares and pressures of life, in that day, with the dolls displayed about the complex, took her back to kinder and more civil times.

Because of her father and their family name Asami Fujinaka had everything she could imagine. She did not want for anything. Asami went to the best schools. As she grew older, she went to the best clubs. There was few places that barred Asami Fujinaka from their establishments.

The celebrity came at a price. Asami had little private life. She traveled with bodyguards for fear of kidnap. Her friends, her true friends, were few and far between. Too many saw Asami Fujinaka as a paycheck or easy touch for the endless money that seemed abundant. So, Asami found herself on the outside looking in most times, in those early days of being Asami Fujinaka.

Asami felt in that world, in that constructed world that was overseen by her father, that she was nothing. She was just a chit. Asami was a bargaining chit. Her father, in his far reaching thoughts, had set up a number of meetings with various families as soon as Asami turned fifteen.

Asami Fujinaka had deluded herself for eighteen years that she was in control of her life. She had unwittingly been a part of a melodrama that played out everyday before her eyes. Her father, the money maker, the rule maker, the final word when it came to anything involving money, was always building his family business. Her mother, dutiful and devoted, worried about Tanaka, her wayward and unmotivated son and Asami. In that order.

Tanaka was seven years Asami's senior and the heir apparent. Tanaka was a bit of a wildcard in the family. He had been in and out of trouble as he grew up and kind of settled into the role of privileged and entitled son of Hiro Fujinaka. Tanaka Fujinaka got in and out of trouble as a playboy millionaire who did not seem to want to be a businessman. He instead, seemed more interested in parties, pretending to be a member of the Yakuza and the American lifestyle of excess wealth and hobnobbing with movie stars.

It only made sense that Tanaka had moved to Los Angeles with hopes of being the next big thing. He wanted to be a movie star though he had never acted on stage or off. Tanaka Fujinaka was a bit of a dreamer. After a year of struggling in Hollywood Hiro Fujinaka had given his son a position at the newly created Signet Industries in Los Angeles.

With Tanaka falling in love and seemingly getting his life together the focus of Hiro and Keiko Fujinaka suddenly pivoted. The family melodrama shifted and focused on the baby of the family; Asami.

By then, she was seventeen or eighteen and learning that her father was still grooming Tanaka for a role in Signet Industries. Asami became aware that she was not being considered for anything other than possible marriage to a powerful businessman.

Asami had been labeled as one of the most eligible bachelorettes in Japan when she turned twenty-one. Prior to her twenty-first birthday the Japanese gossip columns attempted to link her with some of the most eligible bachelors in the nation. Asami Fujinaka was smoke. She was always in attendance at the high profile events of the Japanese social crowds. Yet, she was never seen with any men of note.

There were rumors of her sexuality. When interviewed Asami vehemently denied living an alternative lifestyle. She loved men. She wanted to find someone to love. Asami pointed out that no one held her attention.

"My biggest issue in a relation is feeling like the other person is paying attention to me. I sometimes feel as if I am alone in the room. Or worse, that no one is listening to me. That is the worst."

"So, do you have a preference?"

"I know where you are heading and because I have not settled down as of yet you and everyone wants to know if I like boys or girls. I think that is none of your business. I know that we live in a world that seems to live and die on the need for trivial information. Yet, no one wants to know where I stand on abortion. No one asks me about gun control. No one wants my opinion on water pollution. Instead, you trivialize my life to sound bites that are manageable and sell papers, get eyeballs looking or whatever."

The reporter persisted.

"I just want to ask you to answer this question, first. What was your last sexual experience? What is your favorite sexual position?"

The reporter was stymied.

That was the end of the interview.

Asami Fujinaka found herself the center of attention unintentionally. Her blog; "Asami's Kooky and Spooky Insights in the Nausicaa Valley" struck a chord with Japanese girls struggling with identity issues, fashion and the pressures to conform in a society fractured by traditional and modern cultures.

Chapter Fourteen.

Leverage, simply meant to gain an advantage through the use of a tool. Leverage is the easiest way to move things that seem unmovable. Teddy Dee was called in all the time. He was the tool used for leverage.

So, Teddy Dee waited. Plotted. Schemed. Rather than getting angry and strangling Rupert Williams in his office, as he had desired Teddy Dee took one of the Parole Officer's business cards and left the office. He knew that Rupert Williams was going to be a problem that he had to solve. As he sat in his rental car and waited for Rupert Williams to leave work he hatched a plan.

"Know your enemy," Teddy Dee reminded himself.

Oscar Easton was always going on and on about the Art of War, The Book of Five Rings, Six Secret Teachings and books that he was reading or had read.

He followed Rupert Williams from his office. Williams went from his offices to a nearby bar. He had a drink. Teddy Dee watched in the shadows of the close and neighborhood bar.

When Rupert Williams had his fill, the Parole Officer walked back to his car and folded himself inside. Teddy Dee waited for the Parole Officer to drive off and get going before he slid into traffic, a good distance away. Teddy Dee had followed his number of cars in the shadows. He did not get too close or lag back too far. Teddy Dee used the traffic to hide his pursuit of Rupert Williams.

Rupert Williams went to a local grocery store and bought some fruit and milk. Teddy Dee waited in the grocery store parking lot for the return of Rupert Williams. The Parole Officer came out of the grocery store and back to the waiting car.

The last stop of Rupert Williams night, before home, was a fast food southern fried fish joint. Rupert Williams ordered catfish, hush puppies and greens two cars ahead of Teddy Dee. Teddy Dee did not go through the drive through for fear that he would lose Rupert Williams. He parked his rental car and overheard the order.

Following Rupert Williams up North La Cienega Boulevard toward the Hollywood Hills. Teddy Dee followed at a discreet distance. The Lexus turned onto one of the avenues where Black Hollywood had lived before the color barriers were knocked down in Los Angeles.

Teddy Dee turned onto the quiet and quaint blocks that were dominated by Valentine homes. Teddy Dee could not help but marvel at the beauty of the homes that sat away from the curb. Teddy Dee imagined the area that he was in was what old Hollywood had looked like back in the fifties. It was a neighborhood still relatively untouched by time and Hollywood. People probably raised families here, Teddy Dee thought. People knew of the movies back then and their proximity but they were not influenced by the movies the way that most were today.

The Valentine homes and the quaintness of the Hollywood neighborhood shrank in the rearview mirror of the rental car that Teddy Dee drove. He drove away from where Rupert Williams lived and back to the Los Angeles International airport. Teddy Dee parked his rental car three blocks from the hotel and weaved his way back to the hotel watching for stray tails. He returned unmolested.

The next day Teddy Dee was sitting in his car, waiting for Rupert Williams to arrive at his office at nine o'clock. Teddy Dee sipped a cup of coffee as Rupert Williams climbed out of his car and made his way to the office dressed in a navy blue suit and aqua blue collared shirt. He was wearing sunglasses and carrying a briefcase that morning.

Teddy Dee sat in his car for fifteen minutes before driving from South Central to Ladera Heights.

The traffic was light from South Central to Ladera Heights. Teddy Dee took the Baldwin Hills scenic route. He had a hopefulness about him.

Teddy Dee wanted to give the workmen and gardeners a chance to begin work. It wasn't in his best interest to arrive too early. Teddy Dee wanted to blend in.

Parking the car two blocks from Rupert Williams house Teddy Dee climbed out of the car and slipped on his coveralls. Up the street where he had parked he noted that there were two gardening crews trimming the hedges and mowing the lawns of an adjacent apartment complex. It was nearly ten o'clock in the morning when Teddy Dee walked down the sidewalk toward Rupert Williams house.

Teddy Dee was carrying a lunch pail as he walked down the street and made a left hand turn onto the quiet street where Rupert Williams lived. There was a cable van parked outside of a house. Teddy Dee noticed that there were a couple of trucks on the street advertising landscaping. Up the street Teddy Dee saw two men cutting the grass of two separate homes.

Teddy Dee turned up the driveway of the house closest to Rupert Williams and as he reached the gate Teddy Dee climbed over the fence as quiet as a cat. Teddy Dee slipped into the quiet of Rupert Williams backyard and around to the shadowed side of the house. Teddy Dee slipped in through the side entrance of the garage.

Once inside the garage Teddy Dee headed to the door that was usually unlocked and entered.

Teddy Dee bee-lined for the bedroom of Rupert Williams. The bedroom looked just like the pictures he had taken a few days before. The only difference was that the sheets had been a bronzed autumn color with embroidered "RAW" in the middle of them. Now, the sheets were powder blue with coffee highlights.

Teddy Dee moved to the night table closest to the door where the iHome alarm clock sat next to the modern lamp. Teddy Dee opened the one drawer. In the drawer were a dozen condoms, a .45 ACP Browning pistol, a Bible, three porn magazines, and various sex toys. There was nothing too surprising.

Teddy Dee had gone to the first night table to be sure. So, Teddy Dee crossed to the matching side night table to see if the exact same things were there. Teddy Dee noted the matching modern lamp. Rupert Williams believed in symmetry.

Teddy Dee opened the drawer expecting more of the same from the other side of the bed but been surprised to find very little inside. In the drawer was a pair of handcuffs, lubricating oil, and an envelope containing half a dozen pictures of girls in various stages of undress.

Teddy Dee felt around in the drawer for a moment looking for something. Then Teddy Dee caught hold of a small leather fob that would have been missed by most. Teddy Dee reached in his hand and found the matching leather fob on the opposite side of the drawer. Teddy Dee lifted the false bottom up to reveal Rupert Williams hidden secrets.

A few hours later, Teddy Dee was back in his hotel near the airport looking over what he had taken from Rupert Williams residence.

Teddy Dee took out a legal pad that he had bought and studied what he had gathered from Rupert Williams home. There were eighty pictures that he had taken inside of Williams' home.

Teddy Dee took the pictures to see what Rupert Williams moved day to day. There were pictures of each room. There were pictures of the bedroom.

There were pictures of the kitchen. There were pictures of the living room. There were pictures of the bathroom. Teddy Dee had a picture of the laundry room. Teddy Dee had even taken pictures of the garage and backyard.

In the bedroom, was Williams' queen sized bed with a sleigh headboard in white ash. On either side of the bed were nightstands. On both nightstands were high tech lamps. Over the bed was an abstract piece of art, a painting in three bold colors: red, black, and white. The only piece of furniture in the room was a dresser drawer. He had looked through the drawers and found nothing unusual. There was underwear in a drawer. There were socks in a drawer. There was a drawer specifically for his watches, rings, and jewelry. In one drawer was a pistol. No surprise there. Rupert Williams dealt daily with ex-convicts.

On the nightstand, where there was an alarm clock was Rupert Williams personal electronics. An iPod sat on the alarm clock. There was a jack for a charging station that was hidden in the nightstand.

The bed sheets were changed on the third day for some reason. His bed was made everyday very similar to military perfection.

In the kitchen, Teddy Dee noted that nothing too significant occurred there. Teddy Dee had taken pictures of the garbage and noted that Williams ate out often. There were a number of Chinese take out boxes in the garbage can. Teddy Dee had a picture of several receipts from a Chinese restaurant called: Shczewan Garden.

The living room held the leather couch and entertainment center. Teddy Dee studied the photos and noticed that the living room didn't seem to see much foot traffic. Teddy Dee noted that the extensive DVD collection of porn and gay porn was in heavy rotation at Rupert Williams home. In the living room on a desk near the kitchen was Rupert Williams' makeshift office. On the desk was a laptop computer that Teddy Dee had already downloaded the hard drive from. There was nothing that stood out in the living room as unusual.

After looking over the photos, Teddy Dee narrowed his eyes and opened up the thumb drive that held Rupert Williams hard drive. Teddy Dee was no techno-geek and could not trust anyone with the information he had. So, Teddy Dee had called up his handler who was a techno-geek and asked some innocent questions.

"Roberta, I need a quick and easy turnkey computer. Recommendations?"

"Teddy, as you know the easiest is the most popular. So, you are looking for something fast? Get the largest hard drive memory you can at Apple. I would go to the Apple Store and tell the Apple Genius that you want a Mac Air with all the bells and whistles on it. Tell them to load the Office

Suite on it for Mac. They will offer you a bunch of other options that don't matter."

"Thanks, Roberta."

Teddy Dee called the concierge and asked for the closest Apple Store.

Thirty minutes later, Teddy Dee bought his first computer since leaving Kulani. Teddy Dee had a brand new Mac Air book with all the bells and whistles on it. The Mac Air was a genius machine Teddy Dee had to admit. The Apple Genius, some high school kid by the name of Michael with an earring in his left ear, had been more than willing to explain how the computer worked.

Teddy Dee slipped the thumb drive into the laptop and in seconds Rupert Williams hard drive was before him. There was a bunch of files that seemed to be dead ends. After an hour Teddy Dee had broken the e-mails into two piles. Rupert Williams' e-mails were either inane and meaningless or cryptic to the extreme.

Immediately, Teddy Dee concentrated on the e-mail and personally created documents. If there was any incriminating evidence it would be there, he figured.

There was a file dedicated to Ingrid. There were a number of files that focused on poetry and some classic poets. Williams had a file of classical pictures that seemed connected to the poetry.

Teddy Dee browsed those files and stopped when he found a file labeled: "Georgia." Immediately, Teddy Dee tried to recall in his searches of Rupert Williams life if he had been born in Georgia or gone to Georgia for college. Teddy Dee paused.

Teddy Dee opened the file. There was a long list of names there. With a cursory glance Teddy Dee noted twenty-five names. Last name first, first initial last. Date of birth. Six numbers followed each entry and a letter. The next thing was a date. The last entry was a city and location.

Teddy Dee narrowed his dark eyes and read through the list trying to see the connection.

Teddy Dee read: "Sanchez, V. 11/29/96 C 5/29/xx San Diego Queen Mary" curiously. Sanchez had been in San Diego at the Queen Mary when Rupert Williams met him or her? Was this a date book? A fudge report? Teddy Dee didn't want to hazard a guess.

"Georgia" stood out in the sea of e-mails, papers, notes, and various data that Williams had gathered on his older laptop.

Teddy Dee skimmed through all the other information looking for anything that related to "Georgia" and found nothing. There were no references to the file anywhere on the hard drive. Teddy Dee took a moment to gather his own thoughts.

Teddy Dee returned to the pile of photos and leafed through them again. There was the living room and its museum like quality. There was the kitchen and bathroom with their obsessive cleanliness. The bedroom looked like some photo shoot of Zen Buddhist Monthly. The laundry room looked like any laundry room in America.

Then, quite by accident, Teddy Dee stopped and looked through his notes about the second time Teddy Dee had slipped into Williams home. There was something there, Teddy Dee knew.

Teddy Dee smiled at his notes finding what he had overlooked. In that bedroom there was something wrong. Teddy Dee had noticed but he couldn't be sure what was wrong with the bedroom. Then he remembered. Teddy Dee took pictures.

The night table closest to the door held the iHome alarm clock as well as the modern lamp. In the night table was one drawer. The table had a deep drawer. In that drawer were a dozen condoms, a .45 ACP Browning pistol, a Bible, three porn magazines, and various sex toys. Teddy Dee had noted the contents and closed the side table without much ado.

In the matching side night table next to the bathroom was the very same modern lamp, sans the iHome alarm clock. There was nothing atop the night table. Teddy Dee had opened the drawer expecting more of the same from the other side of the bed but been surprised to find very little inside. In the drawer was a pair of handcuffs, lubricating oil, and an envelope containing half a dozen pictures of girls in various stages of undress.

Teddy Dee studied that one picture again wishing that he had taken a picture of the interior of the night table to be sure. Teddy Dee had a sudden belief. Teddy Dee had discovered what he imagined was Rupert Williams secret.

“Leverage,” Teddy Dee smiled.

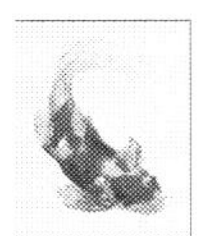  

By 2001 Signet Industries was one of Japan's biggest employers. It had two offices in Tokyo and Kyoto and three plants in each region of the island nation producing everything from hair darkening dyes to sleep inducers. It's CEO and president, Akira Fujinaka, was unquestionably one of the richest and most powerful individuals in Japan.

There had been rumors that Bayer and another global pharmaceutical corporation had attempted to take over Signet Industries. Signet Industries was a billion-dollar business, but small compared to Bayer Industries and others and seemingly easy pickings. The businessmen didn't understand that Signet Industries was a family business and that all the Fujinaka family would fight to the death to protect their heritage.

Needless to say, Bayer and then the next hostile takeover contestant withdrew its bid to buy Signet Industries for no apparent reason. Everyone in Signet Industries knew the reasons.

In 2008 Hiro Fujinaka IV took over the duties of CEO of Signet Industries against the protests of my faithful wife Cherry Blossom. His uncle Akira Fujinaka had an unexpected heart attack and Hiro Fujinaka IV, the eldest Fujinaka, took over despite the seeming negative decision for Hiro Fujinaka IV to become the new CEO of Signet Industries. His family, like most of the Fujinakas was business savvy but the board of directors was lukewarm toward Hiro Fujinaka IV. They, the board, were considering an outsider from the family and even a female to lead the Signet herbal venture when Hiro Fujinaka IV took the helm of one of Japan's most powerful herbal companies.

Almost immediately Hiro Fujinaka IV bought a piece of property in Los Angeles and began to develop a presence in the American market. A year after Signet Industries was up and running in a defunct pharmaceutical facility in Torrance Hiro Fujinaka IV placed his power hungry son in the Los Angeles branch of Signet Industries as the President and head of Research and Development. The move to become a more global company was looked on by the board of directors as a miss play by Hiro Fujinaka IV of Signet money. Hiro F On the far side of the world Japan was all a stir over the second interview with Asami451. The second interview made the Tokyo nightly news. Asami451 appeared and her appearance was a pop culture phenomenon.

There were two interviews that Asami451 gave online. She had been tempted to do an interview with Wired. The interview was very professional. It was published online and in the January publication. The second interview was in another online publication that was Japan's version of Rolling Stone. Both interviews focused on the formula that Asami451 had used to gain all of her followers. Asami451 had explained that her followers had gravitated to her because of her honesty. They, the kooks, were like her. They were young, powerless, female, mostly outsiders, excluded from the bright lights and technology that surrounded them. Asami451 had touched something that the kooks had needed and could not find elsewhere.

"This is not a business. I know that there are people that go online to hock things, sell things and influence others. I never intended it like that. It was more a need to capture things that were going on around me so that I could revisit them and try to figure out the deeper meaning to those moments," she had explained. "It was as simple as that."

Both interviews asked about the nightclub video. Was it staged? Some believed that Asami451 had paid the man to be beaten up. Fujinaka IV refused to listen to the board when it came to the direction of the family run herbal corporation.

Results would trump negative opinions the leader of Signet Industries would trumpet and for the first eight quarters Hiro Fujinaka IV was right. The Oxford trained businessman had surprised many with his business acumen. He was, at 46, Japan's herbal wizard.

In 2010 Hiro Fujinaka IV was on half a dozen Japanese business magazine covers. He had successfully steered Signet Industries into a deal with a smaller competitor and become Japan's premier herbal company. Signet Industries was suddenly at the table with Sony Entertainment, Honda Motors, Suzuki Engines, and Toyota.

The growth of Signet Industries was a blessing and curse. It was a blessing in that everyone associated with the suddenly powerful herbal company was wealthy. It was a curse simultaneously because suddenly everyone associated with Signet Industries had something to lose. The stakes became incredibly high overnight.

Then one night in May, at a club that everyone wanted to get into Asami and six of her friends went out to dance. It was a girls night out. They had wanted to go out and enjoy each other. No strings attached. They were not interested in hooking up with anyone. They just wanted to dance.

The night had been punctuated with a video that went viral that night. It showed the petite Asami stopping a handsy guy from groping one of her friends and that guy attempting to backhand Asami. Asami had launched into a physical beating of the bigger man that ended with him being pummeled senseless in the club. It was all caught on video.

Asami was an instant Internet celebrity.

The Japanese media wanted to interview the pocket sized ninja. They nicknamed her: Danger Mouse. She was the talk of Japan for the next few months.

On the far side of the world Japan was all a stir over the second interview with Asami451. The second interview made the Tokyo nightly news. Asami451 appeared and her appearance was a pop culture phenomenon.

There were two interviews that Asami451 gave online. She had been tempted to do an interview with Wired. The interview was very professional. It was published online and in the January publication. The second interview was in another online publication that was Japan's version of Rolling Stone. Both interviews focused on the formula that Asami451 had used to gain all of her followers. Asami451 had explained that her followers had gravitated to her because of her honesty. They, the kooks, were like her. They were young, powerless, female, mostly outsiders, excluded from the bright lights and technology that surrounded them. Asami451 had touched something that the kooks had needed and could not find elsewhere.

"This is not a business. I know that there are people that go online to hock things, sell things and influence others. I never intended it like that. It was more a need to capture things that were going on around me so that I could revisit them and try to figure out the deeper meaning to those moments," she had explained. "It was as simple as that."

Both interviews asked about the nightclub video. Was it staged? Some believed that Asami451 had paid the man to be beaten up.

Chapter Fifteen.

Teddy Dee walked into Rupert Williams' office as he had done so many times before. Rupert was sitting behind his desk when Teddy Dee arrived. Rupert Williams was reading a report of some kind when he walked into the one room office.

"Sit," Rupert Williams gestured to the overstuffed chair in front of the desk. Teddy Dee looked at the chair and nodded. Teddy Dee would play the game one last time.

"Here," Rupert Williams had said sliding a box across the desktop.

Teddy Dee looked at the box but did not move.

"This is to make my job a little easier with someone like you Theodore," Rupert Williams said not paying attention to him at all. He had a clipboard and a pen in front of him, as he sat behind the desk, dressed in a canary yellow collared shirt and blue and gold spotted silk tie.

Teddy Dee listened.

"Open up the box and put on your new piece of jewelry," Rupert Williams advised with an evil smirk. "Once a week one of Los Angeles' finest will be knocking at your door to check on your new present."

Teddy Dee reached out for the box that sat on Rupert Williams' desk only to pause. He decided then to stop the charade. He had enough of Rupert Williams.

That moment Teddy Dee decided again to rid himself of Rupert Williams. He leaned back in the overstuffed chair and reached down toward his shoes.

"I thought you would like the new jewelry," Rupert Williams said.

Teddy Dee sat up and thought absently that he could snap Rupert Williams neck easily. He could strangle the pain in his side without struggle. Teddy Dee could shoot him inside or outside of his office.

Teddy Dee paused and tried to think of how he would broach the new terms of his relationship. Should Teddy Dee be direct or matter-of-fact? Should Teddy Dee pretend to care? Should Teddy Dee be cold and distant?

"Theodore, I am disappointed in your progress," Rupert Williams said closing the report he had been reading. He pulled a file from the pile of reports on his desk and leafed through it absently. "I thought I made myself clear as to what I expected of you and the consequences of your defiance," Rupert Williams said.

Right then Teddy Dee decided that he had enough of Rupert Williams. There was no way that Teddy Dee was going to listen to Rupert Williams berating him. He was no child. He had not been anyone's child in years. Teddy Dee smirked at Rupert Williams and the Parole Officer furrowed his brow never having seen Teddy Dee show any facial expression. The expression stymied Rupert Williams for a second.

"Stop," Teddy Dee said and watched Rupert Williams recoil at the deepness of his voice. Teddy Dee's voice was more a growl than rhythmic. There was a gravelly nature to his voice as well.

"What--"

"Listen, I came here to tell you that this," Teddy Dee waved his hand around the office. "This won't work. I can't work like this. I'm too old to have a whatever you think this is. I am no slave. You are not my master. So, you and me are over."

"What?"

Teddy Dee was now on his feet. Teddy Dee was a lean two hundred and ten pounds of USDA beef. Few dared face him when he had a full head of steam under him. So, as he placed his hands on the desk of Rupert Williams and leaned toward the Parole Officer he watched as the pencil pusher leaned back frightened.

"Rupert, you know who I am? You know that before I went to prison I was connected to some very powerful people. I didn't get those connections playing nice. I got those connections breaking fingers, double-crossing, and knowing where the bodies were buried." Teddy Dee paused for effect. Teddy Dee was enjoying scaring Rupert Williams. "I tried to play nice with you but you ain't giving me space. You keep cutting off my legroom. That ain't going to work for me. If it ain't working for me then it ain't going to work for you either."

"Theodore--"

Teddy Dee raised a finger for silence.

"Today, until my parole ends, you and I are through. If you try and contact me again I will be sending some of your superiors details of your sick fascination." Teddy Dee removed a manila envelope from his jacket and tossed it on the desk.

"Are you threatening me," Rupert Williams questioned with his hands on his armrests. Rupert Williams studied the envelope for a long minute. Teddy Dee reached out and slapped a hand on it with a loud pop.

"I don't threaten anyone, Rupert. I make promises. You will keep sending in reports and telling the Parole Board how I am a model citizen and a benefit to society and all the bullshit you Parole Officers like to say about your star parolees. I'll be watching. I'll be listening. If you need to contact me you will leave a message at this number. Otherwise, you and I are finished."

Rupert Williams seemed to have a million questions.

"Before I leave Rupert let me assure you that everything that I said I can do. That's a promise. I know things about you that no one else knows. I know things that you thought you had hidden. So, realize that in this relation I have the power. I am in control. The contents of the envelope will prove that power. I am the growling bear that you don't want to poke or even look at wrong. I'll eat you alive. The worst part is that no one will know about it but you and I. I have connections. Those connections are still in place. I just chose not to pull them out."

"But," Rupert attempted.

"This is the easy part," Teddy Dee explained. "You are going to tell everyone that reads your reports that I am a model citizen. You are going to tell them that I am working at that job you tried to send me to or any job you wish. No one will check. That's your job. You won't get in any trouble. No one will be the wiser. Now, if you bother me or make waves in my pool Rupert, I will bring down holy hell upon your head. I will make your sick fascination public and ruin you and all that you have accomplished. If you are feeling suicidal then I will be the last face you see before you go to hell. Is that understood?"

Rupert Williams opened his mouth as if he was about to say something. Teddy Dee stopped and stared.

Rupert Williams was realizing that the man, the parolee, was nothing like he had seemed in the handful of meetings.

The idea of being duped by a parolee had surprised Rupert Williams. He had spent his career reading the criminals that had been assigned to him. To be tricked by any parolee was an affront to his training and skills. It, the deception, had caught him off guard.

Teddy Dee could see Rupert Williams trying to figure out how he had missed the king cobra coiled and ready to deliver the deadly strike in his bedroom. Teddy Dee wanted to smile but chose not to give into gloating. It was a wasted emotion. Teddy Dee knew the pitfalls of counting out an opponent. So, he studied the man in front of him curiously. Rupert Williams had weaknesses. He also had strengths. It was the strengths that Teddy Dee had to pay attention to if he was to remain in control of this tenuous situation.

Rupert Williams was a small man, Teddy Dee noted. The parole officer was struggling with the concept of being bettered by someone he had thought inferior. Rupert Williams continued to open and close his mouth, unable to speak but still using his jaw muscles. Teddy Dee wanted to laugh at the parole officer with his picture of the governor and him shaking hands at some social event. Yet, Teddy Dee remained quiet. The man behind the desk suddenly reminded me of a fish out of water trying to catch his breath.

"Close your mouth Rupert. You might catch flies," Teddy Dee said as he turned on his heels and walked out of the office without another word.

Asami Fujinaka had gone to the corporate offices of Signet Industries with Tanisha Emerson. Tanisha Emerson was always with Asami Fujinaka, when she left the family compound. Tanisha Emerson was an ex-Marine and Asami's bodyguard and a non-negotiable part of her life as Asami Fujinaka.

"Where are you going today?"

"I just wanted to look at the archives," Asami Fujinaka said to Tanisha with a smile. Crusher, her adorable puppy, was sitting on her lap. Tanisha shook her head.

The trio drove into downtown Tokyo and miraculously avoided most of the traffic. Tanisha drove. She was the driver. She parked the car in front of the offices and headed in with Asami and Crusher.

"How long you thinking?"

"Maybe one or two hours, at most. Then we can go to Uoriki Kaisen for lunch."

Tanisha Emerson nodded. The bodyguard stood at the Signet Industries archive door and waited.

Asami walked into the small library and noted the history of the ninety-six-year-old company. She wanted to check something out. It did not take her long. Asami took out her phone and took pictures of valuable information.

At the passing of Akio Fujinaka lawyers noted the changes that the innovative son of Fujiko Fujinaka had implemented. Before his death, Akio Fujinaka had given every member of the Fujinaka family 10,000 shares of the company. Husbands and wives received 10,000 shares between them. Everyone that was a member of the Fujinaka family had shares in the company.

There were only ten members of the Fujinaka family. Each had shares in the company. The brothers of Akio Fujinaka: Oda and Rishuko were ambitious individuals and wanted to run the company. The next in line was Oda. Oda had a daughter named: Miyoki.

Rishuko had a son and two daughters: Ayi and Pachi and Vuel. Ayi married a delightful woman named: Midori. She gave Ayi two sons: Aki and Beppu. Aki was a simpleton. Beppu was a more ambitious individual.

In 1902, Oda Fujinaka became the President of the Royal Family Remedy Company. Oda Fujinaka was in charge of the family business for nearly twenty years.

After Oda Fujinaka stepped down Ayi Fujinaka took over as president of the Royal Family Remedy Company. He was a ruthless leader and spent most of my time in office brokering deals and gobbling up smaller companies across Japan and expanding the Royal Family Remedy Company. Ayi Fujinaka died of mysterious causes after nearly seven years in office.

The board of directors voted in Miyoki Fujinaka as the first female president of the Royal Family Remedy Company in 1930. Miyoki Fujinaka took over Royal Family Remedy Company and made history in her presidency. Having a woman in charge of the now national company was controversial.

Miyoki Fujinaka was a good and steady President. She was President of Royal Family Remedy Company for twenty years. Miyoki Fujinaka and the Royal Family Remedy Company became significant in Japan when the United States of America dropped two atom bombs on the small island nation.

Royal Family Remedy Company was pressed into service to address radiation poisoning. The company was asked to create solutions that eased pain for hundreds of thousands. During this time, without any intention to do so, Miyoki Fujinaka built the family business into a national herbal and pharmaceutical corporation.

So, by her end as president Miyoki Fujinaka had taken the one-time family business that struggled to make a profit and turned it into Japan's premier pharmaceutical corporation.

Miyoki Fujinaka handed her presidency to her daughter: Aisha. Aisha Fujinaka had clear goals left by her mother.

Royal Family Remedy Company changed its name in 1955 to Signet Industries. After the name change Aisha Fujinaka was summarily removed from the board of directors. Her replacement was Riyushi Fujinaka, the grandson of Rishuko Fujinaka.

Signet Industries was moved from Okayama in 1961. The company was relocated and is headquartered in Tokyo, Japan but did a majority of its business outside of the island kingdom.

By 2001 Signet Industries was one of Japan's biggest employers. It had two offices in Tokyo and Kyoto and three plants in each region of the island nation producing everything from hair darkening dyes to sleep inducers. It's CEO and president, Akira Fujinaka, was unquestionably one of the richest and most powerful individuals in Japan.

There had been rumors that Bayer and another global pharmaceutical corporation had attempted to take over Signet Industries. Signet Industries was a billion-dollar business, but small compared to Bayer Industries and others and seemingly easy pickings. The businessmen didn't understand that Signet Industries was a family business and that all the Fujinaka family would fight to the death to protect their heritage.

Needless to say, Bayer and then the next hostile takeover contestant withdrew its bid to buy Signet Industries for no apparent reason. Everyone in Signet Industries knew the reasons.

The growth of Signet Industries was a blessing and curse. It was a blessing in that everyone associated with the suddenly powerful herbal company was wealthy. It was a curse simultaneously because suddenly everyone associated with Signet Industries had something to lose. The stakes became incredibly high overnight.

Akio introduced Royal Family Remedy Company to detailed organization. Akio Fujinaka was a forward thinking individual. He was the first to suggest the name change of the family business. At the time, no one in the family saw the significance of a name change. Few knew that Akio Fujinaka had put into place a five-year plan to modernize the Royal Family Remedy Company.

While in office, as the president, he brokered several small deals with local herbal companies and bought their companies. Before his death in 1901 Akio Fujinaka had secured the dominance of Royal Family Remedy Company.

Chapter Sixteen.

"I love the Rembrandt section. I really love Lucretia. She is so beautiful and so sad," Samantha Morris smiled. "I was an art major before I began working here. So, I like art," Morris confessed with a shake of her head and easy smile.

"Lucretia," Teddy Dee said with a nod. He had never heard of the woman. He couldn't have told anyone if it was a painting, a photograph, a sculpture but Samantha Morris had mentioned it and that meant that when he had some free time, and if he was in Minnesota, he might find her in the museum near Lucretia.

One of the managers walked past the conference room and suddenly Samantha Morris looked down and onto the conference table for something to do. Gone was the ease. Suddenly, Samantha Morris, tensed. Gone was the flirtation.

Teddy Dee looked at the three managers walking past and noted that there were two men and a woman. One of the men was a tall, well built man with blonde hair. He was dressed in shirt sleeves and blue trousers. The second man was a shorter, stockier Asian with spiky black hair. He was wearing a black suit that fit him well. The woman had her black hair pulled back into a ponytail. She was the shortest of the three and dressed in a red jacket and blue skirt.

Cataloging the three managers Teddy Dee tried to figure out the reason for the tension in Samantha Morris. He tried to figure out what caused the tension. Was Samantha Morris in a relation with one of the managers. Teddy Dee did not give enough attention to the managers to determine if one of them had paid attention to the conference room and more particularly, Samantha Morris. He might need to investigate.

The managers passed and as quickly as the moment appeared the moment, the fencing, the ease and opportunity, passed. It was like smoke, Teddy Dee recalled. It was all like smoke.

Teddy Dee tried to figure out which manager had caused Samantha Morris to stiffen and transform into the woman that had greeted him the first time that he had come to Global Corp with Oscar Easton. That Samantha Morris had been stiff and an automaton more than the bubbly, bright and vibrant beauty that had asked him about visiting the art museum.

Before Teddy Dee now was a Samantha Morris that did not want to appear too comfortable with a dumb and plodding brute. Her mood change, reminded Teddy Dee that he was nothing more than a hired arm breaker to most in the corporations. They tolerated the existence of the men and women that made a living inflicting pain for them but they did not want them to be a part of their lives beyond that.

Teddy Dee took a deep breath and found himself looking at Samantha Morris differently. She was human. She was fallible. Like everyone, she caved to pressures for the most convenient reasons. Watching the managers moving back and forth in front of the glass windows of the conference room Teddy Dee understood. When Teddy Dee left Global Corp those managers, friends and colleagues would have a long discussion with Samantha Morris and her interaction with the help, Teddy Dee imagined. He was in Minnesota.

The director appeared at the conference door and smiled. Teddy Dee knew the director from Oscar Easton's initial introduction, when Teddy Dee had been new and green. Barry Granger, forty something, dressed in a charcoal gray suit, with a blue pinstripe collared shirt, green silk printed tie, and matching dress socks. He opened the conference door and smiled as Samantha Morris bowed and made her exit form the conference room.

"Hope you were entertained by my assistant," Granger smiled, his brown eyes sparkling with the question. Teddy Dee gave his attention to Barry Granger but watched as Samantha Morris exited and made her way back to her desk, wherever that was in Global Corp.

Teddy Dee turned his attention to Barry Granger. He was a small, dark haired man that could not have weighed 150 pounds with two five pound bricks in his pockets. He had a $2,500 watch on his wrist and a platinum wedding ring on his finger. Teddy Dee noted as he climbed to his feet and stuck out his hand to greet the director of Global Corp.

"Come with me. We can talk in my office. I had intended to talk here but I think it better to discuss why you are here in my office," Barry Granger repeated, ushering Teddy Dee into his office.

Barry Granger's office was spacious. It was a corner office. To the north the view was of the rolling hills of Minnesota. To the east there was a spectacular view of the cityscape of Minneapolis. The office was 850 square feet. It was the average size of a studio apartment.

He could not help but scan the office for Samantha Morris. Teddy Dee decided he would check into the managers just for his own peace of mind. He usually did not think about or care about things not involving a client. But he wanted to make sure to check on those three managers that had made Samantha Morris hesitate. He just like wanted to know. Prior to Samantha Morris things like why or what was inconsequential to him but suddenly he wanted to know.

“Can I offer you something to drink?”

Barry Granger poured a cup of tea for himself and Teddy Dee. Teddy Dee sat in the overstuffed chair in front of the oaken desk where Barry Granger worked while at Global Corp. The two men sipped their tea, silently.

“This is some of the best tea available. I love it. I get it shipped in from India.”

Teddy Dee nodded, thinking about Samantha Morris. He tried to shake the image of the curly haired beauty from his mind, knowing that whatever he had imagined he had between Samantha Morris would come to a head when he finished his conversation with the director.

Teddy Dee was not a romantic. He could not afford to be romantic. Romantics died everyday.

Teddy Dee did not plan on dying as a romantic. He knew that he was destined to die, as everyone was, but he did not want to go out like a normal. Teddy Dee imagined that when his time came he would determine his own ending. That was the warrior’s way, he told himself.

“So we had to fire an employee about a week ago. We noticed that a few things were missing. Checked our videotapes and found that the items were taken by the guy we fired.”

Teddy Dee did not blink. This was a domestic situation that no one other than the top echelon knew about, it seemed. Joseph Beardsley had been fired and decided to make Granger regret the termination by stealing artwork. It did not make sense to him. It didn't have to make sense to him. My job was simple: retrieve the stolen artwork. So, Teddy Dee nodded to Granger's words.

"We looked at the tapes. It was Joseph. It is delicate dealing with Joseph. We don’t want this to be contentious. We want it handled quietly. No fuss. No muss," Granger smiled. "I would love this whole thing to be over by this time next week. You think you can get that done?”

“Well, I have to find the items first,” Teddy Dee explained.

“I have to believe that the art is in one of two places; his house or his new offices." He pursed his lips as if he had tasted something bitter in his mouth. "Joseph is a bit of an ass. We ended our relationship on a bit of a bitter note. So, he decided to take it out on our bottom line by stealing the four art items. The items are sentimental more than valuable. They were the first things that we bought together when Global Corp was offering its IPO."

Teddy Dee listened and did not say anything. It wasn’t his place. It was just another job. Sometimes, he got good jobs. Sometimes, he got shit jobs.

The job was trivial and meaningless in the realm of corporate affairs but he had stopped caring or paying attention to who was winning these petty pissing wars between the bees, the executives, and the rich kids with too much money. All he knew or cared about was that he was paid for retrieving four priceless items that were either in the multi-million-dollar home or new penthouse offices of an executive that could have bought his own priceless goo gads and trinkets but wanted to thumb his nose at his old employer while making a boatload of money at a new company.

“Samantha, will give you the essentials,” Granger said standing up and shaking hands with Teddy Dee. Teddy Dee shook hands with Barry Granger and Granger could not help but notice how big Teddy Dee’s hands were.

“Jesus, man, I don’t want to be on the receiving end of those meat hooks,” Granger smiled opening his office door and pointing to Samantha Morris and heading in the opposite direction for another meeting.

“Mister Dandridge,” Samantha Morris smiled, climbing to her feet and handing Teddy Dee a padded envelope. Inside the manila envelope was all the information that Teddy Dee needed. He smiled and left Global Corp.

Teddy Dee headed to his hotel near the airport. He did a little research and plotted out two thrift stores on the way to the multi-million-dollar home. Teddy Dee did not plan on fighting anyone but it was always better to be safe than sorry.

When Teddy Dee arrived at the hotel he opened the envelope and looked over the information. There was ten pages on Joseph Beardsley. Teddy Dee only skimmed that information.

Beardsley was an executive. He played tennis and golf. He was no threat. He lived in one of the multi-million dollar homes in the better part of Minneapolis. He worked on Nicollet Mall in one of the insurance buildings.

Before Asami turned twenty-one she had been a part of the last Seijin no Hi, a celebration of people turning twenty in Japan. Asami Fujinaka and thousands of people who had reached adulthood went to shrines and a municipal ceremony that was marred by the appearance of a group of rowdy people who fought and seemed to lack the respect of the ceremony. Obon, New Years day, was another event that Asami Fujinaka dressed in traditional attire and went to a shrine in Tokyo to listen to the ringing of the bells. Yet, it was the Doll Festival that Asami Fujinaka looked forward to each year. It was a miraculous time the Doll Festival. It made Asami feel as if all the cares and pressures of life, in that day, with the dolls displayed about the complex, took her back to kinder and more civil times.

Because of her father and their family name Asami Fujinaka had everything she could imagine. She did not want for anything. Asami went to the best schools. As she grew older, she went to the best clubs. There were few places that barred Asami Fujinaka from their establishments.

The celebrity came at a price. Asami had little private life. She traveled with bodyguards for fear of kidnap. Her friends, her true friends, were few and far between. Too many saw Asami Fujinaka as a paycheck or easy touch for the endless money that seemed abundant. So, Asami found herself on the outside looking in most times, in those early days of being Asami Fujinaka.

Asami felt in that world, in that constructed world that was overseen by her father, that she was nothing. She was just a chit. Asami was a bargaining chit. Her father, in his far reaching thoughts, had set up a number of meetings with various families as soon as Asami turned fifteen.

Asami Fujinaka had deluded herself for eighteen years that she was in control of her life. She had unwittingly been a part of a melodrama that played out everyday before her eyes. Her father, the money maker, the rule maker, the final word when it came to anything involving money, was always building his family business. Her mother, dutiful and devoted, worried about Tanaka, her wayward and unmotivated son and Asami. In that order.

Tanaka was seven years Asami's senior and the heir apparent. Tanaka was a bit of a wildcard in the family. He had been in and out of trouble as he grew up and kind of settled into the role of privileged and entitled son of Hiro Fujinaka. Tanaka Fujinaka got in and out of trouble as a playboy millionaire who did not seem to want to be a businessman. He instead, seemed more interested in parties, pretending to be a member of the Yakuza and the American lifestyle of excess wealth and hobnobbing with movie stars.

It only made sense that Tanaka had moved to Los Angeles with hopes of being the next big thing. He wanted to be a movie star though he had never acted on stage or off. Tanaka Fujinaka was a bit of a dreamer. After a year of struggling in Hollywood Hiro Fujinaka had given his son a position at the newly created Signet Industries in Los Angeles.

With Tanaka falling in love and seemingly getting his life together the focus of Hiro and Keiko Fujinaka suddenly pivoted. The family melodrama shifted and focused on the baby of the family; Asami.

By then, she was seventeen or eighteen and learning that her father was still grooming Tanaka for a role in Signet Industries. Asami became aware that she was not being considered for anything other than possible marriage to a powerful businessman.

Asami had been labeled as one of the most eligible bachelorettes in Japan when she turned twenty-one. Prior to her twenty-first birthday the Japanese gossip columns attempted to link her with some of the most eligible bachelors in the nation. Asami Fujinaka was smoke. She was always in attendance at the high profile events of the Japanese social crowds. Yet, she was never seen with any men of note.

There were rumors of her sexuality. When interviewed Asami vehemently denied living an alternative lifestyle. She loved men. She wanted to find someone to love. Asami pointed out that no one held her attention.

"My biggest issue in a relation is feeling like the other person is paying attention to me. I sometimes feel as if I am alone in the room. Or worse, that no one is listening to me. That is the worst."

"So, do you have a preference?"

"I know where you are heading and because I have not settled down as of yet you and everyone wants to know if I like boys or girls. I think that is none of your business. I know that we live in a world that seems to live and die on the need for trivial information. Yet, no one wants to know where I stand on abortion. No one asks me about gun control. No one wants my opinion on water pollution. Instead, you trivialize my life to sound bites that are manageable and sell papers, get eyeballs looking or whatever."

The reporter persisted.

"I just want to ask you to answer this question, first. What was your last sexual experience? What is your favorite sexual position?"

The reporter was stymied.

That was the end of the interview.

Asami Fujinaka found herself the center of attention unintentionally. Her blog; "Asami's Kooky and Spooky Insights in the Nausicaa Valley" struck a chord with Japanese girls struggling with identity issues, fashion and the pressures to conform in a society fractured by traditional and modern cultures.

Chapter Seventeen.

He had done a little research. There were a few loose ends that he had to tie up before meeting with Roland Cambridge.

Teddy Dee drove the Lexus 450h to the San Fernando Valley. Paul Sawyer lived in the newest housing development near the ESPN offices. Teddy Dee shook his head at the sight of the ESPN offices. Teddy Dee knew that the ESPN headquarters were in Connecticut but Teddy Dee wanted to go there and see what was in that office.

Teddy Dee drove and parked the Lexus 450h two blocks from the entrance to the new housing development where Paul Sawyer lived. Teddy Dee found a gate open and entered into the gated community without much notice. Teddy Dee found the house of Paul Sawyer and walked around looking to see if anyone was home.

It was just his luck to find that Paul Sawyer was sitting in his kitchen by himself eating a pizza and watching television. Teddy Dee made his way around the house and jimmied a window and entered while Sawyer ate.

Home invasion was a crime. Well, so was stealing, as far as Teddy Dee saw it. So, it was a wash. The only thing was that Teddy Dee had kidnapped Anjo Hiroki and assaulted three others that same night.

So, when Teddy Dee made his way into the kitchen Teddy Dee hadn't intended to do anything but talk to Paul Sawyer. Teddy Dee had the thumb drive. Teddy Dee had Anjo Hiroki. Teddy Dee knew where the money was coming from. All Teddy Dee needed was for Sawyer to give him all the information that he had stolen in the last six months. It sounded easy.

Teddy Dee stepped into the kitchen and found Paul Sawyer eating a pizza slice and drinking a beer. Instantly, Paul Sawyer's eyes widened and he stopped eating mid-bite.

"Be cool, Paul. Be cool," Teddy Dee said raising his hands and keeping his voice calm. In Teddy Dee's right hand was the Walther PPQ pistol that he preferred.

Paul Sawyer started to tremble seeing the gun. He held the pizza in front of his mouth. His right hand was shaking and holding the beer bottle.

"You have been a bad boy, Paul. I am the ghost of Christmas Past and I'm coming to correct some bad things you did," Teddy Dee said stepping to the counter and watching Paul Sawyer's hands. Teddy Dee added, "Do me a favor, Paul. Put down the beer, really easy."

Sawyer looked down and jittering placed the beer bottle on the kitchen island. He lifted his hand from around the bottle. Teddy Dee watched every movement and nodded.

"That wasn't so bad now was it?"

"What do you want?"

"Well, Paul, what I want is enough money to live out the rest of my life in the Mexico or Costa Rica. What I need from you, tonight, is the stolen information you took from Arch Corporation."

Paul Sawyer closed his eyes. He nodded. When he opened his eyes he seemed relieved.

"I'm glad you came. I'm not a thief. I'm not a bad guy. I just got into a bind."

Teddy Dee raised his gun and Paul Sawyer stopped as if all the air and words had run out of him.

"Paul, I don't give a shit about the whys and wherefores of your piddly little life. I just want the information no ifs, ands, or buts. So, put down the pizza and get me all the shit you took from Arch Corporation pronto. Chop. Chop."

Paul Sawyer nodded. He spun on his heels and walked with Teddy Dee following closely behind, to his first floor office. In the office was a walnut desk. In front of the desk were two overstuffed claw footed chairs. Behind the desk were bookshelves filled with science books. On the desk was a laptop, an iPad, a printer and old-fashioned architectural lamp. On the walls of the office were several framed pictures of Einstein, Neil Grayson Tyson, and another guy that Teddy Dee figured was another notable scientist. The oddest thing in the office was a model of the USS Enterprise on a pillar near the desk.

"Paul, don't make me shoot you," Teddy Dee said. "I know that you are at your desk and you might have been preparing for this day and maybe, just maybe, you have a gun in the top drawer to scare off the bad guys if it comes to that."

Paul Sawyer was behind his desk and opening the top drawer. He paused. Teddy Dee knew there was a gun sitting there in that drawer. Paul Sawyer's hand hesitated as he looked up and saw Teddy Dee's Walther PPQ pistol aimed at his head.

"If you pull anything out of that drawer that isn't paper or that looks like a jump drive or hard drive know that you are going to be deader than VCRs and eight track tapes," Teddy Dee said placing his finger on the trigger of his pistol.

Paul Sawyer pulled out an envelope and placed it on the desktop.

Teddy Dee gestured for Paul Sawyer to come around the desk. Sawyer complied.

"Sit down," Teddy Dee said and Paul Sawyer sat in one of his claw-footed chairs. Teddy Dee retrieved the stolen information and smiled at Paul Sawyer.

"What now?"

Teddy Dee liked Paul Sawyer. Teddy Dee liked that he hadn't had to beat or threaten the research and development manager. It was refreshing to be able to simply do his job without a bunch of muss or fuss. So, Teddy Dee decided to give Paul Sawyer a little advice.

"What now? Well, I'm about to leave. You might want to turn on your alarm when you are here alone." Teddy Dee said. Teddy Dee raised his hand joking. "You, Paul, well you have a few decisions to make," Teddy Dee continued. "Paul, you got caught. No biggie. People get caught. They don't throw their lives away over getting caught. They get hired by the competition. They get raises. They write books. They do reality shows. They capitalize off of getting caught."

Paul Sawyer closed his eyes and Teddy Dee walked out of the house without incident.

The last errand of the night was to text Fujinaka on Anjo's cell phone and tell him that he needed to meet with Teddy Dee, who would be Theodore Dandridge, the next day.

"Who is this Mr. Dandridge?" Fujinaka shot back.

"A friend interested in helping us with our international problems."

There was a long pause that stretched out to a handful of seconds and then a minute. Then and there, Teddy Dee believed that he might have overplayed his hand. But ninety seconds later Fujinaka responded:

"Very well. My schedule is very tight in the morning. Have him come by tomorrow at two o'clock. You plan on being here at three."

"Yes sir." Teddy Dee replied. Teddy Dee then took Anjo's phone and slipped it in his jacket for safekeeping. The way Teddy Dee saw it Teddy Dee had twelve hours to hammer out the problems between Arch Corporation and Signet Industries. More than enough time.

After the phone conversation Teddy Dee made another phone call. Teddy Dee drove from the San Fernando Valley and over the 405 and back to Los Angeles proper. He exited the 405 at Baldwin Hills and made his way east and toward South Central Los Angeles. Teddy Dee found Slauson Avenue and took that street all the way to Denker Avenue. He turned left on Denker Avenue and negotiated the several side streets that bordered the four blocks of warehouses that were no longer in use.

Teddy Dee parked the Lexus in front of the warehouse. He planned on dumping it in a couple of hours. So, he did not try to hide it. It would be gone in the next hour.

Anjo and Teddy Dee sat in the warehouse silently while Teddy Dee checked his e-mail and arranged a few things with his handler and stockbroker. Anjo was still tied to the wooden chair. He had a black eye. His lip was split. He was not too beat up.

Elijah Graham drove up in a white Chevrolet Avalanche. The giant climbed out of the truck and studied the situation without saying a word. Teddy Dee climbed to his feet and greeted the giant dressed in worn construction boots, carpenter pants, a gray T-shirt, and a throwback Los Angeles Dodgers car coat.

"Well, E, need your help, as always."

Elijah Graham nodded.

"Need you to dump the car somewhere in Venice so the cops find it. Then meet me back at that restaurant, to get you back to your truck." Teddy Dee paused. "How long you think?"

"Give me two hours," was the response from the gravelly voiced Elijah Graham.

"Cool," Teddy Dee said. "You need any getting around money?"

Elijah Graham shook his head: no.

The giant climbed into the Lexus and started the luxury SUV. The music was immediately changed. Suddenly, the warehouse was filled with the sounds of electro-pop. It was as if the warehouse was suddenly some type of ethereal countryside where elves ran and played as young girls wept somewhere.

"Seriously? You listen to the worst English synth pop on earth. You know that the world is filled with all this great music and you pick this trash. If you weren't my friend I might end our friendship based on this drivel."

Elijah Graham smiled in the driver's seat. He did not put the Lexus in gear but instead just let the SUV's incredible sound system fill the warehouse with the electro-pop of William Fitzsimmons.

Teddy Dee smiled and shook his head at Elijah Graham's choice of music. He rarely spoke to anyone about anything. But Elijah Graham was one of Teddy Dee's oldest and closest friends. They had known each other since grade school.

Elijah Graham cut his dark eyes toward Teddy Dee. He studied him for a long silent moment.

"I'm cool, man. I'm cool."

Elijah Graham nodded and put the Lexus into gear. He drove away without a word as the music changed from the ethereal instrumental to a haunting song about goodbyes. Teddy Dee said, a bit embarrassed, knowing the song was by William Fitzsimmons.

Teddy Dee knew much about the singer that Elijah Graham, his lifelong friend seemed to appreciate. For some reason, Teddy Dee had once been compared to Fitzsimmons when Teddy Dee took the stage at an open mike in Hollywood. So, Teddy Dee had done a little research and found that Fitzsimmons was a very talented individual and that the comparison was complimentary.

Maybe, Teddy Dee thought, Elijah and he were close friends for more reasons than Teddy Dee understood. Teddy Dee smiled at the idea. Elijah and Teddy Dee were connected in ways that defied definition. Maybe, Teddy Dee imagined, he and Elijah had been drawn closer to one another through the innumerable fights, scrapes, and battles that we survived. With so many life and death events, his thinking went; perhaps their thoughts overlapped and were intertwined in some way.

Teddy Dee wasn't sure of his thinking or if it was merely coincidence that Elijah and Teddy Dee listened to William Fitzsimmons. Then and there it didn't matter. All that mattered was that Teddy Dee had to dump Anjo some place safe for the next twelve to sixteen hours. So, Teddy Dee took Anjo to a motel near the freeway in South Central and paid for two nights.

"Anjo, give me 24 hours and you will be free to go."

Teddy Dee placed a "Do Not Disturb" sign on the door and left Anjo handcuffed to the toilet.

 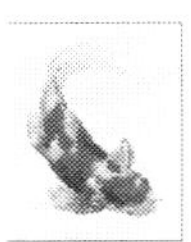 

When the meeting began most that watched the entrance of Hiro Fujinaka IV. He was the man in charge. He was the president of Signet Industries. His decisions effected the day-to-day of Signet Industries.

Hiro Fujinaka sat in the conference room with his son, Tanaka, who had been named the US delegate of Signet Industries. In the room sat the seven elders of the Fujinaka family and board members of Signet Industries. The only people in the conference room other than the Fujinaka family were the three members of the advertising firm tasked with creating the video and Aito Fukui, managing COO of Signet Industries.

"Who has controlling interest in our family business, right now," Akimitsu Fujinaka asked.

Akimitsu Fujinaka, the miniature sumo wrestler, sat at the conference table dressed in a dark blue three-piece suit that made him look like an overstuffed pillow, was flanked by his two sons; Fumihiro and Gakuto.

"So, between the other six members of the family there is 23% interest remaining?"

Next to Akimitsu sat the dapper Arashi Fujinaka. Arashi Fujinaka, like the other members, sat in their designated seats. Akimitsu Fujinaka nodded to his cousin who was still making news for a reported relationship with one of the national Kabuki dance troupe.

Next to Arashi Fujinaka sat the be-speckled Bishamon Fujinaka, who looked always looked as if he should be in a bank somewhere, instead of at a board meeting for one of Japan's biggest pharmaceutical manufacturers.

Bishamon Fujinaka had tried three times to become the chairman of the board of directors and failed. He was a cold and calculating individual and no one to play with.

Next to Bishamon sat Aito Fujinaka. Aito Fujinaka was the peacemaker. He got along with everyone for some reason. He posed no threat to anyone. Aito was an average looking individual with black hair, a slight potbelly and a friendly face. He was the first cousin of Hiro Fujinaka. He sat the closest to his cousin.

On either side of him were his brothers; Choukichi and Chiko Fujinaka.

Choukichi, the eldest, was a dull witted bully who drank too much and gambled recklessly. He liked fast cars and fast women. Too often Choukichi had brought shame upon the Fujinaka family name. Choukichi was the bad boy in the boardroom. He had been arrested a half a dozen times for drunkenness and belligerence. Aito Fujinaka had admitted to Hiro more than once that he wouldn't shed too many tears if he got news that Choukichi had been found dead in a gutter somewhere.

Unlike Choukichi, Chiko Fujinaka had graduated from university and become a manager for one of the peripheral businesses created by Signet Industries. Chikoi Fujinaka had decided to open a sushi bar at one of the offices for the pharmaceutical firms. He had begun humbly and after five years had nearly a dozen sushi shops catering to the influential and powerful in Japan's corporate world.

The monthly board meeting began and the members listened to the minutes of the meeting before. The news was not real news. It was Signet Industries news that was discussed.

Yet, few knew that the quiet and unassuming Asami Fujinaka was orchestrating a bloodless coup within the family. She had been rebuffed by her father and not given a chance to demonstrate her business acumen. So, Asami had decided to wrest power away from her father and take control of Signet Industries.

She did not tell anyone. She did not take out a billboard and announce it. She simply began to talk to her family.

Asami lowered her dark eyes and did the calculations. Her father had 17% of the Signet Industries stocks in my name. Her mother had 6%. Yet, that morning she had given Asami 3% of her shares. Her brother had been given 6% and when he was frustrated with his father, when he had been 17 or 18, he had given Asami 2% of his 6% to teach his father a lesson. So, she, Asami, had originally been given 6% interest that had increased secretly seven years ago to 8%.

When Asami gained Tanaka's interest she had advised the family attorney and asked him to hide the exchange for as long as possible. So, only four people knew that the heir of Hiro Fujinaka IV had given 2% of his interest to his sister. Asami Fujinaka had reached out secretly to her cousins to see who in the family was interested in helping her wrest control from her father. In less than 24 hours later, Asami Fujinaka had become the most influential member of the Signet Industries board of directors.

The responses had come from the most surprising parts of the family. Her mother, Keiko Fujinaka, had spoken to the mothers and daughters of the families and asked them to give Asami at least one share if they didn't mind the idea of a female in charge of the future of the Fujinaka fortunes.

Asami, the devoted daughter, dressed in a traditional kimono was now a voice to be reckoned with in Signet Industries.

Chapter Eighteen.

The man that Teddy Dee was going to see was the son of Hiro Fujinaka IV, the President of Signet Industries.

The next day at two o'clock Teddy Dee went to Signet Industries. The security at the Fujinaka building was top of the line. The lobby had ten visible guards. Two guards monitored the entrance to the lobby. Two more guards maintained the security scan.

Beside those two male guards were two women guards to take care of women visitors. The other four guards were placed near the two elevator banks.

Teddy Dee took the elevator to the 30th floor and sat in the waiting room of Signet Industries. The oval faced woman behind the counter smiled and said that she would inform Mister Fujinaka that Mister Dandridge was in the office. Teddy Dee sat waiting to talk to Mister Tanaka Fujinaka.

Mister Tanaka Fujinaka's assistant showed up. He was a small Asian with one of those kewpie doll hairdos that looks as if his hair was not combed but kneaded atop his head. The assistant was dressed in a dark blue striped suit with white shirt and patterned blue silk tie, Teddy Dee noted. The assistant bowed, said his name, apologized for Mister Fujinaka's inability to greet him personally and smiled again.

Fifteen minutes later the kewpie doll hairdo that defined the assistant to Tanaka Fujinaka was bowing again in front of Teddy Dee. Teddy Dee looked up and smiled at the constant bowing. The assistant finished his bowing and smiled.

"I will take you to see Mister Fujinaka," the assistant finally said and Teddy Dee stood up to dwarf the man in the dark blue striped suit. The assistant bowed again and with Teddy Dee moved quickly to the corner office of the 30th floor where the son of the President was waiting.

The assistant opened the door and ushered Teddy Dee into the office and backed out reverently. Teddy Dee watched as the assistant left and closed the door silently. Tanaka Fujinaka was standing behind his desk as Teddy Dee walked in and he lifted a finger for a moment while he finished a phone call.

"Okay, we need to sell 12 million shares ASAP. Can you also pick up 10 million shares of General Electric once it goes below 30? Dump the airline stock to cover the General Electric purchases." He paused. "Right. Thank you."

The 31-year old Fujinaka was five foot six inches tall if that. Dressed in a dark suit, lavender shirt, and matching striped tie. Mister Fujinaka was a dark haired businessman with the slightest streaks of gray in his temples. On his wrist was a $10,000 dollar Breitling watch.

"My apologies, Mister Dandridge. Business is 24 hours everyday, as you probably know."

Teddy Dee, now Theodore Dandridge, nodded. Business was 24 hours everyday in the shadow world as well. Some deluded themselves and believed that business only happened during business hours. Teddy Dee knew better. Business happened all day everyday.

Fujinaka crossed the expanse between himself and Teddy Dee. Teddy Dee watched as Tanaka Fujinaka approached. As the shorter man approached the bigger and stronger man, Teddy Dee thought of a dozen ways that he could kill Tanaka Fujinaka and no one know of it.

Teddy Dee could blind him. No, Teddy Dee rethought the initial attack. Teddy Dee had to silence Tanaka first. Teddy Dee would have to crush his larynx if he was to attack him in the office. Then, Teddy Dee would hit his shoulders and paralyze his arms. Then Teddy Dee would blind him. All those cruel ideas faded as Tanaka Fujinaka drew closer and extended a hand to the corporate chaos creator and controller.

Tanaka Fujinaka had the blackest hair Teddy Dee had ever seen. He was a solidly built man; Teddy Dee could tell. He probably worked out regularly. He moved like he was comfortable with his body and had a bit of physical acumen.

The two met near the middle of the room and the 31-year old Tanaka Fujinaka had a firm grip when he shook hands with the bigger Teddy Dee. He was a handsome man with perfect and lineless face. Teddy Dee noted his perfectly straight and white teeth. He smelled of fresh flowers and hickory wood.

"Please, let's sit," Tanaka Fujinaka, said gesturing toward his desk. There were two uncomfortable chairs in front of his ultra-modern desk.

Following the shorter Mister Fujinaka Teddy Dee could not help but think how this meeting was going to turn out. The choices were limited. They could only end in one of two ways. Teddy Dee would leave alive. Choice one. Or Teddy Dee would not leave. He would be dead. Choice two. Teddy Dee was leaning heavily on choice number one.

Teddy Dee noted the three oversized familiar abstract art pieces framed on the walls. Teddy Dee had never seen the art before. Two bonsai trees sat on either side of the door on pedestals. The trees were only twelve inches tall. Teddy Dee was no expert but Teddy Dee noted that the miniature trees had to be one hundred years old at least and a treasure in and of themselves.

In the far end of the office was the only office furniture: a glass tabletop desk. The office, the pair moved through, was roomy and dominated by a floor to ceiling window that was the main focus of the room. The window and view overlooked the 405 and the undeniable stretch of Los Angeles magic: Santa Monica Boulevard that lead to the Pacific Ocean.

"What brings you here, Mister Dandridge," Mister Fujinaka asked behind his glass desktop. On top of his desk sat a transparent analog clock. Beside the clock sat a picture frame that randomly flipped from one picture of Mister Fujinaka skydiving, parasailing, practicing kendo, and sitting at a table with several members of his family. In front of the picture frame was a miniature samurai sword and katana, the only thing on his desk that seemed to suggest that Mister Fujinaka was Asian.

Fujinaka was cordial. He was inviting. Teddy Dee also knew that to be in his position he was also calculating.

"I had a meeting with Anjo the other day and discussed some international issues that my expertise might be useful in smoothing over," Teddy Dee said, knowing that all corporations faced international issues because they crossed boundaries. It was a part of every corporation. The better and more efficiently international issues like distribution or outsourcing was addressed the better the profit margin. Thus, any official of an international business was always trying to figure out ways to cut corners.

Teddy Dee studied the office noticing the telltale signs of a rich kid that had become the rich man behind the glass desk. There were great pieces of art on the long white walls that seemed to suggest Pop Culture and Americana, for some reason. One of the pictures was of a blonde haired woman leaning forward and beside her was a child of seven or eight dressed in a partial suit and dress.

Fujinaka had asked Teddy Dee something and Teddy Dee had missed it. Teddy Dee had learned anytime that he missed something someone said it was always easy to smile as an answer. So, Teddy Dee did nothing.

It was time to lay his cards on the table. The worst thing that would happen would be that Fujinaka pressed a panic button and the trained guys with the shotguns showed up.

Teddy Dee closed his eyes. Teddy Dee climbed to his feet and crossed his arms. The giant of a man had to figure how to get to Fujinaka before he could press a button or do something to alert the people outside. Teddy Dee put his finger to his upper lip and stroked it before making his move.

Teddy Dee moved swiftly over the glass tabletop and bowled Fujinaka over in his high backed chair. In less than five seconds Teddy Dee was sitting on Mister Fujinaka's chest smiling at the feat he had accomplished. Teddy Dee was no gymnast, and weighing 220 pounds never considered himself agile or swift, yet Teddy Dee hurdled the glass top desk and landed atop Tanaka Fujinaka without knocking over anything on the desk.

Teddy Dee looked back briefly and noted his physical feat. He wanted to smile and laugh at the accomplishment but did not. He instead looked to the miniature katana sword that was still in place as well as the two bonsai trees. Teddy Dee looked down and into the dark and panicked eyes of Tanaka Fujinaka and saw him begin to speak. Teddy Dee clamped his gigantic hand over the smaller man's mouth. The only thing that Teddy Dee ever had working for him was his sheer ability to outlast the punishment of most.

In that moment, he had the element of surprise on his side. Teddy Dee smiled at the smaller man beneath him, for the moment. He had no time to congratulate himself or revel in the moment.

So, as Teddy Dee sat on the small man's chest Teddy Dee had to think quickly. There were only seconds to make critical decisions. Teddy Dee looked at Fujinaka and deftly slipped off his $200 dollar striped satin tie and shoved the expensive silk into Fujinaka's open and surprised mouth.

Fujinaka blinked in reply, as if Teddy Dee was a part of a dream and that blinking might awaken him from. Teddy Dee studied the man on the floor. Teddy Dee was always amazed when the rich kids, who owned the world, were surprised by simple, brutal violence.

"You know that life always boils down to the choices that we make. People get confused and think it is something else or that life is based on a big decision. I don't. I know that some of you believe that. I don't," Teddy Dee said.

Teddy Dee studied the President of Signet Industries beneath his knees and considered his next steps. He spoke and scanned the office. The attack, if jumping over a desk and pinning Tanaka Fujinaka was an attack, had not raised any alarms. Tanaka Fujinaka had not had time to ring an alarm. His assistant would not dare disturb a meeting between her boss and Teddy Dee unless it was an emergency. Teddy Dee did not imagine that there were any "emergencies" looming that day, or at least that moment. So, he had time to think.

"I could have played the long game and been found out eventually or done the unexpected. Either choice was a choice that had to be made. Choices, big or small, happen everyday and every second," Teddy Dee paused. "I am a little distracted. Sorry." Teddy Dee climbed off of the executive. Teddy Dee instantly grabbed a handful of Tanaka's shirt and sat him back upright in his chair. He seemed stunned and trying to regain his breath.

"I know you, Fujinaka," Teddy Dee said pulling out four plastic zip ties. Before Fujinaka could protest or resist, his wrists and ankles were lashed to the arms of the high back chair by the plastic restraints. "You know the one thing that I always have on me wherever I go? Zip ties. They are a modern marvel. Most people don't even pay them any mind. They are innocuous. Meaningless."

Teddy Dee frowned. "Wait a minute. I was talking about something important. Oh, yeah. I remember. I know you."

Teddy Dee had Fujinaka seated upright again in his chair with his wrists and ankles secured by zip ties to the chair arms and legs, respectively. In seconds, Teddy Dee had removed everything from the executive's pockets and tossed them on the glass desktop behind him.

On the table were two cell phones: one iPhone and one Samsung. There was a thumb drive that could hold 50 gigabytes of information. There were several business cards. Fujinaka's wallet lay open on the tabletop. He had about $500 in cash. Car keys to a Mercedes Benz were inches from the wallet.

Teddy Dee surveyed the room again and his eyes fell on what he was looking for; adhesive tape. Teddy Dee frowned at the small roll of adhesive tape. He stepped to the bookshelf and noted that the office had a private bathroom. Teddy Dee smiled. Of course, Tanaka Fujinaka had a private bathroom.

"How do you know me? Why do you know me? Where do you know me from," Teddy Dee said in a singsong fashion and as he did he began to feel the first moments of being out of control. This was the high of the capture. The exhilaration of besting someone else. Teddy Dee was aware that the injection of excitement could derail the best plans of the best blooder.

So, Teddy Dee took a breath and tried to focus. He focused on the task at hand. He wrapped the adhesive tape around Tanaka Fujinaka's mouth securing the tie. It was a shoddy job but it would suffice until Teddy Dee left the office.

He stopped and studied Tanaka Fujinaka who struggled but could not loosen the zip ties that held him to the high backed chair securely.

“You are thinking that I’m crazy, huh?” Teddy Dee said. Teddy Dee brushed Fujinaka’s shoulder and leaned in with a mischievous grin.

“You are the type of person that I never grew up around.” Teddy Dee paused. Teddy Dee looked around the office that overlooked Santa Monica Boulevard. It was a spectacular view.

“I know you and your type Fujinaka. You were pampered in Japan. You probably went to the best schools back there. Coming to the States you had to succeed,” Teddy Dee smiled. “A lot of pressure, huh?”

Teddy Dee spoke and Tanaka Fujinaka struggled and fought against the zip ties. Teddy Dee seemed unconcerned about the struggling. He had done this before.

“Me, I grew up with nothing. I lived with the bare minimum. I have been through all sorts of crap. I slept in mud. I’ve been shot at, stabbed, kidnapped, and nearly killed. The only pressure I’ve ever had has been if I want to live or die." Teddy Dee paused. He checked his watch.

“You probably have a house that is worth a couple of million dollars somewhere in the hills, near a celebrity. That stuff don’t mean anything to me. I’m a minimum wage kid. I’m happy to be the muscle for others and beat up on a few rich kids that need to be beaten up."

Teddy Dee was looking through the items on Fujinaka's desk when he saw a picture of Fujinaka holding a kendo stick. “You do kendo? I have studied that but I’m not impressed. I don’t really see any value in it. I suppose that it doesn’t make sense nowadays. No one I know walks around with a sword. The idea of training in some ancient art that you will very likely never use in your lifetime is over my head."

Teddy Dee was searching for something. He had lost his train of thought again. “You know what Fujinaka? If the security walked in right now I’d kill you and take my chances. I might get away. I might not. Life is a crapshoot." Teddy Dee gathered the various items from the desk.

"The bigger the risk," Teddy Dee said starting to feel the thrill of conquest. It, the conquest, was intoxicating. Teddy Dee teetered on the edge of euphoria and a downward spiral into the dynamic pull of power. Teddy Dee paused trying to regain his composure.

“You probably don’t take too many real risks. You have too much to lose. I bet you have the latest and greatest of everything. You have to. You have to keep up with the competition. All that technology and schooling don't amount to squat when you come up to deal with someone like me. All the technology won't help you when I punch you in the nose. You might even know a little martial arts. You might think that matters. It doesn't. Not when you face someone that has nothing to lose."

He paused. He closed his eyes to a slight pain behind his right eye. "You see I came here because I needed something you got." Teddy Dee studied the man who was watching him with hatred in his eyes. "The world breaks down to two types of people: those that get and those that take. I take, and the worst thing about it is that you can't do anything about it even though you own this building. It ain't about the security. It ain't about the brains. You probably have bigger brains than me but I beat that. I am the berserker with a battle axe in the boardroom. I am the bloodthirsty savage at the office door. I am the drooling killer with a chainsaw in the conference room. I'm the bad man. The fight in me beats everything else."

Teddy Dee looked out the window and found himself appreciating the Los Angeles view. He turned and looked at Fujinaka. "What do you want? I see you asking that with your eyes," Teddy Dee smirked, a tightening of muscles in his face that he rarely used.

Teddy Dee grabbed the jump drive and cell phones. He plugged the jump drive in the laptop computer on Fujinaka's desk and downloaded everything on it before leaving. As he left Teddy Dee knocked the miniature katana and samurai sword off the desk. He considered for a long moment of tipping one of the bonsai trees off of its pedestal but instead gently tapped the bonsai on the right side of the office as he left.

Teddy Dee walked out of Fujinaka's office with more than he ever imagined. It was not his plan to get more than needed but being in the lion's den Teddy Dee got greedy. He had gagged Fujinaka and tied him up in his ergonomically designed high tech chair and knew that he had overstepped the bounds of the game. Retrieval was never supposed to humiliate the executives.

Executives understood the rules as well as everyone in the shadow world. Humiliation was like roughing the kicker in football. Block the punt but you could not run into the kicker for fear of a lasting injury. There would be a penalty added on after the fact. Teddy Dee knew that but he had gotten caught up in the retrieval and despite the fact that he was supposed to just retrieve the stolen Arch Corporation information he had mistreated Tanaka Fujinaka.

Information was a tricky thing. Anytime a client asked me to get information Teddy Dee never knew exactly what they were referring to, exactly. It could have been a single file. It could mean the whole hard drive. So, as Teddy Dee looked around the office of Tanaka Fujinaka and in a split second decided to burn everything down. Better safe than sorry was and always had been Teddy Dee's motto. So, Teddy Dee had downloaded the hard drive of the laptop and desktop and Teddy Dee knew that doing that simple thing had set Signet Industries back three months if not a year in valuable research and essential internal security in so doing.

Teddy Dee forecasted his immediate future. He was headed to Arch Corporation in Newport Beach to hand over the information that he had gathered to Roland Cambridge. Teddy Dee knew simultaneously that as he headed to Newport Beach Tanaka Fujinaka would be untied and that he would be unleashing the dogs of war on his heels. The dogs of war would be after Teddy Dee.

There was video of Teddy Dee as he entered the building. There was video in the Signet Industries offices. Teddy Dee had to make a decision. Teddy Dee had to decide if he was going to fight or run. Fighting was not feasible. The dogs of war, the Fujinaka security detail, would be coming for bear. They would be given the go ahead to shoot to kill Teddy Dee to retrieve any and all things taken from Tanaka Fujinaka.

Running, based on the sheer number of men that would be sent to ventilate Teddy Dee, made the only sense. Any other thought was suicidal. Running simultaneously meant that Teddy Dee would be hunted by the dogs of war until Roland Cambridge signed off and a few days had calmed the hunt for Teddy Dee's scalp.

Teddy Dee, in the best case scenario, needed to swing by South Central and free Anjo. Teddy Dee was many things to many people but he prided himself on being a man of his word. The blooder planned on dropping Anjo off in Inglewood now that Tanaka Fujinaka was aware of the game. Teddy Dee could have killed the moneyman but there was no need. Anjo wasn't essential. Besides Teddy Dee had bigger problems.

Being the bagman was never a good thing. Getting caught with the bag was even worse. So, the moment that Teddy Dee walked out of Tanaka Fujinaka's office and passed Tanaka Fujinaka's assistant Teddy Dee knew that he only had about fifteen minutes to get out of Signet Industries alive.

So, despite sending Tanaka Fujinaka's assistant a text message from Fujinaka's Samsung not to disturb him for 30 minutes after the meeting with Teddy Dee. Of course, Teddy Dee knew that the assistant or security or anyone might supersede the text message.

So, Teddy Dee climbed into an elevator and hoped to make it to the parking garage before the dogs of war were unleashed. Teddy Dee knew the game and despite knowing the game his heart jumped every time the elevator stopped. Here, in this moment of escape, the game of backstabbing, double dealing, deception, and trickery all came together to make Teddy Dee alive and electric. All of his senses were in overload. If the elevator door opened and a security guard stepped into the small confines of the elevator Teddy Dee imagined, he would have to dismantle the guard as quickly as possible. The possibility excited Teddy Dee.

The three-minute descent to the parking garage was interminable. Four times the elevator doors opened on the descent to the parking garage. The first two stops were the most troubling. Teddy Dee figured that if the guys with the shotguns were going to show up they were either going to be at the start or finish of the elevator ride. When the elevator door opened and allowed Teddy Dee to head to the rental car in the parking lot he tried not to think about the security guards jumping out of the dark to subdue or kill him.

When Teddy Dee finally reached the parking garage he still expected the guards to be waiting with shotguns. The fact that no one was waiting to stop or detain Teddy Dee or more likely cut him in half was surprising. Teddy Dee exited the elevator and wasn't killed then and there, thankfully. So, Teddy Dee headed toward his awaiting rental car.

At the parking garage, with ten minutes until Fujinaka's assistant poked her head in the office and freed Fujinaka, Teddy Dee figured, walking past the security office he purposely made some rookie mistakes. Teddy Dee didn't want to appear too professional. Teddy Dee was working against the clock and knew that his time, fifteen minutes or less in the Fujinaka Towers was limited.

Teddy Dee suddenly had an expiration date if he couldn't get out of the Fujinaka Tower parking structure. If Teddy Dee couldn't get away from Fujinaka Towers before Fujinaka was discovered, he was dead. If Teddy Dee couldn't get out of the parking lot before the alarm was sounded, he was dead. If he wasn't headed toward the 405 and cutting across Los Angeles and toward Newport Beach, Teddy Dee was dead.

There was safety everywhere but not in Fujinaka Towers. Once Teddy Dee was outside of Fujinaka Towers, the safest place, in his world, was at Arch Corporation. If Teddy Dee didn't make it to Arch Corporation to hand off the stolen items that he had taken from Tanaka, he knew he was dead.

It was a bleak forecast, in general. It was a blooder's life. A blooder bloodied others and waited for the repercussions of those bloodied. It was a continuous swinging pendulum of action and reaction based on the needs of the shadow world of corporations. Blooders did not act unless directed to by very powerful men or women. Blooders did not react unless instructed to by the very same powerful men and women in the lofty heights of the untouchable and unassailable corporations.

As Teddy Dee walked to the rental car in the underground parking lot of Fujinaka Towers he had to thank “Alabama” for her heads-up about hatchets seeking to eliminate him after the operation. Thanks to “Alabama” Fleming he was aware that once he dropped off the information to Rollo and Arch Corp there was an open bounty on his head. The bounty lasted usually 24-48 hours after the operation ended. So, Teddy Dee had 48-72 hours to worry before the bounty hunters were called off. Three days after the Arch Corp op Teddy Dee could stick his head out and not worry about someone blowing his head off for a reward. It was as simple as that.

Teddy Dee climbed into the Ford Mustang he had rented and for the first time thought that a muscle car might be a bonus in Los Angeles. Thank God it wasn't red or black. His rental was white. Even though it was a Mustang, being white, it blended in, to a certain extent, with other cars.

Teddy Dee drove to the ticket booth, paid his parking fee and exited. No security guard stopped Teddy Dee or ran up to his car with a shotgun to blow his head off. Instead, Teddy Dee let the Mustang climb up the ramp and out onto Santa Monica Boulevard unhampered.

Teddy Dee smirked at being able to overcome the initial hurdle: escape from Fujinaka Towers. Teddy Dee headed toward the freeway. Arch Corporation was easily thirty minutes away by freeway. Teddy Dee tried to call Roland Cambridge but no one answered. Teddy Dee would call him en route. Teddy Dee called back and left a message.

"Roland I'm coming in hot. I have all the missing information. Need to disappear for awhile though, until things cool down. Standard procedure," Teddy Dee said as he made his way toward the 405. "I think that I might have overstepped my bounds, just a little. Need someone to mediate. It could be ugly for me, for awhile."

Teddy Dee was making his way, like everyone else that afternoon, in a rental car, north or south, heading for the 405 Freeway. Unlike everyone else around him Teddy Dee had kicked a nest of cannibalistic bees, just a few minutes ago and they were pissed and were coming to eat him.

In his mind, Teddy Dee could see the SUVs being loaded and the dark suited Yakuza wannabes sharpening their knives as they piled into the fleet of SUVs and were directed to find and kill the escaping Theodore

Dandridge. They would have a description of the Mustang. They might even have the license plate.

Tanaka Fujinaka would have told them that Dandridge was headed to Arch Corporation. So, the Yakuza posse would be angling for the freeways. The freeways were the quickest way to cut the corporate pirate off, before arriving at Arch Corporation in Newport Beach. They might be on motorcycle, Teddy Dee imagined. Motorcycles would be the best alternative to cut off the Mustang.

Teddy Dee shook the idea of motorcycles shutting down the freeway and systematically searching for him. The dogs of war, the kill team, would be fired up to bring back Teddy Dee's scalp. It was guaranteed that Tanaka had offered a bounty for the man that brought back anything stolen from his office. Teddy Dee knew that he had a bounty on his head, as well.

Teddy Dee knew he had destroyed Tanaka Fujinaka's desktop and disabled the hard drive on the West Coast President of Signet Industries laptop before leaving his corner office. The iPhone, he had taken in the office, was in a trashcan in a parking lot. The chip in his jacket pocket. The Samsung was on Santa Monica Boulevard somewhere. Teddy Dee had dropped it before climbing onto the 405. The Samsung chip was in his pocket. The thumb drive that Teddy Dee had taken from Anjo was in his jacket pocket.

Getting to the freeway would be a great way to escape the dogs of war. They would be scanning video of the parking lot and outside cameras looking for Teddy Dee and which car he was driving. If they were good they might be a few minutes behind. They would be driving at breakneck speeds knowing that when Teddy Dee made it to the freeway he was going to be nearly impossible to find.

Teddy Dee knew that getting the information to Rollo wouldn't stop the dogs of war that the 31-year old hothead Tanaka Fujinaka would have unleashed. Perhaps, Tanaka Fujinaka would decide to call them off. Perhaps not. After every smash and grab operation there was a 48-72 hours given for laying low and giving the offended parties time to squash beefs. The corporate blowback might take longer but for the blooder, who committed the act the whole incident would be in the rearview mirror, literally in three days.

For three days Teddy Dee had to lay low. He just had to find somewhere to be invisible for the next two to three days. Teddy Dee had several places that he usually hid out in. His usual location was a three or four-star hotel near the closest airport.

After two to three days of the dogs of war hunting him Teddy Dee imagined he could return to the normalcy of the shadows of corporations. Three days and Teddy Dee would be persona non grata for most corporations following his romp in Signet Industries. To get the wheels rolling again Rollo Cambridge would inform Tanaka Fujinaka that he had been caught and that Arch Corporation had retrieved and removed all of the Signet Industries double agents while retrieving all the stolen information taken by the spies thanks to Teddy Dee. Tanaka Fujinaka would deny Signet Industries involvement and threaten a lawsuit. The dogs of war would be called off. The whole smash and grab would blow over in three days. That was the best case scenario.

The worst case scenario, was that Tanaka Fujinaka, after being untied and ungagged, took the humiliation personally and sought a very public way to teach Teddy Dee that he had overstepped his bounds. There was a precedence for public humiliation by others in the corporations. It was important to keep the appearance of the big wigs pristine. Big wigs protected their self-image jealously. Teddy Dee knew that big wig self-image was the cause of many of jobs that he had undertaken.

Self-image overrode the idea of calling off the dogs of war. If Tanaka Fujinaka played the self-image card, then the three day cooling off period would be meaningless. Rollo Cambridge talking to Tanaka Fujinaka would be insignificant. The only options Teddy Dee had was flight or fight.

Teddy Dee had to rely on Rollo and the power of Arch Corporation to identify the button men that Tanaka Fujinaka might be sending. That was little solace but at least it was something tangible. The corporate battles were bloodless usually. Bagging a blooder was never good business. It was a part of business to be caught with your hand in the cookie jar and to have your wrist slapped. The corporate world was a school playground to a certain extent and there were unwritten rules.

Of course, if Tanaka Fujinaka had hired some new button men that Rollo and Arch Corporation knew nothing about then Teddy Dee needed to be a light sleeper.

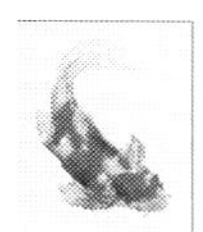  

"Mother, can you tell me why women are not running the family business?"

"Why would they?"

"Let me ask that again. Mother, can you tell me why you are not running the family business or a part of running the family business?"

Keiko Fujinaka twisted her lips, swallowing her words before she could speak.

"Everyone knows how good you are with numbers and contracts," Asami responded.

Keiko smiled awkwardly. She pulled on her earlobe and replied: "Your father is doing a great job doing what he does. Don't you think so?"

"Mother, that was not my question," Asami Fujinaka attempted. "Everyone tries to say that only men should run Signet Industries. But that is not true. There is a history. There have been women that have run Royal Family Remedy before. There is no reason that we cannot run Signet Industries now."

Keiko Fujinaka shook her head.

"The problem with education is that you cannot act stupid when you know something. The problem with knowing things and knowing right from wrong is that it makes us more complicated, Asami," Keiko Fujinaka whispered.

Asami smiled.

"Not everyone is meant to be a leader. Everyone has a role. Even the followers."

Chapter Nineteen.

A week into his forced hiding Teddy Dee found himself in Westchester. Westchester was a small airport close neighborhood. It was a bedroom community that found itself one of the closest cities to the Los Angeles International airport and as a result the police presence was better.

Teddy Dee liked the view from his hotel. He was just on the other side of the airport. After a week in his hotel he decided to take a walk.

For some reason, Teddy Dee decided to stretch his legs and after a few minutes found himself near the Westchester Public Swimming Pool trying to clear his head. He had a mild pain in the back of his head but nothing that suggested danger.

He took a deep breath and tried to think of the last time he had gone swimming. It had been years. He tried to recall if the last time he had worn swim trunks and gone swimming in a swimming pool was when he was a teenager back in Chicago.

Tourists seemed to be everywhere suddenly. It was a strange day and on a sunny and clear day there were a number of tourists in the area. Teddy Dee did not think too much of it. There was a tour bus. Teddy Dee assumed that the tourists were there to take pictures near Loyola-Marymount.

There were Japanese tourists everywhere. Teddy Dee tried not to overthink the tourists. Yet, he was ever vigilant. The first attack came at the hands of a pie-faced woman, who separated herself from the approaching crowds and attempted to poison Teddy Dee with a hypodermic needle. It was very black bag and covert, like in the movies. The first attack had been thwarted because Teddy Dee was hyper vigilant in crowds as he knew that he stood out and was an easy target in crowds.

The first poisoner, armed with a hypodermic, was a woman dressed in a baseball cap, jogging top and ¾ length workout tights. She looked like a typical tourist as she made a direct line toward Teddy Dee in a crowd near the swimming pool. The unerring, unflinching direction that the woman took across the crowd put Teddy Dee on alert. He knew that attacks did not only come from men. Being a sexist in the shadow world of corporations only ended badly as far as Teddy Dee was concerned. “Alabama” Fleming had taught him that the greatest threat might be in the one person that you underestimated.

The woman had gotten close enough to remove the hypodermic and nearly inject Teddy Dee with whatever toxin she had. Unfortunately for the assassin, Teddy Dee was faster and stronger than the woman and turned the tables on the would be killer injecting her with the toxin instead.

“I don’t know what you were trying to give me but you only have a few minutes to get an antidote,” Teddy Dee explained dragging the surprised and drugged assassin to a walkway that had fewer people around. They stood on a little used stone bridge that stretched over a footpath twenty feet below where joggers were moving back and forth.

The woman, trying to keep her composure, smiled and narrowed her gaze. She reached for her small purse that was slung across her chest. Teddy Dee stopped her from putting a hand in the purse instantly.

“Antidote,” the woman said.

Teddy Dee snatched the purse from her neck and opened it. Inside of the purse was a Lady Smith and Wesson pistol. Instantly, Teddy Dee unloaded the chambered bullet and the magazine from the pistol. He slipped the magazine in his pocket for safekeeping.

Teddy Dee poured out the interior of the purse in front of the woman. In the jumble of tissue, loose change, lip balm, lipstick, little sampler of hand cream, there was a small injector that looked like a smaller, silver version of the allergy pens people used.

The woman grabbed the allergy pen and pressed it into her thigh.

“Tell your bosses that they might want to rethink this whole operation. The next person that attacks me I may not be so generous.”

Teddy Dee walked away from the woman and left her purse on the bench.

Teddy Dee returned to his hotel and tried to think how he had been marked. Obviously, the assassins were out and waiting for him like some demented whack-a-mole game. They were poised and ready to take his scalp if he stuck his head out.

So, Teddy Dee moved. He changed hotels. He moved to a more expensive hotel. The expense was for security. There were doormen. There were hotel detectives. It was very high-end.

In that hotel he rented a car. The car arrived and Teddy Dee drove to Pepperdine to get some distance from the threat of hatchets.

Pepperdine was above Malibu and definitely out of the range of the hatchets, Teddy Dee imagined. Hatchets knew Teddy Dee's profile. So, Teddy Dee imagined that if there was to be an attack it would be at or around the airport. It made sense.

After the first attack Teddy Dee had thought to go to Pepperdine and research something the Japanese assassin had in her purse. There was this unusual herbal hand cream that Teddy Dee had noted when he dumped her purse and took her cellphone. It was unusual because it was distinct and not some non-descript hand cream bottle. The jar was a miniature white jar that had a dragon sculpted around the base of the jar and two painted koi on the outside.

Teddy Dee did a little research and was not surprised to find that the maker of the hand cream was none other than Signet Industries. The very same Signet Industries that Teddy Dee had stormed and taken back all the data from their president; Tanaka Fujinaka.

"Fuck knuckles," Teddy Dee said, realizing that he had not shaken Tanaka Fujinaka or Signet Industries. At least, he had not thrown off the dogs of war that were still hunting for him.

For an instance, Teddy Dee thought to call Roberta and complain about his current situation. He smiled at the idea.

He then thought of calling Roland. Almost immediately, he shook that thought out of his head. Roland had done his job. Roberta had done her job. There was no one to call.

If Teddy Dee wanted the attacks to stop there was only one person to stop it and that was him. He could go back to Fujinaka towers and try and reason with Tanaka Fujinaka. That did not seem feasible. If Tanaka Fujinaka was reasonable he would have cut bait and realized that he had been caught and that there was nothing left to do but move on.

So, Teddy Dee considered leaving Pepperdine and returning to his hotel. He paused and noticed that there was a volleyball game that day. He decided to go and watch a volleyball game in the glass walled gymnasium. There was a crowd there. Instantly, Teddy Dee was on alert. He watched everyone until he found his seat in the bleachers and tried to simply enjoy the volleyball game.

A young and attractive Asian girl/woman moved toward Teddy Dee on the bleachers. Teddy Dee was instantly on alert having dealt with the Japanese poisoner just weeks before. The girl sat down a few rows below Teddy Dee. Teddy Dee sat and watched the game and the girl. Two more of the girl's friends showed up and Teddy Dee decided then and there to leave. As he was leaving one of the girls climbed to her feet and headed for the aisle ahead of Teddy Dee. Teddy Dee slowed and noticed that another of the girls that had been seated was on her feet.

Teddy Dee cut across the bleacher and over people to make it to the second stairway of the bleachers. The three girls followed. Teddy Dee bounded down the bleacher stairs and out of the gymnasium and into the lobby. Three against one were not optimal odds but Teddy Dee figured that only one of the three had a hypodermic needle. The worst case scenario would be that they started shooting. Teddy Dee was unarmed.

So, instantly Teddy Dee headed for the exit. If he was going to fight, then he wanted to have an advantage. Space was his advantage.

Outside of the gymnasium and at the bottom of the stairs Teddy Dee stood by a tree and waited. The first girl with her hair in a long black ponytail and blue T-shirt with fluorescent green letters on it that read: Make History, stepped out all piss and vinegar. She had black tights on and like the woman Teddy Dee had faced on the stone bridge a small purse slung across her chest. She looked to be in her twenties and angry.

The second girl to exit the gymnasium was a round faced, thin lipped Asian with thin eyebrows and pug nose. She was shorter than the first girl and dressed in a gray sweat top with hood and blue jeans. Her black hair was piled into a raven black bun on her round head. It was the round faced killer that had spotted Teddy Dee standing near the tree.

"There he is," the girl said and pointed out Teddy Dee to her two accomplices.

The third girl was close behind the first two. She was dressed in black tights, T-shirt, and Nike gym shoes. She had shoulder length black hair, big, expressive anime eyes, and no visible chin. Though she looked to be the same age as the other two her body did not seem to have gone through puberty as she had the body of a teenage boy more than a twenty something.

The three women moved cautiously down the stairs and toward Teddy Dee. Teddy Dee backed up and into the small grove of trees that lined the walkway to the entrance of the gymnasium. Teddy Dee wanted to use the trees to his advantage.

The ponytailed woman was the first to attack. Teddy Dee felt sorry immediately after blocking her feeble attack and punching her unconscious. He opened her purse and like other assassin there was a Lady Smith and Wesson inside. Teddy Dee saw a dozen zip ties inside the purse. He zip tied the attacker and grabbed a handful of ties as the next girl attacked. He unloaded the pistol and prepared for the next attacks to come on the Pepperdine campus.

Teddy Dee fought off the two women as they simultaneously tried to subdue him and inject him with a toxin. The boyish woman attacked with martial arts confidence. Teddy Dee liked using his hands and though the girl was fast and agile nothing that she did with her hands hurt the giant. Her kicks were annoying and constant. Teddy Dee concentrated on the woman's feet and after only a few moments the boyish woman was not willing to get close to Teddy Dee. Teddy Dee looked at the boyish woman just out of reach.

While Teddy Dee was concentrating on the boyish woman the round faced attacker struck and nearly jabbed the hypodermic into his bicep. Teddy Dee did a swimming motion and avoided the attack and without thinking punched at the attacker hitting her wrist and knocking the hypodermic needle from the hand of the round faced girl. The boyish woman attacked again and Teddy Dee punched the boyish girl in the stomach, just hard enough to drop her to her knees. He zip tied them all in the grove of trees and gave the same warning to them that he had to the first attacker.

"Whoever sent you needs to know that I'm not the guy that is attacked. I'm the guy that does the attacking."

The boyish figured woman was the one, that instead of simply accepting her situation, sneered and looked as if she wanted to go another round with Teddy Dee. Teddy Dee shook his head at the incompetence of the three and was about to turn and leave when the boyish figured woman spoke.

"This is not over," she spat.

"Shut up Miki," growled the ponytailed killer whose left eye was already swelling shut.

"No, I want this black bastard to know that beating up a few women has done nothing but made it worse for him," Miki hissed. Her dark eyes glared at Teddy Dee.

Teddy Dee shook his head.

"You think this is funny?"

Teddy Dee turned and walked away.

"You have awakened a dragon," Miki growled. "You have awakened a dragon."

Teddy Dee smiled at the bravado of Miki. He thought absently of walking back and slapping her silent. Teddy Dee paused for a moment and chose the higher road.

Three days after Pepperdine, on a Sunday, Teddy Dee was attacked near Manhattan Beach. He was there to try to see "Alabama." When he was in Manhattan Beach he always thought of seeing "Alabama" Fleming.

The third attack was a combination of hypodermic needle and assassin squad. Teddy Dee was in Manhattan Beach trying to enjoy one of the busiest tourist spots after seeing a movie to beat the heat. Teddy Dee was walking down the beach boardwalk the evening of the third attack.

Three men approached Teddy Dee dressed in jeans, and hooded sweatshirts. Teddy Dee was dressed in a car coat, collared shirt, and khaki pants, noted the three men and his defenses went up. He took in the three men immediately and tried to think of the best attack or retreat. On the section of the boardwalk where Teddy Dee was there were just a few homes and no retail stores. To the right was the Pacific Ocean. He noticed there was a street exit one hundred yards ahead of him and behind the three threats.

"Hey, bro, you have the time," one of the three men that looked a little like an Asian Justin Bieber asked stepping out of the group. He was dressed in baggy jeans, Nike gym shoes, and a black hooded sweatshirt. He had a retractable baton in his hand.

"Hey, man, my friend asked if you have the time. What is wrong with you? You stuck up and can't talk," the second Asian man who had his dark hair sculpted into a faux Mohawk said with a knife in his hand. He was dressed in black baggy jeans, Nike gym shoes, and short sleeve white T-shirt.

Teddy Dee shook his head at the not so veiled threat.

The third person had the hypodermic needle.

The first man with the retractable baton was the first to attack. Teddy Dee watched as the first man telegraphed his attack. Teddy Dee stepped forward and under the arc of the baton and simply fired a knife hand into the angry man's throat driving him pin wheeling into the sand holding his throat and trying to breathe. Teddy Dee grabbed the retractable baton out of the air just long enough to turn and aim the steel rod at the second attacker.

Instinctively, the faux Mohawk man holding the knife swatted at the baton like it was a gnat or annoying bee. Teddy Dee used the moment of distraction to step forward and stop the knife thrust effortlessly. Teddy Dee used his up close proximity to attack and dismantle the man in seconds all the while watching the last man with the hypodermic needle.

The last man with short hair and a diamond in his earlobe and holding the hypodermic needle watched as Teddy Dee stepped over the crumpled man that had attempted to attack him with a knife. The hypodermic wielding man paused and smiled at Teddy Dee. Teddy Dee was surprised at the bravado of the third attacker.

"What? No words?"

The third attacker shook his head; no.

Teddy Dee nodded and the fight began without any other fanfare. The two men circled one another clockwise. One, a giant and the other, a foot shorter and seemingly more confident than the other.

Teddy Dee had just his mitts. The attacker held the hypodermic needle as if it were a dagger. On the sidewalk sat the retractable baton. Perhaps, Teddy Dee thought absently, the attacker had a gun and was going to pull it out and shoot him dead before he could mount a fight.

Teddy Dee waited for the attack. Teddy Dee waited for the smaller man to pull a gun. Teddy Dee waited for the man to make his move.

The attacker upon making a complete circle feigned a left-right-left stabbing motion only to spin to the left and kick at Teddy Dee expertly. Teddy Dee blocked the kick and watched the attacker more closely. The two circled each other, now counterclockwise, looking for an opening, a weakness or soft spot to exploit. Teddy Dee kept his gnarled hands out and his elbows close to his sides, waiting for the next attack, that had to come.

The second attack was three overhead left-right-left stabs at Teddy Dee with the hypodermic needle. Teddy Dee avoided each stab and in the third attack noted a weakness in the attacker's attack. So, Teddy Dee circled around the attacker to the left and kicked the baton into the sand. As Teddy Dee kicked the baton the attacker again did an overhead left-right-left stab attack. In the pulling back for the second stab Teddy Dee rocketed a punch into the jaw of the unguarded attacker. The punch dropped the attacker. He zip-tied the three men together and walked away.

He took their phones and slipped them into his pocket. The phone that the hypodermic needle attacker used Teddy Dee held onto. He checked the two phones that he had grabbed in the first two attacks. Teddy Dee looked for similar numbers. He found three numbers that each phone had in common.

Teddy Dee sent the phone numbers to his handler.

"Tanisha, I want to go into the city today," Asami Fujinaka announced to her personal bodyguard. Tanisha Emerson was Asami's daytime bodyguard. At night, between the hours of midnight until six in the morning there were two others; Kendrick and Zachary. Kendrick was this ex-rugby player with no neck and thin eyes that never seemed to blink. Zachary was this Korean military type that had spiky black hair, a sharp nose, thin lips and a swimmer's physique. Of the three, Asami had to admit that she preferred Tanisha Emerson to the pair of testosterone driven night nurses.

Tanisha Emerson, dressed in a worn motorcycle jacket, white V-neck T-shirt, black jeans, and black motorcycle boots, studied the smaller girl curiously.

"I think I need to settle this whole thing with my dad," Asami continued.

"Are you sure you want to go to Tokyo today," Tanisha Emerson inquired when Asami told her that she wanted to go see her father.

"Why not?"

"It's raining," Tanisha Emerson pointed out.

"What are you afraid you'll melt?"

Tanisha Emerson just smirked in reply.

"It is round trip an hour. We can stop by X for lunch."

Tanisha Emerson did not bat an eye.

"You and your dad made up," Tanisha Emerson finally said, her slight Southern drawl noticeable.

Asami Fujinaka rested a hand on her hip.

It was Asami Fujinaka's time to smirk as an answer.

"Yeah, well, this will not end well."

"You know that he will be happy to see his little angel," Asami smiled and tried to be extremely cheerful. "He loves me. He will drop everything once he realizes that I want to clear all this craziness up."

Tanisha Emerson had not said a word. Instead she went to retrieve the keys to the Mercedes GLC SUV from the seven car garage fob and and prepared for a fast trip to Tokyo. The diminutive bodyguard walked toward her room and after a brief visit returned wearing a thick rain slicker and knee high black rubber boots with yellow ducks holding umbrellas over her black jeans and white V-neck shirt. She was also wearing her driving glasses.

"Are you sure that my father told you that you could drive the GLC?"

"He didn't buy it to sit in the garage," Tanisha Emerson smiled.

"I know that. I know. He just rarely takes the time to drive any of his cars of late."

Tanisha Emerson shrugged her shoulders in response.

"Remember you are supposed to make sure that I am safe," Asami smiled in the seven car garage and slipping into the sleek and fast car with her one piece of luggage; a dog carrier. Tanisha Emerson had smiled as she saw the black toy poodle's eyes and face appear at the top of the carrier.

"You and that dog," Tanisha Emerson said shaking her head. "You two are inseparable."

"Is there a problem?"

"No, not at all," Tanisha Emerson smiled.

"How different would your life be if you weren't Asami Fujinaka?"

Asami Fujinaka shook her head at the question. She had heard all her life how privileged she was to be the daughter of Hiro Fujinaka. She had no control over who she was when she was born. All the control she possessed manifested itself in the person that she was now. So, though Asami understood the point of Tanisha Emerson's question Asami knew that her response would simply be: But I am Asami Fujinaka. Although, Asami liked her bodyguard and felt comfortable with her she chose not to respond at all as Tanisha Emerson eased the black supercar out of the Fujinaka complex.

The car slid through the gates of the complex and into the streets of the rich and powerful of Japan suburb. The rain poured from the skies as Tanisha Emerson put the SUV into gear and began the short drive to the expressway. For what seemed an eternity neither person spoke as the rain washed over the Mercedes Benz SUV.

"If you are giving me the silent treatment then leave the audio off and I can listen to Spotify on my phone... for a little traveling music?"

"I'm not giving you the silent treatment. I just think that you ought to call your dad first. He is the president of one of the nation's largest herbal businesses," Tanisha Emerson said stopping the Mercedes at a roundabout just long enough to make sure that the path was clear and navigating it through the suburban streets heading to the expressway.

"Leave that to me," Asami Fujinaka said fishing her cellphone out of her bag opening an app that suddenly took over the radio of the Mercedes. Music that had initially been something akin to Jacuzzi jazz on Spotify was suddenly usurped and replaced by Asami's musical bent. Hip hop and R&B had replaced the Jacuzzi jazz that had been bathing the Mercedes in easy going music.

Asami Fujinaka sat like a petulant teenager tapping on her cellphone as rap music poured out of the car speakers. She was instantly engrossed in the cellphone screen and typing away. She tapped the screen and was on another app suddenly.

Tanisha Emerson looked to Asami once and then concentrated on driving. The rain and the road to Tokyo could be a bad combination on dry days but in the rain most issues fell away. In Japan, and in Tokyo in particular, when it rained people seemed to avoid the roads.

Asami seemed focused on the cellphone, that she never left home without, as Tanisha Emerson drove. The only daughter of Hiro Fujinaka texted several people as Tanisha Emerson navigated the roadways. Tanisha Emerson did not pry or prod. That was not her job. She was paid to protect Asami Fujinaka.

The road trip was filled with the sounds of Lil Wayne, Eminem, Kendrick Lamar, Public Enemy, NWA and Asami's latest fascination; Lil Kim. Tanisha Emerson smiled at the ironic situation that she had grown up in America and listened to those artists when she was growing up and now, as an adult, a bodyguard licensed to kill, she was once again listening to music she listened to as a child, a world away from Florida.

The drive, once on the expressway, was relatively short. Tanisha Emerson was an excellent driver and even in the rain she drove like a professional. Once inside the city limits of Tokyo the speed limit ground to a stuttering snail's pace.

"I hate all the traffic in the city," Tanisha Emerson hissed more to herself than to Asami.

"We will be at the offices pretty soon," Asami Fujinaka offered.

About ten to fifteen minutes of negotiating through crowded streets, pedestrians and the continuous rain found Tanisha Emerson turning off the busy streets and onto the avenue where the headquarters of Signet Industries was located. Tanisha Emerson parked the Mercedes in the front of the Towers and jumped out of the SUV with an umbrella for Asami Fujinaka. Tanisha Emerson walked Asami Fujinaka into the Tokyo Towers.

"You can't park there," one of the security guards pointed out.

Tanisha Emerson shook her head and gave him a card. The pair walked into the lobby and the security guard read the card. He turned back as Asami Fujinaka and Tanisha Emerson walked to the bank of elevators, escorted by two security guards.

There were layers of security at the Tokyo Towers that Asami and Tanisha Emerson had to traverse. Asami was oblivious. The layers could have been cotton candy for all the attention she gave the various men dressed neatly in dark blue uniforms. Asami was sending a text message or updating her blog or something when she looked up and found Tanisha Emerson by her side and two men that had not been there a moment ago.

"Hey, guys," Asami smiled awkwardly at her fixation on her cellphone. "Are you guys new?"

"No, ma'am," one of the two guards smiled. "I'm Louis," he grinned at Asami from beneath a mop of black hair, thick eyebrows, brown eyes, a small round nose and a pointy chin. He was a tall man compared to Asami and Tanisha Emerson. Louis was of an average build. "Your father hired me himself two years ago."

Asami nodded. She looked to Tanisha Emerson who was mouthing the words: "He likes you." Asami narrowed her eyes at her bodyguard. Asami wanted to punch Tanisha Emerson all of a sudden. Yet, Asami knew how that would end. Tanisha Emerson was one tough mother. Asami had witnessed the power of her bodyguard on more than one occasion. Tanisha Emerson had a very short fuse. Anyone foolish enough to test her bodyguard deserved to be dismantled by the ex-Marine that her father had hired for her personal protection.

"Oh, yeah, I remember you Louis," Asami lied watching Tanisha Emerson loving the awkwardness of the conversation. Suddenly, all she only wanted, in that moment, was to get to the penthouse offices and headquarters of Signet Industries.

Usually, Asami noted, Tanisha Emerson ran interference when they were in the public eye. Tanisha Emerson only stepped in to address those thinking that they needed to touch the daughter of Hiro Fujinaka. It was strange that Tanisha Emerson had not stopped Louis from getting close to Asami Fujinaka and Crusher.

Asami shook her head at her bodyguard and the ongoing lesson about being oblivious to the various requests of the security on each floor that required ID for entry. Crusher seemed to note the tension rising in his owner. He lifted his head and effortlessly licked at Asami's chin.

Asami smiled. Asami smiled at Crusher. Asami became absorbed by Crusher suddenly.

A security guard unlocked the penthouse elevator and the second guard smiled and waited on the opposite side of the elevator door for the elevator to arrive. Tanisha Emerson looked at Asami Fujinaka who was carrying Crusher, her toy poodle in her arms.

Tanisha Emerson held the dog carrier for Crusher. The twenty-eight-year-old bodyguard could not help but smile as the guard closest to Asami Fujinaka tried to get eye contact with one of the most eligible bachelorettes in Japan. When the elevator doors finally opened not Louis held the door.

"Do you need one of us to go up with you," Louis asked.

Tanisha Emerson looked at Asami for an answer. Asami was playing with Crusher and not paying attention to the security guard. Tanisha Emerson looked to the security guard closest to Asami and responded.

"I think that we will be fine," Tanisha Emerson announced.

By the time the two had reached the penthouse and made their way past the second bank of security they were greeted by Hiro Fujinaka's personal assistant; Rai "Ginger" Sato. Rai was an attractive Japanese woman with big anime eyes, thin lips, arched eyebrows and a bit of a shape to her twenty something body. Rai was dressed that day in dark blue jacket, blue and white striped blouse, jeans and brown leather high boots. She tilted her oval head upon seeing Asami, Crusher and Tanisha Emerson.

"This is quite a surprise," Rai "Ginger" Sato smiled.

"Why? I drop in often to see my father when I am in the city,"

"Yes, that is true," Rai "Ginger" Sato smiled. "Usually, you call and we are aware of you possibly dropping in."

"I'm here now. Is my father in his office?"

"No."

"No?"

"No. Sorry."

"Is he coming back?"

"Your father has been in the air for at least thirty minutes."

Asami felt the eyes of Tanisha Emerson burning into the back of her head but she refused to turn around. Of course, her father was not in the offices. He had flown to Singapore earlier on business.

"When is he back?"

"Two days," the assistant answered. "Don't you and your father talk," "Ginger" smiled.

"Fuck," Asami exhaled out of frustration. She knew she should have known all this. She was simply frustrated by the inability of her father to talk directly to her.

Act Three.

Teddy Dee tried to think if it counted to love someone that did not know that he loved them at all? For the heck of it Teddy Dee imagined that love was love. He loved someone that did not even know that he had feelings for her. Her name was Samantha Morris. She was a statuesque beauty that dressed like a model. She was the assistant to Barry Granger.

Samantha Morris lived in Minnesota. He had seen and talked with her, maybe she made Teddy Dee smile just by looking in his direction. Thankfully, Teddy Dee thought, she was in Minneapolis. If she had been closer, Teddy Dee would have found that the dreams and ideals would have all fallen through.

That was the benefit of unrequited love.

Chapter Twenty.

Arch Corporation sat on the two-acre rectangular plot of property in Harbor City, CA. It was located just minutes from the Pacific Coast Highway and Torrance. The entire property was gated and secured by armed guards.

The main building was eight stories of modern glass and steel that dominated the skyline of Harbor City near the 110 freeway. Entry to the main facility of five buildings was through the main entrance guarded by a ten foot reinforced gate and guard tower.

Teddy Dee had entered Arch Corporation after showing his identification and been directed to the main building where a woman dressed in dark blue jacket and and skirt waited with a clipboard. The girl was wearing a golden blouse and her hair was whipped up into into a pile of loose blonde curls atop her heart shaped face.

“Mister Douglass,” the woman had smiled. “I am Tammy. I am Mister Cambridge’s assistant. I will take you to see Mister Cambridge.”

“We need you to help us with this rather delicate situation,” Cambridge added.

“You know that I have been out of the game for nearly two years,” Teddy Dee said.

“Yeah, you know that I do my research. The type of work you do doesn’t have an out of touch feature. If you can still kick ass.” Rollo paused. “Teddy, I need you to do this for me,” Roland Cambridge said. He added, “We are friends Teddy.”

Teddy Dee listened to Roland Cambridge. Teddy Dee wanted to be back in the game, he had to admit that. He was in Minnesota because of that desire. He was working with Barry Granger to see if he still had his chops.

Teddy Dee closed his dark eyes and thought about climbing back in the corporate world. Teddy Dee longed to regain his essential corporate influence. Yet, at the same time, Teddy Dee knew that returning to the corporate world also held the threat of complete and utter failure.

"So, what do you say, Teddy?"

"I say that this ain't something that I take lightly," Teddy Dee explained. "You know what I do."

Roland Cambridge laughed.

"So, you turned soft in prison?"

Teddy Dee laughed. "I'm not soft. I just wanted to make you aware of the situation." Teddy Dee paused and added, "The best thing about me is that I don't really sweat the politics of the job. I just do it. You know Rollo when we met two years ago I was riding high. I had everything."

Roland Cambridge cleared his throat. "Dee, I remember. I know who I am talking to."

Teddy Dee paused. Teddy Dee smiled despite the seriousness of the conversation and the stakes at hand. Going back to the corporate world held endless possibilities of success and failure. Returning and accomplishing what Rollo wanted would give him all that Teddy Dee desired. If Teddy Dee failed then he could end it all on his terms.

"Teddy, I called because I know you. You and I have a relationship. We go back."

"If I come back and they catch me you know what will happen."

Roland Cambridge deflected his comment and was talking about this being something that would keep Arch Corporation ahead of its rivals. Roland Cambridge was a company man and focused on the needs of the company. Arch Corporation needed Teddy Dee.

Teddy Dee decided that he wanted to return to the world of corporate espionage and black bag operations that protected the interests of the corporation for Roland and for himself. Teddy Dee had made many enemies, powerful enemies, and the news that he was back in circulation would cause many to salivate at the chance to remove him from the corporate world.

Teddy Dee didn't care about the inevitable particularly. Teddy Dee had faced death before. Everyone had to die, Teddy Dee understood. Yet, it was HBR, Alabama, and Samantha Morris that came to mind as he thought about the offer.

"Teddy, think of it this way. Arch Corporation will open the door and give you one more chance to be bigger than the muckety mucks that daily trample over the rights and lives of so many," Rollo Cambridge said on the phone.

Teddy Dee smiled despite knowing that Rollo was trying to play a player. Rollo knew him well. Roland Cambridge was smart. He was not from the rough and tumble streets where Teddy Dee had learned to measure someone quickly and attack suddenly and without notice.

Teddy Dee didn't make any pretense of the fact that Roland Cambridge was smarter than him. There were a whole bunch of people smarter than him. Smarts, school smarts, business smarts, worked in the corporate world. That world was filled with lawyers, doctors, scientists, politicians, and their police, rules, and consequences. Teddy Dee worked outside of that world as an outsider who had access to the fringes of that powerful corporate world.

Teddy Dee was the 800-pound gorilla in the corporate boardroom with all the high-tech equipment and geeks managing the equipment like it was their child. As the 800-pound gorilla Teddy Dee was the one that all the rich kids feared in their multi-million dollar homes and super sports cars. They knew that Teddy Dee didn't give one whet about their money or pleas or tears. Teddy Dee would torture, threaten, and kill anyone if needed to protect the corporation's interests.

Teddy Dee was the loaded gun that the Presidents and Vice Presidents used to threaten each other while playing Russian roulette. Teddy Dee was the sharp knife that they pulled out when they wanted to play mumbly peg. Teddy Dee was the rough and tumble kid that beat up the bullies that threatened this group of rich kids and that group of rich kids depending on who was paying.

There were four main items Teddy Dee was struggling with. The first and preeminent thought that drove him was in Hawaii. Teddy Dee wanted to catch up with and beat the living shit out of Elliott Winslow. Teddy Dee wanted to hurt Elliott Winslow and his family's business and the corporations that they represented for the betrayal and 24 months that he could never get back.

The second ball in the air was that nagging thought of HBR. He had, since being released from Kulani, been thinking about HBR often. He had tried to connect with her in New York. He had wanted to tell her so many things that he had decided for one reason or another not to tell her. HBR was now in college and in a year or two graduate and start her career. Teddy Dee thought about all this and knew that he did not deserve to hope that HBR would ever see him as anything more than a protector and friend of her mother. HBR was unaware of who Teddy Dee really was. He had lied to her to protect her and now.... the lies had become a prison that kept him at a distance from HBR. It was paradoxical that the person that he wanted to be closest to he could not break down the walls that he had built unless he dared to risk everything in telling HBR the truth.

The third ball in play but not in play simultaneously was Alabama Fleming. She was elusive. She seemed only interested in Teddy Dee being a casual play thing more than anything else. Teddy Dee knew that Alabama was a dead end but she was bewitching in so many ways. Unlike every woman that he knew Alabama knew and understood every aspect of the shadow world of corporations.

The fourth ball in play was Samantha Morris in Minnesota. For some reason, when Teddy Dee was not engaged in some heavy lifting his mind would gravitate back to the brown curly haired beauty and thoughts of walking into the Minneapolis Museum of Art with her one day. It was perhaps, the most outlandish thought Teddy Dee entertained but nonetheless it was a thought that permeated his usually pragmatic thinkings.

The fifth ball, was the idea that Samantha Morris had mentioned in passing that Teddy Dee did not want to consider. It was the idea of slowing down. Teddy Dee needed to figure out if there was a way to leave the corporate world alive. All tall orders to say the least.

Teddy Dee returned to Global Corporation one last time before leaving for Los Angeles. He had made arrangements to see Barry Granger one last time before leaving. He hoped to see Samantha Morris one last time as well.

Teddy Dee hesitated. Getting back in the business was nothing to be taken lightly. Teddy Dee had made more enemies than he cared to admit. Before Kulani, daily, Teddy Dee was placed in a shark tank. Teddy Dee, after fourteen years as a chaos controller, was not the biggest shark in the tank but few bothered him. Teddy Dee had a reputation. Most knew that Teddy Dee was not to be played with.

Having been imprisoned publicly put him on the outside of the shark tank. 24 months out of the game put Teddy Dee on the sidelines. There were new sharks swimming in the corporate waters. Oscar Easton was dead. Easton had been Teddy Dee's mentor. So, returning to the shadows was going to be a tap dance instead of a flamenco.

Teddy Dee was no longer a player to the sharks and as a result inconsequential to the others. Teddy Dee posed no threat to anyone, initially. Teddy Dee, secretly, liked his life outside of the shark tank. Teddy Dee didn't have to worry about phone calls in the middle of the night. There were no urgent flights to parts unknown to clean up a mess that he didn't care about. Teddy Dee was free of the ugliness of the corporate world.

Teddy Dee had to admit leaving the shark tank was a blessing in a way. Being out of the tank meant that no one was trying to lie to him, cheat him, or kill him. Teddy Dee was just a normal man-eater.

Well, Teddy Dee was not normal. Teddy Dee was capable of living outside of the shark tank without any income. Teddy Dee had amassed a large sum of money and secreted it away for just such emergencies.

Now, if and when Teddy Dee stepped back into the shark tank and the corporate world Teddy Dee was re-entering a world filled with intrigue, mystery, and double-crossing. That world, that shark tank, was dangerous but simultaneously entrancing for the lack of clear cut lines in the shark tank. It, everything, was always in flux.

Today, Teddy Dee might be the hero. Tomorrow, Teddy Dee might be the goat. An hour from now, Teddy Dee might be a target. A day following, Teddy Dee might be targeting someone that got in the way of someone's leveraging.

"I'll get back to you," Teddy Dee said. It seemed as if Teddy Dee wasn't talking any longer but someone else. "I have some questions," Teddy Dee added.

"Yeah, yeah, no problem. E-mail them to me. You have my email? I'll text it to you in a few minutes."

"Okay," Teddy Dee said and hung up the phone.

A few minutes later Teddy Dee got a text message with Roland Cambridge's e-mail.

Teddy Dee thought all this and sent Rollo a message: "Let the games begin."

Teddy Dee checked out of his hotel and dropped off his rental car and headed to the airport. He checked in and after boarding read the information that Roland Cambridge had sent him while Teddy Dee was on the midweek flight back to Los Angeles. No one was on either side of him as Teddy Dee read, dressed in a gray suit and powder blue button down shirt and matching tie.

Teddy Dee got comfortable in his seat and prepared for his flight from Minneapolis back to Los Angeles. As he sat and prepared to read the information that Rolland Cambridge sent the corporate bloodletter noticed that the stewardess continued to walk past him and smile. He knew the type. Older women found him strong and powerful. Teddy Dee was their hero; fearless and mysterious. He was this bigger than life character. No woman or man that knew him worried when Teddy Dee was with them. There was an invisible shield of protection that Teddy Dee exuded.

For the women that gravitated toward him Teddy Dee knew that they really longed for a guardian and sentinel. Teddy Dee was the big dog. Teddy

Dee was the proverbial bad guy that made everyone with bad intent cross the street.

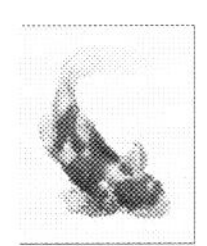  

Hiro Fujinaka IV and his son, Tanaka, were headstrong and determined to globalize Signet Industries. The effort to expand Signet Industries put incredible stress on the corporation and the Fujinaka family. There was dissension in the ranks of Signet Industries. There was dissension in the families of the Fujinakas from the bottom to the top.

For all his success Hiro Fujinaka IV had as many detractors as supporters. The surprising thing about the detractors was that the most vocal were inside his home and family. An internal struggle had been launched between the women of the Fujinakas and the men that controlled Signet Industries. As Hiro Fujinaka IV groomed Tanaka Fujinaka for the eventual takeover of Signet Industries many saw other alternatives to the brash, power hungry Tanaka Fujinaka especially his wife Keiko and Oxford educated and trained daughter Asami. The once quiet herbal company with success had awakened a sleeping dragon.

Hiro Fujinaka IV sat in the conference room with my son, Tanaka, who had been named the US delegate of Signet Industries. In the room sat the seven elders of the Fujinaka family and board members of Signet Industries. The only people in the conference room other than the Fujinaka family were the three members of the advertising firm tasked with creating the video and Aito Fukui, managing COO of Signet Industries.

The dour Akimitsu Fujinaka, who looked like a miniature sumo wrestler, sat at the conference table dressed in a striped three-piece suit that made him look like an overstuffed candy cane, was flanked by his two sons: Fumihiro and Gakuto. Next to Akimitsu sat the dapper Arashi Fujinaka.

Arashi Fujinaka was reportedly in a relationship with one of the national Kabuki dance troupe. His sexuality was always at issue, especially with the publicly reported tryst with a still unidentified Kabuki performer. Next to Arashi Fujinaka sat the bespectacled Bishamon Fujinaka, who looked as if he should be in a bank somewhere, instead of at a board meeting for one of Japan's biggest pharmaceutical manufacturers.

Bishamon Fujinaka had tried three times to become the chairman of the board of directors and failed. He was a cold and calculating individual and no one to play with. Next to Bishamon sat Aito Fujinaka.

Aito Fujinaka was the peacemaker. He got along with everyone for some reason. He poised no threat to anyone. Aito was an average looking individual with black hair, a slight potbelly and a friendly face. He was the first cousin of Hiro Fujinaka. He sat the closest to his cousin. On either side of him were his brothers: Choukichi and Eiichi Fujinaka.

Choukichi, the eldest, was a dull witted bully who drank too much and gambled recklessly. He liked fast cars and fast women. Too often Choukichi had brought shame upon the Fujinaka family name. Choukichi was the bad boy in the boardroom. He had been arrested a half a dozen times for drunkenness and belligerence. Aito Fujinaka had admitted to Hiro more than once that he wouldn't shed too many tears if he got news that Choukichi had been found dead in a gutter somewhere.

Unlike Choukichi, Eiichi Fujinaka had graduated from university and become a manager for one of the peripheral businesses created by Signet Industries. Eiichi Fujinaka had decided to open a sushi bar at one of the offices for the pharmaceutical firms. He had begun humbly and after five years had nearly a dozen sushi shops catering to the influential and powerful in Japan's corporate world.

Everyone that sat at the conference table was impressed with the seven-minute montage narrated by Chow Yun Fat. Hiro Fujinaka IV beamed with pride at my vision. Everyone at the table was richer than they could have ever imagined. They, the seven families, had become wealthy because of Signet Industries and few now did anything that represented the old Royal Family Herbal Company of old. Most of the assembled had diverted their families from working with the family business and relegated others to work at Signet Industries. The Fujinakas owned controlling interest in one of the most influential pharmaceutical companies in Japan. Yet, most in the boardroom that night did very little in the pharmaceutical giant other than collect checks as board members.

"It was an honor to portray the history of the great name of the Fujinaka family and the Signet Industries. It is our hope that you will be able to utilize this video in events where the audience is unaware of the wealth and rich history of the pharmaceutical giant and the Fujinaka family."

Aito Fukui smiled and clapped at the end of the speech. The Fujinaka clan clapped politely.

On the surface, the board of directors seemed cordial and polite. Yet, all that knew the Fujinaka family knew that there was so much more to the family of farmers and fishers. They sat in the boardroom and smiled and nodded but offered little to the conversation about the corporate image of Signet Industries.

The video began with Teddy Dandridge, dressed in a dark blue suit, light blue collared shirt, blue striped tie, sitting at the glass table of Tanaka Fujinaka. On first observation, it looked like an ordinary meeting between two men. The only exception was that Teddy Dandridge looked like a NFL linebacker dressed in a suit. He was gigantic and extremely muscular. Tanaka Fujinaka was dressed in a dark suit open collared shirt looked as if he was pretending to be the director of operations in Los Angeles. He appeared to be more Hollywood than business.

The black giant looked around the office, taking in all the knick knacks that stood out.

Fujinaka had asked Dandridge something and Dandridge simply smiled as an answer. There was a moment it appeared when it seemed that the black man did nothing. He seemed to be listening.

The black man closed his eyes. He climbed to his feet and crossed his arms. The giant of a man put his finger to his upper lip and stroked it before making his move.

The giant jumped over the glass tabletop from just standing on the other side. He did not run or build up speed. The giant bowled Fujinaka over in the high backed chair. In less than five seconds Dandridge was on the other side of the glass table sitting on Mister Fujinaka's chest smiling at the feat he had accomplished.

The smiling giant looked back briefly and noted that the miniature katana sword was still in place as well as the two bonsai trees. Dandridge nodded looking back at the office door and looked down and into the dark and panicked eyes of Tanaka Fujinaka and saw him begin to speak. The giant of a man clamped his gigantic hand over the smaller man's mouth.

So, as the giant sat on the small man's chest and slipped off his $200 dollar striped satin tie and shoved the expensive silk into Fujinaka's mouth.

Fujinaka blinked in reply. The giant studied the man on the floor.

"You know that life always boils down to the choices that we make. People get confused and think it is something else or that life is based on a big decision. I don't. I know that some of you believe that. I don't," Teddy Dee said.

The black man identified as Theodore Dandridge studied the President of Signet Industries beneath his knees and considered his next steps. He spoke and scanned the office. The attack, if jumping over a desk and pinning Tanaka Fujinaka was an attack, had not raised any alarms.

"I could have played the long game and been found out eventually or done the unexpected. Either choice was a choice that had to be made. Choices, big or small, happen everyday and every second," Theodore Dandridge paused. "I am a little distracted. Sorry." Teddy Dee climbed off of the executive. Theodore Dandridge instantly grabbed a handful of Tanaka's shirt and sat him back upright in his chair. He seemed stunned and trying to regain his breath.

"I know you, Fujinaka," Theodore Dandridge said pulling out four plastic zip ties. Before Fujinaka could protest or resist, his wrists and ankles were lashed to the arms of the high back chair by the plastic restraints. "You know the one thing that I always have on me wherever I go? Zip ties. They are a modern marvel. Most people don't even pay them any mind. They are innocuous. Meaningless."

Theodore Dandridge frowned. "Wait a minute. I was talking about something important. Oh, yeah. I remember. I know you."

Dandridge had Fujinaka seated upright again in his chair with his wrists and ankles secured by zip ties to the chair arms and legs, respectively. In seconds, Theodore Dandridge had removed everything from the executive's pockets and tossed them on the glass desktop behind him.

On the table were two cell phones: one iPhone and one Samsung. There was a thumb drive that could hold 50 gigabytes of information. There were several business cards. Fujinaka's wallet lay open on the tabletop. He had about $500 in cash. Car keys to a Mercedes Benz were inches from the wallet.

Dandridge surveyed the room again and his eyes fell on what he was looking for; adhesive tape. Theodore Dandridge frowned at the small roll of adhesive tape. He stepped to the bookshelf and noted that the office had a private bathroom. Dandridge smiled. Of course, Tanaka Fujinaka had a private bathroom.

“How do you know me? Why do you know me? Where do you know me from,” Theodore Dandridge said in a singsong fashion.

So, Dandridge took a breath and tried to focus. He focused on the task at hand. He wrapped the adhesive tape around Tanaka Fujinaka’s mouth securing the tie. It was a shoddy job but it would suffice until Theodore Dandridge left the office.

He stopped and studied Tanaka Fujinaka who struggled but could not loosen the zip ties that held him to the high backed chair securely.

“You are thinking that I’m crazy, huh?” Dandridge said. Theodore Dandridge brushed Fujinaka’s shoulder and leaned in with a mischievous grin.

“You are the type of person that I never grew up around.” Dandridge paused. Theodore Dandridge looked around the office that overlooked Santa Monica Boulevard.

“I know you and your type Fujinaka. You were pampered in Japan. You probably went to the best schools back there. Coming to the States you had to succeed,” Theodore Dandridge smiled. “A lot of pressure, huh?”

Theodore Dandridge spoke and Tanaka Fujinaka struggled and fought against the zip ties. Theodore Dandridge seemed unconcerned about the struggling.

“Me, I grew up with nothing. I lived with the bare minimum. I have been through all sorts of crap. I slept in mud. I’ve been shot at, stabbed, kidnapped, and nearly killed. The only pressure I’ve ever had has been if I want to live or die." Theodore Dandridge paused. He checked his watch.

“You probably have a house that is worth a couple of million dollars somewhere in the hills, near a celebrity. That stuff don’t mean anything to me. I’m a minimum wage kid. I’m happy to be the muscle for others and beat up on a few rich kids that need to be beaten up."

Dandridge was looking through the items on Fujinaka's desk when he saw a picture of Fujinaka holding a kendo stick. “You do kendo? I have studied that but I’m not impressed. I don’t really see any value in it. I suppose that it doesn’t make sense nowadays. No one I know walks around with a sword. The idea of training in some ancient art that you will very likely never use in your lifetime is over my head."

Theodore Dandridge was searching for something.

“You know what Fujinaka? If the security walked in right now I’d kill you and take my chances. I might get away. I might not. Life is a crapshoot." Theodore Dandridge gathered the various items from the desk.

"The bigger the risk," Dandridge said and paused.

"You probably don't take too many real risks. You have too much to lose. I bet you have the latest and greatest of everything. You have to. You have to keep up with the competition. All that technology and schooling don't amount to squat when you come up to deal with someone like me. All the technology won't help you when I punch you in the nose. You might even know a little martial arts. You might think that matters. It doesn't. Not when you face someone that has nothing to lose."

He paused. He closed his eyes. "You see I came here because I needed something you got." Theodore Dandridge studied the man who was watching him with hatred in his eyes. "The world breaks down to two types of people: those that get and those that take. I take, and the worst thing about it is that you can't do anything about it even though you own this building. It ain't about the security. It ain't about the brains. You probably have bigger brains than me but I beat that. I am the berserker with a battle axe in the boardroom. I am the bloodthirsty savage at the office door. I am the drooling killer with a chainsaw in the conference room. I'm the bad man. The fight in me beats everything else."

Theodore Dandridge looked out the window and at Fujinaka. "What do you want? I see you asking that with your eyes," Dandridge smirked, a tightening of muscles in his face that he rarely used.

Dandridge grabbed the jump drive and cell phones. He plugged the jump drive in the laptop computer on Fujinaka's desk and downloaded everything on it before leaving. As he left Teddy Dee knocked the miniature katana and samurai sword off the desk. He considered for a long moment of tipping one of the bonsai trees off of its pedestal but instead gently tapped the bonsai on the right side of the office as he left.

Teddy Dee walked out of Fujinaka's office.

No one disturbed or checked on Tanaka Fujinaka for thirty minutes. At thirty minutes after the black giant left his assistant entered.

Asami Fujinaka sat and tried to comprehend what she had just watched. A smile spread across her round face. She was surprised at the sound that came from her but it was a laugh. Asami heard herself laugh out loud.

"Jiminy Cricket," Asami Fujinaka giggled.

Chapter Twenty-One.

Teddy Dee had to go downtown for his final Rupert Williams meeting and could not imagine that anyone would attack him in the center of downtown with so many police and law enforcement officers traipsing back and forth in the highly populated downtown. So, he dressed and caught the Metro downtown. He checked in with Rupert Williams and as he left found his Spidey senses tingling.

A dark haired man dressed in a gray suit was walking toward Teddy Dee. On his left was another dark haired man wearing a dark blue suit, carrying a leather valise. The man, as far as Teddy Dee could ascertain, had come from one of the buildings to the right but Teddy Dee could not be sure. The man in the gray suit was moving quickly toward Teddy Dee. The other man was slowing and crossing the street. They seemed to smell of professionalism to Teddy Dee. Professional killers? Teddy Dee was impressed.

Downtown Los Angeles was a weird place, Teddy Dee thought as he surveyed the area that he would have to fight. He had just walked past Angel City Brewing and was making his way to the Tristan Eaton mural on Traction Avenue when he had to double back toward Little Tokyo. Teddy Dee figured that in Little Tokyo he might stand a fighter's chance against the two killers tracking him.

Teddy Dee cut across Rose Street and headed quickly to East Second Street and behind him the two killers separated and took either side of the street as they followed. Teddy Dee walked up the seemingly deserted street and at the first intersection turned left and back onto East Second Street. Teddy Dee crossed Alameda Street and South Central Street trying not to look back as one of the killers tried to get ahead of him. At Azusa Street Teddy Dee turned right and into the small streets of Little Tokyo. He wanted to use the tightness of the small streets to limit the attacks that he expected to come at any moment.

The Japanese Village Plaza became the battleground. Teddy Dee stepped into the mall entrance and waited for the two men to pass. Like in a horror movie, Teddy Dee slipped out of eyesight just long enough to reach out and grab the second killer and slam him headfirst into a pillar. The intensity of the violence and surprise attack allowed Teddy Dee to pull his pistol, cell phone, and wallet. The attack had taken seconds. He placed the unconscious killer on a bench near the storefront of Kula Revolving Sushi Bar. Teddy Dee followed behind the lead killer. The lead killer turned around and noticed that instead of his fellow killer he saw Teddy Dee. The killer instinctively reached for his gun but did not complete the action as tourists milled around the Japanese Village Plaza.

Teddy Dee turned and the assassin followed. Teddy Dee cut through the Japanese Village Plaza and made his way toward the Shabu-Shabu House. The tourists and shoppers moved through the Japanese Village Plaza unaware of what was about to happen. The families, the children, the grandparents smiled and took pictures and went to eat as the Japanese killer made his move in front of Mikawaya Mochi Ice Cream.

The attack was simple and direct. The assassin stepped in front of the family of tourists that were all wearing T-shirts that read: Kansas City Royals. The man was wearing a dark blue suit, white collared shirt, and blue tie. The small courtyard seemed to freeze as the two men eyed one another.

Teddy Dee checked his surroundings as the killer circled. The killer moved cautiously to his left, with his hands slowly and methodically moving into a crane pose. His feet were positioned to offer him the greatest balance as he moved closer to Teddy Dee.

"So, who sent you?"

The assassin did not speak but watched Teddy Dee as he drew closer to the scarred giant. When the assassin was just out of reach of Teddy Dee he paused and measured Teddy Dee one last time. Teddy Dee was six foot four inches tall and two hundred and twenty-five pounds of street toughened beef. If there was fat on him, it was only the essential fat needed to power him if the weather changed. Teddy Dee was formidable. He was built for inflicting and taking damage.

The hired killer, on the other hand, gave up at least a foot to the giant. Unlike Teddy Dee the assassin was built for speed and quickness. He did not seem to be afraid of the drastic differences between Teddy Dee and himself.

As a result, it only made sense that the assassin attacked Teddy Dee in front of Mikawaya Mochi Ice Cream and forced the tourists and families to scatter for safety. The smaller man had literally sprung into the air and kicked expertly at Teddy Dee. Teddy Dee, seeing the man hurtling toward him, dodged the first attack and moved from in front of the ice cream shop to the far side of the courtyard. Teddy Dee pressed against the Mitsuru Cafe front window and prepared for the second attack from the killer.

He did not have to wait long. The assassin landed and ran headlong toward Teddy Dee. Instantly, Teddy Dee observed, the assassin had a length of wooden stick in his right hand. Teddy Dee moved to the right and away from the cafe as the attacker had to adjust his attack and slow to correct his trajectory.

Teddy Dee snapped off a piece of bamboo in front of Mitsuru Cafe and used the bamboo to protect himself against the attack of the killer with the wooden stick. The wooden stick was a lethal weapon used in the right hands. The assassin was vicious with the stick slashing and hitting Teddy Dee about the thighs, forearms, and shoulder. Teddy Dee used the bamboo to fend off most of the wooden stick attack.

Teddy Dee knew that the assassin was skilled and dangerous. So, if he was to survive this attack he had to disarm the killer as quickly as possible and use his size and power to his advantage.

The assassin knew that the advantage that he had would be nullified if Teddy Dee was able to disarm or get close enough to make it a fight in a phone booth. So, the killer kept away from Teddy Dee.

"We don't have a lot of time here, Bruce," Teddy Dee pointed out. "The police are on their way and you get to Kung Fu your way out of a hail of bullets. Me, I just get to fade into the shadows if you can't close this deal."

The assassin listened but did not respond. He simply attacked again with the wooden stick that he used as a baton to try and bash in Teddy Dee's brains. Teddy Dee had weathered rougher storms before and as the assassin became bolder and bolder thinking that he was winning Teddy Dee sprung upon the smaller man. The assassin was lightning fast and powerful. He used his feet and kicks to keep Teddy Dee at arm's reach.

Teddy Dee noted that the killer was like a swarm of gnats that you swung at and they scattered only to form up again to harass and annoy in another location. The killer was looking for ways to break down Teddy Dee's defenses. Teddy Dee had twice blocked attacks to his eyes and groin. The assassin had changed his strategy and was now concentrating on Teddy Dee's knees and throat.

Teddy Dee allowed the killer to get closer pretending to tire and be slower than he actually was. The killer was cautious. The killer was wary. Yet, he had stepped forward and into Teddy Dee's trap. Teddy Dee knew that as soon as the smaller killer got within arm's reach all his speed and quickness would suddenly no longer be an advantage.

So, when Teddy Dee got ahold of the assassin's left arm the battle scarred giant smiled through a busted lip. The killer had attempted to throw a punch that Teddy Dee simply slipped under. Controlling the killer's hands stopped 50% of the attacks against Teddy Dee.

"This is where you lose," Teddy Dee spat.

He head-butt the smaller man and stunned him for an instant. The first thing that Teddy Dee did, after the head butt, was twist the wooden stick out of the man's hand so violently that he was sure that he had broken the killer's wrist. The wooden stick had pin wheeled through the air and clattered on the courtyard pavers loudly.

Teddy Dee then, up close and holding the killer, systematically dismantled the smaller man, starting at his elbows. He had thought to ask the man questions but knew that he would not answer Teddy Dee. So, Teddy Dee crushed every joint and muscle as he moved from the elbows to the killer's shoulders and then with six bone crushing punches to the ribs. He knew that those punches had left the assassin harmless and on the verge of death. The killer wheezed loudly for air as Teddy Dee stood up and walked away from the unmoving body lying near the Nijiya Market.

Security guards were gathering and rushing toward the commotion but when they arrived they only found the still and broken body of the nameless killer. Teddy Dee had exited the Japanese Village Plaza and was back on Second Avenue.

Hours later, Teddy Dee flew to Boston. There was no upside to the trip. In the best-case scenario Teddy Dee imagined that he would fly into Boston and talk to the Rogers and put them on alert. He might have them move out of Boston for a couple of weeks while he tried to root out the men or women trying to disco him. It would take time to find and then cut off the head of the snake. That was the best-case scenario. In the end, if he failed, then the killers only killed him.

The worst-case scenario would be that the Rogers, to a person, stonewalled him and refused to listen to or believe him and jeopardized everyone in their family in so doing. Teddy Dee would then have to wage a war on two fronts, one trying to protect the Rogers and mending fences at the same time as preparing for the killers coming to attack.

The Rogers were stubborn and proud Bostonians. They were tough bastards. The killers were just as tough but they were also money motivated. In that worst case scenario situation Teddy Dee knew that no one won. Everyone died if he failed.

Teddy Dee tried to sleep on the plane flight but he could not get comfortable. So, to while away the time, he started thinking of ways that he could move the worst case scenario into a best case scenario.

It, the chance to change anything, was dependent on Mrs. Rogers, the matriarch of the family. If she agreed, then everyone agreed. If she disagreed, then everyone in the Rogers disagreed. It was as simple as that.

Of course, Teddy Dee had a rocky relation with Mrs. Rogers. She did not think that Teddy Dee should have been with Katherine, her daughter. Mrs. Rogers tried to stop the short relation between her daughter and Teddy but it was Katherine and her stubbornness that had superseded Mrs. Rogers disapproval.

The plane landed and Teddy Dee snapped out of sketching scenarios. He was in Boston to protect the Rogers and send a message to the people that thought that he was a liability. In the world of shadows, the only thing that mattered was power. Teddy Dee had to show that he was in control. Power determined everything, Teddy Dee concluded as he deplaned.

As Teddy Dee walked through the airport he found himself thinking about Katherine Rogers. He tried to submerge the memories of the second love of his life. She was a brilliant, beautiful and gentle soul that should have never been with Teddy Dee. Katherine Rogers was a modern day princess, somehow attracted to the Chicago bruiser.

Teddy Dee knew that Katherine Rogers was not destined to be with him but he could not stop hoping. Katherine Rogers had nearly cost him everything. It was the appearance of Oscar Easton who had redirected Teddy Dee and put him back on line in the rough and tumble of the shadow world.

Climbing out of the rental shuttle Teddy Dee headed to the counter. Renting his car Teddy Dee left the airport and headed to Granary Burying Ground. He made a short stop at Five Guys and bought a burger and a milkshake. Though many suggested that Five Guys was crap Teddy Dee loved the Boston fast food chain.

From Five Guys he made his way to Back Bay. From the airport and Five Guys Teddy Dee headed toward Fenway Park and weaved his way toward Boston Public Park. Teddy Dee headed toward Boston Public Park where Granary Burying Ground was situated.

Parking his car, Teddy Dee walked into the Back Bay area cemetery. It was a cool day and Teddy Dee was dressed in a light car coat. He walked from the entrance to the marble headstone that had a pair of marble doves resting on the stone marker. Teddy Dee walked toward the doves and was surprised that when he arrived at the headstone that the doves that he thought were marble lifted off the headstone. Teddy Dee watched the pair of doves rise into the air and bank away from him. Teddy Dee watched the doves disappear behind a grove of trees. He looked and found that he was at the grave site of Katherine Rogers. He placed flowers on the grave and tried to regroup.

Teddy Dee left the graveside of Katherine Rogers a little heavier than when he arrived. Each step away from the headstone seemed harder and harder. He paused and looked back and wished that he had words then and there to say what was on his heart.

The loss of the perky woman had left a hole in his heart. Teddy Dee turned back and looked out at the cloudy day and toward the part of the city where Katherine resided. It hurt, the loss. He returned to the car and took a moment to compose himself.

There were two men sitting in a car on the edge of Granary Burying Grounds, Teddy Dee noted, as he sat trying to compose himself. Teddy Dee noted the two men and the first few numbers of the license plate, just to check if they decided to follow. He slowly pulled away from the Back Bay area cemetery. All the while watching to see what the two in the car would do. They followed.

He drove from Granary Burying Ground and back toward downtown. It was nearly noon and traffic was heavy, but not so heavy that it was stop and go. So, Teddy Dee did a slow drive through downtown. At a light, he slowed and just before the light changed, punched the gas and tore through the intersection as the light turned red. Behind, the following car was stuck as Teddy Dee turned at the next street and doubled back on the two men to avoid them.

As Teddy Dee drove he knew that there were a few things that he knew for certain. If nothing else, Teddy Dee knew that he was not paranoid. There were people out for him. There were also people in Boston preparing to harm the people that he was tenuously connected. He needed to contact Bethany and the Rogers.

Teddy Dee cut through downtown and headed back to the airport and found his hotel. For a moment Teddy Dee thought that he should beeline it to the Rogers but he thought better of it. If there were people waiting for him at the cemetery, then there had to be people at the Rogers.

Teddy Dee had to figure out how to attack the problem of shadow world hatchets in Boston. There were at least two men looking to take Teddy Dee's scalp. Teddy Dee detoured.

Teddy Dee drove to the Boston Waterfront and his self-storage unit. Teddy Dee punched in a code that he used for all Teddy Dee's self-storage units and entered the quiet grounds through an electric gate. Teddy Dee parked the rental car and walked up one flight of stairs to his unit.

At the unit was another lock but this one was the same that protected all of Teddy Dee's storage units. Teddy Dee preferred the combination as it was electronically enabled and scrambled. Teddy Dee punched in the day's code and the lock opened silently.

Teddy Dee opened his Boston storage unit and flicked on the strip lights above his head. Inside of the storage unit were the only things that he seemed to have any attachment to or care about. It was the same in all of his two dozen storage units spread out over the world. There were twelve suits. The color range spanned from black; pinstriped black; three-piece black; blue; pinstriped blue; three-piece blue; gray; pinstriped gray; three-piece gray; and chocolate brown; brown pinstriped; and finally a three-piece brown suit. In boxes beneath the suits were the matching dress shoes. Teddy Dee preferred lace-up shoes although he had slip-ons as well. In a box labeled: "Recreational" Teddy Dee had more sporting and active wear including gym shoes.

In one of the several leather wallets was $500 in cash, a number of driver's licenses, at least six passports, and three credit cards. Teddy Dee unlocked a small gun safe and looked at his Boston arsenal. There were three handguns there: a blue Glock 26 Gen 3; a Browning Hi Power 9MM pistol; and a Beretta 92F. Teddy Dee took the Glock 26 and slipped it into his waistband, as it was a more compact and less visible weapon, compared to the other two when walking on the street. Teddy Dee grabbed a black leather jacket and left his storage unit.

He walked to his rental car watching everyone as he did. Teddy Dee had learned quickly that a moment of being unaware in the shadows was just long enough for someone to drop a pill in the back of your head and steal your wallet, rumple you up just enough to make the local police think that the killing had been a botched robbery. Botched robberies happened pretty regularly in most urban settings.

So, Teddy Dee climbed into his rental and headed back to the airport, checking for tails. He drove around for an extra ten minutes before parking on the opposite side of the hotel and slipping through a fence that put him on the back of the parking lot. From the parking lot it was just two minutes to the hotel lobby. He checked in the airport hotel and took his one piece of luggage to his room. In the room he took stock of what he was planning to do in Boston.

The hotel had a restaurant. Teddy Dee opted out of going down to the restaurant. He needed to have a low profile while in Boston. The fewer people that saw him the less likely it was that anyone could tell the hatchet men where he was in town.

Teddy Dee had gone back and forth on if he should reach out to Bethany Rogers or any of the Rogers. Teddy Dee was not suicidal. He was not insane. He just did not know how to do anything but protect and ensure the safety of others.

His release from Kulani meant that the list of hatchet men that were out there were suddenly sniffing the air and looking for easy advancement. Teddy Dee would be an easy target to many of the hatchet men trying to prove their worth in the shadows. Teddy Dee knew this coming out of Kulani. He had left Kulani and Hawaii before anyone could signal his release on the island paradise. So, to shake the threats he caught a plane to Los Angeles. He knew instinctively that there was a target painted on his back.

Returning to the world of shadows was like diving back into a tank of piranha. It was not for everyone. It was nothing easy. It was nothing where you let your defenses down. Even in a tank of piranha no one piranha slept too deeply. If you were a piranha, then you knew what you were about to face jumping back in. Teddy Dee was a piranha and before his twenty-four months in Kulani he had been one of the best piranhas in the tank. Now, he knew that he could not guarantee that he was the best or one of the bests. He could not rest on his laurels if he wanted to stay alive.

Teddy Dee knew that he had few options. He had been marked immediately. If he could not get an exec to vouch for him then he was going to be discoed. Teddy Dee would become like those old time funky records and the platform shoes and bell bottom pants of days gone by; a thing in the past, history.

That night, after arriving in Boston, Teddy Dee stayed in his hotel and ordered room service. He would approach the whole Boston mess in the morning when he was fresh. Teddy Dee ate and rested and watched bad television.

The next morning, he worked out in what passed as a gym in the airport hotel. There was a treadmill, stationary bicycle, a bench and leg press machine and two flat screen televisions hanging from the ceiling and after ninety minutes headed to his room to shower. Teddy Dee dressed and went to have breakfast in the hotel restaurant.

The threats, being followed, being chased, avoiding threats were part and parcel of Teddy Dee's life since stepping into the shadows nearly a decade prior. Few, in the shadows, just gave anyone a pass. The shadows tested everyone. There was too much at stake in the shadows of corporations. Passes were a luxury that no one in the shadows allowed. Tests were given daily and if you failed you were toe tagged.

Yet, it was his friends and their families that Teddy Dee worried about. Teddy Dee was bulletproof, in terms of family. His mother was dead. His aunt had died. There was no immediate family to threaten or kidnap that Teddy Dee cared about. So, the hatchet men would focus on Teddy Dee's closest friends and their family to flush him out, for an easy kill.

The Rogers, good or bad, were connected to Teddy Dee by Katherine Rogers. Foolishly, against Oscar Easton's advice, Teddy Dee had hitched his heart to the rising star of Katherine Rogers for twenty-four months. All the hatchets knew this. So, when Teddy Dee had been released from Kulani with a question mark on his loyalties it only made sense to the hatchets to start circling around the Rogers knowing that Teddy Dee would eventually show up or contact them. It was a shadow world technic. Find the weak point and apply pressure.

So, despite all the negatives Teddy Dee dressed and left the airport hotel and found himself moving toward Dorchester. He drove to the Dorchester neighborhood where the Rogers had lived for years. He parked the rental on the street three blocks away from the Rogers home and climbed out of the non-descript rental. He walked to the edge of the block and watched the green house with its shingled roof not sure of his next step. He knew that it was essential to talk to the Rogers. It had to be done.

He watched the traffic, with his micro high powered binoculars, go up and down the street. There was a park at the end of the street. Teddy Dee walked to the park and sat on a bench in the dark. While he sat in the dark Teddy Dee tried to figure if he could walk up to the house and talk to the Rogers he noted that there was a car that had two men in it. He checked the license plate and noted that it wasn't the same as from the cemetery. The two men, were just sitting in their car; waiting.

Teddy Dee climbed to his feet and walked counter clockwise around the block so that he could end up at the far end of the street when he saw the men and they saw him. He needed cover. He wanted to make sure that there were cars and traffic between himself and the car, in case the passengers were hatchet men.

Teddy Dee walked around the block and played out his inevitable pulling out of the Glock to fire or return fire if the hatchet men attacked. One block from the block where Teddy Dee believed the hatchet men were waiting Teddy Dee took a deep breath and prepared for the unavoidable staring down death.

Turning the corner, he was on the far side of the street compared to the Rogers' home. If there was a second team they would notice him first. His attention and senses became acute as he walked. He noted the two cars parked in the Rogers driveway. Teddy Dee listened for car doors opening. He listened for anyone running toward him.

The few hundred steps that Teddy Dee took to reach the Impala were the tensest. He had slipped out his Glock as he came up on the driver side and noted that the driver was distracted and on his cellphone. The passenger, though, was not on his cellphone. He was seated with a submachine gun on his lap.

Teddy Dee pressed the Glock's barrel to the window, even with the driver's head and pulled the driver's side door handle. Instantly, Teddy Dee had the pistol's barrel under the driver's jaw and simultaneously reaching in and removing the driver's handgun. Teddy Dee crouched down behind the open door using it as cover.

"Gentlemen," Teddy Dee smiled. "You know how this goes, right? Let's not mess up this interior with a bunch of blood and brains. Now, hand over the burner nice and easy and you two will have a story to tell. Get twitchy and no detail shop is going to get all the blood and brains out of this leather interior."

Teddy Dee paused as the driver reached across and handed Teddy Dee the passenger's submachine gun. Teddy Dee placed the submachine gun in the gutter as the passenger passed his handgun to him from inside of the car.

"Okay, handcuffs?"

The driver nodded.

"Give."

The driver cautiously handed Teddy Dee handcuffs. Teddy Dee refused the handcuffs.

"Cuff him and you to the steering wheel."

The driver cuffed the left wrist of the passenger and his right wrist through the steering wheel.

"Phones," Teddy Dee ordered. Two cell phones were handed to Teddy Dee. "Okay, have a nice day," Teddy Dee said reaching in and pulling the key from the ignition without much effort. Teddy Dee climbed to his feet and walked away with the submachine gun barely concealed under his black leather jacket. He walked back in the direction that he had initially come from. Teddy Dee figured that if there was danger it would be ahead of him and not behind. So, he turned the corner laden with two extra handguns and a submachine gun and two cell phones. After turning the corner, he deposited the keys to the Impala in the hedges of a ranch home that he passed on the way to his rental.

Teddy Dee drove slowly away trying to figure out how he was going to contact the Rogers. He pulled over and tried to think. He had a mild headache throbbing in the back of his right eye. He closed his eye and tried to breathe. Breathing, slow breathing, usually helped with the mild headaches. He opened his eye and there were small spots before his eyes. As he was trying to breathe and shake the spots from before him Bethany Rogers, Katherine Rogers older sister, drove by. Teddy Dee put the car in gear and followed.

He checked his rearview for any tails. Teddy Dee did not see anyone following. Bethany Rogers drove for another ten minutes before stopping at a big box mall. Teddy Dee could only smile at the absurdity of going to the mall. He drove behind and watched as she parked. Teddy Dee parked a few aisles over.

Bethany Rogers, petite, athletic, with big brown eyes and broad smile, dressed in a parka, jeans and ankle boots, walked into the mall. Teddy Dee took in her red and blue parka. It was distinct.

Teddy Dee waited and allowed Bethany some space. He entered the mall and almost immediately lost Bethany. He had attempted to follow at a discreet distance.

Teddy Dee looked left and right and spotted the red and blue parka going into one of the big box stores. He shadowed Bethany Rogers through the mall. He approached her as she came out of a store.

"Hey," Teddy Dee smiled. He was dressed in a black leather jacket and wearing black trousers and comfortable black zippered boots.

Bethany Rogers stopped, shocked to see Teddy Dee.

"I thought you were dead," Bethany Rogers breathed.

"Not yet," Teddy Dee replied.

 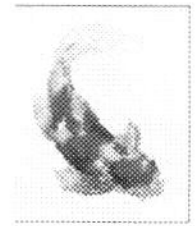 

When Asami stood in her father's office she was trying to resolve the ongoing problems that existed in modern day Japan where the storied past and Japanese history was displayed everywhere and on everything. There was modern elements and historical Japanese remnants wherever the eye rested. It was the schizophrenic nature of the country.

Yet, as Asami Fujinaka studied herself in the reflection of the ornate mirror that hung on the northern wall in her father's office she knew that she had come to Tokyo for another reason. She could study her imperfections endlessly. But today she was not to focus on those imperfections. Asami Fujinaka had told herself that she was not going to beat herself up this month. She was going to concentrate on the things that she liked.

So, she looked in the gold trimmed mirror and made a concerted effort to find something that she liked. She liked her shoulder length raven black hair. She liked the red highlights she had insisted her hairdresser add just a month ago. The highlights brought out her dark eyes. The dark eyeliner made her almond shaped eyes thinner, purposely.

The girl with the red highlights turned her pie shaped head to take in her pencil thin nose. Beneath her nose were the paper thin lips and just a suggestion of a chin. She was not unattractive. She was not beautiful either. Some might think that Asami Fujinaka was pretty or possessed pretty qualities.

Asami Fujinaka twisted her thin body in the reflection of the mirror. It was a child's body that twisted and turned beneath that red highlighted hair, thin nose and thin lips. She leaned forward and closer to the mirror's surface hoping that if she got closer there would be a discernible difference in the reflection. Sadly, the reflection showed what Asami Fujinaka was trying to understand. Her body had stopped developing. Well, her body had not developed at all was a better estimation.

Asami Fujinaka had the body of a twelve-year-old boy. That would not be that unusual but she is nearly twenty. She had small hips and the faintest hint of breasts. Asami Fujinaka studied the beginnings of breasts and nipples. It looked as if she might be wearing another shirt underneath her graphic T-shirt more than breasts and nipples.

There was a slight curve to her body, Asami Fujinaka admitted reluctantly, but not like the girls that strut up and down the avenues to get the attention of boys and men. When she looked in the mirror in the morning she did not see a curvaceous full figured girl but what she imagined a teenage boy without male genitalia must see if he dared to look into a mirror in the morning naked. Asami Fujinaka showered and dressed never concentrating on her undeveloped areas. Sadly, Asami knows that her lack of external femininity comes from somewhere in her fabled and well-documented lineage. All the parts are there, Asami Fujinaka concluded, but they seem to be dormant.

Asami Fujinaka smiled cupping the space where her burgeoning breasts were to fill in gently, while looking at the dim reflection of herself in the floor to ceiling window that overlooked the seaport.

Chapter Twenty-Two.

"How long you in town?"

"I have some business here."

Bethany Rogers narrowed her eyes. She looked Teddy Dee up and down as they stood near her car. He was not uncomfortable in the silence. Teddy Dee stood with his hands in his coat pockets, silent and unmoved.

"No one in my family likes you," Bethany Rogers finally said.

"Nobody," Teddy Dee smirked.

"Well, the dog sort of likes you," Bethany Rogers smiled.

Teddy Dee did not fill the silence with idle words. He stood and watched as cars parked and cars drove around the mall parking lot looking for parking spots closer to the doors of the stores. Teddy Dee looked down at Bethany Rogers who suddenly looked like Katherine Rogers younger sister.

"What about dinner?" Bethany asked. She had opened her car door only to turn around.

"I don't think that I would be a welcome sight, if I showed up at the homestead tonight," Teddy Dee suggested.

"No, no," Bethany began with a smile. "I wasn't saying at my parents. I was saying at a restaurant."

Teddy Dee nodded.

"Where?"

"How about Neptune, on Salem? Say eight?"

"Okay," Teddy Dee agreed.

Bethany Rogers and Teddy Dee ate from the raw bar. The warm, buttered lobster rolls were sensational. Bethany Rogers, dressed in a slate gray fur lined parka, red scarf, red cardigan sweater, black jeans, and gray fur lined boots. She was cute.

"You and your family are in danger," Teddy Dee said at their table.

"What kind of danger?"

"My kind of danger," Teddy Dee said. "I have some people looking for me and you and your family happen to be in the way."

Bethany narrowed her brown eyes, skeptically.

"I'm thinking that it might be safer for you and your family to get out of town for a few days, no more than a week. On me. Just pick some place out of town while I shut this all down."

"I don't know, Teddy," Bethany smiled.

"You know I wouldn't gaslight you," Teddy Dee responded.

"What does that mean?"

"Doesn't matter. Trust me, things are going to go from good to bad pretty quickly now that I'm in town. The bads wanted me to be here and that is not a good thing," Teddy Dee explained.

"Don't know if I can sell that to my mom and dad. They would have to watch an alien invasion a block away for them to consider leaving Dorchester. Now, I am sure that Isaac and Jacob would be easy to sell for a week away," Bethany said.

Teddy Dee stopped. He knew that there was nothing else he could add. He would let Bethany think about what he had said.

They finished eating. Teddy Dee paid for the dinner. He left a generous tip. Bethany and Teddy Dee left the restaurant and Teddy Dee tried to casually take in his surroundings. As they walked away from Neptune Teddy Dee saw a pair of men discreetly following them at a distance. Teddy Dee did not panic or sound an alarm. Distance meant that the men were watching and not threatening.

"Thanks for dinner," Bethany Rogers smiled, pulling her jacket closer to her throat.

"Want to take a walk, before I leave," Teddy Dee asked.

The pair were a block away from Fenway Park when Bethany Rogers said: "Have you ever gone to a baseball game at Fenway Park?"

Teddy Dee shook his head; no. He looked back and noted where the two men who had been shadowing them since the Neptune Oyster restaurant were in relation to them. Teddy Dee did not feel that the threat was too high until he noticed that there were two other men at the head of the street.

"We should turn here," Teddy Dee advised. He guided Bethany down a narrow street that moved slightly uphill and back toward Neptune. Behind him came two of the men that were following the pair.

He fast walked Bethany Rogers to a site where a two story office was being built and entered.

"What is going on?"

"Remember what I told you earlier?"

Bethany nodded.

"These are the bads I was talking about," he gestured behind him to the two men in the shadows.

Bethany Rogers had a heart shaped face and a sprinkle of freckles across her high cheekbones. Teddy Dee noted that she, then and there, looked like a slightly darker version of Katherine. Bethany Rogers bit her lower lip, afraid.

"They seem like they were waiting for me. They haven't made a move yet. So, we have time. We need to keep moving."

"Is this bad?" Bethany balled her gloved fists, suddenly. "You going to get me killed?"

"That's not the plan," Teddy Dee smiled. "If we make it through this, right now, then you got something to complain about," Teddy Dee said directing Bethany Rogers to a safe spot in the construction area.

"Should we call the police?"

"For what? Two men following us down a street at night?"

Teddy Dee directed Bethany Rogers through the construction site. The office was being given a new life as something more trendy, but there was still a framework to hide in. Teddy Dee looked around and found a retaining wall where Bethany Rogers could hide.

"Stay here," Teddy Dee advised, leaving Bethany to deal with the men tasked to kill him.

He returned and found Bethany Rogers, crouched in a ball. She was wearing gray mittens to keep her hands warm.

"There's three of them now," Teddy Dee said.

"Fuck," Bethany exhaled.

In the dark, somewhere lurked three men sent to dispatch the man that had loved Katherine Rogers. Teddy Dee knew that if he did not kill the men they would kill him and Bethany Rogers. They were tasked to finish Teddy Dee. They would kill him and then silence Bethany because she was there. They could not leave witnesses.

"Are we going to get out of this," she whispered.

Teddy Dee nodded.

"Tell me: 'We are going to get out of this,'" Bethany Rogers corrected, her voice a little above a whisper.

"We are going to get out of this," Teddy Dee repeated.

Bethany Rogers studied Teddy Dee for an instant before responding. She looked sideways at the scarred giant that was nearly a foot taller than every man she knew crouched behind a retaining wall dressed all in black, from his three-quarter length black leather steampunk coat, a wool watch cap, collared blue shirt, black jeans, and combat boots. As long as she had known Teddy Dee she had never felt afraid when he was near. In any situation, when Teddy Dee was near, there was no reason to worry.

"I want to believe you, but I am a little skeptical," Bethany Rogers said more to herself than to the big Cro-Magnon beside her. Her brown green eyes were big and bright in the darkness of the Boston night.

Teddy Dee smiled despite the seriousness of the moment. He could not argue with Bethany Rogers. She was right. Teddy Dee wanted to say something to ease Bethany Rogers' distress but there were no words that could do that task. He had to act. He had to act quickly.

Teddy Dee lowered his brown eyes for an instant understanding what the caramel skinned woman who was three years older than Katherine said. It was his fault that they were in this situation. He had come to Boston to protect Bethany Rogers and instead walked into a trap that had jeopardized everyone that Bethany Rogers knew and loved. So, it was his responsibility to eliminate the men that had come to kill him and make the men that had hired these men understand that their fight was with Teddy Dee and no one else.

“Might be good to cover your ears and close your eyes until I come back,” Teddy Dee advised as he walked away.

“I'm not some child,” Bethany Rogers hissed, covering her ears and closing her eyes.

The craziest part of the Boston standoff, in Teddy Dee's mind, was that once Teddy Dee was back in the shadows the threats would dissipate. The shadow world was a shark tank. There was always blood in the water. Yet, when working for someone there was a small bit of protection around the shark. The bigger the corporation the thicker the protection.

Teddy Dee knew that there was no such thing as being safe in the shadows. Everyday, in the shadows, someone fell off the earth. People were ventilated. Discoed. Eight-tracked, Teddy Dee smiled thinking of all the terms that rich kids coined to make them feel that sending out men like Teddy Dee to do their dirty work was cute and a part of business.

Being out of circulation and in Kulani put a crimp in Teddy Dee's perceived defense. He was vulnerable. Well, he was more vulnerable because he had not been working, in the world of shadows, in twenty-four months. Not working, in the world of shadows, was the most dangerous time for any blooder. It was the most dangerous time because the heads of corporations, that had used Teddy Dee, got nervous and antsy when Teddy Dee was not working. They feared that Teddy Dee might get religion or write a book or worst of all become a pie-in-the-sky whistleblower. Whistleblowers were the pond scum that Teddy Dee and most blooders found themselves silencing and stopping from handing over videos or audio or whatever of sensitive information that might ruin great corporate empires.

As it was, during this time, when Teddy Dee was not attached to a corporation or working for anyone, corporations feared blooders because the blooders were secret keepers. In the minds of those in charge of secrets it was always best to burn down the forest than just prune the trees. The corporations feared those that knew all of the secrets. Their biggest fear was that the blooders would spill the beans and topple the empires. Working in the shadows meant loyalty. Any secrets divulged in the world of shadows was usually punished by those higher up and above the pay grade of Teddy Dee.

Teddy Dee thought in all the time that he had been in the world of shadows that no one had ever written a tell all book about this corporate world of lies, backbiting, double crosses, hostile corporate mergers and the men behind it. There was a reason, he surmised. The suits, the highest echelon, did not want others to know of the inner workings of the corporations. It was not in their best interests to allow anyone to know the dirty part of the business of business.

The giant block of scarred obsidian stood up, chalking up the need to silence a threat that was now reaching out toward the Rogers, in the darkness with his Glock 26 in his right hand. No one shot. So, Teddy Dee closed his eyes, for an instant, and listened to the snow falling outside. He could hear the sounds of traffic just two blocks away on Beacon Street. Teddy Dee stood in the middle of the unfinished housing development and listened. The scrape of a boot to his left alerted him of the attacker and Teddy Dee estimated that he had to be maybe twenty or thirty feet away.

Teddy Dee turned and fired three shots in the direction of the man and suddenly he could see, in the muzzle flash, the second attacker just five or ten feet to the left of the man he was aerating. Teddy Dee reacted. He did not think.

Teddy Dee simply spun and fired again grouping the shots where he had seen the second attacker in the muzzle flash of his own gunfire. There was one shot that whizzed by Teddy Dee but no more. There was silence as the shell casings tumbled from the Glock 26 and Teddy Dee scanned the area for the last man. Teddy Dee listened and looked into the dark for the third attacker.

Bethany Rogers had her eyes squeezed shut and her gloved hands cupping her ears. Teddy Dee grabbed Bethany Rogers and lifted her to her feet. She opened her eyes and let her hands down.

"Are we safe now," she asked.

Teddy Dee wanted to explain that no one was ever safe. There were threats everywhere. There were continuous threats based on wealth, celebrity, accessibility and so many factors. He was in the business of providing a modicum of safety to those that feared the loss of their lives, businesses, family or whatever. Teddy Dee listened and for the moment thought that Bethany and Teddy Dee were not in imminent danger.

He nodded though Teddy Dee knew better. Teddy Dee guided her through the construction site, shielding her from the two men that lay dead in the interior of the building. Teddy Dee allowed Bethany to clasp his right arm as he moved her out of the killing zone.

The pair moved quickly and silently from the construction area to the nearby streets of Boston. Teddy Dee slipped the Glock into his waistband and he instantly transformed back into a big, black man but not a killer or maniac. Bethany Rogers tilted her head studying the black giant trying to figure out how someone like Teddy Dee could be in her life. Or more importantly, how Katherine, the more conservative of the two, had brought Teddy Dee into their lives.

"This kind of stuff happen to you often?"

"Not often," Teddy Dee lied.

They walked in silence with Teddy Dee looking back every once in awhile to see if anyone was following. The third gunman was somewhere near. They did not run. They just looked for better opportunities.

"We need to head toward people," Teddy Dee said as they walked.

"We need to head toward people," Bethany repeated.

Teddy Dee was impressed with Bethany Rogers. She had been in a gunfight and been unarmed and come out unscratched and not a babbling mess. She was not crying. She seemed to be adjusting to the live firefight pretty quickly.

Despite, Bethany Rogers toughness Teddy Dee knew that the sooner they could blend in with a crowd the sooner that he would feel less like a hockey puck on an ice rink. So, they walked. They walked up the hill and back toward Neptune.

The gunfire would attract police attention. Teddy Dee guided Bethany Rogers away from the place where three men had tried to kill him. At a busy street Teddy Dee hailed a cab.

"We catching a cab?"

"Yeah, but we headed downtown."

"Downtown?"

"Yeah, lots of people downtown. Less chance of running into people with bad intentions."

Bethany Rogers fell silent as the yellow cab slid to a stop. Teddy Dee opened the door and Bethany Rogers entered. Teddy Dee followed the petite beauty into the musty smelling cab.

"Can you take us to Four Seasons," Teddy Dee said and sat back in the rear of the cab.

"No one in my family trusts you," Bethany Rogers said as a matter of fact as the cab pulled away from the curb. Teddy Dee cut his dark eyes in the direction of Bethany Rogers and then back to back of the head of the cab driver.

"Well?"

"Well, what?"

"What do you have to say?"

"Nothing," Teddy Dee said.

Bethany Rogers studied Teddy Dee for a long moment and then turned away. Teddy Dee simply sat and checked his hands and watch. He silently calculated the time and distance to the luxury downtown hotel.

"You are something, Teddy," Jessica Rogers finally spat.

"I am," Teddy Dee replied.

"What is that supposed to mean?"

"Nothing," Teddy Dee said.

"You ain't going to comment about my family not trusting you?"

"Trust is smoke. No one can hold onto it forever."

"What does that mean?"

"I guess it means that things change. Nothing is permanent."

"What about love? Or gold? Or land?

"Love is used to sell carpet. Gold? We don't have gold anymore. We put more trust in Bitcoin. I ain't a house cat, Bee. I'm just this big, old, untamed black cat. Big cat don't worry about love, gold or land. I ain't a pussy cat and I didn't come to Boston for the chowder," Teddy Dee said trying to keep his voice low and just above a growl.

"You ain't a pussy cat and you didn't come here for chowder," Bethany Rogers smiled despite all the chaos and destruction she had just survived. "You got jokes Teddy Dee?"

Teddy Dee looked out the window as Boston appeared in the window. Bethany tried to continue the conversation but Teddy Dee did not respond. So, Teddy Dee and Bethany Rogers sat in the rear of the cab and rode in silence.

The cab navigated through the night traffic and headed for downtown. Boston stores, cars, people dressed in parkas and all forms of winter wear, flitted by as the cab rolled down Boylston Street.

Boston at night was an interesting place filled with beauty, ugliness, adventure, and danger. It was a major metropolitan and it had changed and remained exactly the same since the 1700's.

"When we get to Four Seasons I need to check you in. Four Seasons is bigger and better," Teddy Dee added. "Just stay there for a few days. You order in, pamper yourself. I'll foot the bill."

Bethany Rogers smiled. Bethany Rogers hesitantly reached out and placed a hand on Teddy Dee's giant paw. Teddy Dee looked down surprised at the show of affection. He smiled.

"Don't get any ideas," Bethany Rogers hissed. "I just had a moment that I thought that this might be the last time that I see you."

"I'll be around for awhile," Teddy Dee said as he looked out the window and the traffic drifted by just inches from the passengers in the cab. "I'm the one that people don't want to see."

Bethany Rogers and he walked into one of Boston's landmark hotels: Four Seasons. Teddy Dee smiled at Bethany Rogers. She was a tough cookie. She had been through the fire and come out unburned. The shootout in the Back Bay was only minutes before and Bethany was already moving on, compartmentalizing the incident. Teddy Dee did not know what to say to Bethany but he smiled at her.

"Harbor view or city view?"

"Surprise me," Bethany Rogers smiled taking in the elegantly appointed lobby.

Teddy Dee checked Bethany Rogers into the Four Seasons and gave her the hotel room key. Bethany took the hotel key and hooked her arm around Teddy Dee's arm. She guided him to the elevator bank.

The pair climbed into the elevator and went to the seventh floor. Teddy Dee walked Bethany Rogers to her hotel room. At her hotel door Teddy Dee stopped.

"I will call you when this is all over."

"Will it ever be over?"

"Has to end at some point," Teddy Dee had to say to Bethany Rogers.

She seemed shocked by his words.

"Has to?"

Bethany opened her hotel room door. She entered. Teddy Dee reluctantly entered the hotel room. Bethany examined the hotel room. Teddy Dee stayed near the door.

"You shy?"

"I don't have time for this," Teddy Dee scolded.

Bethany sat on her king sized bed.

"There are some very powerful people that are after me. To get to me they are going after the people that I care about. You and your family are important to me. So, I have to make them rethink threatening you to get to me." Teddy Dee paused. He was thinking. "Until I stop those people or make them understand that it is not worth their time or energy to attack those that they think mean anything to me then this is not over."

"How long?"

Teddy Dee twisted his lips, thinking. He did not answer immediately. He knew that Bethany and everyone that he put in danger needed to hold onto simple ideas of a return to normalcy. They did not want to hear that as long as Teddy Dee was alive and they were connected to him they were in danger.

"Give me two days," Teddy Dee said, knowing that he had the assassin's phones and that the number of the man that had started this had to be there. It was a simple thing in the world of shadows. The rich kids always wanted evidence of the deeds done. They always called and tried to confirm the dirty work. Sadly, they sometimes called to call off things already in motion. That was the nature of shadow work. Blooders and hatchets all had cell phones to send messages to the rich kids and calm their fears. That was also the easiest way to figure out who was behind any attack.

"What now?"

Teddy Dee said nothing.

Bethany nodded. Teddy Dee headed for the hotel door. Bethany Rogers climbed up from her the bed and reached out for Teddy Dee.

"Tell me that everything is going to be okay," Bethany Rogers said, sleepily.

"Everything is going to be okay," Teddy Dee repeated more for Bethany Rogers than for himself.

There was a moment between Bethany and Teddy Dee that Teddy Dee allowed to pass. She was suddenly close. He could smell her perfume in his nostrils. Her hand was on his forearm. He did not have the time to reassure Bethany beyond words. He took a deep breath and allowed Bethany Rogers her moment. She was scared. She had seen real danger. So, Teddy Dee waited. He waited for Bethany Rogers to realize that Teddy Dee was not going to stay with her. He was going to try and find the men that were foolish enough to think that he was a soft target.

"Got it," Bethany Rogers said. "Stay put until you call." She paused. "Pamper myself. Order room service. Enjoy all the amenities."

Teddy Dee nodded. He walked out of Bethany Rogers hotel room and found the elevator. Teddy Dee climbed in the elevator and descended. He exited the elevator at the lobby.

He headed for the revolving door entrance. Once outside and back in the cold of the Boston night Teddy Dee caught a cab back to the airport. He planned on retrieving his rental car in the morning.

Leaving Four Seasons Teddy Dee scanned the street and was not surprised to see two more of the hatchets on the sidewalk on the opposite side of the street. There were people walking up and down the street. There were taxicabs everywhere. The occasional policemen either walked by or drove by the biggest hotel and tourist spot in Boston.

Teddy Dee took a deep breath and walked across the street toward the two men watching him. He expected the two men to walk away. They did not move. They waited for Teddy Dee to cross the street and smiled as he approached.

"Gentlemen, my name is Teddy Dee, I suppose you know that already," Teddy Dee said as he got within in arm's reach of the two strangers. The two strangers, one a square-faced man with thin eyebrows, squinty eyes and a small mouth that was always in a half smile and the other a triangle-faced man with a round nose, thin lips and one of those flat top military haircuts, smiled and nodded.

"I need you to get a message to whoever you work for, tell them that I am here, in Boston, to end this here and now. Tell your boss that I don't want anymore craziness. I just want it over."

While in Boston, Teddy Dee learned that the present fight was with a low-level Vice President of one of the many companies that he had worked for or against that had decided Teddy Dee was a troublemaker. The jerk weed was named: Louis Martin.

The name was familiar. It had a connection with Teddy Dee but he was not sure why Louis Martin wanted to disco Teddy Dee. That was another of the realities of the shadow world.

Louis Martin had been born into wealth in one of those exclusive Boston neighborhoods with gates and private security. His father had been one of the many that rose to success in the Mars candy dynasty. Teddy Dee had come in contact with Martin when one of his flunkies made a deal with a research company in Clovis, CA for an experimental chemical that was reported to improve chocolate in some fashion. Teddy Dee did not know the details. Nor did he care. He had gone to Clovis, CA and taken the chemical that everyone wanted and driven it back to the safety of the chemist that had invented it.

That had been over three years ago and a year before Teddy Dee was in Kulani Correctional. Three years, Louis Martin had plotted and planned and gathered the hatchets to cut off his water. Before Teddy Dee climbed aboard his plane to New York City he had confronted Louis Martin in Boston.

The meeting was a trap and Teddy Dee knew it but he had little choice. He went to the meeting spot just a few blocks from a boating supply company. Teddy Dee arrived and four hatchets were waiting with Louis Martin.

"I wanted to see your face when you realized it was me that brought all this on you," Louis Martin smiled with his triangular head, big forehead, big ears and nearly invisible chin. He was dressed in one of those military coats with the fake fur around the collar and about a dozen pockets. He was wearing jeans and lace-up brown boots. Beside him were the four men that he had hired to kill Teddy Dee. They all looked the same to Teddy Dee. They only wore different clothing. The tallest was maybe six foot two or three inches tall and dressed in a puff coat. He wore jeans and comfortable boots. The shortest was wearing a watch cap on his round head. The two others were nearly identical in that they were white, nearly six feet tall, wearing watch caps, dark eyes and dressed in black leather jackets and wearing gloves. The only distinction that Teddy noted was that one had a more weather beaten face.

Teddy Dee noted that one of the men had a gun tucked in his waist belt as he leaned forward. Teddy Dee assumed that everyone, except for Louis Martin were armed. Teddy Dee took a deep breath and took one step forward to see what was in store for him if he played the victim.

The four men moved in concert. The tallest was the lead, Teddy Dee noted. Everyone cued on him. When he moved everyone else moved. The weather beaten character in the black leather jacket reached for his weapon and the others seeing him reach all reached. The tall leader stood his ground trying to decide what to do.

Louis Martin stepped back, behind the tall leader. The tall leader threw out an arm to protect his boss. Louis Martin narrowed his eyes seeing that Teddy Dee opened his hands, showing the men that he was unarmed.

"So, what do you want?"

"I suppose that I want you to get my chemical back and the ten million dollars that it cost us in loss of revenue," Louis Martin said, stepping forward as the tall leader relaxed and in so doing all the others did as well. Teddy Dee smiled.

"I don't believe in science fiction," Teddy Dee said. The four men, together, all frowned at Teddy Dee's words. The tall leader looked back at Louis Martin trying to figure out what to say or do.

"You know that I took my time to get this operation rolling," Louis Martin began. Teddy Dee rubbed his hands together for warmth, realizing that Louis Martin was a blowhard who just carried a grudge.

Teddy Dee moved so quickly that it seemed that only the tall leader saw him go from warming his hands to pulling his Glock, aiming his Glock and firing his Glock and killing Louis Martin under the disused train trestle that spanned the Boston river. Teddy Dee aimed his Glock at the tall leader of the three men surrounding him.

"There's two ways this ends. You walk away alive. You are found dead. You decide."

The tall leader twisted his lips considering that Teddy Dee was outnumbered. Teddy Dee continued to aim his Glock at the tall leader. He knew that the three others would not shoot him unless the leader gave them the green light. Teddy Dee took two steps forward and pressed his pistol in the leader's chest, simultaneously stepping behind him and using the leader as a shield.

"The way I see it our contract ended when you ventilated the suit," the tall leader calculated.

"That's the way I saw it too. Tell your goon squad to drop their weapons and I'll leave and won't look for you and you don't look for me."

"Sounds good."

That was the last time that Teddy Dee saw the four men or Louis Martin. Teddy Dee disassembled the Glock and deposited the parts around the city before heading to the airport.

 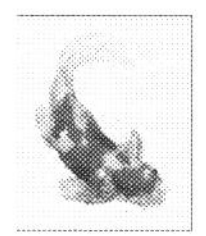 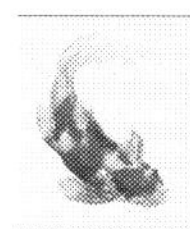

Asami Fujinaka never saw herself as a trendsetter. She was awkward and uncomfortable with her own self. She could not have ever imagined that nearly two million people religiously paid attention to what she wrote, thought and posted. The idea was a bit overwhelming.

She was an artist with a business mind and her art reflected her steely eyed competitive personality that did not believe in coming in second. She was a social commentator and her art mirrored that social judgment. Her art was in your face and quirky and sometimes over the top but at all times honest and genuine.

Japan's culture was pulled backwards to preserve the past while simultaneously being pulled forward to the ever burgeoning future and the continual need for innovation.

This schizophrenia was seen in one of Asami's paintings entitled: Neo-Samurai. Her latest photo commentary was entitled: Prince(ss). There were a dozen pictures of brothers and sisters from some of the most powerful families dressed similarly and blown up and plastered on the sides of several downtown buildings. The art was a condemnation of the male-dominated patriarchal driven chauvinism of an outdated mechanism that promoted male heirs over female heirs. The dozen pictures had captions placed beneath that exposed all the crimes and foibles committed by the male heirs of these influential families.

Asami Fujinaka, by a trick of fate, was not the heir to the riches of her family because she had been born the only daughter of one of Japan's largest herbal companies; Signet Industries. Her brother, Tanaka Fujinaka, was next in line for leadership of Signet Industries despite Asami's richer experiences in business.

So, she had come up with a plan. She came up with a blog. That blog, ""Asami's Kooky and Spooky Insights in the Nausicaa Valley"" gave her a platform and voice and that platform and voice gave her plan legs. Her blog was far reaching. Millions of eyes read the blog posts.

Chapter Twenty-Three.

On his flight to New York City Teddy Dee tried to figure if aerating Louis Martin meant that all the threats from the hatchets was over. The threat against the Rogers, as far as he could figure, was over. In the world of shadows there were no absolutes. Teddy Dee in a decade had stepped on some toes along the way. It was inevitable in his line of business. He forced people to do things that they did not want to do for a living. So, people held grudges. People plotted and planned.

Yet, as the plane prepared for arrival in New York City, Teddy Dee believed that eliminating Louis Martin had eliminated the threat against the Rogers. At least, Teddy Dee had eliminated the threat created by him with the Rogers. If there was anyone else thinking about threatening the Rogers Teddy Dee did not know about it. So, as he landed in New York City's LaGuardia airport with the desire to protect his only other loose end; Heather Beckham Rogers he was hopeful. He hoped that HBR was well and unaware of any threats toward her.

He had not been in New York City in years. Teddy Dee arrived in New York just as the snow arrived. The cold had finally come and many of the students were preparing for finals. Some were preparing for trips home. He decided to stay in New York City for the night.

Since he was going to be in New York City for the night he considered seeing Heather Beckham Rogers, the niece of Katherine Rogers. In New York City, he knew a few people but of all the ones that he might see, Teddy Dee was willing to go out of his way to see HBR.

HBR was attending NYU. Teddy Dee knew of HBR and when he and Katherine Rogers were close they had taken her niece to New York to visit NYU because she was interested in attending that school. Teddy Dee liked HBR. Before Kulani, Teddy Dee recalled, she had written him to tell him that she was heading to NYU. So, she would be either a sophomore or junior now at school.

Teddy Dee left the airport and caught a train to Greenwich Village. The ride was shortish. It took only thirty minutes.

The train dropped Teddy Dee off at Washington Square Park. Washington Square Park was busy when Teddy Dee stepped out of the subway. It was still relatively early in New York City. It was just an hour before five o'clock and Teddy Dee watched as people moved back and forth on the snow covered streets.

Teddy Dee walked toward the park knowing that it was the locus from where the NYU campus buildings radiate. He moved to the edge of the park dressed in a dark blue suit. He scanned the park and the streets around it and took in the businesses just on the other side of the street. There were several places to get warm and have a cup of coffee or tea. The snow was still falling as Teddy Dee noticed there were easily four coffee shops just a stone's throw away from the park.

Crossing the street Teddy Dee made his way to the closest cafe named: Java Time. The cafe doubled as an Internet cafe. Teddy Dee headed to that cafe because he knew that he might need to get online and search for a thicker coat while on the east coast.

Inside Java Time Teddy was met with a small interior that sat no more than 50 people. There were four people working the counter when Teddy Dee walked in. Two cashiers and two baristas. The counter and kitchen were half of the interior. The remaining space was reserved for ten cafe tables crammed in the interior. At the counter were bakery goods. Teddy Dee noted that in the rear of the cafe was the Internet cafe.

Teddy Dee ordered a Chai tea latte from a diamond faced woman with black curly hair and brown eyes. Her hair framed her angular cheeks. Teddy Dee noted that she had a nose ring.

"What is the rate per hour for the computers?"

"Are you a student?"

Teddy Dee smiled. He looked around the café. Most people in the café were dressed in jeans, polo shirts, T-shirts and sneakers or boots. The men and women in the café were tattooed on their necks, arms, and backs. Teddy Dee noted that there were a few with hand and finger tattoos.

"We have discounts for students," the cashier smiled. "That's why I asked," smiling awkwardly.

Teddy Dee shook his head; no.

"There are four computers in the back. They aren't great. They aren't crap either. You can use a credit card and use the computers for four hours at a time. It is pretty reasonable."

"Thanks."

Teddy Dee took his tea and walked to the rear of the cafe. In the back of the cafe were four desktop computers bolted to the wall. There was a printer available as well. Four more cafe tables were in the rear of the cafe.

Teddy Dee walked to one of the desktop computers and read the Internet cafe instructions. He found a NYU student ID card sitting on an adjacent computer kiosk. Teddy Dee scooped up the ID and sat down. He used his credit card for four hours of computer use. He did not need the computer that long but it allowed him to not be rushed.

He did a quick Internet search for Heather Beckham Rogers. Stranger things had happened. The search came back and Teddy Dee noted that there were easily 231 Heather Beckham Rogers in the world.

Of the 231 names Teddy Dee found that there were 57 Heather Beckham Rogers in the United States. Of the 57 names only 13 Heather Rogers were in New York. Of the 13 Heather Rogers only three had attended NYU. Three chances to find his Heather Beckham Rogers.

It was nearly half past five when Teddy Dee checked his watch. He did another search and found the closest library. Finishing his tea, Teddy Dee logged out of the computer and left the Internet cafe.

Teddy Dee checked for the closest clothing store to the Java Time location. He walked two blocks to the clothing store and picked up a three-quarter length leather motorcycle jacket. He paid cash for the jacket, hat and gloves.

Teddy Dee headed to the library after getting his new old and battered leather jacket. He crossed the NYU campus and found the library. He entered and walked directly to the librarian.

"Hi," the brunette librarian with smoky eyes and shoulder length hair, dressed in a pink sweater smiled at Teddy Dee. "May I help you?"

"Would you have any yearbooks available for the past five years?"

The librarian listened and nodded.

"Are you a student here?"

"Yes," Teddy Dee lied.

"Can I see your ID?"

Teddy Dee fished in his pocket and found a ID badge that he had swiped at Java Time.

The librarian examined the ID and nodded.

"I'll be right back," the librarian announced.

The librarian brought back an armful of yearbooks from NYU. Teddy Dee reached out and received the yearbooks.

"You have an hour with the yearbooks."

"Thank you," Teddy Dee said as he turned and walked to the closest stall to examine the yearbooks.

Teddy Dee sat and looked through the oldest yearbook. He skimmed the book for pictures. Teddy Dee flipped to the rear of the book and scanned the ladder for Heather Beckham Rogers. No Heather Beckham Rogers.

In the oldest issue there was no Heather Beckham Rogers either.

He found a mention of Heather Beckham Rogers in the third yearbook. Teddy Dee flipped to the page and found his first picture of Heather Beckham Rogers in the Art department standing beside a sculpture of what looked like two wooden hands coming out of a solid block of wood.

Heather Beckham Rogers had a slight family resemblance to Katherine Rogers. She had the high cheekbones, the dark curly hair and slightly upturned nose. Heather Beckham Rogers was dressed in a school girl outfit with a blue V-neck sweater and red tie. On her feet were combat boots.

The second yearbook featured another picture of Heather Beckham Rogers. This time Heather Beckham Rogers was in a gallery in front of several abstract paintings. This time Heather Beckham Rogers was dressed in a black and white striped dress that fell to her knees. On her feet were a pair of worn cowboy boots. Again, Teddy Dee noted, Heather Beckham Rogers was listed as a part of the Art Department.

The last yearbook had a number of news clips and art installation of Heather Beckham Rogers art exhibit. Heather Beckham Rogers had her hair piled upon her head. She was dressed in a short-sleeved blouse, short skirt and sandals.

Heather Beckham Rogers was a notable artist. Teddy Dee went to the library computer center and did a cursory search of Heather Beckham Rogers, the artist and suddenly found himself looking at the high cheekbones and freckles across her nose, dark curly hair and slightly upturned nose that marked the Rogers women.

Teddy Dee tried to see if there was a gallery with Heather Beckham Rogers artwork anywhere near. He hoped for an art show but did not put too much hope into that being a reality. The closest thing that Teddy Dee found was a handful of galleries downtown that had Heather Beckham Rogers art. Teddy Dee wrote the names of the galleries and their addresses on a scrap of paper.

After 50 minutes Teddy Dee headed for the exit. The librarian smiled and waved to Teddy Dee. Teddy Dee hesitated for an instant and continued on toward the exit. He left the library frustrated.

Was he going to see HBR on this trip, Teddy asked himself as he took a short ride to a hotel near Greenwich. He paid the cab driver and found himself at one of the bigger hotels in Manhattan. He checked in and headed to the hotel room.

Teddy Dee dropped his carry on in the hotel room and went back to the lobby. At the counter was an Eritrean woman on the phone. She looked to be in her twenties with dark eyebrows and the caught in the headlight eyes that made her distinctive. Next to her was a pointy nosed brown haired white girl with oversized glasses that were perched on her nose. Teddy Dee walked to the counter and the Eritrean woman smiled and spoke to him first.

"How can I help you?"

"Just wanted to get pointed in the right direction if I wanted to go and not have to hang out with NYU students," Teddy Dee said.

"Well, just don't head toward Washington Square or that area. Stay downtown. Go to Broadway," the Eritrean woman said very knowingly.

Teddy Dee fished out his phone and called for a cab. He got a ride back to Washington Square Park. It was just two or three hours' difference since Teddy Dee had been there and the area had changed drastically.

It was night. It was no longer snowing. The snow was melting and making the sidewalks wet.

Teddy Dee stood on the sidewalk and tried to think if this was a possible task to find Heather Beckham Rogers.

Heather Beckham Rogers had been sixteen or seventeen when Teddy Dee had met her with her aunt, he thought as he walked on the border of the NYU campus thinking that he might run into HBR. He had not seen HBR in at least four years, if not longer.

Finding Heather Beckham Rogers in New York and in Greenwich Village seemed an impossible task. He had not thought too much about the difficulty of finding that quirky little girl that he had met nearly four years prior.

It was starting to get cold and Teddy Dee found himself returning to Java Time to hold up and think over how to find Heather Beckham Rogers. While in the cafe Teddy Dee considered all of the possibilities of coming upon HBR in New York City.

He sat in the Internet cafe and tried to recall where Heather Beckham Rogers stayed. Teddy Dee sat for an hour in Java Time when he glanced a tall girl dressed in boots, skin tight jeans, a thick leather coat and a Russian Cossack hat. Teddy Dee could not be sure but he thought that he saw the familiar reddish brown traces of Katherine in the tall, thin girl.

Teddy Dee smiled at the idea of the tall girl being HBR. She seemed too tall. She seemed too stiff to be HBR. He knew that his luck did not fall like that, since Kulani. There was nothing simple, since Kulani.

The gruff and sometimes cruel man sipped at his tea and tried to remind himself of his promise to Katherine Rogers. He was to help HBR until she graduated from NYU. Teddy Dee was supposed to check in on HBR twice a year, at the least. However, Kulani had put a crimp in that plan.

It was during his mental stroll down disappointment lane that the tortured Teddy Dee looked up and saw the tall, beautiful girl that looked strikingly similar to the girl he had seen earlier exit her apartment dressed in a black trench coat and black high heels. She, the HBR substitute, was carrying a small hand purse and walking arm and arm with another tall girl with brown shoulder length hair dressed in a black motorcycle jacket and a white wraparound dress and matching white motorcycle boots.

Teddy Dee exited the cafe and crossed the street as the two tall beauties talked and laughed loudly. Teddy Dee slow walked past the pair that appeared to be a little drunk already as they hailed a taxi and headed uptown. Teddy Dee walked to the end of the street and hailed a taxi and followed the pair at a discreet distance.

Teddy Dee knew that the girl was not HBR but in the back of his mind he imagined that this random girl might lead him to HBR. So, he followed the girl and her girlfriend to an uptown club where they danced for several hours.

It was during his recollections that the tortured corporate enforcer looked up and saw the tall, beautiful woman that he had seen before on the streets near Washington Square Park, dressed in a black trench coat and black high heels. Her hair was loose and a stair step of brushed and pinned hair that gave the impression of a Mohawk. She was carrying a small hand purse and walking arm and arm with another tall girl with a brown cinnamon bun hairstyle dressed in a black motorcycle jacket and white skintight jeans and matching white closed toe boots.

The pair laughed loudly and appeared to be a little drunk already as they leaned on each other and eventually hailed a taxi and headed uptown. Teddy Dee hailed a taxi and followed the pair at a discreet distance.

The two women went to an uptown club. Teddy Dee had bypassed the line and entered the club and immediately felt like a fish out of water. The club, during the day, was a small restaurant. It seated maybe fifty or sixty people as a cafe. As a club it was an exclusive hotspot near Battery Park where celebrities occasionally came to shake the paparazzi. There was a constant rumor that some rapper or model was in the rear of the club. Teddy

Dee shook his head at the rumors and tried to keep an eye out for the only person that he cared about in mind as he walked around the small club.

At about midnight the two tall girlfriends left the uptown club and caught a cab to another club a few blocks from the financial district. Teddy Dee followed. He followed because he hoped that this pair of beauties would attract Heather Beckham Rogers, if she was still going to NYU.

Teddy Dee followed the pair also because they seemed to know where the cooler places young and hip NYU students went. As he went to the second dance club Teddy Dee also marveled at the duality of businesses in New York. The second club, during the day was a car repair shop, but after midnight it became another downtown hotspot.

Teddy Dee entered the collision shop club through the service entrance and followed the stanchions that led the club goers to a garage where fifty cars sat against the wall of the New York garage dance club. Teddy Dee noted the two portable bars situated one on the North wall and the South wall and situated himself near a Tesla electric sports car that had extensive front end damage and sipped at a weak rum and coke. Teddy Dee scanned the small crowd for Heather Beckham Rogers. She was not there. He knew it was a longshot at best but it was the only hope he had that night.

The most notable event at the uptown club was that cinnamon buns had a shouting match with a thick necked bull of a man dressed in a tight shirt and expensive jeans. The argument it seemed was based on the fact that the man really was interested in cinnamon buns and wanted to take her to another club without her friend.

"Get lost, loser, we don't break up the team," the tall beauty hissed near Teddy Dee who was invisible in the small club. He watched the exchange from the shadows.

At about 1AM Teddy Dee watched as a touchy thick armed man with a ponytail, a thick gold chain, and dressed in baggy jeans and a Mark Ecko long sleeve shirt trying to dance with the Mohawk woman. The man had a gold earring in his earlobe.

The man stopped dancing and raised his hand to hit the nameless woman. To her credit Mohawk took three steps back and shook her head and walked away from the thug.

Teddy Dee thought for an instant that he needed to intervene. His fists were clenched and ready to lay waste to the ponytailed thug. The tall Mohawk beauty walked off the dance floor and to her friend's side. The man with the ponytail walked back to the table where the tall Mohawk beauty and her friend were sitting. The friend with the cinnamon bun hairstyle and the man shouted at each other and the Mohawk girlfriend jumped in. It was quite a scene. The man with the ponytail shook his head and left the two angry women for other women.

The men weren't dancing to relieve stress. They were dancing looking for opportunity. It was not rocket science. These two needed to be more careful.

Teddy Dee watched silently. He considered his options. This was New York City. There were a bunch of creeps here. Mohawk and cinnamon buns were out dancing with a bunch of creeps. What did he expect? What did they expect?

Then and there, Teddy Dee found himself doing something that he never did. He walked up to the ponytailed thug and the two women he was trying to impress and whispered these words to the stranger:

"I was told to find you. Someone said you have a friend trying to get in."

The ponytailed man looked at Teddy Dee skeptically.

"A woman," Teddy Dee added.

The ponytailed man narrowed his eyes, thinking.

"If you don't want them to let her in then tell me," Teddy Dee said, deadpan.

"No, no. I got this," the ponytailed stranger said.

Teddy Dee and the ponytailed man walked to the exit of the club. Teddy Dee had decided that the ponytail wasn't going to make it to the front door. Teddy Dee paced the man toward the front of the club and into a quieter part of the club.

He slowed and waited for the ponytailed stranger to come even with him before he shoved the unsuspecting stranger into the bathroom. Teddy Dee followed the shocked and shouting stranger into the small confines of the bathroom.

"You know that this will not take too long," Teddy Dee breathed.

The ponytailed club hopper slid to a stop in the bathroom and braced for an attack. He crouched. He balled his fists in preparation for the fight to come.

"You messed with the wrong guy, amigo. This ends all sorts of bad for you," the ponytailed clubber said with a wicked grin. "They call me K.O. Castro. You might have heard of me."

Teddy Dee stepped forward and K.O. Castro stepped forward and the pair met near the sink. K.O. Castro was a strong and confident street fighter.

Teddy Dee felt the first punch to his shoulder and then a right grazed his left ear.

Teddy Dee lifted his fists and blocked Castro's initial attacks. Teddy Dee launched his first assault. He bobbed and weaved as he threw his first combination of punches. Teddy Dee was no slouch in hand-to-hand combat.

Grabbing Castro, Teddy Dee kneed him in the kidneys and then punched him a dozen times. K.O. Castro was a dirty fighter but so was Teddy Dee. The fight was not a slam dunk.

Castro punched Teddy Dee in the head and busted his lip. He scratched Teddy Dee across the cheek before Teddy Dee shut the whole commotion. He grabbed a towel and mopped at the scratch on his cheek. K.O. Castro lay on the floor of the car dealership toilet, unconscious and bleeding.

Teddy Dee checked his knuckles and smiled. He had scraped his knuckles in the bathroom fight. Teddy Dee stretched and enjoyed the brief exercise. Teddy Dee felt that suddenly he wanted to fight everyone for the next five hours.

He rubbed his bald head. He shook the berserker inside of him and tried to return to normal. Teddy Dee walked back into the club only to turn around and go back outside and onto the streets.

Teddy Dee stood outside in his three-quarter length leather coat. Out of doors, in the cold of the night, he thought that he should leave and try and find HBR. Yet, he dawdled. He waited. For some reason he decided to stay until the Mohawk and cinnamon bun left the club.

At about 2AM the Mohawk and her friend left the car dealership and hailed a cab. Teddy Dee watched the Mohawk and her friend drive away. He had thought to head back to Washington Square. Instead, he hailed a cab and followed the cab.

Near 120th the cab pulled over and allowed cinnamon bun to exit the cab.

"Can you pull over here," Teddy Dee asked the cab driver. The cab driver pulled over.

"Let's just wait."

"Is this something that I am going to regret, pal?"

"No, just making sure that the two get home safely," Teddy Dee told the cab driver.

"She your daughter?"

"Niece."

The cab driver picked up his cellphone and read his text messages while Teddy Dee watched as the girl with the cinnamon buns turned and talked to her friend in the cab.

Teddy Dee assumed that cinnamon bun lived near the location. Cinnamon bun ran into an apartment as Mohawk and the cab waited for Cinnamon bun to get safely inside. The cab with Mohawk pulled away from the curb.

The cab Teddy Dee was in pulled away from the curb and headed to Washington Square. Teddy Dee checked his watch and told the cab driver to pull up at the end of the street. He watched Mohawk climb out of the cab and walk up the walkway to her apartment.

Teddy Dee gave the cab driver instructions to drive him to his hotel. He was in his hotel room and in bed by 3AM. He asked for a wake up call at 9AM. Teddy Dee went to sleep feeling that if he did not see HBR while he was in New York City he wouldn't feel bad.

At nine o'clock Teddy Dee woke up and prepared for a ten o'clock breakfast at Craftbar.

He caught a cab to Madison Square Park and walked two blocks to Craftbar a little before ten o'clock. Teddy Dee was dressed casually in black jeans, his warm three quarter length black leather jacket, and comfortable shoes and a gray collared shirt that he buttoned to the throat. Wrapped about his neck was a black and white muffler. On his head was a matching black and white watch cap.

After eating Teddy Dee walked around downtown looking for the art galleries where Heather Beckham Rogers artwork was on display. He went to two of the three galleries before hitting the HBR jackpot.

The first gallery had only one of Heather Beckham Rogers sculptures on display. The sculpture was in wax. It was a surprising Lego sculpture that was a parody of and very similar to the Lenticular Images of Arthur Gugick. The sculpture was of Batgirl and Harley Quinn. Teddy Dee was impressed by the creativity of Heather Beckham Rogers.

The second gallery had a painting of something that Heather Beckham Rogers had made. The painting was a variant of a Flash cover that was stunning. It was surprising how detailed the painting was for something so small. It was another pop culture reference that the gallery owner suggested was Rogers newest phase in art.

"How much is this?"

"It is a limited edition," the gallery owner said.

Teddy Dee waited.

"There are only one hundred prints."

"$1,500," the gallery owner said.

"If I buy it can you have the artist write a thank you note for me and get me a picture with her?"

The gallery owner twisted his lips, thinking.

"I think I can arrange that."

Teddy Dee smiled at his ingenuity.

He arranged to pick up the framed painting and get the picture before catching a plane to parts unknown.

Teddy Dee headed to the hotel, had lunch, and returned to the hotel and picked up his carry on and then headed back to the gallery and meeting with Heather Beckham Rogers.

Heather Beckham Rogers was dressed in a black and white dress and combat boots. Her hair was in those Afro puffs that reminded Teddy Dee of Mickey Mouse ears. She was cute and such a small thing suddenly in front of Teddy Dee.

Heather Beckham Rogers began running headlong to Teddy Dee as he entered the gallery. She was all arms, smiles, and energy when she felt herself slam into the solid form of Teddy Dee. Teddy Dee could only smile as HBR hugged the giant with all her might.

"I didn't believe Andre when he said that someone wanted me to take a picture with me and my art that they bought. I couldn't turn it down though. Then he told me the name. I could not believe it."

They were sitting in a cafe on one of the busy streets in New York City. Teddy Dee smiled and listened to Heather Beckham Rogers. She was like this energetic ball that just suddenly had all of his attention.

"So, how long are you here?"

"I'm leaving in a couple of hours."

Heather Beckham Rogers looked down disappointed suddenly. She noticed that Teddy Dee's knuckles were scraped and bloody as if he had recently fought someone.

"Are you okay?"

Teddy Dee cocked his head; unsure.

"Why are you here, in New York?"

"I had some business here," Teddy Dee lied.

Heather Beckham Rogers exhaled. For the first time she got serious.

"I thought you would be at the funeral."

"I wanted to but I was unable to make it."

Heather Beckham Rogers nodded.

"Have you ever heard of Lucretia?"

Heather Beckham Rogers narrowed her eyes and furrowed her brown, thinking.

"I think it was done by Rembrandt. It's a painting."

"Yeah, yeah," Heather Beckham Rogers nodded.

"Are you lying," Teddy Dee asked.

"Yeah, yeah," Heather Beckham Rogers admitted. "You know there are about a million paintings in the world that matter. Well, there are more than that but I don't know them all." Heather Beckham Rogers paused. "Why did you ask?"

"I was just broadening my learning."

Heather Beckham Rogers laughed.

"I can learn too."

Heather Beckham laughed and raised her hands in surrender.

"I have to go," Teddy Dee said and climbed to his feet. He and Heather Beckham Rogers exited the coffee house and he walked the talented artist back to the gallery. The gallery owner had taken the painting down from the wall and was preparing it to be mailed.

Heather Beckham Rogers hugged Teddy Dee for a long moment. Teddy Dee did not think that he needed or wanted a hug until Heather Beckham Rogers released. Heather Beckham Rogers smiled and tilted her head the way that Katherine Rogers had, so long ago.

"Thanks for coming to New York and all," Heather Beckham Rogers said, suddenly a vapid twenty-something.

Teddy Dee smiled despite himself. Heather Beckham Rogers turned to leave and instantly Teddy Dee reached out and stopped himself from touching her.

He balled his fist and realized that this was the last time that he would see Heather Beckham Rogers or Bethany Rogers. Teddy Dee narrowed his eyes and watched as the twenty-something walked to the gallery owner. He was a danger to Heather and Bethany and anyone that wanted to hurt him as long as they knew that they were important to Teddy Dee. So, he steeled himself to the fact that he would never see or return to see Heather Beckham Rogers or the Rogers. Teddy Dee took a deep breath and turned and walked to the gallery exit. In moments, he was out of the gallery and down the street. He caught a cab and headed to the airport.

The Rolls Royce was luxurious. It was such a large and extravagant car to drive in Tokyo. Yet, the Rolls Royce Phantom was a status vehicle. There were not a number of people driving in the sleek and elegant Phantom. Asami knew that everyone that saw the Rolls Royce and Hiro Fujinaka IV recognized him as a captain of industry. Her father was a powerful man. Everyone knew him. Everyone respected him.

"Asami, your mother and you and Tanisha are going to Shibuya. Kogu will be with you also. They will take you to the restaurant and then home." Her father announced as Keiko, his wife, skimmed the paperwork that had to be signed that day. Keiko had been a lawyer before deciding to be the wife of Hiro Fujinaka. She had an eye for detail. Whenever Keiko and her father sat in a car or boarded a plane Keiko would go over the paperwork of Signet Industries that was soon to be renamed the Royal Family Herbal Company. The renaming was the biggest change in the family business in the last five years.

"I cannot believe that you have me look over these papers. You hired a General Counsel," Keiko said without looking up from the paperwork she was reading over.

"Yes. We have a General Counsel but I like when you look over the important stuff," Hiro Fujinaka IV smiled.

Asami looked at her mother from the rear of the luxury car.

Keiko Fujinaka looked up briefly and shook her head at her daughter. She smiled despite herself.

"Are you not going to the restaurant with us?" Asami asked a little alarmed. The tone in Asami's voice made Keiko stop her scanning of the documents that her husband was carrying to one of her meetings this morning.

Hiro had his tablet open and an eye on the Nissei Stock Market when Asami made her outburst.

"Of course I am," Hiro Fujinaka IV smiled focusing his attention on his daughter. The businessman reached out to his daughter and placed a manicured hand on her wrist. "I just have a few business dealings that I have to take care of before lunch. As I said, I will be meeting with Muramata before we all have lunch," Hiro Fujinaka IV smiled sitting next to his wife.

The Rolls Royce Phantom pulled to a stop in front of Kugo who was waiting at the curb. Kugo was dressed in a blue jacket with a short-sleeved pinstriped shirt and dark blue washed jeans and brown suede lace-up shoes. Tanisha climbed out of the Rolls Royce wearing lace-up combat boots, a black jean jacket and gray hooded sweatshirt. Tanisha had a light weight backpack she carried as well.

Asami and Tanisha went to Shibuya and did a little shopping. With them was their constant protector: Kogu. Kogu was 6'4" tall and weighed 241 pounds. He looked like an American football player more than a Japanese bodyguard.

Tanisha was a lithe beauty with shoulder length hair that was dyed at the tips fire engine red. She was 5'3" tall and weighed 103 pounds. Tanisha was the polar opposite of Kogu, physically. They both were more than professional in their undying effort to protect the Fujinaka clan.

Tanisha took Asami to several stores looking for a very specific look for her 12-year old charge. Asami had seen a dress that she had to have. The quartet of Keiko, Kogu, Tanisha, and Asami Fujinaka had traipsed back and forth through the Shibuya fashion district looking for a very specific dress. They went to every boutique and clothing store. They thought that they had found the specific dress at Shibuya 109 but the dress at Shibuya 109 was by a different designer. Of course, they went to Parco department store. Asami and Tanisha loved Parco department store. There at the always-crowded department store Asami and Tanisha found a pair of new shoes.

Chapter Twenty-Four.

Teddy Dee detested the fact that he had no backbone or a whit of courage to talk to Samantha Morris. His feelings were unrequited. He was the lowest of individuals because he tortured himself for no reason not knowing if Samantha Morris entertained any affection for him or not. He had not allowed her the opportunity to dismiss him or encourage him and that, in and of itself, had infuriated and depressed Teddy Dee. He thought he was better than that.

So, flying back to Los Angeles, from Boston via New York City, he had detoured and landed in Chicago and then gone to Minnesota. He had called Barry Granger after landing at the airport and talked briefly to Samantha Morris as she located her boss. Teddy Dee wanted to engage Samantha Morris in small talk but could not think of anything relevant to say.

"He will be right with you," Samantha Morris smiled on the phone and Teddy Dee suddenly felt awkward.

Teddy Dee had switched gears upon hearing Barry Granger pick up the phone. "Hey, Teddy," Barry Granger had rung in his ear.

With Granger Teddy Dee was a different person. He was clear, confident and concise. He explained his desire to the president of Global Corporations.

Granger had asked a few clarifying questions before disagreeing or agreeing to anything. The request was unusual Teddy Dee knew.

"I'm not a pimp or anything, but I will see what I can do."

"That's all I can ask," Teddy Dee said.

"Let me have thirty minutes to an hour. If I can swing it you should get a call back from my assistant," Barry Granger said and hung up.

Teddy Dee registered at a hotel close to the airport and hired a driver and a Cadillac CTX for two days.

An hour later Teddy Dee was crossing the parking lot of Global Corp and at the desk of Samantha Morris. It was only ten o'clock in the morning.

Samantha Morris narrowed her hazel eyes and cocked her head to the right seeing Teddy Dee. She smiled. She batted her eyes and smiled more, showing her perfectly white teeth.

"How can I help you, Mister Dandridge?"

"Was wondering if you were available for lunch?"

"Lunch?" Samantha Morris repeated. "With you?"

"Lunch with me," Teddy Dee nodded. "We can go to the Minneapolis Institute of Art. I heard that it is a great place to go while you are in Minneapolis."

Samantha Morris smiled and stroked her bottom lip, thinking.

Teddy Dee waited. He knew that most would try to fill the silence with words. He was not most people. Teddy Dee had learned to be silent and patient.

"I only get an hour, Mister Dandridge," the petite blonde pointed out. "The Museum of Art is just about that far away."

"I pulled some strings. I think you can have a longer lunch, if you want to have lunch with me," Teddy Dee said.

"You pulled strings?"

"You said so much about the museum and I leave tomorrow," Teddy Dee trailed off.

"Fine, lunch it is," Samantha Morris agreed. Her hazel eyes narrowed for an instant and Teddy Dee thought that was Samantha Morris being wicked then and there. The moment was gone as quickly as it had appeared and what remained was the Samantha Morris that Teddy Dee had first found by the side of Barry Granger, dressed impeccably and with that curly brown hairdo.

"We can go now, if you want or I can come back and pick you up at noon," Teddy Dee added. "Your choice."

"It's not ten o'clock yet, Mister Dandridge," Samantha Morris smiled, blushing just a bit, suddenly flustered.

"Okay, then I will come back and pick you up at noon. Is that okay?"

"Yes, that is fine," Samantha Morris smiled and shook her head.

Teddy Dee spun on his heels and walked away and left Samantha Morris. He left the offices and sat in the car that he had rented for two days. Teddy Dee sat in the back seat and listened to music while the driver sat waiting for instructions.

"We will be going to lunch at the Minneapolis Institute of Art. We have a couple of hours to kill. What is close to here?" Before the driver could answer, Teddy Dee said, "Let's go to a comic book store."

"Yes sir," the driver, a man in his forties with white hair, said. The driver, a thick necked man, typed in search items and upon seeing the search results drove to the closest comic book store. It was only a few miles away from the Global Corp offices.

Teddy Dee and the driver browsed the titles of the comic book store looking for things that struck them. Teddy Dee loved the superhero comics. His favorite was Batman. He liked the detective mind of Batman.

"I used to like Batman too," the driver pointed out, holding a Crying Freeman comic book in his hand. "I think that I look at Batman as a franchise more than a comic book nowadays. His stories have become more cinematic and less about the character. They have changed Batman. He is not as gritty and damaged as he was when he donned the cowl."

"I can see your point," Teddy Dee said. "There is this belief that Marvel and DC have been stealing each other's characters for a long time. The first was Superman. DC created a real superhero. Marvel responded with Thor. So, Man of Steel versus God of Thunder. When DC created Batman Marvel Comics took those same traits and created Iron Man." Teddy Dee paused. "I am a Batman fan. I like that there's a billionaire trying to protect the little man. Batman is one of the greatest superheroes in the DC Universe without super powers. When you think of it Batman can go toe to toe with most superheroes and win because he is so smart."

"Yeah, I lost interest in Superman after Man of Steel. How can they have Superman kill someone?"

Teddy Dee and the driver picked up a few comics. Teddy Dee paid for all of the comics. He had opened the envelope that he had inside of his jacket. In the envelope were five bundles of new $100 dollar bills.

Teddy Dee returned to the offices of Global Corp and picked up Samantha Morris at noon. He simply smiled as he walked her to the waiting car.

"We are just going to lunch Mister Dandridge?"

"Of course," Teddy Dee said a little shocked by the question. He quickly added, "Please call me: Teddy."

"Okay, Teddy," Samantha Morris said sitting in the back seat of the car as they drove to downtown Minneapolis. The three in the car were silent. Teddy Dee was content to sit in the silence and presence of Samantha Morris but the assistant to Barry Granger seemed to have a number of questions.

"Can I ask you a question?"

"Of course," Teddy Dee said, noting how small Samantha Morris' hand was compared to his gigantic paw. He could fit three or maybe four of her hands in his palm.

"Why did you want to go to lunch with me?"

"Seriously? You are bright, friendly, and knowledgeable," Teddy Dee admitted. "I don't get to have lunch with anyone that usually has one of those qualities let alone all of them." He paused. "It doesn't hurt that you are drop dead gorgeous either," he added.

Samantha Morris fell silent. She smiled. She studied Teddy Dee silently as the car hurtled down the highway toward Minneapolis.

"Mister— Teddy, I don't want to lead you on," Samantha Morris said suddenly serious.

"I am not being led on. I just want to take you to lunch. Is that wrong? Is that an indecent proposal? Are you worried that you are going to want to rip off my clothes while we sit in the museum?" Teddy Dee said. "That was a joke." He continued. "I just want to take you to lunch. Besides, I am not that kind of guy."

"Teddy, no, that is not indecent," Samantha Morris smiled. "It is just that you made arrangements with my boss and got me a day off with pay."

"I really wanted to have lunch with you," Teddy Dee admitted. "I am leaving tomorrow. I won't have another opportunity to have lunch with you once I leave."

"How do you know that?"

Teddy Dee did not answer. He looked out the car window. The Minnesota prairie flashed by as they drew closer to the city.

"When you go to the museum where do you usually eat?"

Samantha Morris hesitated.

"It's okay, I promise I just want to use it as reference." Teddy Dee said from his side of the back seat of the car. The driver looked back into the rear view mirror and his eyes crinkled. Teddy Dee continued nonplussed. "People don't ask you to lunch? You don't eat lunch? I suspect that many a man has asked you to lunch in your lifetime."

Samantha Morris nodded. "I have to admit that no one has asked my employer if they could go to lunch with me." Samantha Morris said.

"I understand. Do you not want to go to lunch with me? If that is the case, I will have the driver turn around and take you back. I don't want you to do anything under duress."

"It's not that," Samantha Morris smiled.

"Is it because I am black?" Teddy Dee asked with a slight smile. "It is a new day if you didn't realize it. We have had a black President. We had a woman President. Before I die I believe we will have a Hispanic President. Times they are a changing, Samantha Morris. Blacks and whites and everyone can get along. There are some notable interracial couples," Teddy Dee heard himself say. He paused. "If going to lunch with a black man is too painful or against your beliefs then tell me now. We can turn around and call it a day."

"No. No, I didn't mean to.... Teddy, I'm black."

"You might be black but you aren't stomped on the ground and scarred from head to toe black, like me," Teddy Dee smiled.

Samantha Morris smiled. She added, "I just have a sort of relationship. I suppose that going to lunch is not going to be something that I need to mention." Samantha Morris smiled and looked at Teddy Dee with those hazel eyes and thin nose. "I usually eat in the museum cafe," Samantha Morris responded.

"Good. That is where I made reservations," Teddy Dee said. He quickly added: "I was kidding. I don't think that they take reservations."

"They do not."

Teddy Dee nodded.

They wandered through the museum for an hour before Samantha Morris stopped in front of one of the paintings that she absolutely loved. They had meandered around the Minneapolis Institute of Art before arriving in front of a painting by Eugene Delacroix. It was vibrant and an explosion of colors. Teddy Dee studied Samantha Morris who was riveted to the spot smiling at the painting.

"I love this painting."

Teddy Dee nodded.

"It is one of the 900 donated paintings from the St. Paul railroad magnate James J. Hill."

Teddy Dee nodded.

"Every time I am here I have to find this painting and just enjoy the sheer power of the paint."

"Have you ever been to Africa?"

Samantha Morris narrowed her eyes.

"The painting says: Tangiers Convulsionists." He paused. "Tangiers is in Africa."

Samantha Morris nodded. She smiled. "I know that."

Teddy Dee nodded and smiled. He liked the sound of her voice. Teddy Dee liked everything about Samantha Morris. She was so unlike everyone that he saw daily.

The pair were in another part of the Minneapolis Institute of Art when Samantha Morris asked Teddy Dee a question that seemed to come out of nowhere. They had stopped in the African gallery. They were in front of the Bis pole sculpture.

"Art is an incredible vehicle to express complex ideas and emotions that we cannot, sometimes express clearly for whatever reason. Do you have a favorite piece?"

Teddy Dee remained silent.

"This Bis pole is made of a single nutmeg tree," she explained. Teddy Dee nodded. He liked that Samantha Morris had a vast art knowledge.

"The pole is created after someone dies and is commissioned to be carved by the grieving family. There is always a canoe featured in the carving as the most common means of transportation to the other world." Samantha Morris continued. "The pole is given to the family in a big ceremony and there are mock battles to drive away any evil spirits and then it is burned."

"Burned?"

"Yes," Samantha Morris said.

Teddy Dee nodded, leaving the question unasked.

"This is an art piece and so it was preserved," Samantha Morris smiled, answering the unasked question.

Teddy Dee nodded.

"When do you return to Los Angeles?"

"Tomorrow afternoon."

Samantha Morris paused and twisted her thin lips on her freckled sprinkled diamond shaped face.

"I have to work."

Teddy Dee listened. He did not know where Samantha Morris was going with her line of thinking. It did not matter. He had done all that he wanted to do with the assistant to Barry Granger that day or any day.

Teddy Dee and Samantha Morris had lunch at the Minneapolis Institute of Art. They ate lightly. Teddy Dee had a chef's salad and a lemonade. Samantha Morris had a spinach salad and a sweet tea.

"Okay, now that we have had lunch and looked at paintings, sculptures, and vacuum cleaners can you tell me what this is all about," Samantha Morris said as they walked away from the Delacroix painting.

"I just wanted to spend one of my last days in Minnesota with someone that I thought was... interesting...different and wonderful. That is what this is all about. Nothing more," Teddy Dee said.

"Nothing more," Samantha Morris repeated.

"Nothing more," Teddy Dee said again. "If you are bored we can go back to Global Corp now."

"I didn't say that," Samantha Morris protested.

Teddy Dee nodded and smiled.

Teddy Dee looked up and saw that Samantha Morris was quietly studying him.

"Are you ready to see some more of the museum?"

Teddy Dee nodded. The pair climbed to their feet. Samantha Morris placed a tiny hand on Teddy Dee's bicep, guiding him from the gallery and to the next exhibit.

"Can you show me Lucretia?"

Samantha Morris paused, and for the first time, she seemed to hesitate. Her impeccable pluck seemed to waver for just a moment. Her hazel eyes glittered for a moment as she narrowed her view. Teddy Dee stood beside the petite curly haired beauty expressionless.

"Lucretia?"

Teddy Dee nodded.

Samantha Morris led Teddy Dee to the permanent painting gallery of the Minneapolis Institute of Art. There the two stood in front of one of the museum's central art pieces. The painting hung in the Rembrandt Collection section of the museum.

"What do you think," Samantha Morris asked after a few minutes of standing in front of the painting.

"It is sad," Teddy Dee admitted.

"Yes, I agree," the reddish brown curly haired assistant to Barry Granger agreed with a smile. "Do you know the story?"

Teddy Dee had learned of the story the first time Samantha Morris had mentioned Lucretia to him. Yet, he did not stop her from telling the story again.

"Lucretia was the wife of a Roman nobleman, known for her virtue and loyalty, who was raped by Sextus Tarquinius, the son of a ruling tyrant. The next day Lucretia revealed the crime to her husband and father, and in their presence took her own life, choosing death over dishonor."

"Sad," Teddy Dee repeated.

"Every time I come here I find myself here in front of Lucretia," Samantha Morris confessed.

Teddy Dee nodded. He stood in front of the painting silent. The painting said so much to Teddy Dee. He wanted to be like Lucretia. He wanted to be honorable despite the work that he did. Teddy Dee wanted to be seen by Samantha Morris as someone loyal and virtuous, if just for the day. As he thought that, Teddy Dee realized that Samantha Morris too was seeking something like himself. Perhaps, he thought, the reddish brown beauty had darker secrets than she cared to admit. Teddy Dee studied the Rembrandt again and reconsidered Samantha Morris and Lucretia.

Samantha Morris was the first to move from the Rembrandt and Teddy Dee followed. They moved away from the painting and toward another part of the museum and then eventually toward the exit. Though they had seen many things that day Teddy Dee knew that he could not monopolize Samantha Morris' complete day even though he had called in a favor with her boss.

"Can we sit down for a few minutes?"

Samantha Morris nodded and pointed to an empty bench. Teddy Dee nodded. They sat down in front of a small gallery.

"Can I make a confession?"

Samantha Morris nodded.

"I have wanted to ask you to lunch for days, months, years. I just didn't have the nerve."

"I cannot believe that," Samantha Morris smiled.

"Look at me, I am not the type of guy that gets the girl. I am the guy that fights and fights and when everything is over in walks a Barry Granger or another rich kid with all the shiny toys to sweep the girl off her feet."

"You never know," Samantha Morris smiled. "The girl that walks away with the rich kid and the shiny toys may not be the right girl for you."

Teddy Dee nodded.

"Maybe you have fought for the wrong girls?"

Teddy Dee remained silent. He tilted his head, considering what the assistant said.

"I always seem to fight for the wrong girls," Teddy Dee stated. "That's my job."

"You ever think of doing something else?"

Teddy Dee knitted his brow with the question. For six years he had been a part of the chaos and attempts to control the chaos for corporations. He had dipped his hands in the blood of shadows with the guidance of Oscar Easton when he was naive but quickly become aware of the hard truths of the darker side of multi-nationals and global economies. Teddy Dee had learned that inside the multi-global conglomerates there were no morals or ethics. Instead, all that mattered was results and the bottom line. Results mattered more than the methods that were taken to achieve those results.

As a result, Teddy Dee had learned to ignore the tailor made suits, luxury cars, Presidential suites, and executive bathrooms because he knew that all those extrinsic items were gained and bathed in the corruption, blackmail, extortion, deceit, cutthroat dealings, intimidation, and bloodletting.

It was Teddy Dee's job to insure that the executives and bigwigs stayed safe and secure in their multi-million dollar homes. He had in a dozen years in the shadow world of corporations learned and honed very specific skills and talents. Teddy Dee did not know of any place that would recruit or hire someone that was a paid enforcer for corporate executives.

"What are you going to do when this is all over?"

Teddy Dee narrowed his eyes again, looking at Samantha Morris curiously.

"You mean this afternoon?"

"No. I mean when you stop working," Samantha Morris smiled. "You know, at some point, you will stop working. Maybe, you will retire."

Teddy Dee knew that when he stopped working his retirement was already planned by others more powerful than himself. He had learned that a peaceful retirement on the beach with his feet in the sand was not a realistic conclusion to a life spilling blood in the shadows of corporate lies and deception. His end, like all blooders that had come before him, would end with someone discovering his body in an alleyway or on a set of stairs in some nameless place and his death declared a failed robbery, accident, or suicide.

His mentor had been found dead in his home in South Carolina, an apparent suicide. Oscar Easton did not own a home. Teddy Dee knew that.

The corporations silenced any and everyone that had too much leverage on any one corporation. So, Teddy Dee knew that when his usefulness for his corporate leaders had drawn to an end he would be found dead by a botched theft or an apparent suicide in a house that he did not own sucking on the barrel of a 9mm pistol. Yet, Teddy Dee knew that he could not say any of that to Samantha Morris. Instead, he thought about a more acceptable answer.

"I've always wanted to see Crazy Horse," Teddy Dee said.

"Crazy Horse? In South Dakota?"

Teddy Dee nodded.

"I wouldn't have guessed that you would have said that," Samantha Morris smiled.

"I am full of surprises," Teddy Dee half smiled.

Again Samantha Morris smiled.

They walked around the museum one last time. Teddy Dee took Samantha Morris to the gift shop and bought her a Flappy the Elephant stuffed toy to mark the memory of the day at the museum.

"Thank you for a memorable museum visit," Teddy Dee said.

He left Samantha Morris at Global Corp. He walked out of the doors and texted Barry Granger: Thanks for allowing me to steal your assistant.

The afternoon with Samantha Morris was magical and still had Teddy Dee uncharacteristically on an emotional high as he told the driver that he wanted to go back to Minneapolis and grab something to eat.

Teddy Dee walked to the Cadillac and folded himself inside the luxurious interior. The driver drove on the slightly congested highways and stopped briefly to try out Hell's Kitchen in downtown Minneapolis. Teddy Dee ordered a turkey burger with cheese, fries, and a strawberry milkshake. He took his order to go just as the band began to play.

He returned to the airport hotel where he would spend the evening before his flight the next day. Teddy Dee dismissed the driver and the Cadillac CTS and grabbed his meal for the evening. Teddy Dee entered the hotel and was greeted by a man in jeans and baseball cap. Instantly, Teddy Dee went on hyper-alert. He immediately became aware of his surroundings and the threat level in front of him in the hotel lobby.

"Are you Teddy?" The man was in his twenties and unshaven. He had dark eyes and thick eyebrows and an angular face that seemed somehow familiar. Teddy Dee noted that the man was wearing a pretty expensive wristwatch.

Teddy Dee did not respond. He simply watched the man's hands.

"I was told to give you a package," the man continued, raising a manila envelope that had Arch Corporation's logo in the left hand corner.

"Are you related to Cambridge?" Teddy Dee asked taking the package from the man that resembled Roland Cambridge a little.

"Nephew," the courier smiled.

"Okay. Thank you," Teddy Dee said and the nephew left the hotel.

In Teddy Dee's hand was one manila envelope that read: Teddy.

Teddy Dee read the dossier on the plane ride back to Los Angeles and thought what he had to do to stop the flow of information seeping out of Arch Corporation. Roland had told him that the key information was coming from a division of research in the Newport Beach laboratory.

"If you don't believe in the business you know that you can sell your stocks and interest in the business at any time," Hiro Fujinaka IV smiled.

"Speaking of stocks," Aito beamed, standing up. "I was made aware that there have been some family members contacted about that exact matter. Have you anything to say or do with that Hiro?"

Hiro Fujinaka IV stared at Aito coldly.

Aito Fujinaka glared at his cousin.

The conference room fell silent.

"Hiro," another cousin hissed, making the President of Signet Industries change my stare. "What are you trying to do?"

"I am always responsible to the greater good of the company. There have been a few family members that have expressed some concern over the direction of the company and their involvement. As you know the family has grown. Some are involved in the business of Signet Industries. Some are not. Those that are not have suggested that their stocks are available for purchase to buy them out."

"Sonuvabitch."

Daiki raised my hands and came between Hiro Fujinaka IV and Aito Fujinaka.

"At present, of the 51% interest in Signet Industries, the Fujinaka family still has controlling interest." Daiki explained. He quickly added, "As a publicly owned company we have sold 49% of our interest in the company to those speculators and investors around the world."

"How much do you possess?" Aito growled glaring openly at Hiro Fujinaka.

"I would suggest that you read the board meeting notes. They are posted and archived on the corporate website."

"How much of the company do you own?" Aito repeated, a vein rising from the left side of my throat.

"The individual with the most interest in Signet Industries is myself," Hiro Fujinaka IV admitted. "I possess, with my wife, my son, and my daughter, 28% interest in the company."

Asami lowered her dark eyes and did the calculations. Her father had 17% of the Signet Industries stocks in my name. Her mother had 6%. Yet, that morning she had given Asami 3% of her shares. Her brother had been given 6% and when he was frustrated with his father, when he had been 17 or 18, he had given Asami 2% of his 6% to teach his father a lesson. So, she, Asami, had originally been given 6% interest that had increased secretly seven years ago to 8%.

When Asami gained Tanaka's interest she had advised the family attorney and asked him to hide the exchange for as long as possible. So, only four people knew that the heir of Hiro Fujinaka IV had given 2% of his interest to his sister. Asami Fujinaka had reached out secretly to her cousins to see who in the family was interested in helping her wrest control from her father.

In less than 24 hours later, Asami Fujinaka had become the most influential member of the Signet Industries board of directors. The responses had come from the most surprising parts of the family. Her mother, Keiko Fujinaka, had spoken to the mothers and daughters of the families and asked them to give Asami at least one share if they didn't mind the idea of a female in charge of the future of the Fujinaka fortunes.

"So, between the other six members of the family there is 23% interest remaining?"

Hiro Fujinaka IV sneered at his cousin.

There was a murmur that rose and Aito pushed back away from the conference table.

Hiro Fujinaka IV didn't move. He looked to his left and saw Aito Fukui standing trying to form words to defuse the suddenly volatile situation. Hiro Fujinaka IV sneered at the theater created by his younger cousin Aito. The President of Signet Industries reached out and touched Daiki on the forearm gaining his immediate attention.

"Aito, can you leave? This is suddenly a family matter about the business."

Aito Fukui nodded and exited.

Hiro Fujinaka IV stood at the head of the conference table studying his fuming family members. Next to him stood Tanaka Fujinaka, a brash and reckless young man, more boy than man, at the age of 31.

The President of Signet Industries looked to his right and there was his wife, Keiko, and his brilliant daughter Asami. They, Tanaka, Keiko, and Asami, were the only ones that Hiro Fujinaka IV could rely on. Within the immediate family there had always been in fighting and political wrangling. Whoever was in power was always the target of the Fujinaka clan. Hiro had learned that lesson long before taking control of Signet Industries.

“If you don’t like the way that I am running the business then I will step down immediately and one of you can take over.”

The board members hesitated.

Chapter Twenty-Five.

Teddy Dee was walking in Westchester near the Westchester Public Swimming Pool trying to clear his head. It was a strange day and there were a number of tourists in the area. Teddy Dee did not think too much of it. There was a tour bus. Teddy Dee assumed that the tourists were there to take pictures near Loyola-Marymount.

The Japanese women approached in crowds and attempted to poison Teddy Dee with hypodermic needles. It was very black bag and covert, like in the movies. The first two attacks had been thwarted because Teddy Dee was hyper vigilant in crowds as he knew that he stood out and was an easy target to find in crowds.

The first poisoner was a woman dressed in a baseball cap, jogging top and ¾ length workout tights. She looked like a typical tourist as she made a direct line toward Teddy Dee in a crowd near the swimming pool in a park. The unerring, unflinching direction that the woman took across the crowd put Teddy Dee on alert. He knew that attacks did not only come from men. Being a sexist in the shadow world of corporations only ended badly as far as Teddy Dee was concerned. "Alabama" Fleming had taught him that the greatest threat might be in the one person that you underestimated.

The woman had gotten close enough to remove the hypodermic and nearly inject Teddy Dee with whatever toxin she had. Unfortunately for the assassin, Teddy Dee was faster and stronger than the woman and turned the tables on the would be killer injecting her with the toxin instead.

"I don't know what you were trying to give me but you only have a few minutes to get an antidote," Teddy Dee explained dragging the surprised and drugged assassin to a walkway that had fewer people around. They stood on a little used stone bridge that stretched over a footpath twenty feet below where joggers were moving back and forth.

The woman, trying to keep her composure, smiled and narrowed her gaze. She reached for her small purse that was slung across her chest. Teddy Dee stopped her from putting a hand in the purse instantly.

"Antidote," the woman said.

Teddy Dee snatched the purse from her neck and opened it. Inside of the purse was a Lady Smith and Wesson pistol. Instantly, Teddy Dee unloaded the chambered bullet and the magazine from the pistol. He slipped the magazine in his pocket for safekeeping.

Teddy Dee poured out the interior of the purse in front of the woman. In the jumble of tissue, loose change, lip balm, lipstick, little sampler of hand cream, there was a small injector that looked like a smaller, silver version of the allergy pens people used.

The woman grabbed the allergy pen and pressed it into her thigh.

"Tell your bosses that they might want to rethink this whole operation. The next person that attacks me I may not be so generous."

Teddy Dee had walked away from the woman and left her purse on the bench.

Two days later, Teddy Dee had been at Pepperdine college researching something about Japan and decided to go and watch a volleyball game in the glass walled gymnasium. There was a crowd there. Instantly, Teddy Dee was on alert. He watched everyone until he found his seat in the bleachers and tried to simply enjoy the volleyball game.

A young and attractive Asian girl/woman moved toward Teddy Dee on the bleachers. Teddy Dee was instantly on alert having dealt with the Japanese poisoner just weeks before. The girl sat down a few rows below Teddy Dee. Teddy Dee sat and watched the game and the girl. Two more of the girl's friends showed up and Teddy Dee decided then and there to leave. As he was leaving one of the girls climbed to her feet and headed for the aisle ahead of Teddy Dee. Teddy Dee slowed and noticed that another of the girls that had been seated was on her feet.

Teddy Dee cut across the bleacher and over people to make it to the second stairway of the bleachers. The three girls followed. Teddy Dee bounded down the bleacher stairs and out of the gymnasium and into the lobby. Three against one were not optimal odds but Teddy Dee figured that only one of the three had a hypodermic needle. The worst case scenario would be that they started shooting. Teddy Dee was unarmed.

So, instantly Teddy Dee headed for the exit. If he was going to fight, then he wanted to have an advantage. Space was his advantage.

Outside of the gymnasium and at the bottom of the stairs Teddy Dee stood by a tree and waited. The first girl with her hair in a long black ponytail and blue T-shirt with fluorescent green letters on it that read: Make History, stepped out all piss and vinegar. She had black tights on and like the woman

Teddy Dee had faced on the stone bridge a small purse slung across her chest. She looked to be in her twenties and angry.

The second girl to exit the gymnasium was a round faced, thin lipped Asian with thin eyebrows and pug nose. She was shorter than the first girl and dressed in a gray sweat top with hood and blue jeans. Her black hair was piled into a raven black bun on her round head. It was the round faced killer that had spotted Teddy Dee standing near the tree.

"There he is," the girl said and pointed out Teddy Dee to her two accomplices.

The third girl was close behind the first two. She was dressed in black tights, T-shirt, and Nike gym shoes. She had shoulder length black hair, big, expressive anime eyes, and no visible chin. Though she looked to be the same age as the other two her body did not seem to have gone through puberty as she had the body of a teenage boy more than a twenty something.

The three women moved cautiously down the stairs and toward Teddy Dee. Teddy Dee backed up and into the small grove of trees that lined the walkway to the entrance of the gymnasium. Teddy Dee wanted to use the trees to his advantage.

The ponytailed woman was the first to attack. Teddy Dee felt sorry immediately after blocking her feeble attack and punching her unconscious. He opened her purse and like other assassin there was a Lady Smith and Wesson inside. Teddy Dee saw a dozen zip ties inside the purse. He zip tied the attacker and grabbed a handful of ties as the next girl attacked. He unloaded the pistol and prepared for the next attacks to come on the Pepperdine campus.

Teddy Dee fought off the two women as they simultaneously tried to subdue him and inject him with a toxin. The boyish woman attacked with martial arts confidence. Teddy Dee liked using his hands and though the girl was fast and agile nothing that she did with her hands hurt the giant. Her kicks were annoying and constant. Teddy Dee concentrated on the woman's feet and after only a few moments the boyish woman was not willing to get close to Teddy Dee. Teddy Dee looked at the boyish woman just out of reach.

While Teddy Dee was concentrating on the boyish woman the round faced attacker struck and nearly jabbed the hypodermic into his bicep. Teddy Dee did a swimming motion and avoided the attack and without thinking punched at the attacker hitting her wrist and knocking the hypodermic needle from the hand of the round faced girl. The boyish woman attacked again and Teddy Dee punched the boyish girl in the stomach, just hard enough to drop her to her knees. He zip tied them all in the grove of trees and gave the same warning to them that he had to the first attacker.

The boyish figured woman was the one that instead of simply accepting her situation sneered and looked as if she wanted to go another round with Teddy Dee. Teddy Dee shook his head at the incompetence of the three and was about to turn and leave when the boyish figured woman spoke.

"This is not over," she spat.

"Shut up Miki," growled the ponytailed killer whose left eye was already swelling shut.

"No, I want this black barbarian to know that beating up a few women has done nothing but made it worse for him," Miki hissed. Her dark eyes glared at Teddy Dee.

Teddy Dee shook his head.

"You think this is funny?"

Teddy Dee turned and walked away.

"You have awakened a dragon," Miki growled. "You have awakened a dragon."

The word: "dragon" had made Teddy Dee's ears perk up. His anonymous friend had said the same word. Teddy Dee catalogued the incident. In less than a week three women had attempted to poison him.

That night Teddy Dee received another message.

To: Teddy Dee
Fr: anonymous123113751971114111
Subject: hatchet face
Dear Teddy,
You are being watched. There is a lot of attention on you right now.
Sleep with one eye opened.
Do not give up.
You are inspiring.
Usually, people just quit and give up.
Hold on.
Get jacked up.
Think that you may get one big attack soon.
Watch your back.
This is not over. There was talk of stopping after the first two failures.
But it is not stopping. At least, not yet.
Think blitzkrieg.
This is purely a personal attack. Be cautious.

They are not going to focus on downtown only for attack. There is also a suggestion that a friend near a beach may be used to draw you out. Insider information.

Your friend.
NVWAF

Three days after Pepperdine on a Sunday, Teddy Dee was attacked near Manhattan Beach. The third attack was a combination of hypodermic needle and assassin squad. Teddy Dee was in Manhattan Beach trying to enjoy one of the busiest tourist spots after seeing a movie to beat the heat. Teddy Dee was walking down the beach boardwalk the evening of the third attack.

Three men approached Teddy Dee dressed in jeans, and hooded sweatshirts. Teddy Dee was dressed in a car coat, collared shirt, and khaki pants, noted the three men and his defenses went up. He took in the three men immediately and tried to think of the best attack or retreat. On the section of the boardwalk where Teddy Dee was there were just a few homes and no retail stores. To the right was the Pacific Ocean. He noticed there was a street exit one hundred yards ahead of him and behind the three threats.

"Hey, bro, you have the time," one of the three men that looked a little like an Asian Justin Bieber asked stepping out of the group. He was dressed in baggy jeans, Nike gym shoes, and a black hooded sweatshirt. He had a retractable baton in his hand.

"Hey, man, my friend asked if you have the time. What is wrong with you? You stuck up and can't talk," the second Asian man who had his dark hair sculpted into a faux Mohawk said with a knife in his hand. He was dressed in black baggy jeans, Nike gym shoes, and short sleeve white T-shirt.

Teddy Dee shook his head at the not so veiled threat.

The third person had the hypodermic needle.

The first man with the retractable baton was the first to attack. Teddy Dee watched as the first man telegraphed his attack. Teddy Dee stepped forward and under the arc of the baton and simply fired a knife hand into the angry man's throat driving him pin wheeling into the sand holding his throat and trying to breathe. Teddy Dee grabbed the retractable baton out of the air just long enough to turn and aim the steel rod at the second attacker.

Instinctively, the faux Mohawk man holding the knife swatted at the baton like it was a gnat or annoying bee. Teddy Dee used the moment of distraction to step forward and stop the knife thrust effortlessly. Teddy Dee used his up close proximity to attack and dismantle the man in seconds all the while watching the last man with the hypodermic needle.

The last man with short hair and a diamond in his earlobe and holding the hypodermic needle watched as Teddy Dee stepped over the crumpled man that had attempted to attack him with a knife. The hypodermic wielding man paused and smiled at Teddy Dee. Teddy Dee was surprised at the bravado of the third attacker.

"What? No words?"

The third attacker shook his head; no.

Teddy Dee nodded and the fight began without any other fanfare. The two men circled one another clockwise. One, a giant and the other, a foot shorter and seemingly more confident than the other.

Teddy Dee had just his mitts. The attacker held the hypodermic needle as if it were a dagger. On the sidewalk sat the retractable baton. Perhaps, Teddy Dee thought absently, the attacker had a gun and was going to pull it out and shoot him dead before he could mount a fight.

Teddy Dee waited for the attack. Teddy Dee waited for the smaller man to pull a gun. Teddy Dee waited for the man to make his move.

The attacker upon making a complete circle feigned a left-right-left stabbing motion only to spin to the left and kick at Teddy Dee expertly. Teddy Dee blocked the kick and watched the attacker more closely. The two circled each other, now counterclockwise, looking for an opening, a weakness or soft spot to exploit. Teddy Dee kept his gnarled hands out and his elbows close to his sides, waiting for the next attack, that had to come.

The second attack was three overhead left-right-left stabs at Teddy Dee with the hypodermic needle. Teddy Dee avoided each stab and in the third attack noted a weakness in the attacker's attack. So, Teddy Dee circled around the attacker to the left and kicked the baton into the sand. As Teddy Dee kicked the baton the attacker again did an overhead left-right-left stab attack. In the pulling back for the second stab Teddy Dee rocketed a punch into the jaw of the unguarded attacker. The punch dropped the attacker. He zip-tied the three men together and walked away.

He took their phones and slipped them into his pocket. The phone that the hypodermic needle attacker used Teddy Dee held onto. He checked the two phones that he had grabbed in the first two attacks. Teddy Dee looked for similar numbers. He found three numbers that each phone had in common.

Teddy Dee sent the phone numbers to his handler.

 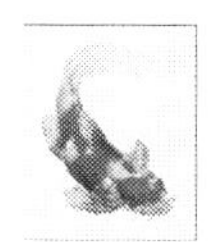 

The video began with Teddy Dandridge, dressed in a dark blue suit, light blue collared shirt, blue striped tie, sitting at the glass table of Tanaka Fujinaka. On first observation, it looked like an ordinary meeting between two men. The only exception was that Teddy Dandridge looked like a NFL linebacker dressed in a suit. He was gigantic and extremely muscular. Tanaka Fujinaka was dressed in a dark suit open collared shirt looked as if he was pretending to be the director of operations in Los Angeles. He appeared to be more Hollywood than business.

The black giant looked around the office, taking in all the knick knacks that stood out.

Fujinaka had asked Dandridge something and Dandridge simply smiled as an answer. There was a moment it appeared when it seemed that the black man did nothing. He seemed to be listening.

The black man closed his eyes. He climbed to his feet and crossed his arms. The giant of a man put his finger to his upper lip and stroked it before making his move.

The giant jumped over the glass tabletop from just standing on the other side. He did not run or build up speed. The giant bowled Fujinaka over in the high backed chair. In less than five seconds Dandridge was on the other side of the glass table sitting on Mister Fujinaka's chest smiling at the feat he had accomplished.

The smiling giant looked back briefly and noted that the miniature katana sword was still in place as well as the two bonsai trees. Dandridge nodded looking back at the office door and looked down and into the dark and panicked eyes of Tanaka Fujinaka and saw him begin to speak. The giant of a man clamped his gigantic hand over the smaller man's mouth.

So, as the giant sat on the small man's chest and slipped off his $200 dollar striped satin tie and shoved the expensive silk into Fujinaka's mouth.

Fujinaka blinked in reply. The giant studied the man on the floor.

"You know that life always boils down to the choices that we make. People get confused and think it is something else or that life is based on a big decision. I don't. I know that some of you believe that. I don't," Teddy Dee said.

The black man identified as Theodore Dandridge studied the President of Signet Industries beneath his knees and considered his next steps. He spoke and scanned the office. The attack, if jumping over a desk and pinning Tanaka Fujinaka was an attack, had not raised any alarms.

"I could have played the long game and been found out eventually or done the unexpected. Either choice was a choice that had to be made. Choices, big or small, happen everyday and every second," Theodore Dandridge paused. "I am a little distracted. Sorry." Teddy Dee climbed off of the executive. Theodore Dandridge instantly grabbed a handful of Tanaka's shirt and sat him back upright in his chair. He seemed stunned and trying to regain his breath.

"I know you, Fujinaka," Theodore Dandridge said pulling out four plastic zip ties. Before Fujinaka could protest or resist, his wrists and ankles were lashed to the arms of the high back chair by the plastic restraints. "You know the one thing that I always have on me wherever I go? Zip ties. They are a modern marvel. Most people don't even pay them any mind. They are innocuous. Meaningless."

Theodore Dandridge frowned. "Wait a minute. I was talking about something important. Oh, yeah. I remember. I know you."

Dandridge had Fujinaka seated upright again in his chair with his wrists and ankles secured by zip ties to the chair arms and legs, respectively. In seconds, Theodore Dandridge had removed everything from the executive's pockets and tossed them on the glass desktop behind him.

On the table were two cell phones: one iPhone and one Samsung. There was a thumb drive that could hold 50 gigabytes of information. There were several business cards. Fujinaka's wallet lay open on the tabletop. He had about $500 in cash. Car keys to a Mercedes Benz were inches from the wallet.

Dandridge surveyed the room again and his eyes fell on what he was looking for; adhesive tape. Theodore Dandridge frowned at the small roll of adhesive tape. He stepped to the bookshelf and noted that the office had a private bathroom. Dandridge smiled. Of course, Tanaka Fujinaka had a private bathroom.

“How do you know me? Why do you know me? Where do you know me from,” Theodore Dandridge said in a singsong fashion.

So, Dandridge took a breath and tried to focus. He focused on the task at hand. He wrapped the adhesive tape around Tanaka Fujinaka’s mouth securing the tie. It was a shoddy job but it would suffice until Theodore Dandridge left the office.

He stopped and studied Tanaka Fujinaka who struggled but could not loosen the zip ties that held him to the high backed chair securely.

“You are thinking that I’m crazy, huh?” Dandridge said. Theodore Dandridge brushed Fujinaka’s shoulder and leaned in with a mischievous grin.

“You are the type of person that I never grew up around.” Dandridge paused. Theodore Dandridge looked around the office that overlooked Santa Monica Boulevard.

“I know you and your type Fujinaka. You were pampered in Japan. You probably went to the best schools back there. Coming to the States you had to succeed,” Theodore Dandridge smiled. “A lot of pressure, huh?”

Theodore Dandridge spoke and Tanaka Fujinaka struggled and fought against the zip ties. Theodore Dandridge seemed unconcerned about the struggling.

“Me, I grew up with nothing. I lived with the bare minimum. I have been through all sorts of crap. I slept in mud. I’ve been shot at, stabbed, kidnapped, and nearly killed. The only pressure I’ve ever had has been if I want to live or die." Theodore Dandridge paused. He checked his watch.

“You probably have a house that is worth a couple of million dollars somewhere in the hills, near a celebrity. That stuff don’t mean anything to me. I’m a minimum wage kid. I’m happy to be the muscle for others and beat up on a few rich kids that need to be beaten up."

Dandridge was looking through the items on Fujinaka's desk when he saw a picture of Fujinaka holding a kendo stick. “You do kendo? I have studied that but I’m not impressed. I don’t really see any value in it. I suppose that it doesn’t make sense nowadays. No one I know walks around with a sword. The idea of training in some ancient art that you will very likely never use in your lifetime is over my head."

Theodore Dandridge was searching for something.

“You know what Fujinaka? If the security walked in right now I’d kill you and take my chances. I might get away. I might not. Life is a crapshoot." Theodore Dandridge gathered the various items from the desk.

"The bigger the risk," Dandridge said and paused.

“You probably don’t take too many real risks. You have too much to lose. I bet you have the latest and greatest of everything. You have to. You have to keep up with the competition. All that technology and schooling don’t amount to squat when you come up to deal with someone like me. All the technology won’t help you when I punch you in the nose. You might even know a little martial arts. You might think that matters. It doesn’t. Not when you face someone that has nothing to lose.”

He paused. He closed his eyes. “You see I came here because I needed something you got." Theodore Dandridge studied the man who was watching him with hatred in his eyes. "The world breaks down to two types of people: those that get and those that take. I take, and the worst thing about it is that you can’t do anything about it even though you own this building. It ain’t about the security. It ain’t about the brains. You probably have bigger brains than me but I beat that. I am the berserker with a battle axe in the boardroom. I am the bloodthirsty savage at the office door. I am the drooling killer with a chainsaw in the conference room. I’m the bad man. The fight in me beats everything else.”

Theodore Dandridge looked out the window and at Fujinaka. "What do you want? I see you asking that with your eyes,” Dandridge smirked, a tightening of muscles in his face that he rarely used.

Dandridge grabbed the jump drive and cell phones. He plugged the jump drive in the laptop computer on Fujinaka’s desk and downloaded everything on it before leaving. As he left Teddy Dee knocked the miniature katana and samurai sword off the desk. He considered for a long moment of tipping one of the bonsai trees off of its pedestal but instead gently tapped the bonsai on the right side of the office as he left.

Teddy Dee walked out of Fujinaka’s office.

No one disturbed or checked on Tanaka Fujinaka for thirty minutes. At thirty minutes after the black giant left his assistant entered.

Asami Fujinaka sat and tried to comprehend what she had just watched. A smile spread across her round face. She was surprised at the sound that came from her but it was a laugh. Asami heard herself laugh out loud.

“Jiminy Cricket,” Asami Fujinaka giggled.

Chapter Twenty-Six.

Teddy Dee was in Inglewood when he noticed that two men were ghosting him. Then Teddy Dee noticed that the two men were Asian. So, instantly he knew that this was not a normal ghosting but a possible attack.

Teddy Dee was at Hollywood Park watching the horse racing on satellite with about three or four thousand other horse fanatics. Teddy Dee was at Hollywood Park not to bet but to talk with an executive that was being harassed by some jack weasel named: Scott Evans. Teddy Dee had been asked to meet with Scott Evans and explain to him the foolishness of harassing an executive that had the power to hire men like Teddy Dee. Scott Evans was a gambler and liked the horses. Scott Evans, the two dick wads, and Teddy Dee were all at Hollywood Park the same day.

The Asian dick wads followed Teddy Dee to the third floor of the Hollywood Park horse racing section. Teddy Dee decided to send a definitive message as he reached the third floor of the near empty Hollywood Park horse racing seating area. There were a number of concession stands, but only two were open Teddy Dee noticed. The floor was nearly empty except for the ticket windows in the middle of the floor guarded by armed guards. Scott Evans, Teddy Dee noted, was one floor below and having a good day at the track from what Teddy had seen.

So, Teddy Dee upon reaching the third floor turned around and pushed the door open and into the face of one of the two Asian ghosts. The force of the door against the ghost threw the unexpected dick wad down the stairs followed closely by Teddy Dee. The man, dressed in a black suit, white collared shirt, black tie and polished shoes tried to grab the railing and brace himself as he fell back and down the stairs. Teddy Dee jumped down the stairs and grabbed a hold of the falling man's shirtfront and launched a rocket into the man's suddenly relieved face thinking that he had been saved.

The man took the punch as Teddy Dee grabbed, punched and released him simultaneously. The man crashed down the seventeen steps and slid to a stop on the landing in between the second and third floor. Teddy Dee jumped down the remaining steps and relieved the man of his weapon; a nine-millimeter pistol and his cell phone.

Teddy Dee lifted the unconscious man and placed him so that he looked as if he was sleeping on the stairwell. The whole attack had taken less than two minutes. Teddy Dee climbed back up the stairs to the third floor and sought out the second jack weasel trying to intimidate him or kill him.

On the third floor, Teddy Dee walked from the far end of the third floor to the opposite end looking for the second killer. Teddy Dee had thought that he had lost the second killer when he felt the prick of the hypodermic needle in his arm as the assassin tried to walk past him. The injection had come quite by surprise. The man had been hiding somewhere in the crush of people and Teddy Dee had missed him.

Teddy Dee spun around and took a few steps grabbing the retreating man by his jacket and shoving him into the closest bathroom.

"I need the antidote," Teddy Dee said.

"I don't speak English," the cocky Asian man that looked as if he should have been in a boy band instead of paid assassin smiled and tilted his heart shaped head.

Teddy Dee knew that he did not have much time to stop the toxin coursing through his veins. So, he had to act. Hesitation meant death.

Teddy Dee stepped forward and the man snapped a kick into Teddy Dee's groin. Teddy Dee expertly blocked the kick and grabbed the man's leg and spun and threw him against the bathroom stall with a crash. The action had caught the man off guard. Teddy Dee did not stop. As the man crashed to the tiled floor Teddy Dee fell upon him and beat him savagely on the bathroom floor until he stopped struggling or fighting back. Instantly, Teddy Dee braced the man looking for the injection pen. He found the pen and jabbed it into his thigh. He did not know how long the antidote would take to counteract the toxin. Teddy Dee did not care. He climbed to his feet and found himself face-to-face with an armed guard who had come to the bathroom to investigate the commotion.

"Freeze," the guard said with his gun drawn and aimed at Teddy Dee.

Teddy Dee was climbing to his feet and when he heard the order he stopped.

"What the hell is going on here?"

"This asshole tried to touch me while I was doing my business," Teddy Dee lied. "I gave him a little street justice for his unasked for attention."

The guard looked at the unconscious man on the ground and back to Teddy Dee and back to the man on the floor.

"Now, what happened," the guard said lowering his weapon and scratching his chin.

"Man, I was in here, doing my business, and in walks this faggot and all of a sudden he gets close and touches my ass. I freeze up. What the fuck, I say. Don't you like nasty boys, he says," Teddy Dee lies. The guard holstered his weapon and is listening to the story.

"Fuck, man," the guard said.

"Yeah, can I leave or do you need me to do something," Teddy Dee asked.

"It's cool," the guard said.

"Thanks. You should make people aware that they might get harassed in the bathrooms at Hollywood Park. If I had known that I would have tried to hold it."

Teddy Dee exited the bathroom and headed to the second floor and Scott Evans. He knew that the two dick wads would be fine. They would tell their sides of the story and embellish it so that they looked good in the end. Teddy Dee didn't care. He just wanted the testing to stop.

Then, Teddy Dee stopped himself. He was made of tougher stuff. They could throw all sorts of shit at him and Teddy Dee was supposed to be able to take it. He reminded himself that he was not just a blooder. He was a wolf. He was a hunter. He was a killer.

He had learned his lineage early, while in Chicago. His lesson came not in a classroom but on the street while he walked to the corner store for his mother. He was not twelve then.

"Where you headed, little man?"

"To the store'" Teddy Dee recalled telling the man sitting in a shiny, new Cadillac who everyone knew as Miles.

Miles had driven up in his red and white Cadillac convertible and matched Teddy Dee's slow, young stride on the streets of Garfield Park. Teddy Dee was on an errand for his mother to the corner store. Teddy Dee knew Miles. Everyone in the neighborhood knew Miles. He was a pimp. He drove a new Cadillac convertible and was always with the prettiest women. Miles had lots of money and a short temper. Few tested the pimp in the neighborhood. Even the cops gave Miles a wide berth.

"You going to the store? Cool. You mind doing me a solid and picking me up a pack of smokes while you are in there?"

Teddy Dee had blanched at the idea of buying cigarettes for Miles. He was only seven or eight in his memory. Miles smiled at the confusion that danced on the seven-year-old Teddy Dee's face.

"Don't worry little man. I got you covered. You just go inside and tell them that Miles is outside waiting for a pack of smokes. They know me. They know that I smoke Kools. They are in the blue box. Don't let them try to sell you the green box. Blue box is for me."

Teddy Dee hesitated.

"I see you thinking here little man. That's good. Thinking is a good thing. Now, you thinking that you going to go into that store and get in trouble trying to buy some smokes for me while I'm sitting outside." Miles paused and stopped the Cadillac. He stuck his hand out of the driver's side window. In his hand was a wrinkled five dollar bill. "Take this. If they won't let you buy my smokes you can keep the money. That fair?" Before Teddy Dee could reply Miles added: "If they sell you the smokes I expect my change back."

"I get the five if they don't sell me your smokes in a blue box," Teddy Dee said.

"That's what I said."

"They ain't gonna give me cigarettes," Teddy Dee explained to the man dressed in a green and yellow silk shirt and wearing several gold chains around his neck in his red and white Cadillac.

"Bring me back a pack of Kools?"

Teddy Dee thought about arguing but chose not to a that moment.

"Little man, just tell them that Miles sent you to get him a pack of Kools," the pimp smiled. Teddy Dee was going to complain or refuse but then he saw the golden lion headed pinky ring that seemed to dance on the pimp's small finger. Miles added with a smile, "Tell them I don't want to get out my car."

Teddy Dee hesitated.

"Go on."

"He's not--"

Miles narrowed his eyes and the look froze Teddy and stopped his protest. Miles sitting behind the wheel of his car then and there went from friendly to serious.

"You will learn that this world is filled with two type of people: wolves and sheep, little man. Wolves are wild and dangerous. They are hunters. They kill to live. By their very nature they frighten the sheep. Me, I'm a wolf. I didn't drink anything or do anything to become a wolf. I was born a wolf. They tried to tame me and make me a sheep. That didn't work for me. So, today little man you met a wolf. Meeting a wolf and petting a wolf is two different things. You can pet a sheep. You pet a wolf and you might come back with one less hand. Wolves and sheep," Miles concluded. "Wolves and sheep."

Teddy Dee nodded not understanding what the street hustler was trying to get him to understand at that moment. All he really understood was that Miles wanted a pack of cigarettes. More importantly, he wanted Teddy Dee to go in the store and buy and bring them to him.

"The person in that store is a sheep. He may look like a wolf to you but he's a sheep to me. When he hears my name he will act just like a sheep. If he doesn't you can keep that fiver."

"I keep your money if the man inside won't give me your cigarettes?"

"That's what I said."

Teddy Dee hesitated.

"Go and get my motherfucking cigarettes little nigger," Miles hissed and scaring Teddy Dee.

Teddy Dee ran then walked into the corner liquor store and found himself shaking. Miles, the pimp, had frightened Teddy Dee. At ten years old Teddy Dee knew that men like Miles were no one to test. They were violent and unpredictable men. Teddy Dee had been sent to the store for somethings his mother needed but he decided to get Miles his cigarettes first. Having never bought cigarettes Teddy Dee looked around the store for the packs of cigarettes. When he didn't see them out he walked to the cash register and said: "Hey, I'm supposed to buy some Kools for Miles. He's waiting outside."

The man behind the counter did not even blink when Teddy Dee asked for the cigarettes. The man reached back behind him and pulled out a pack of Kool cigarettes. He placed the cigarettes on the counter.

Teddy Dee reached out for the cigarettes but the man behind the counter pulled the cigarettes back easily.

"That's $1.77 kid," the merchant breathed.

Teddy Dee handed him the five dollars that Miles had given him.

The man behind the counter made change and handed it to Teddy Dee. Teddy Dee took the change and the pack of cigarettes and exited the store. Teddy Dee did not count the change. He simply walked out of the store and to the red and white Cadillac and Miles.

Miles was listening to some music when Teddy Dee approached the car. Miles cut his dark eyes at Teddy Dee as he drew closer to the Cadillac. He smiled and in that smile Teddy Dee felt a bit of comfort. Miles was no longer the mean and threatening Miles that Teddy Dee had seen only minutes before.

Teddy Dee handed Miles the change and the cigarettes. Miles took the money and handed Teddy Dee a dollar for his trouble.

“That’s for you,” Miles said. He unwrapped the cigarettes cellophane and slowly produced a single cigarette from the newly purchased pack. He lit the cigarette and closed his eyes for an instant before talking.

“It’s your money,” Teddy Dee said. Miles looked at Teddy Dee who was still standing on the curb.

"You know little man, I know you must be thinking: Why did this man give me a dollar? Well, the way the world works, little man, is on this system of give and take. You give and someone takes. You take and someone gives." Miles was talking but Teddy Dee didn't understand anything he was saying. Teddy Dee just stood there on the curb holding the dollar that Miles had handed him. "You take me and you. I gave you a job. You took the job. So, I need to pay you for what you did. Give and take. Now, the problems of the world are based on the same system. Give and take. You take these bitches," the pimp gestured to the street. "I give them the chance to make money. They take that chance and fuck it up trying to take my share of that money. So, I have to give them an education of who is the boss in this relationship." Miles paused for dramatic effect. Teddy Dee listened as Miles sat in his car listening to music and teaching street lessons. "Bitches ain't just bitches with tits and a wet spot little man. There are bitches all over the world, men and women, and they all need to be re-educated to the whole who's in charge dynamic. The thing is that bitches are bitches by nature. They don't stop being bitches because they get older or married. A bitch is a bitch is a bitch. If a bitch is a bitch, little man, and they start thinking they ain't a bitch then shit gets out of whack. A bitch needs to know her place. They need re-education. They need it and if they don't get it they get all beside themselves. Shit, I see it everyday. Bitches who ain't re-educated fuck things up for the other bitches and all hell breaks loose." Miles was a pimp philosopher. "The worse thing you can do is let a bitch think that she is running shit. Half the problems we are having in this world come from bitches doing shit they ain't got no right to be doing."

"Bitches," Teddy Dee said wanting to say the word at least once in front of Miles.

"Now, little man, don't let your mouth get you in shit your ass cannot handle," Miles pointed out. "You ain't Miles and Miles ain't you. Know that. I can say all types of shit that your little ass would be beat down for. Be aware of your limits, little man."

Teddy Dee nodded.

"Classes over. Now, go and get your narrow ass home."

Miles drove away from the liquor store and left Teddy Dee there on the curb with a dollar for getting the pimp a pack of cigarette.

She could not help but smile at that experience. She had learned so much in such a short time. Asami Fujinaka thought of what Mister Masamoto had told her when she was still trying to be a teen.

"Everything you want is on the other side of fear."

Everything that Asami ever wanted was always found on the other side of fear. It was so true that Asami Fujinaka wanted to hug Mister Masamoto every time she saw him for his invaluable lesson. His words had redirected her trajectory when her father had denied her entry into the family business.

At the edge of the deck she could hear the koi. They were always near when she was on the deck. Asami smiled at the simplicity of the koi.

From the left Asami noted one of the inner doors open and her father, Hiro Fujinaka IV, step out of his study. He was dressed in a business suit, collared shirt and tie. He made his way to his daughter sitting near the koi pond. He smiled. He always found Asami near the koi pond when the caretaker showed up. Asami seemed to gravitate toward the workers for some reason.

The father of the Fujinaka clan watched his daughter, that morning, sitting and entranced by the koi as she sat beside the great koi pond.

Chapter Twenty-Seven.

Teddy Dee had to go downtown for his final Rupert Williams meeting and could not imagine that anyone would attack him in the center of downtown with so many police and law enforcement officers traipsing back and forth in the highly populated downtown. So, he dressed and caught the Metro downtown. He checked in with Rupert Williams and as he left found his "Spidey" senses tingling.

A dark haired man dressed in a gray suit was walking toward Teddy Dee. On his left was another dark haired man wearing a dark blue suit, carrying a leather valise. The man, as far as Teddy Dee could ascertain, had come from one of the buildings to the right but Teddy Dee could not be sure. The man in the gray suit was moving quickly toward Teddy Dee. The other man was slowing and crossing the street. They seemed to smell of professionalism to Teddy Dee. Professional killers? Teddy Dee was impressed.

Downtown Los Angeles was a weird place, Teddy Dee thought as he surveyed the area that he would have to fight. He had just walked past Angel City Brewing and was making his way to the Tristan Eaton mural on Traction Avenue when he had to double back toward Little Tokyo. Teddy Dee figured that in Little Tokyo he might stand a fighter's chance against the two killers tracking him.

Teddy Dee cut across Rose Street and headed quickly to East Second Street and behind him the two killers separated and took either side of the street as they followed. Teddy Dee walked up the seemingly deserted street and at the first intersection turned left and back onto East Second Street. Teddy Dee crossed Alameda Street and South Central Street trying not to look back as one of the killers tried to get ahead of him. At Azusa Street Teddy Dee turned right and into the small streets of Little Tokyo. He wanted to use the tightness of the small streets to limit the attacks that he expected to come at any moment.

The Japanese Village Plaza became the battleground. Teddy Dee stepped into the mall entrance and waited for the two men to pass. Like in a horror movie, Teddy Dee slipped out of eyesight just long enough to reach out and grab the second killer and slam him headfirst into a pillar. The intensity of the violence and surprise attack allowed Teddy Dee to pull his pistol, cell phone, and wallet. The attack had taken seconds. He placed the unconscious killer on a bench near the storefront of Kula Revolving Sushi Bar. Teddy Dee followed behind the lead killer. The lead killer turned around and noticed that instead of his fellow killer he saw Teddy Dee. The killer instinctively reached for his gun but did not complete the action as tourists milled around the Japanese Village Plaza.

Teddy Dee turned and the assassin followed. Teddy Dee cut through the Japanese Village Plaza and made his way toward the Shabu-Shabu House. The tourists and shoppers moved through the Japanese Village Plaza unaware of what was about to happen. The families, the children, the grandparents smiled and took pictures and went to eat as the Japanese killer made his move in front of Mikawaya Mochi Ice Cream.

The attack was simple and direct. The assassin stepped in front of the family of tourists that were all wearing T-shirts that read: Kansas City Royals. The man was wearing a dark blue suit, white collared shirt, and blue tie. The small courtyard seemed to freeze as the two men eyed one another.

Teddy Dee checked his surroundings as the killer circled. The killer moved cautiously to his left, with his hands slowly and methodically moving into a crane pose. His feet were positioned to offer him the greatest balance as he moved closer to Teddy Dee.

"So, who sent you?"

The assassin did not speak but watched Teddy Dee as he drew closer to the scarred giant. When the assassin was just out of reach of Teddy Dee he paused and measured Teddy Dee one last time. Teddy Dee was six foot four inches tall and two hundred and twenty-five pounds of street toughened beef. If there was fat on him, it was only the essential fat needed to power him if the weather changed. Teddy Dee was formidable. He was built for inflicting and taking damage.

The hired killer, on the other hand, gave up at least a foot to the giant. Unlike Teddy Dee the assassin was built for speed and quickness. He did not seem to be afraid of the drastic differences between Teddy Dee and himself.

As a result, it only made sense that the assassin attacked Teddy Dee in front of Mikawaya Mochi Ice Cream and forced the tourists and families to scatter for safety. The smaller man had literally sprung into the air and kicked expertly at Teddy Dee. Teddy Dee, seeing the man hurtling toward him, dodged the first attack and moved from in front of the ice cream shop to the far side of the courtyard. Teddy Dee pressed against the Mitsuru Cafe front window and prepared for the second attack from the killer.

He did not have to wait long. The assassin landed and ran headlong toward Teddy Dee. Instantly, Teddy Dee observed, the assassin had a length of wooden stick in his right hand. Teddy Dee moved to the right and away from the cafe as the attacker had to adjust his attack and slow to correct his trajectory.

Teddy Dee snapped off a piece of bamboo in front of Mitsuru Cafe and used the bamboo to protect himself against the attack of the killer with the wooden stick. The wooden stick was a lethal weapon used in the right hands. The assassin was vicious with the stick slashing and hitting Teddy Dee about the thighs, forearms, and shoulder. Teddy Dee used the bamboo to fend off most of the wooden stick attack.

Teddy Dee knew that the assassin was skilled and dangerous. So, if he was to survive this attack he had to disarm the killer as quickly as possible and use his size and power to his advantage.

The assassin knew that the advantage that he had would be nullified if Teddy Dee was able to disarm or get close enough to make it a fight in a phone booth. So, the killer kept away from Teddy Dee.

"We don't have a lot of time here, Bruce," Teddy Dee pointed out. "The police are on their way and you get to Kung Fu your way out of a hail of bullets. Me, I just get to fade into the shadows if you can't close this deal."

The assassin listened but did not respond. He simply attacked again with the wooden stick that he used as a baton to try and bash in Teddy Dee's brains. Teddy Dee had weathered rougher storms before and as the assassin became bolder and bolder thinking that he was winning Teddy Dee sprung upon the smaller man. The assassin was lightning fast and powerful. He used his feet and kicks to keep Teddy Dee at arm's reach.

Teddy Dee noted that the killer was like a swarm of gnats that you swung at and they scattered only to form up again to harass and annoy in another location. The killer was looking for ways to break down Teddy Dee's defenses. Teddy Dee had twice blocked attacks to his eyes and groin. The assassin had changed his strategy and was now concentrating on Teddy Dee's knees and throat.

Teddy Dee allowed the killer to get closer pretending to tire and be slower than he actually was. The killer was cautious. The killer was wary. Yet, he had stepped forward and into Teddy Dee's trap. Teddy Dee knew that as soon as the smaller killer got within arm's reach all his speed and quickness would suddenly no longer be an advantage.

So, when Teddy Dee got ahold of the assassin's left arm the battle scarred giant smiled through a busted lip. The killer had attempted to throw a punch that Teddy Dee simply slipped under. Controlling the killer's hands stopped 50% of the attacks against Teddy Dee.

"This is where you lose," Teddy Dee spat.

He head-butt the smaller man and stunned him for an instant. The first thing that Teddy Dee did, after the head butt, was twist the wooden stick out of the man's hand so violently that he was sure that he had broken the killer's wrist. The wooden stick had pin wheeled through the air and clattered on the courtyard pavers loudly.

Teddy Dee then, up close and holding the killer, systematically dismantled the smaller man, starting at his elbows. He had thought to ask the man questions but knew that he would not answer Teddy Dee. So, Teddy Dee crushed every joint and muscle as he moved from the elbows to the killer's shoulders and then with six bone crushing punches to the ribs. He knew that those punches had left the assassin harmless and on the verge of death. The killer wheezed loudly for air as Teddy Dee stood up and walked away from the unmoving body lying near the Nijiya Market.

Security guards were gathering and rushing toward the commotion but when they arrived they only found the still and broken body of the nameless killer. Teddy Dee had exited the Japanese Village Plaza and was back on Second Avenue.

Asami Fujinaka had read about a deadly fight at Nijiya Market in Los Angeles, California that left a man dead near a popular restaurant. She read the news report and marveled at the scarcity of detail. Asami Fujinaka wanted more details. She read the article again and noted that the fight had been in the main court of one of the numerous food courts in the Japanese Nijiya Market.

After an hour of searching she pulled up a grainy video of the last five minutes of the fight between a black man and an Asian with a wooden stick. The Asian was much smaller but unafraid. He was the aggressor. The video came from the Mitsuru Café.

The giant black man snapped off a piece of bamboo in front of Mitsuru Café and used the bamboo to protect himself against the attack of the Asian with the wooden stick. The assassin was vicious with the stick slashing and hitting the black slower man about the thighs, forearms, and shoulder. The black man used the bamboo to fend off most of the wooden stick attack.

There was a low and garbled audio on the video. Asami Fujinaka played the video again and again to decipher the words of the black man. She smiled at the cockiness of the bigger and slower man who was being hit over and over again by the faster man.

"We don't have a lot of time here, Bruce," the black man said in a grumble. "The police are on their way and you get to Kung Fu your way out of a hail of bullets. Me, I just get to fade into the shadows if you can't close this deal."

The assassin listened but did not respond. He simply attacked again with the wooden stick that he used as a baton to try and bash in the black man's brains. The assassin was lightning fast and powerful. He used his feet and kicks to keep the black man at arm's reach.

Asami watched as the killer seemed to be looking for ways to break down the giant's defenses.

The black man allowed the killer to get closer pretending to tire and be slower than he actually was, Asami noted. The killer was cautious. The killer was wary. Yet, he had stepped forward and into the black man's trap.

When the black man got ahold of the assassin's left arm the battle scarred giant smiled through a busted lip. The killer had attempted to throw a punch that black man simply slipped under.

"This is where you lose," the black man spat.

He head-butted the smaller man and stunned him for an instant. The first thing that the black man did, after the head butt, was twist the wooden stick out of the man's hand so violently that he was sure that he had broken the killer's wrist. The wooden stick had pin wheeled through the air and clattered on the courtyard pavers loudly.

The black man then, up close and holding the killer, systematically dismantled the smaller man, starting at his elbows. Asami Fujinaka recoiled as the video documented the methodic destruction of the smaller man that had attacked the black man with a stick. The black man crushed every joint and muscle as he moved from the elbows to the killer's shoulders and then with six bone crushing punches to the ribs. He knew that those punches had left the assassin harmless and on the verge of death. The killer wheezed loudly for air as the black man stood up and walked away from the unmoving body lying near the Nijiya Market.

"Gotdamnit," Asami Fujinaka breathed and smiled.

Chapter Twenty-Eight.

"You know that there is not a bunch of options, as far as I can see, Mister Dandridge," Eric Robinson said. He was sitting in the Beverly Hills Hotel bar. There were maybe a dozen people in the airy and bright restaurant.

Teddy Dee listened as he sipped at his strawberry lemonade and watched the rich and famous walking around the Beverly Hills Hotel. A big bodybuilder with a bald head and dressed in a sports coat and polo shirt was suddenly gathering a lot of attention near the pool. Three women, dressed in nearly nothing, broke toward the cameras and gathering crowd. Teddy Dee watched them and Eric Robinson without any real expression.

"Mister Dandridge, thought you would be upset?"

"I suppose that I expected the news sometime ago."

"But you know what that means?"

Teddy Dee did not respond.

"I feel bad," the sixteen-year-old admitted.

Teddy Dee smiled. He reached out and placed a scarred hand on Eric Robinson's shoulder.

"You did your best," Teddy Dee said.

"I know, but I— "

"It was an impossible situation. I just hoped that with new eyes you or someone might have figured out a way out."

"I tried."

"I know."

"There is no way to get out of—" Eric Robinson stopped, suddenly.

"That's okay," Teddy Dee smiled.

"You know your black knight, by himself, is doomed. There are too many enemies for him, you, to fight."

Teddy Dee listened.

"If you had someone to watch your back you, I mean the black knight, would have a better chance of survival." Eric Robinson paused. "I am not saying that with one more person your odds are significantly higher but they are not abysmal, like they are now."

"Thanks Eric," Teddy Dee concluded. Teddy Dee left the Beverly Hills Hotel and tried to think of who he could ask to risk their lives on a trip to Japan. The list was short. The first person that he called was Elijah Graham.

Elijah Graham and Teddy Dee met in fourth grade. Teddy Dee had been a quiet and calculating kid, who seemed to know all the answers that the teacher asked. He dressed like a painter back then. Teddy Dee wore painter pants everyday. He usually wore a polo shirt and gym shoes with his various colored painter pants.

Elijah, unlike Teddy Dee, dressed like a street thug. He always wore a too big white T-shirt, baggy jeans, and Nike gym shoes.

The two had become friends when they met a boy named: Ryan. Ryan was a thin kid with curly hair and caramel skin. He was a pretty boy.

Neither Teddy nor Elijah liked Ryan. He was a pretty boy. Ryan thought that he was a fourth grade playboy. In fourth grade Ryan decided that he would go after the prettiest girl in school; Rosa Ayala. It didn't help that she was Spanish.

Ryan had been nice to Teddy and Elijah and they had not been aware that Ryan was using them. He had recruited them because they were the biggest fourth graders in the school.

A few days after meeting Ryan the caramel skinned boy had come to them and asked for help.

"Need you to have my back," Ryan had said at lunch. Teddy Dee was sipping his fruit punch juice box. Elijah had been eating an apple.

"What does that mean?"

"It means that if someone comes around and starts trouble you will step in and help me out'" Ryan spat back at Elijah.

The black giant had furrowed his brow for an instant and twisted his lips on his nut brown face, puckering his thick brown lips.

"Don't play with me," Ryan said focusing on Elijah.

"Why someone coming around to hurt you, Ryan?"

Ryan spun around to Teddy Dee.

Ryan was a handsome caramel skinned kid with hazel eyes and curly black hair. He looked slightly Asian, Teddy Dee calculated. Maybe he was part Asian? Ryan was dressed in a strange mix of blue jeans and a collared shirt. Ryan smiled showing a single dimple in his left cheek.. "You guys remember Rosa?" He continued before either Teddy or Elijah could say a word. "Well, I talked to her. We were cool. She seemed cool. Then she went bad when I wanted a kiss." Ryan shook his head. "She screamed at me and said that I was trying to force her to do things that she didn't want to do."

Elijah Graham furrowed his brow, thinking. He stared at Ryan for a long time without words. Then he looked at Teddy Dee silently.

Teddy Dee narrowed his dark eyes and studied Ryan and Elijah as if narrowing his eyes would reveal something he had missed. There had to be something that Teddy Dee had missed. How had Ryan's problem become his problem?

"You my boys," Ryan smiled.

"All right man but remember you owe us,," Elijah Graham stated.

Two days later an eighth grader named: Jose had talked to Ryan and threatened to kill him if he tried to disrespect his sister again. That was the whole Rosa Ayala saga.

Those were gentler, kinder,, more innocent times. Elijah and Teddy had grown older and remained the biggest seventh and eighth graders. Elijah was recruited to Gramercy High School for football and basketball. Teddy Dee was recruited to Jefferson for track.

Elijah went to Gramercy and for four games Gramercy found the Freshmen linebacker phenomenon named: Graham shutting down all the offenses they faced. The coach decided one game to allow Elijah the chance to carry the ball. He was big and powerful and fast.

Elijah Graham was a fifteen-year-old Hershel Walker. He was a man trapped in a boy's body playing against children. Elijah Graham got the ball once on the ten-yard line and it was a simple dive up the middle. Elijah had dived up the middle and when he saw the hole close before he could get there he bounced out and to the right, toward his bench.

His coach screamed at him like he had stolen something. A linebacker was on his heels. A lineman dove at him and Graham had fired out his free hand to knock him off balance. Graham kept running East toward his coach. Outside of containment, Elijah cut up field like he had seen someone he hadn't seen in years. There were five people that could stop him and ninety yards to cover. Elijah Graham didn't run up the sideline like everyone else. He wanted to punish the players on the field.

So, he tore across the field daring the five defenders to stop his march to the goal line. Elijah Graham was an unstoppable force. The only players that had any chance of stopping him were the defensive backs. The linebackers had given up the chase. They were following but they seemed to be moving in slow motion.

Graham ran over a defensive back that tried to arm tackle him mid-field. A back on the far sideline was zeroing in on him and Graham knew that he could outrun him effortlessly but slowed just enough to test himself. The back ran at full speed only to bounce off Elijah Graham.

Elijah Graham had one of the greatest runs recorded at Gramercy High School. He laughed at the idea. He was a linebacker who the coach thought might be able to score touchdowns. Nothing more.

Graham played one more game and then the ugly truth reared its head. Elijah hated school. Well, he hated classes. His grades made him unable to play football. He got tutoring. His grades improved but not by very much. Elijah was not interested in school. After his Freshmen year found it hard to stay in classes. He was still the biggest ninth grader but failing everything. Elijah's chance to shine on the basketball court never occurred his Freshmen year.

The beginning of their tenth grade year Teddy Dee transferred to Gramercy. Once again they, Elijah and Teddy Dee were the biggest tenth graders. Teddy Dee was the brighter of the two. He paid attention in class. He also liked learning. The novelty of new information fascinated Teddy Dee.

"Teddy I don't think that I'm going to make it."

"What?"

"School. It just doesn't make sense to me."

"What about the girls?" Teddy Dee smiled trying to make light of the seriousness of Elijah leaving school and leaving him there to suffer another year without him.

Elijah had not smiled. Teddy Dee knew that Elijah was serious.

"Man, if you leave I'll have to suck it up and be the big dog all by myself."'

Elijah paused, thinking. He hadn't thought about what his leaving would do to the school dynamic of Teddy Dee and himself. Leaving Teddy Dee would become a target of the guppies trying to be piranhas. Teddy Dee would have a year to remember without Elijah.

"I hear you, man. I can't cut it. This has been hard for me. School just isn't working for me." He paused and then added,, "I may not be around after this year," Elijah admitted standing near the fence of the football field. The sky was slate gray, Teddy Dee recalled and there was a threat of rain in the air. Teddy Dee had not spoken and Elijah had filled the silence between them.

"I mean it man," Elijah had said in his unhurried, direct way. Teddy Dee had heard that tone before. It meant business.

"How you going to do that? You ain't eighteen yet," Teddy Dee pointed out.

"Three months, man," Elijah noted.

Like clockwork, three months later Elijah had dropped out. He had stayed in contact for awhile and then fallen off the earth. Teddy Dee heard that Elijah was trying his hand as a drug dealer. That wouldn't last long. Elijah was a blunt tool. He had no people skills.

Being a drug dealer was all about dealing with people.

Teddy Dee ran into Elijah at a party once and the pair talked for an hour. Elijah had become street tough. He was a knockout champion. Elijah had gained that title after a short stint as a drug dealer.

"I don't have the patience to be a drug dealer," Elijah explained at the party with a beer in his hand. He was wearing a hooded sweatshirt that was three times too large. The newest Air Jordan's were on his feet. He was wearing three hundred dollar jeans that night.

"Yeah, I couldn't see that working out."

Elijah laughed and continued with his story.

"This brute from the Disciples tried to rob me one night. He got away and for some reason I decided to hunt him down and teach him a lesson in respect."

Teddy Dee shook his head. He knew where the story was headed.

"Well, I find him in the back yard of a friend of his and there are four or five of his friends there when I show up."

"Oh, shit," Teddy Dee hissed.

"Yeah, shit could have gotten real cowboy all of a sudden but two of my boys were there sort of as my backup. So, no one touched steel."

"Damn," Teddy Dee whistled.

"Well, the story ain't over. Like I said I was there to teach that big, black motherfucker a lesson and that was what I told him." He smiled at the memory. "I told the four or five to step back and let me and dickhead handle our business."

"They pulled up lawn chairs and let us have a back yard brawl.

"The big, black motherfucker had a reputation for being a street fighter. I didn't know that. I didn't care. It was just me against him. We were about to knuckle up, real gladiator style."

Teddy Dee realized that he had heard about the fight between a Disciple in a back yard off Kedzie, near the old Brach's Candy Factory. There was supposed to be a video of the fight online. That fight was supposed to be one of the fiercest ever captured between two street fighters.

"I caught him slipping, when he hit me in the mouth and made me bite my tongue. I was spitting blood and he thought that he could showboat for his friends." Elijah narrowed his eyes. "The taste of blood does strange things to people. For some it frightens them and paralyzes them. For others it just makes them slink away. For me, it made me want to rip off that motherfucker's head."

Elijah had reached out and grabbed a handful of the black motherfucker's shirt and spit a mouthful of blood on his Chuck Taylor's. Simultaneously, he had launched a rocket from China or parts South to catch the black motherfucker square on the chin, lifting him off the ground and into the air.

Everyone in the backyard had screamed at the superhuman feat of strength. When the black motherfucker hit the ground the fight was over. The black motherfucker had a broken jaw from that one punch.

Elijah had stopped being a drug dealer and become a street fighter and enforcer for a short time.

When Teddy Dee left school Elijah was still on the streets trying to beat the brains out of anyone that dared to offer him money to fight.
Teddy Dee went into the Army.

Teddy Dee had come back from Germany and run into Oscar Easton, an old friend that knew his family. Easton was always busy. He was a classy guy. Teddy Dee liked Oscar Easton's style. Teddy Dee liked that Oscar Easton never seemed to talk too much to anyone. Yet, when he spoke he seemed to unleash all the knowledge that he had, His knowledge and understanding of the shadowy world of corporate lies, human behavior, deception, body language, as well as the reason that he had outlasted so many others and was considered a dinosaur in an industry that seemed to focus more and more on youth was imparted to only Teddy Dee.

Elijah Graham had tried his hand at street enforcement and nearly been killed when he beat up a couple of gangsters that tried to rob someone he was tasked to protect. The gangsters had crawled back to their holes and gathered strength and courage with a car full of guns and drugs and tried to level a corner where Elijah had been standing. Elijah had been shot a number of times in his life and being shot was nothing new. Yet when the gangsters tried to kill him they had killed two twin infants, not yet six years old, and that had infuriated Elijah. He knew he had no control over the violence that was aimed at him but it disturbed him that the violence had spilled over to innocents.

He had decided to work for people that he could protect. Elijah was going to be a bodyguard. At six foot four inches tall and nearly 250 pounds Elijah Graham was impressive. He had, for a long season believed that he would go to college and play football. That dream evaporated and reality folded in upon him when he became ineligible to play football his senior year in high school.

Of all the people that Teddy Dee considered there was only one that he contacted. The call was short. The call was mostly Teddy Dee speaking.

"E, need a little help," Teddy Dee had begun.

Elijah had not spoken.

"You up for a trip to Japan?"

Silence.

"You got a passport?"

Elijah grunted.

"We'll be leaving in a couple of days."

"Hit me."

"Cool."

 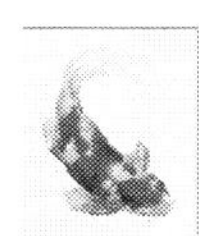 

Asami Fujinaka never saw herself as a trendsetter. She was awkward and uncomfortable with her own self. She could not have ever imagined that nearly two million people religiously paid attention to what she wrote, thought and posted. The idea was a bit overwhelming.

She was an artist with a business mind and her art reflected her steely eyed competitive personality that did not believe in coming in second. She was a social commentator and her art mirrored that social judgment. Her art was in your face and quirky and sometimes over the top but at all times honest and genuine.

Japan's culture was pulled backwards to preserve the past while simultaneously being pulled forward to the ever burgeoning future and the continual need for innovation.

This schizophrenia was seen in one of Asami's paintings entitled: Neo-Samurai. Her latest photo commentary was entitled: Prince(ss). There were a dozen pictures of brothers and sisters from some of the most powerful families dressed similarly and blown up and plastered on the sides of several downtown buildings. The art was a condemnation of the male-dominated patriarchal driven chauvinism of an outdated mechanism that promoted male heirs over female heirs. The dozen pictures had captions placed beneath that exposed all the crimes and foibles committed by the male heirs of these influential families.

Asami Fujinaka, by a trick of fate, was not the heir to the riches of her family because she had been born the only daughter of one of Japan's largest herbal companies; Signet Industries. Her brother, Tanaka Fujinaka, was next in line for leadership of Signet Industries despite Asami's richer experiences in business.

So, she had come up with a plan. She came up with a blog. That blog, "Asami's Kooky and Spooky Insights from the Nausicaa Valley" gave her a platform and voice and that platform and voice gave her plan legs. Her blog was far reaching. Millions of eyes read the blog posts.

Chapter Twenty-Nine.

Teddy Dee was willing to do what others were not willing to do. He was a corporate button man. If someone had to be slapped about a bit, then Teddy Dee received the phone call. If someone needed to be intimidated, then Teddy got paid. If someone had to end up unable to walk without a cane, then so be it. It, slapping around those that were dragging their feet, was the dark part of the business deal and his services were a part of the cost of business.

Teddy Dee and the blooders were professional accident makers. People died everyday. Blooders zapped people when there was no other way. Death, in the corporations, was not always the quickest and easiest way to solve problems. Sometimes, the death of an executive caused worse problems.

The way the blooders and Teddy Dee saw it, death was used only as a last resort and only if the executives green lighted it. Blooders were not paid killers. Some killed. Some did not. Teddy Dee liked to say that knowing that most blooders were hired to intimidate and if things went south to do whatever was needed to insure that the corporation succeeded.

Executives, just like "normals," died. The head of corporations and CFOs and board members were no better than the average Joe in Teddy Dee's dealings. People died in his line of work for one of two reasons; either it was because the person in question was a liability or a negative for the business. Teddy Dee didn't spend much time deciding right or wrong. That was an issue that didn't concern him. He was an artisan. He was a craftsman.

In South Central, there was violence but none of it was aimed at Teddy Dee. Thankfully, at six foot two inches tall and weighing two hundred and twenty pounds and scarred from head to toe, few looked at Teddy Dee as an easy target. There were definitely others to consider compared to Teddy Dee.

So, he walked around the Leimert Park area and enjoyed the quiet of the night. The little neighborhood within the hustle and bustle of South Central was surprisingly like Oak Park in Illinois. The tree lined streets gave Teddy Dee a comfort that he had not felt in a long time. The houses and steps and porches in front of them reminded Teddy Dee of the Shaker homes he had longed to live in when he was growing up, so long ago.

Teddy Dee had found himself recalling thoughts of squares, like him, when he first returned to Los Angeles, and toying with trying to walk away from the world of shadows and trying to have a normal life. Yet, Teddy Dee knew that he was too deep in the shadow world to return to the square life unscathed.

The shadow world and the corporations that the shadow world protected was a black hole of endless power plays, double dealings, misdirection and arm twisting to protect and extend the corporate footprint of the most unscrupulous companies. Those same corporations relied on the shadow world players to keep their backdoor dealings hidden. It was those secrets, that caused the corporations to be paranoid. The corporations did not trust anyone; especially blooders.

That shadow world that protected the old and new money of established and new Fortune 500 companies would not and could not allow Teddy Dee, or any blooder, to step away from the dark world of lies, betrayals, strong arm tactics and worse. The shadow world was built on the idea that they existed but no one knew they existed. Blooders, who found themselves knee deep in the blood of corporations, were always considered liabilities. They, the blooders, knew too much to walk away and possibly spill the secrets that had built the very corporations on the backs of others.

Some blooders stepped over the boundaries and were known to have snapped the lifelines of some. Teddy Dee, initially, tried to think that he was not a killer. He had broken arms, legs, fingers, strangled, intimidated and never killed anyone in the first three years in the shadows. He had nearly killed more times than he liked to admit in those first three years, but that was a part of his job. Killing was not what he did until it was required.

The higher ups worried about moral questions. All that Teddy Dee knew was that the asset called him and gave him an assignment. If the person needed to be threatened, beaten up, injured, or silenced Teddy Dee was more than capable of achieving the desired outcomes.

“Mister Dandridge, I need to know you can finish this operation,” Arthur Reeves said from behind his desk. He was sitting there, the second in command in the office building of the man that owned the building and needed a problem to permanently disappear.

It took 1,551 days in the shadows before Teddy Dee had learned that there were no limits to the depths that he was willing to sink to get a job done. On the 1,551th day Teddy Dee had gone to the golf course where Nelson Christopher Fordham, a vice president of a company that was a competitor for a fashion shoe company was playing with three others. Teddy

Dee had waited for two hours for the vice president to finish his golf game. Nelson Christopher Fordham had headed home and before he could get to his palatial home was cut off at the corner.

Teddy Dee jumped out of the car and apologized. Nelson Christopher Fordham jumped out of his car, a hot head. He was a bigger man. Teddy Dee had feigned an apology and that seemed to enrage the beer bellied vice president.

"I didn't move here to have to deal with your kind," Nelson Christopher Fordham hissed.

Teddy Dee pulled out his silenced Glock 26 and fired one shot to end the vice president. To make it look sloppy and amateur Teddy Dee dropped four more shots on the scene of the dead Nelson Christopher Fordham. He put two in the car door and two more in the vice president's chest and arm. The job was supposed to look like a robbery gone bad. Teddy Dee made sure that the killing was not to seen as anything but a robbery gone bad.

To insure the robbery attempt Teddy Dee had taken the watch, phone and wallet and drove away. When he called the police he anonymously reported that he had heard shooting near Nelson Christopher Fordham's home. He waited until the police arrived before he drove away. He hoped that the police would find Nelson Christopher Fordham and figure that it was a robbery gone bad. Another senseless act of violence.

He had foolishly thought that there were lines that he would not cross. Teddy Dee had tried to say that he would never kill someone for money. Then he killed someone for money. He then said that he would only kill those that were bad. He had crossed that line as well.

Teddy Dee wanted to believe that he was a good guy. Teddy Dee wanted to believe that he was doing good for the world in his own little way. He knew that he was lying to himself. Initially, it was the only way to sleep after getting blood on his hands. He had deluded himself back then. He had believed that he had morals and a point where he would stop. He realized that all that was a lie.

Yet, he wasn't a monster. Teddy Dee had aspirations. He was going to make a bunch of money and get out of this crazy life. Or, he was going to die trying.

Teddy Dee wasn't a rabid dog. He didn't go around killing people just because they annoyed him. He had morals. He was not a murdering savage. Teddy Dee reassured himself that he wasn't a homicidal maniac.

Everything he did was based on logical progressions. He worked within the parameters of the corporate world. Assets and liabilities determined Teddy

Dee's actions. He was handed a contract and asked to complete the contract to the letter. Teddy Dee once he accepted the contract was obligated to fulfill the contract no matter how abhorrent.

Teddy Dee had scruples. He had to have scruples, Teddy Dee told himself. Otherwise he was no better than the gangsters running up and down the blocks shooting out of a moving car with AK-47s.

He was better than the gangsters. He had to be. If he wasn't....

Teddy Dee, the night before his longest air flight, sat on a bench near a school and tried to again try to figure out what he was heading toward with his longtime friend; Elijah Graham. He was taking on the last dragon that threatened to destroy his life and those of people that he cared about. The battle was inevitable.

That night Teddy Dee climbed aboard the United Airlines plane, ahead of Elijah Graham, thinking that the trip was the only way to end the attacks. It, the trip, had been suggested by Eric Robinson and the anonymous leaker. Eric Robinson had been his sixteen-year-old pragmatic self when he suggested: "If you go you will be on unfriendly territory from the moment you arrive until the moment you leave. You can't slack. You can't lag. This is an all in kind of proposition. You come home with your shield or on it."

The other suggestion had come from the anonymous leaker that preferred to be called: Nausicaa. Nausicaa had suggested that the solution for all the attacks were going to be found in Japan. The messages, more than sixty, had all come through a video game website named: IGN. The recommendation came with the subject line: Japanese Condoms. Teddy Dee wanted to smile at the playfulness of the unknown author.

Bon voyage. Can't wait until you get here. Six movies to watch on the flight: 1) Blade 2) Creed 3) Road to Perdition 4) Old Boy 5) Rocky 6) Aliens 2. Get the juices flowing. Get pumped.

--Nausicaa.

An eighteen-hour flight to Tokyo and Teddy Dee was restless. He thought about the six movies that Nausicaa had suggested. After an hour he watched one of the films. It was interesting.

After the boxing movie Teddy Dee took a moment to think about what he and Elijah were heading toward. They did not speak the language. The odds were against them. They were going to be on unfamiliar ground. They were also going to be outnumbered. They had no allies.

"Damn," Teddy Dee breathed.

Elijah Graham sat next to Teddy Dee but did not move. He was sleeping like a three-hundred-pound baby rhinoceros. Teddy Dee shook his head.

Well, Teddy Dee paused and realized that he could name a handful of people in the shadows that he could rely on in a pinch. Of course, his pinch was different than most people. A pinch for most might be a loan or gift of money in a tight situation. For Teddy Dee a pinch was always based on a tight situation but it might mean hundreds of thousands of dollars, a flight on a private jet, access to firearms, entry into a secure facility, or the turning of a blind eye on some questionable activities perpetrated in an unfriendly country.

He tried to recall the handful of people that he could call upon. There was Roland Cambridge. Cambridge was a rich kid that worked in pharmaceuticals and someone that Teddy Dee might call on in a pinch. Carl Fisher was another big wig who relied on Teddy Dee. Michael Prescott ran one of the biggest trucking firms in the USA and Teddy Dee had been to his home on several occasions. Prescott tried to hand Teddy Dee his sister-in-law. The idea still made Teddy Dee smile.

Violet Reese was the CFO of one of the most powerful real estate firms in Las Vegas and she seemed to have a crush on Teddy Dee. André Finch was one of the richest people that Teddy knew. He had a Malibu beach house yet lived in Northern California. Finch was a seemingly unassuming individual until you saw his home and the way he lived. He owned a helicopter and knew how to fly it. Finch was a jokester and someone that Teddy could call on if he needed corporate help.

The exercise widened to include other nations and places where Teddy Dee had stayed longer than six months. In twenty years of being the trash man of the corporate world he smiled at the fact that he traveled all the time but only had stayed in six countries more than six months.

In Egypt, he immediately thought of the Tower of Cairo and the expansive view of the wondrous city and the Great Pyramid of Giza and the Mogaattam Hills on the far valley laid out below the great tower and Amir. Amir Rashad was a powerful investor who had run into trouble when trying to introduce Titan Machinery to the Egyptians as a possible venture capital investment. Amir Rashad had needed his help in negotiating with some stubborn industrialists. Six months Teddy Dee had been in Cairo taking in the wonders of the world. Needless to say, Teddy Dee helped break the logjam that occurred in the final negotiations.

In France, there was Ingrid Beauvois. Beauvois was the daughter of a newspaper magnate who imagined herself France's "It" girl. She had been in one scandal after another but it was the scandal of her younger sister, Claudia, that had brought Teddy Dee to Paris. Claudia Beauvois, only 17, had been linked to a murder in a club in Paris. Teddy Dee had been asked to prove that

Claudia was not at the party despite the overwhelming evidence and video that suggested that she was there.

In Spain, Teddy Dee had become close to a gruff head of corporation of one of Spain's Telecommunication companies. In a peripheral matter that had nothing to do with the head of corporation or the Telecommunication company Ferdinand Estevial had found himself in a battle over bull semen. Ferdinand Estevial owned a prize bull and his semen was extremely valuable. Yet, somehow, with all the safeguards in place, his prize bull had two dozen samples stolen from the laboratories taxed to keep the samples safe by someone and sold in the black-market bull semen exchange for hundreds of thousands of euros. Teddy Dee was not a cowboy by any stretch of the imagination. He didn't even watch cowboy movies. Yet, he was able to find the thieves and retrieve half a dozen samples that the thieves did not sell or destroy.

In England, Teddy Dee had found himself working with a Charles Bellingham. Bellingham was the director of one of England's largest hospitals. He was in charge of several hospitals and one in particular had become a problem; Overhill. Teddy Dee had been asked to help the COO of Overhill retire. It was an easy process for Teddy Dee. He had shown up at the COO's home and told him that it was in his best interest not to return to Overhill. Teddy Dee never understood why negotiations were not done more often at gunpoint?

In Hong Kong, Teddy Dee had gone for a week and stayed nearly a year. Teddy Dee was there initially to bodyguard a corporate son who had decided to do a bit of modeling. After the rich kid's kid had gone back to the States Teddy Dee had returned and gotten his first job in Hong Kong as a theft prevention advisor for the Hong Kong Foreign Exchange. At the Foreign Exchange was his first opportunity to work with Sun Kim. Kim was involved in import and export and had run afoul of a pirate named: Wang. Wang was notorious in the Pearl River Delta.

Sun Kim asked Teddy Dee to do what the Hong Kong government was unable to do; make Wang stop stealing. Sun Kim had been grateful when he learned that Wang had decided to stop stealing because he was found drowned in his own bathtub. Accidents happened all the time Teddy Dee understood. Teddy Dee was in the business of controlled accidents.

Teddy Dee couldn't help but laugh at the situations he had found himself in after nearly a decade as a corporate corporate blooder. He solved problems that others liked to hope would simply disappear. Teddy Dee made problems disappear.

Of course, Teddy Dee had another working list of people that he could call upon who were not considered his friend. That list was immense. He had compiled it from the people that he had worked for in the last twenty years. Those on the working list were not friendly and were more a burn list. Use once and then discard.

Asami read one of the files she had photographed when she was in the corporate offices.

The Signet Industries security report was dated one month ago and was five pages long. The first page detailed the reason for the hiring of the security company: Invisible Protection. There was a detailed history of the five attacks that caused the hire of seven paid protectors assigned to the Signet Industries board of directors, which was made up of the seven immediate members of the Fujinaka clan.

The first attacks had come nearly five years ago at the Fujinaka board of directors. Shokichi Fujinaka, the bachelor, had nearly been kidnapped, robbed, and tricked into paying for a child that was not his all in the span of thirteen months. The kidnapping had been foiled by Shokichi Fujinaka's loyal bodyguards: Ben Williams and Tommy Sharp. Sharp was still in hospital recovering. During the robbery Joshua Ong and Nick Woo had thwarted the attempt and found themselves face-to-face with a hand full of Tong members. The three Tong members had been arrested and jailed.

The second and third Fujinaka to be attacked and nearly killed was Shoto Fujinaka, the fifth Fujinaka son and first to join the board of directors at the nascent company under the direction of Hiro Fujinaka. Shoto Fujinaka had been on his way home when three thugs decided to beat him up. Shoto Fujinaka had been stabbed and nearly killed before a policeman came upon the bleeding board member. Shoto Fujinaka was rushed to a nearby hospital and barely survived the life saving operations before the Fujinakas found him and transferred him to a private hospital with their own private doctors. The third attack happened in downtown Tokyo under similar circumstances. The only difference was that Shoto had not been stabbed but beaten badly enough to be hospitalized.

The fourth Fujinaka to be attacked was Aito Fujinaka. The attack had happened at a nightclub when Aito and another unnamed patron got into a shoving match. The unnamed patron and Aito had a shoving match in the club and both were thrown out. In the rain the two fought only to have two other unnamed men attack Aito. The fight quickly transformed into a much more brutal fight that seemed destined for something lethal. It was only quelled by a passing pair of policemen who stepped in and stopped the three on one attack.

The last attack had happened two years ago and forced Hiro Fujinaka to rethink personal security of his family was the attempted home invasion of Rinko in Ota-Ku. Rinko had not been home. His wife and two daughters were home and terrorized until the police arrived and the home invaders run off.

In the report it listed the seven dedicated paid protectors to the seven board members. Hiro Fujinaka, Tanaka Fujinaka's father and the head of corporation of Signet Industries, had a paid protector assigned to him by the name of: Toshi. In the report there was a mention of an incident with Toshi and HIro Fujinaka in Hong Kong the month before. There was a suggestion that police had been called and an arrest made. Toshi had been detained briefly and released after the altercation. The assailant was hospitalized. He had some ties to a radical research protest group. Teddy Dee was surprised that he did not hear of any problems in Hong Kong with the head of corporation. He was equally surprised to find that Toshi, who was often called the friendly giant, could be formidable. He was a painted as part of the family.

Toshi was the silent giant in the office when Fujinaka was working. He rarely spoke but when he did it, his voice, was deep and rich like chocolate covered honey. The idea of the big Panda bear, a nickname for Toshi, given by the family, and seen more as a family fixture than paid protector seemed to suggest that he was more friendly than dangerous. There was a brief addition to the report that stated that there were three other protectors assigned to the primary's immediate family but no names were mentioned.

Tomo Fujinaka, the second oldest Fujinaka brother to Asami's father, was a board member of the Signet Industries, had a paid protector named:

Sonny. Tomo Fujinaka was Tanaka's uncle and the second oldest Fujinaka male in the family after Hiro Fujinaka. Tomo was 52 years old and a bit frail. He was a banker. Well, Tomo had been a banker before becoming ill and nearly dying before the doctors found a cancerous lump in his back. The doctors had removed the cancer and nearly killed Tomo in the process. Tomo had been sick for five years and when he regained his strength he was too weak to be a banker and opted to assist the family with finances and his banking acumen. The work was too taxing for Tomo who eventually became a board member after working for Signet Industries for three years. Sonny, the paid protector, was the exact opposite of Tomo. Sonny was a young, muscular, and imposing figure next to uncle Tomo. He accompanied him everywhere that Tomo went. In the report there was a cursory mention of Tomo's wife: Lotus, who had divorced Tomo several years ago and was now living in Hawaii.

Rinko Fujinaka, the husband of Leia, father of two twin boys, Ryu and Rin, and an aspiring actress, Shiki, was a board member of the Signet Industries. Rinko Fujinaka had a paid protector named: Jun. Rinko Fujinaka, 42, saw himself as a politician. He was a representative of the Katsu-Shika-Ku district. Rinko loved his work. Jun was always by his side. There was mention of four paid protectors watching over the family as well.

Shokichi Fujinaka, a board member of the Signet Industries, had a paid protector named: Karuma. Shokichi had been a tailor before becoming a board member. Shokichi was always dressed incredibly well. Some said that Shokichi was dating a man that lived in Taito-Ku. There was a brief addendum that suggested that there was a paid protector watching an unnamed man that lived in Taito-Ku paid for by Shokichi Fujinaka.

Aito Fujinaka, a venture capitalist and board member of the Signet Industries, had a paid protector named: Masaka. Aito was the baby of the family and constantly finding himself in trouble. He was mixed up in the underground Japanese hip hop and illegal street car racing. Though he was in his mid-thirties he seemed to believe that age was nothing to determine his passions. So, Aito made himself a target with his lavish lifestyle, big home, fancy cars, and discussion of investments with nefarious types in the seedier areas of Japan. Aito was continuously linked with one singer or actress week to week. He was one of Japan's most eligible bachelors and seemed to crave all of the attention that frenetic lifestyle brought. Masaka was the Signet Industries paid protector but Aito had two personal bodyguards: Ara and Le. They were both trained professionals and highly recommended for their focus and ability to protect the most attention hungry clients. Teddy Dee read the report and noted that the majority of the report focused on Aito and the one-man circus that he had become while dating Kurara Chibana, Miss Japan.

Takeshi Fujinaka, a board member of the Signet Industries, had a paid protector named: Naohito. The older brother, by three years, of Aito Fujinaka was the exact opposite of his attention seeking brother. He was married to his Esha, and the happy father of his first child: Ishi. Unlike the other Fujinaka brothers Takeshi could handle himself. He had served in the Japanese police and was now semi-retired. He had been shot in the shoulder and leg in a raid of a drug den and placed on desk duty. Thankfully, Hiro Fujinaka had offered Takeshi a board position as well as security consultation for Signet Industries.

Rie Fujinaka, a board member of the Signet Industries, had a paid protector named: Teppei. Rie was the oldest member of the Fujinaka clan. She was married to Eita Oka, the relation of the American actor Masi Oka. Eita Oka was a famous landscaper until he became ill. He had not been seen out of their palatial home in years. Teppei was a handsome, young, attentive protector. He was everywhere that the 56-year-old appeared. There were rumors that Teppei had a more intimate relationship with aunt Rie but there was no evidence. Eita Oka had an incredible amount of money based on landscaping some of the most powerful lawns and estates in Japan. He had amassed incredible wealth before marrying Rie.

In the report it stated the date that Hiro Fujinaka mandated that every board member of the Fujinaka clan invest in bodyguards. Each member of the board was given a bodyguard. Any bodyguard above that was paid for out of the pockets of individual board members.

In the light of the various attacks, assaults, and attempts to wrangle money out of one of the richest families in Japan every member of the Fujinaka clan found themselves under the watchful eye of some paid protector. Some protectors were innocuous. Some protectors were invisible. Some protectors were short-lived.

Chapter Thirty.

When he and Elijah arrived in Tokyo, Teddy Dee moved slowly and cautiously. Teddy Dee led the way. Roberta had made all the arrangements.

Waiting for Teddy Dee and Elijah was a young black woman holding up a placard that read: Teddy and Elijah.

"I'm Teddy," Teddy Dee smiled at the black woman dressed in a black pantsuit and white blouse. She nodded and asked:

"Do you have bags?"

"No," Teddy Dee said, looking at Elijah. "Just these."

"Okay, then we can go to the car."

Teddy Dee nodded as the woman turned on her heels and headed for the exit.

The woman moved to a limousine. She opened the door and Teddy Dee and Elijah folded their hulking forms into the backseat of the limousine. The woman closed the door behind them and made her way around to the driver's side of the limousine. She climbed in and started the engine.

"You are registered at the Hotel Ryumeikan Ochanomizu Honten," the woman said in stilted English. "We should be there in about thirty minutes."

"I have to ask," Teddy Dee smiled. "I didn't think there were too many blacks in Japan."

"There are some. Not too many. I am a military baby," the woman said as she drove away from the Tokyo International Airport. She wheeled the limousine expertly. "My father was a soldier stationed here. He got my mother pregnant and then, before my mother knew, he was headed back to the States."

Teddy Dee sat in the back of the limousine and studied Elijah Graham who listened, stone faced. Teddy Dee wondered about the father, the relationship that the woman had or did not have with her father and the mother. It was a strange sensation to want to know those details. Teddy Dee was preparing to face a dangerous and powerful man used to having his way but suddenly, unexplainably, Teddy Dee wanted to know more about the woman.

Elijah Graham reached across Teddy Dee and rose the partition between the driver and the passengers.

"You know that I don't backseat drive, Teddy," Elijah confided. "But, man, you have to get your shit together. You are fucked up something awful right now."

Teddy Dee nodded.

Elijah Graham lowered the partition.

"Can you play some music back here?"

"Sure," the nameless woman smiled. "You have a preference?"

Elijah looked at Teddy Dee. Teddy Dee shook his head. Elijah smiled.

The limousine was suddenly awash in British Pop.

"Nice choice," Elijah smiled as he listened to bass, drumbeat and the haunting sound of a saxophone as English Beat began to sing about "Mirror in the Bathroom."

"Yeah, love ska," the woman said as they drove down the highway. The limousine skated through the busy streets of Japan. The driver exited the highway and began the delicate navigation of the limousine toward the landmark hotel.

"Damn," Elijah Graham intoned as they pulled into the covered driveway of the hotel.

Teddy Dee nodded. Hotel Ryumeikan Ochanomizu Honten is a cultural landmark in Tokyo. It is one of the many unique and signature places in Tokyo. The hotel was opened in 1899. As the driver put the car in gear and exited the driver's side of the limousine Elijah and Teddy could only smile.

"We are here," Teddy Dee said and Elijah Graham nodded.

The pair climbed out of the limousine and stood for a moment in front of the iconic hotel watching as the hotel officials started toward them. The driver made a hand gesture and instantly they stopped their forward progress.

She spoke in Japanese and the hotel officials nodded. One of the hotel officials stepped forward with a clipboard. Teddy Dee noted that the clipboard was actually a notebook computer. It is one of those hotels that goes over and above expectations. The hotel was very intimate.

Teddy Dee and Elijah Graham stood near the limousine. The woman driver made sure that the two passengers got into the hotel without incident.

"Thank you," Teddy Dee and Elijah said as they reached the entry to the hotel.

The woman nodded.

Teddy Dee and Elijah walked into the lobby of Hotel Ryumeikan Ochanomizu Honten. Instantly, two people walked toward them dressed in gray blazers, nametags and big, broad smiles. "Good afternoon," the diamond faced man smiled.

The woman with a heart shaped face and slight almond eyes listened.

"I am checking in for the week," Teddy Dee announced.

"Mister Dandridge?"

Teddy Dee nodded and looked at Elijah with a smile.

"Got you, how was your flight?"

"Long, but manageable."

"Well, if you want you might take a refreshing shower and then enjoy the city before dinner this evening."

Teddy Dee nodded.

"All I will need is a credit card if you have any incidentals."

Teddy Dee fished in his wallet and pulled out a credit card.

"We will also need to make a copy of your passports, if you would be so kind."

Elijah and Teddy Dee surrendered their passports. The woman walked away. She came back and handed the pair back their passports.

The man that had asked for the credit card watched the woman head to the counter. He led Teddy Dee and Elijah Graham to the elevator. The man smiled as the woman returned.

"You are in room number four," the woman smiled.

The four rode the quiet and efficient elevator to the second floor.

"We hope that you enjoy your stay."

Teddy Dee and Elijah entered their hotel room and were truly amazed. The ancient beauty is fused with modernity and function. There was shimmering lights through a shoji/paper sliding door, patina décor inspired by tea ceremony in Edo period, private ceramic bath in a spacious room.

The tatami mats and their golden hues help retain an elegance befitting a Japanese room. There was a large sofa that was used to separate the space between living and bedroom. Teddy Dee was surprised that the room is surprisingly quiet enough that Teddy Dee almost forgot that they were in the heart of the city.

"Are you going to take a shower," Teddy Dee asked Elijah as he slipped out his laptop computer.

Elijah Graham nodded and unzipped his carry on and grabbed his toiletry bag. Elijah stripped down and took a shower. After his shower he dressed in jeans, Nike sneakers and a black T-shirt. He slipped on a black windbreaker.

"Okay, give me ten minutes and I will be ready."

Teddy Dee unzipped his carry on and grabbed his toiletry kit. He stripped down out of his traveling clothes and climbed into the shower. Teddy Dee scrubbed up and climbed out of the shower. He dried off. He slipped on blue jeans, Nike sneakers and a hooded sweatshirt.

The two giants walked down a flight of stairs to the lobby.

"Is there anything we can help you with?"

Teddy Dee shook his head.

The pair stepped outside and Teddy Dee went to the right. The sidewalks were chockfull of people that afternoon. It was warm in Japan. People were dressed in shirt sleeves and shorts. Many of the women were wearing skirts. A smattering of men were wearing suit jackets.

Teddy Dee and Elijah did not have to push through the crowd. The people stopped and stared at the two gigantic black men. They stood head and heels over most men and women.

The stares and pointing was interesting, at first. Five minutes later, there were people still pointing and staring.

"What do you want to do?"

"Ignore them," Elijah grumbled. "We ain't here long enough to really care."

Teddy Dee nodded. He and Elijah walked on and tried to ignore the people that stopped and stared and pointed. Teddy Dee stopped and stared and pointed when he saw a store sign in written in English. The store was a fast food store called: Ringer Hut.

"What do you think they have in there?"

"I'm not sure."

The first sign of Americanization in Tokyo, Japan for Teddy Dee was the sight of Burger King near the train station near Ochanomizu. There was a Print Shop near the Burger King as well. Those three stores had their neon signs in English.

"Think that is the Kanda River," Teddy Dee said.

They crossed to the Kanda River and stood and enjoyed the spectacle of Japanese walking and pointing at them.

"Don't seem like they have a bunch of brothers in Tokyo."

"Yeah, that might be a problem if we are trying to blend in."

"Hungry?"

"Yeah, might as well. I am a bit tired." Teddy Dee pushed off the railing and back toward Ochanomizu. Elijah fell in line. "I am pretty sure if I eat I will be asleep in an hour."

"Yeah, me too."

Green Tea Restaurant 1899 Ochanomizu was the restaurant in the hotel. It was a small and efficient place. The guests looked at Teddy Dee and Elijah and whispered amongst themselves. Teddy Dee and Elijah signed in and waited for about ten minutes before being seated.

When the pair sat the waitress came back and smiled broadly. Teddy Dee waited for her to take his order.

"Can I ask for an autograph," a woman with her son in tow said.

Teddy Dee furrowed his brow.

"Who do you think I am?"

"You are the actor, the movie actor, that played in The Green Mile," the woman smiled.

"John Coffey," her child said from behind her.

Teddy Dee wanted to argue. He wanted to be upset. It was a compliment. Well, it was sort of a compliment. Teddy Dee signed a kind of autograph and the woman bowed and the child bowed and after taking a quick picture allowed Teddy Dee to eat.

Elijah Graham smiled broadly.

"It's because you're bald and you smile at people," Elijah Graham said.

"It's because they don't know shit about black people and think that we all look alike." Teddy Dee wanted to be angry but the woman was nice and apologetic for disturbing his privacy. The child was adorable and Teddy Dee did not like children too much.

"You know that Michael Clark Duncan died, like ten years ago?" Elijah Graham continued. "You do look a little like him, though."

Teddy Dee shook his head.

They ate a good meal. It was a lighter meal than they usually had but after an eighteen-hour flight it didn't really matter. Teddy Dee paid the bill and they made their way back to their hotel room.

"Hey, movie star, think that you can use your celebrity to upgrade my Spotify?"

Teddy Dee laughed and shook his head.

In the room, Elijah Graham was the first to start undressing.

"Okay, you have a preference? Window or door side of the room," pointing to the two beds; one on the side closest to the window, the other closest to the door.

"I'll take the door side. It's closer to the toilet too."

Teddy Dee shook his head.

He took his carry on and placed it next to the window side of the room. He stripped out of the clothes he was wearing and into his pajamas.

Elijah returned dressed in his pajamas as well.

Teddy Dee had his laptop computer with him and was planning on checking his e-mail before going to sleep.

Asami Fujinaka listened and waited for her father to leave the complex and her mother to get busy before she slipped into her father's study. His study was an organized den of efficiency. On two walls of the four were bookcases that rose to the ceiling. In the bookcases were her father's greatest treasures. He had first editions of several Japanese writers. He had signed copies of most of Japan's brightest and brilliant business minds if they had written a book of any kind. Asami Fujinaka always found herself scratching her head at her father's fascination with the written word. His two favorite titles were Sun Tzu and Miyamoto Musashi. He had based Signet Industries on those two military strategists thinking.

Asami Fujinaka loved the lone bonsai sitting in the corner of the study. Her father had explained over and over again the importance of the bonsai. It had come from his great, great, great grandfather's home and it, the bonsai, was a reminder of the importance of family and the connection of the family despite being in Tokyo now. The bonsai was a gentle reminder for Hiro Fujinaka to stay grounded and humble and rooted in the work that his great, great, great grandfather had begun nearly two hundred years ago.

The daughter of Hiro Fujinaka pushed deeper into the study and to her father's desk where he ruled and made all his decisions. On the desk was the desktop computer that he used sparingly. Asami Fujinaka tapped the keys on the keyboard and woke the computer. The screensaver was the logo of Signet Industries. There was the ancient signet ring of the Emperor of Japan in the background of the Signet Industries logo.

The computer was password protected.

Asami Fujinaka did not hesitate. She had helped her father time and time again accessing vital information on his desktop computer. His password was Tanaka and Asami's birthdays.

Asami skimmed the computer and looked for the report that her father had asked for. On the desktop sat a file named: Incident Report-LA. Below the incident report was another file labeled: Video-LA incident.

Chapter Thirty-One.

The next day, after a short sleep, Teddy Dee woke and dressed and went to find a place to do some stretching before the battle that he imagined he and Elijah were going to face. Teddy Dee walked outside and around the streets which were relatively quieter than the day before. He walked down a one-way street at the end of the street came upon a park. At the park there were easily forty people doing Rajio Taiso. Teddy Dee stretched near the Rajio Taiso group.

Thirty minutes later Teddy Dee was back in the hotel room and showering. Elijah and Teddy Dee ate breakfast in their room. The meal came from Green Tea Restaurant 1899 Ochanomizu. The meal was good and filling.

By ten o'clock they were packed and heading to the train station. They bought two tickets to Nakatsu. They would arrive just in time to check in to their second hotel in Japan; Hotel Route Inn Nakatsu Ekimae. It was a short walk from the train station.

The train ride was uneventful. Six hours of watching the Japanese seaside pass by allowed Teddy Dee to just rest and think. The battle ahead was going to be interesting to say the least.

Hiro Fujinaka IV lived like a king. He had purchased one of the state's regional castles for his home. He had a staff of nearly seventy to maintain the household and grounds. The main estate sat on fourteen acres of land. The castle had been badly damaged in a fire but had been fully restored by Hiro Fujinaka IV. The land around the Nakatsu Jo castle includes a forest, river, and Zen garden. In the rear of the castle is a stable and servant quarters. It is a five-tiered castle that was built in 1589. His family owned and run Signet Industries.

Nakatsu-Jo castle was a flatland castle on the shores of the River. It was a five tiered donjon castle and maze of sorts. The castle itself was built on a simple floor plan that resembled an open fan. There were 100 rooms in the castle. Yet in its intricate details and being a one-time museum and five floors the flatland castle's interior made it a modern day labyrinth. Beneath the stone Nakatsu-Jo castle foundation there were two sub-basements. That translated to two extra floors few saw or knew of beside the most trusted members of the staff and family. The history of Nakatsu-Jo's secret sub-basement construction had been done to ensure the safety of the magistrate living there at the time and his family.

Hiro Fujinaka IV and his son, Tanaka, were headstrong and determined to globalize Signet Industries. The effort to expand Signet Industries put incredible stress on the corporation and the Fujinaka family. There was dissension in the ranks of Signet Industries. There was dissension in the families of the Fujinaka clan from the bottom to the top.

For all his success Hiro Fujinaka IV had as many detractors as supporters. The surprising thing about the detractors was that the most vocal were inside his home and family. An internal struggle had been launched between the women of the Fujinaka clan and the men that controlled Signet Industries. As Hiro Fujinaka IV groomed Tanaka Fujinaka for the eventual takeover of Signet Industries many saw other alternatives to the brash, power hungry Tanaka Fujinaka especially his wife Keiko and Oxford educated and trained daughter Asami. The once quiet herbal company with success had awakened a sleeping dragon.

The castle was a symbol of Hiro Fujinaka IV. Outwardly, he was strong. Outwardly, Hiro Fujinaka IV seemed unassailable. He had built a reputation of being inaccessible. No one got close to Hiro Fujinaka IV if Hiro Fujinaka IV did not want you close. Rin, the great panda, made sure that, when in the public eye, that Hiro Fujinaka IV was untouched and unapproached by anyone that he did not wish to see or talk to.

Yet, there was a complexity to the head of corporations of one of Japan's biggest employers. Like Nakatsu-Jo there were secrets that Hiro Fujinaka IV tried to hide from the public. Only his family knew of the inner struggle that the nearly sixty-year-old Hiro Fujinaka IV battled with daily within his own family. There were too many detractors to name attempting to take over the leadership of Signet Industries. Too often, his family heard the rancor of Hiro Fujinaka IV and frustration at the seemingly endless attacks on his leadership.

Few knew of the two sub-basements. Even fewer have seen the second sub-basement, where the magistrate had an elaborate escape route built that led two hundred meters into the woods for speedy retreat if ninjas or enemies swarmed the Nakatsu-Jo castle. Any that came upon the steel gate in between two gigantic boulders may have thought it was a rain grate or water pipe that controlled irrigation not aware of its regal lineage.

Teddy Dee and Elijah Graham knew little about the history or significance of the Nakatsu-Jo castle. They had been two foreigners who had come to Japan for business. Actually, it was Teddy Dee who had come for business. Elijah Graham had come to assist an old high school friend in a bind in Japan.

When they arrived at Nakatsu, Japan and located the Nakatsu-Jo castle everyone in Nakatsu had spoken of the black men dressed like businessmen looking for Hiro Fujinaka IV. Nakatsu was a small village dominated by the castle that sat on the brow of the Red Sea. It was a small village compared to Tokyo but Nakatsu was not that small unless you were Teddy Dee or Elijah Graham. There was neighborhood talk of the black men in Nakatsu. Some speculated that the black men were professional athletes. Maybe, some suggested that they were WWE celebrities. Even though it was the 21st century blacks were not common in Japan, unless they were dressed in military uniforms.

"We aren't blending in, Teddy," Elijah smiled as they climbed out of the cab that had dropped them off in front of Nakatsu Jo castle.

"It's awfully hard to blend into a culture that is five foot nothing, on average, speaks Japanese, and doesn't have a black population," Teddy Dee pointed out.

“They seem to like hip hop music and Nikes,” Elijah Graham laughed.

“Yeah, there is that,” Teddy Dee had to admit.

"What you expecting?"

"Well, I ain't expecting them to be happy to see me.” Teddy Dee paused. “Just hoping to walk out of this alive," Teddy Dee admitted.

Elijah Graham nodded.

The pair had arrived at the gates of Nakatsu-Jo castle. The guards had halted them immediately at the gates. The four men behind the gates were dressed in business suits.

Teddy Dee had stepped to the gate and smiled.

“Any of you speak English?”

“Yes, I speak English,” one of the guards said with a smile.

“I have an appointment to see Hiro Fujinaka,” Teddy Dee announced.

The guard spoke in Japanese quickly to one of the guards. One of the guards retrieved a clipboard and walked to the gate.

“You are Mister Dandridge?”

Teddy Dee nodded.

The gate was opened and Teddy Dee and Elijah Graham entered the outer courtyard of the castle. The guards stopped Teddy Dee and Elijah there as two men with pistols on their hips appeared and walked toward them.

"I thought pistols were illegal in Japan," Elijah said to Teddy Dee.

"Thought Michael Clark Duncan was dead," Teddy Dee smiled.

Elijah Graham smiled at Teddy Dee's response.

The men that checked them for weapons nodded.

"Didn't come all this way to get popped by cops in a foreign country carrying weapons," Teddy Dee said to the guard watching him.

"Can't be too careful," the guard said with a smirk.

"Thought that guns were illegal in Japan?"

"They are," the guard said.

"Come with me," the guard that had spoken to Teddy Dee said, leaving the three others by the first gate. The two guards with pistols followed.

They crossed the courtyard and entered a low doorway. Once inside of the hall Teddy Dee and Elijah noted that the hallways were not built for tall or wide individuals. There was barely room enough for Teddy Dee and another man to walk shoulder to shoulder. If Teddy Dee and Elijah had wanted to walk side by side they could not.

"This is one of three sea castles in Japan," the guard closest to Teddy Dee announced as they stepped down a short flight of stairs that brought them to a wider hall. They snaked through dark halls and ended up in a room that was surprisingly long, wide, and bright. Teddy Dee imagined that this was where the king or emperor met with his subjects about things of import.

The convoy of men crossed the long hall and went through an arched doorway that led to another hallway. The hallway snaked around and for the first time Teddy Dee and Elijah Graham could hear the sound of the sea on the other side of the walls. The pistol carrying guards were joined by two others now carrying sub-machine guns.

"What gives with the heavy weapons?"

"Can't be too careful," the guard smiled.

They continued walking through the stone interior of Nakatsu-Jo castle and noted the lights that ran along the stone walls to illuminate the dark interior of the sub-basement. Teddy Dee looked from Elijah to the Japanese shadow that held a sub-machine gun. Killing the leaders would not stop the others from shooting and cutting Elijah and Teddy Dee down in the midst of Nakatsu-Jo castle. By his estimation, Teddy Dee imagined that they were in the second sub-basement of the castle. It seemed to be the oldest part of the castle and further from the sea.

The four armed shadows, who had escorted the black giants into the meeting room of the castle, bowed and handed over Teddy Dee and Elijah Graham to two others. There was a brief exchange in Japanese before the guard and the four others left the only two blacks in Nakatsu, Japan.

"Move," one of the two men said, gesturing to Teddy Dee and Elijah Graham, as they moved into the room. Teddy Dee noted that the two bodyguards had pistol bulges under their jackets.

"Time to put on our game faces," Teddy Dee said as he led the pair to the first gate.

The man that had led them to the room motioned for Teddy Dee and Elijah to wait. The pair stopped. Teddy Dee looked back and noted that two samurai had appeared from the shadows and were now blocking their exit.

"We are in it now," Teddy Dee whispered. He calculated that to get back to the exit he and Elijah would have to go through no less than a dozen unfriendly and motivated Fujinaka employees. It was going to be an interesting meeting, Teddy Dee told himself. It would more interesting leaving if things went completely off the rails and off the rails was where Teddy Dee felt this meeting heading already.

In the room they entered was a set of steps that lead to a riser where a man in his late sixties, with white hair and a ponytail, was kneeling, dressed in a traditional red and white Japanese kimono. He had an apple pie shaped face and round chin. The dark eyed man looked through a pair of thin framed glasses. Rin, the bodyguard, was dressed in a black jacket, white shirt, and dark gray trousers. He looked like a giant panda.

On the white haired man's left sat/kneeled a beautiful woman in her mid-twenties with raven black hair, pencil thin eyebrows, and big, expressive dark eyes. She was dressed in a yellow and black traditional Japanese kimono very similar to the one that the man to her right wore. She wore no jewelry. Her hair was piled atop her round head, to show off a thin delicate neck and slightly protruding ears. Several ringlets of her dark hair fell to her small, rounded shoulders.

Just to the left of the beautiful Japanese woman stood a small black woman dressed in combat boots, black jeans, and black motorcycle jacket. Teddy Dee did a double take. He had been surprised to see another black person in Japan. Immediately, upon seeing the woman he thought that the woman looked a little like a tougher and younger "Keke" Palmer.

On the right hand side of the white haired man kneeled the apple faced Tanaka Fujinaka, the son of Hiro Fujinaka IV. Tanaka was dressed in a red and black kimono. On his left hand he wore a wedding ring. His left hand was balled into a fist. He looked like he was holding himself back as he stared daggers at Teddy Dee. Surprisingly, Tanaka had no bodyguard present on the riser.

Teddy Dee looked at the head of Signet Industries and then to the women and finally Tanaka. Teddy Dee recalled that Tanaka, the rich kid, was the privileged son of the head of the corporation, who played with wooden swords. He probably thought he was a samurai or ninja, Teddy Dee mused.

"Teddy," Elijah whispered drawing Teddy Dee's attention from Tanaka and to the bigger problem. The pair were in a room with at least eight men on the main floor with them, of the eight, four were holding samurai swords.

Teddy Dee noted the men slowly and quietly spread out around the big room that was dominated by the twelve stone columns that divided the stone interior walkway from the stepped riser. Teddy Dee noted the two bodyguards on the riser and had to believe that they were armed as well.

Of course, Teddy Dee noted, there was only Elijah and himself versus the Fujinaka security. If they got out of the sub-basement and past the samurai sword wielding guards, they still had to wind their way back up and through the gauntlet of a dozen motivated and hungry Fujinaka employees devoted to their President and family. Teddy Dee did not want to throw in the fact that probably the majority knew martial arts as well as how to pull the triggers of their assault rifles.

If there was going to be a fight, then the fight was going to be one-sided and short-lived. Teddy Dee trusted few people. He trusted even fewer in a fight. Elijah Graham was a fighter that once the fight began was not someone that Teddy Dee had to check on. He would take the fight to the fools that dared face him. Teddy Dee was a fighter as well but as he calculated the odds, then and there, it did not seem as if Teddy Dee had planned to leave Japan alive.

“We have our backs up against it,” Elijah pointed out.

“That’s when we shine,” Teddy Dee smiled, despite the odds.

Teddy Dee continued to work out the possible outcome if he and Elijah took out the leaders first and then caused the lesser ranks to have to defend without direction. At first, Teddy Dee thought that removing the leaders would cause chaos and in that chaos and hesitation that ensued a slim chance for he and Elijah to escape. Yet, running from a fight was not something that Teddy Dee or Elijah Graham were comfortable with, be it in Japan, Inglewood, South Central, or wherever.

“This isn’t a meeting. This is a slaughter house.”

"Not even," Teddy Dee figured. "If they wanted us dead they would have killed us already."

"Yeah, there is always that, huh," Elijah said.

"Let's see how this plays out."

"You mean are they going to wine and dine us? Or do you think they are just going to fuck us," Elijah said.

"Not even a little bit," Teddy Dee stated. "They want to talk. They are listening. For some reason they are curious. Maybe it's their first time dealing with black people."

"Okay, say you're right," Elijah said. "What's your plan?"

"I'm still working on that," Teddy Dee admitted.

Elijah Graham didn't blink. He just waited for the first signal. The chaos, if there was going to be chaos, was going to be immediate and intense.

Down the dozen steps that distanced those on the riser descended the woman in her yellow and black delicately designed kimono with the design of a giant koi sewn into the fabric brushing the steps. Behind her came "Keke" Palmer in her motorcycle jacket and motorcycle boots.

She moved effortlessly down the steps like a fish moving fluidly through the water unhindered and unrushed by concerns or time. She kept her eyes on Teddy Dee and Elijah Graham as she descended the dozen steps. The men guarding Teddy Dee and Elijah Graham hesitated as she drew closer. The woman gestured and "Keke" Palmer stepped down another step or two, closer to Teddy Dee and handed him a wood grain box the size of a laptop and three times as thick. Teddy Dee took the wood grain box and furrowed his brows at the unexpected gift. He did not know what to do or say until she spoke.

"This is a gift for you, on your first visit to Japan, from a grateful host," the black woman said, in perfect English.

Teddy Dee furrowed his brow, but did not reply. He was a bit shocked at the gift and the response from the woman.

Elijah had looked and overheard the conversation, what little there was, and remained silent. The men who were escorting Teddy Dee and Elijah paused just long enough to allow the exchange between the woman and Teddy Dee and before Teddy Dee or Elijah could speak the woman turned around and respectfully bowed to the woman in the yellow and black kimono. The woman in the kimono bowed and turned and bowed to Hiro Fujinaka IV, still on the riser next to Tanaka Fujinaka.

Teddy Dee noted the small black woman dressed in black standing near the woman in the yellow and black kimono and imagined that she had been hired as a translator. The black woman stood like someone that could handle herself.

Teddy Dee looked to Elijah and back to the only other black person in Japan. Elijah smiled for the first time the whole trip.

"Check this shit out, Teddy, this chick got a chick bodyguard. Japan is on some stupid shit," Elijah laughed.

"Shit ain't funny," Teddy Dee said to Elijah. He turned his attention to the two men on the dais, both now flanked by two other men. The man near Tanaka was dressed in a black suit, white collared shirt and black tie. He looked young and athletic with a black bush of hair on his round head. The man had appeared out of the shadows at the top of the riser. Teddy Dee had to believe that there were doors and hallways that led back up to the main castle. So, Tanaka Fujinaka had a bodyguard.

The Asian woman bowed and the black woman behind her. Teddy Dee lowered his eyes awkwardly. Elijah Graham smiled and dipped his head just a little, amused at the whole ceremony.

"I hope you enjoy the small gift from me," Asami Fujinaka whispered. "I am Asami Fujinaka, daughter of Hiro Fujinaka. Welcome to Japan," Asami Fujinaka smiled as Teddy Dee held the gift in his gigantic hands. Awkwardly, Teddy Dee sat the gift beside him.

"Thank you," Teddy Dee said to Asami Fujinaka. He narrowed his focus and redirected his attention to Hiro Fujinaka IV.

Tanaka was the first to react. He leaned forward and rocked himself onto his feet. The elder sitting watched as Tanaka Fujinaka began to speak.

"It is the ultimate affront to have—"

The elder, Hiro Fujinaka IV, raised his hand and Tanaka Fujinaka fell silent. He looked toward Teddy Dee and Elijah Graham. Hiro Fujinaka IV gestured for the pair to come closer. The two complied. They moved up to the edge of the steps, where two guards pointed that they sit. Teddy Dee and Elijah Graham complied. Teddy Dee sat uncomfortably on a small pillow beside Elijah Graham and noted that the women and the duo in kimonos all had similar features.

Hiro Fujinaka IV seemed ageless. He looked as if he had seen empires rise and fall. He spoke in Japanese. He spoke for easily one minute from a script that he might have memorized.

Elijah Graham leaned forward as if hearing the words clearly would allow him to understand a foreign language. Teddy Dee shook his head at Elijah's efforts. He smiled at his friend's desire to attempt to decipher what Hiro

Fujinaka was saying as if he had studied Japanese while knocking out people in South Central Los Angeles.

Teddy Dee didn't know what Fujinaka said. He listened and tried to figure out what the old man was saying next to Elijah Graham. Teddy Dee shook his head, confused. He thought that this man could have ordered the men in the hall to cut them to pieces or asked for dancing girls to come out and entertain them. Teddy Dee did not know. The sounds were not angry, at least that was the overall tone but Teddy Dee could not be certain.

"What did he say?" Elijah Graham asked. He, like Teddy Dee, had never graduated from high school.

"I don't have a clue what he said," Teddy Dee whispered to his friend.

"My father has asked you and your friend: If you two are crazy? He is curious if you are aware how powerful the Fujinaka family is? He spoke of the history of the Nakatsu-Jo castle. He mentioned that this is one of three sea castles in Japan and that it is the only one owned by the Fujinaka family. The Japanese government sold this historic landmark to our family because our family is Japan. We uphold Japanese traditions. We embrace the Japanese culture. We are historic and modern at the same time. He mentioned that you have offended our family in your dealings with my brother Tanaka, in Los Angeles. You have embarrassed Tanaka, and caused him great shame. That shame has led to him, making an error in his attempt to right a perceived wrong. We had thought that this matter had ended, but obviously it has not. My father concluded with a question: Why have you come here today," the beautiful woman dressed in a gold and black kimono translated.

She spoke in Japanese and the guards stepped back to allow Asami Fujinaka to get closer to the Americans.

"Tell him that I came here to resolve an issue that his son created. Thank you," Teddy Dee said absently. He studied Asami Fujinaka then he returned his attention to the matter at hand.

The woman nodded and spoke to Hiro Fujinaka IV. Tanaka Fujinaka sat and squirmed as he listened to Asami Fujinaka repeat what Teddy Dee had just said. Tanaka Fujinaka was wearing a traditional kimono with a gigantic black, red and white koi seeming to circle the midsection of the kimono.

Hiro Fujinaka IV did not look to his son but straight ahead as his daughter translated. He was a small man compared to Tanaka. Dressed in his white kimono with red geometric patterns along the sleeves Hiro Fujinaka IV looked even smaller. He furrowed his brow as his daughter finished her translation.

Hiro Fujinaka IV thought over the words that his daughter had translated. The President of Signet Industries paused and after a few seconds replied. He looked at Teddy Dee as he spoke. The young woman translated.

"You have caused my brother great shame. He was tasked to best his competition and failed. You are the cause of that failure. We are a proud people and do not take lightly the loss of face."

Teddy Dee shook his head at the idea. Shame? Failure? It was business. He rubbed at his temples, suddenly frustrated. This was the president of a corporation. This was a big wig. This man probably made more money in a day than Teddy Dee made in a year. He was supposed to be smart. He was supposed to know how business worked. Tanaka had been caught. There was no shame in that. Where was the miscommunication?

"It was only business," Teddy Dee began. "In business, when you are caught with your hands in the cookie jar you apologize or not and move on. Your brother, his son, was caught with his hands in the cookie jar and needs to realize that it was my job to catch him. I'm paid to be a corporate cookie jar-hand-catcher. That's my job. I catch people all the time trying to be sneaky. I'm good at my job. There is no shame in being caught. This is business. That is the price of business."

Asami Fujinaka translated.

"I came here from America to tell your father that Tanaka has overstepped his bounds. He stole from my boss. I retrieved what was stolen. That's business. He sent men to kill me. I get that. That is a part of the job. But there are rules. There are rules that are in play, in the bigger world, that have to be acknowledged and applied. Breaking those rules cause us to fall into chaos. He knows that he didn't recover the stolen information and I got back to my bosses without being killed. That is business. That is part of the crazy world that we live in. He knows this. You are aware of this. You have to be aware of this. That is acceptable. The job ended. The job was over. There is no reason for him to still have the dogs of war out for my head. I did a job. I did my job. When the job was done his chance to exact revenge ended."

Asami Fujinaka translated.

"That is the rules of the business we are in. I don't think that you want me to kill your son. That ain't the business. But, if he doesn't let this shit go someone is going to die. Tanaka is holding a grudge against me, a blooder. Do you have blooders in Japan? Hell, yeah, everyone has blooders. I'm the guy that they send to end other blooders."

Asami Fujinaka translated.

"I am the guy that is tasked, that's what you said, I was tasked to follow the breadcrumbs that were left by your son and his Signet Industries spies. I was hired to find and recover or destroy all the files that had been stolen."

Asami Fujinaka translated.

"I did my job. It's business. I had to rough up Tanaka a little. I had to destroy some of his things. That was the cost of business."

Asami Fujinaka translated.

"I slapped him around a bit," Teddy Dee recalled. Tanaka Fujinaka tried to stand up and Hiro Fujinaka stopped him with a glance.

"I didn't need to rough him up as much as I did, but now that I think about it I should have roughed him up a little more and that might have stopped this whole thing."

Asami Fujinaka translated.

Hiro Fujinaka IV listened and folded his hands in front of his face for a moment. He steepled his fingers before he spoke. The head of corporation spoke briefly.

"My father suggests that the dishonor you demonstrated against my brother is enough to have you beheaded, in Japan."

"Listen Mister Fujinaka, I didn't fly all the way here to be threatened. This ain't feudal Japan. There ain't no beheading happening as long as I am alive. If anyone is beheading, it is me. I'm the executioner. I'm the blooder. I'm the black berserker. Threatening me is something that few people live to talk about in the shadows. I'm not threatening you, Mister Fujinaka. Everything that I am saying is the business of the shadow world. It is truth. Your son's actions are out of line. I did not want to fly to Japan. I did not want to have this meeting, but it seems to be the only way to end all this, one way or another. Now, I came to ask you to call off the dogs of war. Nothing else. I tried to ask your hotheaded son in America and all I got was more attacks. I didn't want to break him because he was out of line, but it seems that I might have to break him for you to get the point. You have spoiled this-- the leader of Signet Industries in the States, and that means that someone like me might have to bend some of his parts, the wrong way, so that he comes to his senses, since he refuses."

Asami Fujinaka translated everything Teddy Dee said.

Hiro Fujinaka IV responded curtly.

"My father...he does not agree with you. He thinks that you are the one that overstepped your bounds in trying to teach Tanaka a lesson," Asami Fujinaka explained. "You are a... I do not know the English term for what he says." She added: "It seems that we have come to an impasse."

Teddy Dee paused and studied Hiro Fujinaka IV. The old man looked steadily at Teddy Dee and Elijah Graham.

Hiro Fujinaka IV spoke.

Teddy Dee and Elijah listened and when the head of the corporation was done looked to Asami Fujinaka for the translation.

"We cannot expect barbarians to understand our ways. Yet, even a barbarian understands that respect is earned and lost with the simplest offenses. As a barbarian you have insulted our family. Tanaka is a hothead. We cannot disagree with that. Yet, he was given a job and you thwarted his efforts. You embarrassed him in stopping him. We, the Fujinaka clan, will not be happy with just an apology. You have gone too far. You have shamed my son and now you have come here to make demands?"

"Well, that's all I got. So, what's next?"

The woman paused. She studied Teddy Dee for an instant.

"You might want to open your present," Asami Fujinaka smiled.

Teddy Dee reached for the gift and opened it effortlessly. Inside of the box were two brand new blue Ruger pistols. Teddy Dee did another double take. In that moment, Teddy Dee flipped one of the Ruger pistols to Elijah and as he armed Elijah they made their moves.

The two giants aimed the pistols and the Japanese guards recoiled. Neither Teddy Dee or Elijah pulled their triggers. The threat of the gun was enough to allow them the chance to attack.

Teddy Dee was the first to remove the gun's magazine and check to see if the gun was loaded. Not surprised, he replaced the magazine and nodded to Elijah. Elijah checked his pistol. He nodded as well. They used that moment to make strategic decisions as to who to attack first.

"Make them come to us, E," Teddy Dee shouted as he attacked the closest guard to him, sweeping his legs out from under him and punching him in the face as hard as he could, as Teddy Dee climbed to his feet and ran headlong at Asami Fujinaka and "Keke" Palmer. Asami raised a hand and "Keke" Palmer did not attack or protest.

Teddy Dee, with gun in hand, moved passed Asami Fujinaka and "Keke" Palmer and toward her father and brother. The reaction from the two bodyguards closest to the two men seated on the dais was a half step slower than Asami Fujinaka who seemed to anticipate Teddy Dee's attack.

Teddy Dee aimed his Ruger at the guard and before the guard could pull his own weapon punched the closest guard and he fell, like a marionette puppet that had just had his strings cut. Teddy Dee dropped the Ruger and fished out the guard's pistol.

The second guard, seeing Teddy Dee approaching prepared himself for the fight ahead. The guard was armed but did not reach for his firearm, Teddy Dee imagined because of concern that shooting could get Hiro or Tanaka Fujinaka dead. Maybe, Teddy Dee thought, the guard thought he could take Teddy Dee hand-to-hand.

Tanaka Fujinaka jumped to his feet. He took two steps forward and instantly pushing past the fumbling guard. Tanaka Fujinaka saw himself as a bit of a badass Teddy Dee recalled. He had a bunch of pictures of himself dressed in a traditional Japanese fighting gear. Teddy Dee did not pay much attention to Tanaka Fujinaka without a sword. Tanaka ran down the steps and stopped realizing that Teddy Dee was armed and not deterred by the one remaining guard.

Behind Teddy Dee, Elijah Graham was moving in a stutter step to the left and then to the right. The giant was using the columns to his advantage. The two closest sword wielding samurai attempted to cut Elijah down instantly but the giant deftly moved next to the closest column to deflect the first two attacks. In an instance, Elijah backhanded one of the samurai and knocked him unconscious with the unplanned and natural lightning attack. The giant followed the backhand and moved gracefully to grab the samurai sword that the unconscious guard had attempted to use to cut off Elijah's head.

That was the last that Teddy Dee saw of Elijah. His attention was suddenly on the last guard, Tanaka Fujinaka and his father. All around them madness and mayhem reigned. Chaos ensued.

Teddy Dee watched as the second guard found himself unable to do anything. He was blocked by Tanaka Fujinaka and as Teddy Dee drew close enough to punch the son of Hiro Fujinaka IV the petulant son tried to pull a Russian pistol from his kimono. Instantly, Teddy Dee had lifted his newly acquired Heckler-Koch that he had taken from the guard and chose not to fire. In one deft move Teddy Dee slipped the compact gun into his waistband and turned his attention to Tanaka Fujinaka. Teddy Dee reached out and grabbed Tanaka's wrist and twisted the Russian pistol out of the man's grip.

Tanaka dropped the pistol and Teddy Dee spun and fired the Russian pistol at the second guard who had finally pulled his pistol. The report was deafening in the echo chamber of the sub-basement. Everyone's ears rang and for a long moment. It was as if they were all suddenly under water. There was just the undulating sound wave that tore through the chamber.

Tanaka recovered quickly and almost immediately twisted free of Teddy Dee's grip and pulled a dagger from the folds of his kimono with his left hand and slashed Teddy Dee across the chest. Teddy Dee without much thought grabbed Tanaka's hand, the one with the dagger, and drove it into Tanaka Fujinaka's chest.

Tanaka Fujinaka stumbled back and tumbled onto the steps of the dais. Blood stained the kimono front of the still body of Tanaka Fujinaka. Hiro Fujinaka IV climbed to his feet, in a fury, and like his son pulled a Russian made pistol from inside of his kimono.

"Fuck," Teddy Dee hissed.

Hiro Fujinaka lifted the pistol. Teddy Dee fired a knife hand at Hiro Fujinaka IV as he fired the first shot from his Russian made automatic pistol in the walls of the Nakatsu-Jo castle. The second gunshot was deafening inside of the sub-basement. Everyone again winced at the unexpected sound. The bullet nicked Teddy Dee's shoulder. Almost simultaneously Teddy Dee turned the Russian-made pistol on Hiro Fujinaka IV and fired a deadly pair of shots into the chest of the President of Signet Industries.

The third and fourth shot that day rang in the Nakatsu-Jo castle inner sub-basement. Teddy Dee narrowed his eyes. He had not intended on killing Hiro Fujinaka. He had come to Japan to negotiate with Hiro Fujinaka and solve this problem. Now, Hiro Fujinaka lay dead at Teddy Dee's feet. Tanaka Fujinaka lay dead at Teddy Dee's feet. One of the bodyguards that had been hired to protect Tanaka Fujinaka lay dead at Teddy Dee's feet. Teddy Dee, still holding the Russian pistol, tried to rethink what had just happened. The whole incident had been less than two minutes. His final actions had been more of a natural reaction to being shot at by Hiro Fujinaka IV than an attack.

Teddy Dee was a trained combat artist. So, his handling of a handgun was unlike anyone that might simply pick it up and try to fire it. Hiro Fujinaka IV fell to his knees and tilted to his left falling face forward, dead. He was the third to die in the ancient Nakatsu-Jo castle.

Teddy Dee walked back down the steps toward Asami Fujinaka. He dropped the Russian made pistol and looked at the empty Ruger on the steps and thought about cramming it down Asami Fujinaka's throat.

As he descended the steps Teddy Dee could not help looking for Elijah. From the left flew a guard across the expanse. Behind the guard Elijah Graham stepped out from behind the column. Three men were snapping at his heels. Elijah Graham reached out and grabbed one of the three guards and slammed him face first into a column.

Teddy Dee did not rush to Elijah Graham's side. He had seen him fight. Teddy Dee was certain that the big brute could handle two Japanese guards.

Teddy Dee looked back to the right and the black woman appeared like a jack-in-the-box to Asami Fujinaka's left. The black woman stepped forward only to be slapped unconscious by Teddy Dee. The small black woman spiraled and lay sprawled on the steps motionless. The slap had surprised Asami.

"You didn't need to do that," Asami Fujinaka said and for the first time Teddy Dee felt that the translator and daughter of Hiro Fujinaka IV was telling the truth.

"Maybe I did and maybe I didn't," Teddy Dee responded, narrowing his eyes at the daughter of Hiro Fujinaka IV.

"You are a thug," Asami Fujinaka said, tilting her head, and narrowing her dark eyes.

"Sometimes," Teddy Dee admitted.

"You can play it that way," Asami Fujinaka said poking out her lower lip and checking on the black woman that lay unconscious on the steps near her. She leveled her gaze at Teddy Dee. "You can make a smart decision now and walk away. Or you cannot. You have to decide; do you want to live or do you want to die? You can leave here or be buried here. It's up to you."

"Well, I am leaning toward living," Teddy Dee admitted.

Asami Fujinaka smiled at Teddy Dee's words.

Chapter Thirty-Two.

Teddy Dee studied the daughter of Hiro Fujinaka IV evenly. From the doors of the sub-basement came the Nakatsu-Jo castle reinforcements. The eight men that had been in the sub-basement earlier were bolstered by another ten heavily armed men carrying assault rifles.

Leaving the sub-basement by force seemed to be an impossibility suddenly. There was no way to physically cut a swath of destruction and exit the sub-basement without either Teddy Dee or Elijah or both dying.

As Teddy Dee was calculating how to escape the sub-basement Elijah Graham stepped up and onto the steps beside Teddy Dee. He was holding a samurai sword and scabbard in his hands and had he been Japanese and two feet shorter he might have pulled off the failed imitation of Toshiro Mifune in the Seven Samurai.

"So, how does this work," Asami Fujinaka asked, the ultimate puppet master pulling all of the strings suddenly.

Teddy Dee looked from Asami Fujinaka to the massing armed men just behind them closing their escape and to Elijah Graham holding the samurai sword and scabbard.

"I know I don't get a vote here, but I want to go with leaving and never coming back to Japan," Elijah Graham whispered.

Teddy Dee smiled and shook his head.

"We will leave and never come back, but before we do, I have a question," Teddy Dee noted.

Asami Fujinaka nodded, amused by the boldness of Teddy Dee.

"Why did you give me the pistols?"

"Thought you might need them," Asami Fujinaka smiled.

"But they were unloaded," Teddy Dee said.

"I didn't want you to shoot my family with pistols that I had given you," Asami smiled. Behind her two men had gathered the two Ruger pistols and bagged them. The gift box had disappeared during the gunfight.

“Now, I have your fingerprints on two weapons that killed my brother and father, if you ever decide to suggest that something different happened here today,” the daughter of Hiro Fujinaka smiled, evilly.

Teddy Dee looked from Asami Fujinaka to the fake Keke Palmer to Elijah and back to Asami Fujinaka. Teddy Dee suddenly wanted to throttle Asami Fujinaka. She was like everyone else. Rich kid with something missing and playing with their family’s money and all that came with to try and fill that void. They had everything and nothing, Teddy Dee calculated.

They lived in this weird bubble world that was insulated from the people around them. They lived but they did not live. It was a weird conscious coma, Teddy Dee decided. As Teddy Dee studied Asami Fujinaka he imagined that with all the money that she would receive as the sole heir of the Signet Industries President’s wealth she was not satisfied. She wanted more.

Rich kids wanted all the toys. They were selfish. They did not want anyone else to have their toys even if they had outgrown them.

Selfish, myopic, short-sighted rich kids, Teddy Dee thought looking at the daughter of Hiro Fujinaka IV. No one mattered to Asami Fujinaka. The whole power grab had been for selfish reasons. Asami Fujinaka was all about Asami Fujinaka and no one else.

“What are you thinking, gaijin,” Asami smiled.

"I came here to stop a fight. That's all."

"The assassins? I will call them off."

"You?"

"Yes, me."

"How?"

"I am now in charge of Signet. So, I run things," Asami Fujinaka smiled.

Teddy Dee paused, thinking.

"You are just starting to realize that you were part of something bigger than yourself."

"Why?"

“My brother and father were misguided. Japan is changing. The world is changing. The world keeps spinning and we must change with the times or be ground underneath by the very machines that we build.”

The men stalked forward. Teddy Dee and Elijah Graham noted the men. Asami held the samurai at bay with a slight gesture of her left hand.

"This was all a power grab?"

"Can you think of a better way to force change?" Asami Fujinaka smiled evilly.

Teddy Dee had seen his share of conniving and power hungry people but he had been surprised to the extent that Asami Fujinaka had gone to gain control and keep control of her new position as leader of Signet Industries.

What fascinated Teddy Dee the most was that the woman that he had thought was initially a demur translator had morphed into an obedient daughter there to help with negotiations between her father and gaijins had gone and been replaced with this cutthroat power hungry cold-blooded killer dressed in a gold and black kimono.

Asami Fujinaka stood unmoving, unafraid, ever observant. The apple faced woman narrowed her almond shaped eyes. There seemed to be a glint there. She did not seem upset that her father and brother had been killed in front of her or that Teddy Dee was still holding a pistol in front of her.

"What's your next move?"

"What?"

"You need to go," Asami Fujinaka smiled as the black woman bodyguard climbed to her feet and rubbed at her jaw. The bodyguard opened her eyes and slowly seemed to recover from Teddy Dee's initial attack. The black woman climbed unsteadily to her feet. She stood blinking, guarding Asami Fujinaka jealously. Teddy Dee noted that the black woman seemed to be recovering quickly and suddenly seemed ready to pull her pistol at any provocation.

Teddy Dee had been played. He had been used to help Asami Fujinaka gain power of the Signet Industries. The realization made Teddy Dee want to rush Asami Fujinaka and the stink eye giving black woman and beat both their brains out. Of course, that wasn't going to happen.

Teddy Dee weighed the choices. The whole trip, the anonymous friend, the advice had all been a set up. He had been used. He had been used so expertly that it was only when the daughter of Hiro Fujinaka IV smiled as the castle guards massed behind him and Elijah Graham that he truly understood the length and depth that Asami Fujinaka had gone to wrest the power from her brother and father's hands. were attempting to impede his exit did he realize his part in the political grab for power.

"You better skedaddle," the black woman, Asami's bodyguard, had laughed. The black woman expertly guided Asami Fujinaka through a doorway that Teddy Dee had not seen. In Nakatsu-Jo castle there had to be numerous secret passages.

Though Teddy Dee had not considered following the pair he knew that there was no chance to follow them in the warren of mazes that made up the secret interior of Nakatsu-Jo castle.

The fifteen guards watched Teddy Dee and Elijah standing on the steps with the Heckler-Koch pistol in his hand, unmoving. They seemed to hesitate seeing the two Fujinaka men lying dead on the stairs and the two guards tasked to protect them lying prone on the stairs near the muscular giant. The guards moved in unison forward toward Teddy Dee without a word.

The guards again seemed unsure as Elijah Graham pushed Teddy Dee toward the exit that they had come in initially, carrying a bloody samurai sword and scabbard and bleeding from his right arm.

"We gotta go," Elijah Graham said. "Let's go."

The corporate blooder blinked and considered his present situation. Teddy Dee was once again a wanted criminal, he thought in the close quarters that was his cabin on the Ghanzou Shipping and Freight cargo ship. Teddy Dee imagined that the cabin he was in had been a makeshift room, just off the galley. The captain had given Elijah and him a few foodstuffs to survive the twelve-hour sea voyage.

While Teddy Dee sat on a small hammock that was secured by two eye bolts in the ceiling of the cabin he found himself recalling the last three days of his international adventure that had begun nearly nine months before after he was released from Kulani Correctional Facility on Hilo. One name came to mind as he looked back nearly a year to the various and seemingly random events that had lead him to the Ghanzou Shipping and Freight cargo ship; Elliott Winslow.

Less than an hour from the port and Yu Li knocked and poked his head into the cabin.

"We should begin offloading in forty-five minutes. You can leave as soon as we begin," he said in broken English.

Teddy Dee nodded.

The Ghanzou Shipping and Freight cargo ship docked and the gigantic ship was suddenly busy. There were men everywhere doing everything to secure the mammoth ship to the Hong Kong dock. Ropes were thrown. Men ran here and there. Yu Li escorted Elijah and Teddy Dee to the gangway and gestured for them to leave with the four crewmen already lined up to climb down the gangway.

Elijah and Teddy Dee fell in line behind the four crewmen as they arrived in Hong Kong. The pair walked the dock following the crewmen. At the far end of the dock Teddy Dee noticed that there was a man dressed in a suit.

On the dock waiting for Teddy Dee and Elijah Graham was a small square faced man with a crew cut dressed in a green checked business suit holding up a placard in English that read: Theodore + One.

“Think you are the plus one,” Teddy Dee smiled at Elijah.

"I am Theodore," Teddy Dee said.

"I am Cho," the driver dressed in a green checked suit and white collared shirt, wearing an earring in his ear said and bowed reverently.

“You pick up a lot of people at the cargo docks?”

“No, but Mister Kim wanted to make sure that you knew that you were safe.” Cho smiled, awkwardly.

"I have been asked to take you wherever you would like to go before taking you to Mister Kim's home," Cho explained.

Teddy Dee looked from Cho to Elijah and back. They could benefit from a change of clothes but it wasn't life threatening. So, Teddy Dee looked back to Elijah and back to Cho.

"We're good. You can take us to Kim."

"Yes, sir," Cho agreed.

He immediately opened the rear door of the Mercedes Benz for Teddy Dee. Teddy Dee climbed in. Elijah Graham followed.

They drove through the relatively quiet morning streets of Hong Kong, still crowded and busy, as they moved toward the downtown area with its lights and bustling businesses that Friday morning.

Elijah Graham, having been patched up on the freighter, sat in the comfort of the Mercedes and sipped a bottled water. His arm was in a sling.

“How you feeling,” Teddy Dee asked.

Elijah Graham smiled but did not answer.

“Well, the best thing to do on the other side of this dumpster fire is to get our minds off this with a little indulgence.”

“What’s that mean?”

Teddy Dee smiled. He tried to think of an easy way to explain what Elijah and he were in store for, thanks to Sun Kim. Sun Kim spent most of his life trying to be the center of attention in Hong Kong. He threw parties. He knew celebrities. He knew political leaders. Kim seemed to have his hand in every influential pot imaginable.

Sun Kim lived over the top. He had unrealistic expectations about everything. When Teddy Dee had met the Hong Kong politico Kim was fighting with another politico that was trying to strangle Kim’s business. Kim refused to allow his business to die without a fight.

He had hired Teddy Dee to release the stranglehold on his business. Doing what no one else was able to do was invaluable to Sun Kim and that put him forever in Teddy Dee’s debt. Teddy Dee told Kim that he had only been a blunt tool used to break the control of the dick wad that had figured out a way to jeopardize Sun Kim's interests.

The celebration, before Teddy Dee left Hong Kong was two days running. The highlight of the two days had to be a scorching performance by Johnny Marr from The Smiths of The Priest with Maxine Peake. There were several celebrities spotted at both day's events. Movie stars loved Sun Kim. Jet Li was at the party briefly. Terrence Howard and Diddy showed up. Nikki Minaj appeared. Sun Kim pulled some strings and had Adam and the Ants play on the last day of the two-day event. Bananarama played at the event as well. There was an appearance of The Cure front man Robert Smith. Soft Cell performed. It was a memory that Teddy Dee recalled fondly for all the over the top things that Sun Kim did in the short time that Teddy Dee worked for him.

"We are in for a treat," Teddy Dee said next to Elijah Graham.

Elijah Graham continued to sip his bottled water silently.

"Kim knows how to throw a party," Teddy Dee continued.

Sun Kim was a powerful and influential person in Hong Kong. Kim was the man to see if you had a project that you wanted to see completed. The little man with the spiky hair and bushy eyebrows knew everyone and more importantly, knew where the bodies were buried.

Sun Kim had become a governmental go between quite innocently a decade ago, when he was looking for a job after graduating from university in the States. He had returned to Hong Kong and gotten a position in the Hong Kong government as a runner and an assistant to a financial attaché. Kim didn't know immediately that the financial attaché was corrupt. Yet, when he discovered that the man was funneling hundreds of thousands of yen to an offshore account the information became more important than the money. The information gave Kim clout. He brokered that information into a promotion that opened more doors of information.

For Sun Kim, information was power.

So, when the driver parked in the front of the Lily Apartments Teddy Dee looked to Elijah Graham with a slight smile.

"High class," was all that Teddy Dee needed to say to his close friend. Elijah Graham only nodded.

The driver climbed out of the Mercedes Benz and scrambled around the car to open the door for Teddy Dee and Elijah Graham. The two exited the Mercedes and took a moment to appreciate Hong Kong in the morning. The Lily Apartments were a group of exclusive apartments built into a complex with washed and cleaned sidewalks. The exterior of the complex was immaculate.

There were two heavy planters on either side of the doorway that housed five foot trees. The planters had imprinted in script lettering: Lily Apartments in English.

Teddy Dee looked up and took in the twenty-five story height of the Lily Apartments. The sky was gray behind the apartment. There were three pale white clouds, more wisps of white, somewhere in between the top ten floors. They were standing in front of Sun Kim's downtown home. Cho was on the phone and moving around the car slowly listening and not talking.

"Be prepared to be impressed."

Again, Elijah Graham only nodded.

The doorman, dressed in a crimson jacket and matching shirt and black pants, opened the door and Cho paused in front of Teddy Dee and Elijah Graham.

"One moment, please," Cho smiled holding the phone to his ear.

Cho looked at the doorman and nodded and the the doorman nodded back. Instantly, a man walked out of the complex to stand beside the Mercedes Benz.

Cho put his cell phone away and smiled.

"This way gentlemen," the driver smiled with a slight bow. Cho led the pair into the bright lobby and to the elevator that was waiting.

Teddy Dee noted the elevator interior. It looked like any other elevator except that the floor panel had a card slot. Mr. Cho, the driver, removed an electronic key card and inserted it in the card slot. The elevator doors closed and gently lifted the trio up and off the ground. The lift moved silently as if on rails.

Three minutes from climbing into the elevator the doors slid open and in front of Teddy Dee and Elijah Graham stood two six-foot-tall Buddha dogs guarding a red door with a golden knocker.

Power brokers lived to impress those that they worked for and those that potentially they might work for, Teddy Dee thought as the driver stepped out of the elevator and waved to he and Elijah Graham to follow. The pair followed behind their driver silently. Teddy Dee was all smiles. Sun Kim was a friend of Teddy Dee, if he had any friends in this dog-eat-dog industry.

"Theodore," the five foot four-inch Sun Kim smiled, dressed in a black monk jacket and black trousers. He was standing in the middle of the entryway stretching out his arms as Teddy Dee walked into the luxurious flat that few that lived in Hong Kong could afford. Teddy Dee brightened as Sun Kim and he exchanged a brief and friendly embrace. While the pair hugged Elijah Graham and the driver stood in the interior of the flat silent observers.

"So, who is this you have brought with you?" Sun Kim smiled stroking his upper lip. Teddy Dee tilted his head and Elijah Graham moved forward, ever the obedient soldier.

"This is my friend, Elijah," Teddy Dee said. He watched as Elijah Graham shook hands with the diminutive Sun Kim. They looked like some bizarro world son and dad picture of some black Hulk family reunion, Teddy Dee thought absently.

"Do they make anyone in America normal sized, Theodore?"

"We are normal sized from where I come from, Sun," Teddy Dee returned with a smile. "You should see the guys that we think are big."

They, Kim and Teddy, shared a laugh. Cho, the driver laughed also. Elijah Graham remained silent.

"Sit down," Kim demanded. "Where are my manners? You want something to drink? Eat?" Kim paused. He poked out his lower lip. "Perhaps, you would prefer a shower and some clean clothes?"

Teddy Dee nodded.

"Good," Kim nodded rubbing his upper lip with his left index finger. He looked to Cho who directed Teddy Dee and Elijah to separate bathrooms where there were showers.

"If you will give me your clothes by the time you are showered and fed we will have clean clothes ready for you. If I am delayed, then I will leave you with bathrobes."

Teddy Dee gave Cho his clothes and took his shower.

When Teddy Dee climbed out of the shower Cho had left him a XXL Nike T-shirt, black and gold tracksuit, underwear, socks, and black and gold Air Jordan basketball sneakers all in his size.

Dressed and surprised at the comfort of the tracksuit Teddy Dee ventured forth, looking for Elijah or Kim. He heard voices to his left and laughter. So, Teddy Dee followed the voices and came to another section of the flat.

"I thought that you Americans all loved relaxing in tracksuits," Cho was saying as Teddy Dee entered the living room of the flat where Kim was seated and sipping on a cup of tea. Elijah Graham was seated on the couch with his back to the wall.

Cho had outfitted Elijah Graham as well. He was wearing the exact same outfit except in blue and gold. Elijah Graham didn't seem to care too much for the track suit it seemed.

"There you are," Kim announced. "You did not tell me that Elijah had been injured."

Teddy Dee didn't respond.

"I have sent for my doctor to check Elijah over. Cannot have a friend of mine in need of medical attention when I have access to one of the best doctors in Hong Kong."

Teddy Dee looked to Elijah and Elijah shrugged his shoulders.

"Yes, as I told Elijah I will not hear any protest on his or your part about this. You are my guests. It would just be bad manners to have you not leave Hong Kong better than you arrived."

"Yeah, sure," Teddy Dee agreed.

Ten minutes later two men and a young woman entered the penthouse apartment home of Sun Kim. The doctor, a Mister Alvin Wong, showed up with a Wilson backpack and no black doctor's satchel. He was nothing like Teddy Dee had expected.

Doctor Alvin Wong was a young man with a broad face and a thin Van Dyke moustache and beard. Wong looked like he was dressed to play golf instead of coming for a medical visit. Wong was wearing long khaki pants belted at the waist and comfortable black tasseled shoes. He had an aqua marine golf shirt on. His jet black hair was coiffed perfectly and cut neatly above his ears. Wong had a phone on his hip and wore no jewelry. He was friendly and had a slight British accent when he spoke in English.

After a cursory examination of Elijah, he returned to Kim and Teddy Dee and explained the problem.

"It seems that your friend has suffered a major trauma above his bicep. It is a wonder that he is able to use that arm in any way," Wong explained.

"Blah, blah, blah," Kim interrupted. "I did not bring you here to tell me things that I will never be able to tell others. I had you come here to fix a problem that I cannot solve."

"Yes, sir," Wong bowed.

"So, when will my friend be patched up and ready to go?"

"Ready to go?" Wong repeated, looking at Kim curiously. "Your friend has suffered a major trauma just above his bicep. If it was anyone else, he would be dead from blood loss having had his arm so severely injured." Wong was reeling at the idea of responding to Kim in some sensible way.

With him were two young colleagues; a Chinese man and woman. Wong described the two with him as his partners. The man, David Pan, was the accountant and legal advisor. Pan was dressed in shorts and a green polo shirt. When he walked in Pan was on the phone. He had an iPad tablet with him. On his wrist was a Breitling watch. He couldn't have been more than thirty, Teddy Dee guessed.

Pan had a slight British accent like Wong. He seemed uninterested in Teddy Dee and talked exclusively to Wong and Kim in Mandarin after a brief introduction.

Kim raised his hand and signaled for the doctor to stop. Pan instantly was beside Kim. He was the go-between for the client and doctor.

Pan spoke in Mandarin to Kim. Kim nodded. Pan smiled. Wong shook his head.

The woman, Mai Li, was his medical assistant in case there was a need for more equipment or medical attention.

Li, unlike Wong or Pan, seemed more professional than either. So, as Wong and Pan and Kim discussed the next steps Lee hooked up her small traveling case in the nearest wall outlet and waited. She, Lee, was calm and collected compared to the two men. Li was a dark haired beauty with alluring eyes and thin and serious mouth. She was dressed in a knee length floral dress with a diamond tennis bracelet and large but not gaudy diamond earrings. Of the three, Li had to be the youngest, Teddy Dee figured. Like Wong, Li carried a backpack that Teddy Dee assumed held medical supplies.

So, Pan returned a few minutes before the doctor had finished patching Elijah Graham up and giving Kim this warning: "He is patched up. He should be fine. His physical nature helps him in more stressful situations. So, he should be fine as long as he doesn't lift anything too heavy or put too much strain on his arm."

"Blah, blah, blah, Wong, thank you so much for all your help," Sun Kim said.

Teddy Dee was sitting near the kitchen, on a bar stool, sipping orange juice as Cho walked into the apartment house carrying four boxes. Cho moved through the chaos of Wong, Pan, and Lee as they packed up to leave Kim's apartment house. Cho noted, as he moved through the apartment, that the guest bedroom where he had put Elijah Graham had been made into the medical room for the moment. He placed the boxes in Teddy Dee's bedroom.

"We are going out after you recuperate, eat, and feel up to it." Kim announced after the doctor left the flat. "The doctor of course wants to write a paper on the disproportionate size of Elijah. He is not used to seeing anyone as big as Elijah. He has worked on the Sumo wrestlers from Japan but does not see them regularly and they are morbidly obese."

Teddy Dee shrugged his shoulders.

"Of course, you both are morbidly obese also but the doctor said that your body fat was surprisingly low, which boggles his mind."

"Well, we are medical wonders," Teddy Dee said. "In shape giants."

"Okay, in shape giants, we are going out to eat. Cho, will arrange everything. After dinner we can go dancing. Always have to go dancing."

"We will leave it in your capable hands, Kim," Teddy Dee said.

"Wonderful."

The quartet of Sun Kim, Elijah Graham, Teddy Dee, and Mr. Cho drove from the Lily Apartment house and to the Hong Kong dining district. They were now in a Mercedes Benz SUV. The SUV was spacious and allowed for the much needed legroom for Teddy Dee and Elijah Graham.

Sun Kim dominated the conversation from the moment that he climbed into the SUV dressed in a black Armani suit, white silk shirt, and butter leather Italian shoes. Cho was wearing a blue suit with a navy blue collared shirt and black shoes. Cho had given Teddy Dee and Elijah Graham two choices for the evening; black or gray. Elijah Graham had to choose between a gray custom tailored Sean John inspired suit and a custom tailored black three-piece suit that had all the telltale signs of a Ralph Lauren down to the subtle jacket liner that read: RLauren. The giant of a man sat in the back of the SUV dressed in the gray Sean John suit.

Teddy Dee had been given similar choices but had decided on the brown checked tweed inspired country gentlemen suit with its seemingly separate brown checked jacket and vest and well made khaki pants. Cho had picked Teddy Dee up a pair of Western inspired ankle boots with the image of horse shoes stitched across the toes.

"How often do you come to Hong Kong," Kim asked. "So, to take you and Elijah out for the night or the next couple of nights is no inconvenience for me or Cho."

Cho was driving and nodding and smiling. He reminded Teddy Dee of those dogs that people put in their cars and they bob their heads based on movement.

"Tonight you and Elijah are in for a treat. Most people come to Hong Kong and get caught up in the nightlife and the international exchange of ideas here. That's good for most people. They love it. They go back to the states and tell everyone how amazing Hong Kong was but they rarely see the greatest parts of Hong Kong. Tonight, you and Elijah will see the best of Hong Kong."

The Mercedes Benz oozed British club music. Kim loved electronic pop music. The funniest thing about that night was that Elijah too loved British pop music. Kim and Elijah had a surprisingly simple bond in the music that they listened to. It was great to see the two exact opposites in size, culture, and purpose simply transformed by the music they listened to. That night Kim Sun and Elijah Graham became fast friends while Teddy Dee learned to listen to electronic pop music and not want to tear off his ears.

"I have always loved the synthesizer laced Kraftwerk, XTC, Depeche Mode, Soft Cell, New Order, and Human League sound of the '80's that had redefined the English sound," Sun Kim explained.

"Love XTC," Elijah smiled. "I love that synthesizer driven music. Just can't get enough of Bauhaus, Depeche Mode, The Cure and English Beat."

Teddy Dee listened and let the bonding of Kim and Elijah dominate the conversation inside the Mercedes. Teddy Dee did not see a reason to interrupt. The two, Teddy Dee noticed, were the oddest couple. Yet, they were enjoying themselves.

Here, in Hong Kong, on the far side of the world Elijah and Sun Kim discussing British synth music made sense. Nowhere else would these two make sense, Teddy Dee calculated and he knew he was right.

Sun Kim was showing Elijah Graham pictures of him and Adam Ant and several other British pop stars.

"Every year I throw a party and invite all the British pop stars out to play for two days," Sun Kim announced.

"You still do that?"

"Yeah, it is sort of my thing now. Everyone loves it. I get all the benefits. The government loves the guaranteed money from the event."

"Always working the angles."

"Always," Sun Kim said smiled. He narrowed his eyes. "Theodore I promised no talk about work or work questions while you were here. This is supposed to be a celebration of my old friend back in Hong Kong. No business."

Sun Kim pouted, having broken his own rule. The pouting would not last, Teddy Dee knew.

"You like Dim Sum? Who doesn't like Dim Sum?" Sun Kim paused having found a song that he wanted everyone to hear then and there. He instantly turned the volume up and the Mercedes was filled with the sound of British alternative music.

"This is what I miss most about British rule, Theodore," Sun Kim confessed and for a long moment Teddy Dee didn't know if Sun Kim was being serious. He continued, now screaming, "The British have some truly marvelous music, without question."

"We'll be out of your hair by tomorrow at the latest," Teddy Dee said to Sun Kim. Kim was in the front passenger seat playing with the stereo and directing Cho to the dining district.

"We are going to Gough," Sun Kim reminded his driver pointing to a sign in Chinese. Cho nodded and obediently slowed down to turn left onto a street that was already packed.

"Some of the greatest food in Hong Kong is here," Sun Kim continued as Cho slowed the SUV down and looked for a parking space. "We will start at the tea house. You cannot come to Hong Kong and not experience a tea house."

Cho inched along finally stopped in front of a well lit door with four or five men standing on the sidewalk.

Cho stopped.

"We are here," Sun Kim smiled opening the door and climbing out of the SUV. Teddy Dee and Elijah Graham followed. Cho smiled awkwardly until one of the men moved to the car and climbed in behind the steering wheel.

Cho walked around the SUV and followed a few steps behind the group that was moving up the stairs and into the second story tea house.

"After we have tea we can get some seafood. If you want, we can get Chinese BBQ. I don't have a taste for BBQ here. I would prefer to have a little dessert after dinner and then we can go dancing."

Teddy Dee and Elijah Graham just looked at one another and remained silent. Sun Kim had been the perfect host. How could they say no to him? The pair knew that Sun Kim was unquestionably the best host they had.

While the two exchanged looks Sun Kim continued talking about the Hong Kong dining district.

"So, tonight we have fun."

After dinner the quartet climbed back in the Mercedes Benz SUV and headed to the best dance spot in Hong Kong.

"You will love this. You will really love this place. The music is banging. The DJs are incredible." Sun Kim smiled from ear to ear. "The women are amazing. Some of them are American models. Men, too. It is going to be memorable."

"Don't like to dance too much," Teddy Dee pointed out to Sun Kim again as they pulled up to the hottest dance club in Hong Kong; Magnum.

Sun Kim looked suddenly dejected.

"I'm not much of a dancer Sun," Teddy Dee said. "I like clubs. I like listening to music. I just don't dance."

Sun Kim brightened and nodded. "I understand. Gangsters don't dance, eh?"

Teddy Dee laughed and shook his head at his old friend. He had missed the point completely.

"We won't be here too long. Just going to pop my head in and say: 'Hello' to a few people. It should take me less than an hour." Sun Kim added, "Just pretend to be my bodyguards for the night. Make everyone think twice about messing with me tonight."

Teddy Dee nodded. He and Elijah had little choice in the matter. They were Sun Kim's guests. Sun Kim was knocking himself out to make sure that they had a memorable time.

"I mean it gives you and Elijah something to do while we are in the club."

Teddy Dee again nodded. He was not going to screw up this relationship with Sun Kim.

"You and Elijah can't get into that much trouble in less than an hour? Can you?"

Teddy Dee didn't answer. He and Elijah left to their own devices could wreak havoc. They could level the club in less than an hour if needed. Teddy Dee hoped that there was no need for that type of behavior in Hong Kong that night.

The next morning Teddy Dee woke up and found that he was in the guest bedroom in Sun Kim's apartment house. He climbed out of bed and found in the closet three white collared shirts in his size. Hanging beside the shirts were three pair of pants and a pair of Levi jeans in Teddy Dee's size. Teddy Dee slipped on one of the collared shirts and the jeans. He pulled on the Nike gym shoes that he wore only the day before and padded to the kitchen to find Cho sitting at the kitchen island checking something on a laptop.

"Don't you ever sleep?"

"Of course, sir," Cho smiled.

Teddy Dee paused.

"Would you like some coffee, sir?"

"Sure, and can you tell me where the closest Internet cafe is," Teddy Dee answered.

"Mister Theodore, you can use any computer here. There is a private room near the entertainment area that has complete privacy."

Cho directed Teddy Dee to the small room that was used as Kim's library and study. On one wall was a built-in dark wood bookcase that held easily over two hundred books. In the small but comfortable room was a small desk and on that desk was a MacBook Air.

So, Teddy Dee opened the computer and went to the homepage of a news source. He did not have to do much to find the Fujinaka family story. It was big news. There were dozens dead and injured. The deaths of Hiro and Tanaka Fujinaka in a historic castle was national news.

The newest information about the Fujinaka Family Murders suggested that the killers had fled Japan even though police were stationed at all airports and ports. There was grainy photos of Teddy Dee and Elijah but no one seemed to have revealed their names or identities. Teddy Dee tried to recall if he or Elijah had signed anything when they entered the castle. He did not recall. In one story there was a reference to a surveillance camera and recording that police were reviewing.

Teddy Dee read another report looking for the surveillance recording and found that the report, though more detailed, was tied into an unsubstantiated theory that suggested that the Fujinaka Family Murders was a corporate plot of the envious pharmaceutical powers to wrest power from the influential Japanese company. The report noted that the Fujinaka family had fought a hostile takeover of the company years before.

Several reports from Japan read that two black ex-military Americans were wanted criminals and suspected murderers of Hiro and Tanaka Fujinaka. The reports had no distinct descriptions of the murderers. There were no clear photos used. There was a blurry surveillance photo taken of two black men near the gate of the castle but they could have been any two black men in Japan.

The last report that Teddy Dee read said that the two black men were assassins of some unknown enemy of the Fujinaka family. The report noted that there had been several witnesses who had been happy to give details of the double murders. One witness said that the killers were possibly Nigerian. Another witness said that the killers were big, black American giant football players. One witness said that one of the giants was able to lift a car.

Teddy Dee shook his head at what was now seen as news. The Internet and its immediacy had destroyed the credibility of news reporting. Teddy Dee checked a few more reputable Internet news sources before deciding to take a different tact.

Chapter Thirty-Three.

There was a video link that suggested that Asami Fujinaka would take over the leadership of the pharmaceutical giant. Teddy Dee watched the video skeptically.

The video was labeled as a board meeting that had happened two years before the murders. The scene was filmed in a building that overlooked the night sky of Tokyo. The speaker, Asami Fujinaka, was dressed in a golden formal kimono and her hair was swept up and away from her thin neck to show off her almond shaped eyes and thin red painted lips.

"Uncles, I cannot begin to express my concern about the need for women, in general, and me, specifically, having the chance for advancement in our country.

"An ancient Sanskrit saying says, woman is the home and the home is the basis of society. It is as we build our homes that we can build our country. If the home is inadequate—either inadequate in material goods and necessities or inadequate in the sort of friendly, loving atmosphere that every child needs to grow and develop—then that country cannot have harmony. No country, which does not have harmony, can grow at all." Asami paused. She continued.

"Our country is a very rich country. It is rich in culture, it is rich in many old traditions—old and modern tradition. Some would say that we are in a fight for Japan. There are two Japans now; old and new. Of course, Japan has a lot of bad things too and some of the bad things are in the society—superstition, which has grown over the years and which sometimes clouds the shining brightness of ancient thought and values, eternal values. Then, of course, there is the physical poverty of large numbers of our people. That is something which is ugly and that hampers the growth of millions of young boys and girls. Now, all these bad things we have to fight against.

"But, we must not allow this dark side of the picture which, by the way, exists in every country in the world, to frighten us into paralysis. Even the richest country in the world has its dark side. Here in Japan, we seem to want to project only the best side of society. But there is a need to see the worst side as well. How are we to address the problems if we do not acknowledge that we have problems? Before anybody does anything, he or she has to have, of course, knowledge and capability, but along with it he or she has to have a certain amount of pride in what he or she is doing. He or she has to have self-confidence in his own ability. If your teacher tells, "You cannot do this," even if you are a very bright student I think every time you will find, it will be more and more difficult for you to do it. But if your teacher encourages you by saying, "Go on, you have done very good work, now try a little harder," then you will try a little harder and you will be able to do it. It is the same with societies and with countries.

"This country, Japan, has had remarkable achievements to its credit, of course in ancient times, but even in modern times, I think there are a few modern stories, success stories, which are as fascinating as the success story of our country. Our company rose on the simple desire to find a remedy for a powerful man who had fallen ill. Our ancestor did not begin this business for money alone. He was in the business of helping others.

"It is true that we have not helped everyone. We have not banished poverty, we have not banished many of our social ills, but if you compare us to what we were just about 20 years ago, I think that you cannot disagree that we have done much good in our time as a company.

"As I said, we do have many shortcomings, whether it is the government, whether it is the society. Some are due to our traditions because, as I said, not all tradition is good. And one of the biggest responsibilities of the educated women today is how to blend what has been valuable and timeless in our ancient traditions with what is good and valuable in modern thought. All that is modern is not good just as all that is old is neither all good nor all bad. We have to decide, not once and for all but almost every week, every month what is coming out that is good and useful to our country and company and what of the old we keep and enshrine in our society. To be modern, most people think that it is something of a manner of dress or a manner of speaking or certain habits and customs, but that is not really being modern.

"What is important is how we are thinking. Sometimes, I am very sad that even people who do science are quite unscientific in their thinking and in their other actions—not what they are doing in the laboratories but how they live at home or their attitudes towards other people. Now, for Japan to become what we want it to become with a modern, rational society and firmly based on what is good in our ancient tradition and in our soil, for this we have to have a thinking public, thinking young women who are not content to accept what comes from any part of the world but are willing to listen to it, to analyze it and to decide whether it is to be accepted or whether it is to be thrown out.

"So, I hope that you, father, who have this great advantage of power, privilege and education and my uncles will not only do whatever work you are doing keeping the national interests in view, but you will consider how allowing women to be a part of the deciding body of Signet Industries, as my mother before me and her mother before her were allowed in the decision making process of the family business and to make my own contribution to bringing beauty and balance to the lives of our people and our country. I think this is the special responsibility of the women of Japan."

Teddy Dee watched the video twice and marveled at the smoothness of the Japanese snake hiding beneath the skin of the daughter of Hiro Fujinaka.

The video was chilling in its completeness and insightfulness.

He went to Signet Industries website to see what they were saying and to check a hunch.

The splash page of Signet Industries had a black and white notice centered on the screen. On either side were Japanese characters that scrolled down the screen. The notice read:

Dear Reader,

You probably have heard the reports of the recent murder of our President and son at the Nagatsu-Jo castle. The Fujinaka family and Signet Industries cannot express our collective appreciation for the outpouring of sympathy and support in this trying and traumatic time. We, our family, and Signet Industries suffered an incredible loss. Hiro and Tanaka Fujinaka have been silenced by outsiders.

The police are investigating and seeking the arrest of the killers. At the writing of this letter we can only say that there were two Americans who came into our home as guests and deceived and duped our staff and security. The attack was unprovoked and brutal in its intensity. We are an herbal company and were not prepared for the murderous attack that occurred. More importantly we had no knowledge of the reasons or motivations of the two men that perpetrated this heinous act. They introduced themselves as Mister Smith and Mister Jones and potential clients of Signet Industries.

As has been reported these two strangers brutally murdered Hiro and Tanaka Fujinaka while killing and wounding several trusted unarmed employees. We are cooperating with the police in their investigations but the killers seem to have been very aware of cameras in the castle and avoided most of them in their escape. At this time, we believe that the murders were premeditated and planned against Hiro and Tanaka Fujinaka perhaps as a retaliatory strike for Signet Industries expansion into America but this is only speculation.

We are relying on the investigations of the police to bring these criminals to justice. The Fujinaka family is in a state of shock. The loved ones of each member of the Fujinaka family has asked that everyone respect their privacy in this time of loss. We ask that all tread lightly in approaching and requesting further information from members of the Fujinaka clan. We have a number of public media members in place if there is a need to discuss anything other than the loss that the Fujinaka family has suffered. The board of directors of Signet Industries have already moved quickly to ensure the stability of our family, brand, and our national business.

To ensure stability of our brand we have succeeded in temporarily putting Asami Fujinaka in as acting President of Signet Industries. Asami Fujinaka, daughter of Hiro Fujinaka, is well versed in corporate affairs. She graduated from Oxford at the top of her class. She has an excellent business mind and was groomed to take over various operations in Signet Industries by her late father. Signet Industries is in great hands, at present, and the brand and work continues to improve the health of all our clients. it is our good fortune in this horrific situation to be able to rely on someone that cares so much about the Fujinaka family and Signet Industries.

With Asami Fujinaka at the helm of Signet Industries we will have no questions of the future and the seriousness of our brand. Although, only a temporary fix, until an official election can be held, Asami Fujinaka offers stability for the Fujinaka family, the Signet Industries brand and our particular niche in the growing pharmaceutical industry.

Sincerely,

大毅 黒澤

Aito Fukui
Public Relations
Signet Industries

The flight back to Hawaii from Hong Kong was uneventful, but another eighteen-hours in the air.

Elijah Graham slept most of the flight.

Teddy Dee struggled to sleep. He had much on his mind.

The last time he had been in Hawaii was his release from Kulani Correctional facility. So, almost instantly, Teddy Dee found himself reliving that sentencing.

He had been arrested at the Honolulu airport and the arrest was news worthy. The Honolulu police had rushed through the airport and caught Teddy Dee as he was browsing the magazines in a news stand, near an airport gate. The police had guns drawn.

It was quite an arrest.

Teddy Dee, because he was arrested in the airport had to be released from Homeland Security to the Honolulu police. The FBI got involved for a brief moment. It was chaotic.

While all the legal filings were being made Teddy Dee tried to unravel what had brought him to being locked up in the Honolulu jail awaiting a meeting with a judge.

For reasons that seemed inconsequential, Teddy Dee had broken nearly half of his own rules in taking the contract in Hawaii. Three rules out of seven were just like telling everyone that Teddy Dee wanted to be caught.

The rules were there to remind Teddy Dee of the treacherous nature of the people he had to deal with in the shadow world of corporations. Yet, he ignored half of the rules that he relied on to keep him focused and point out things that he might forget while in the madness of the corporate milieu.

It was as if his rules meant nothing, suddenly, dealing with Elliott Winslow. It was as if Teddy Dee was on his first job and trying to tear the heads off the people that paid him.

"You know that you can make this easier on yourself by cooperating. You are already caught. It's up to you how this goes. Make it easier on yourself and tell us the name of the man behind the operation."

Teddy Dee listened to Homeland Security first, then the FBI and finally the Honolulu policeman trying to play good cop or bad cop in the small interrogation room. He had not said anything to Homeland Security or the FBI and had no intention of saying anything to Honolulu's Finest so he remained mute until his lawyer showed up.

"This guy ain't talking. Put him back in holding. Let him stew there a bit. Maybe then he will loosen his tongue," one of the cops said.

Teddy Dee was escorted back to holding. He sat in his jail cell and after an hour his corporate lawyer arrived.

Teddy Dee let his lawyer, a dark haired Latina named: Gabriella Cabrera, do her job. All the while Teddy Dee figured that Gabriella Cabrera was going to say the magic words and Teddy Dee would walk out of the Honolulu Correctional facility and board a plane.

Instead, Cabrera explained: “Mister Dandridge I am not going to be able to get you a bail hearing. The Feds have locked you and your co-conspirators down.” The Latina corporate lawyer whispered, “Elliott Winslow has given you and the others up for a deal.”

Up until that moment, Teddy Dee thought that he would get bail and then jump bail and get out of Hawaii. After Cabrera spoke, Teddy Dee made it up in his mind that he would have to do some time. Teddy Dee was the fall guy.

“I am here to make sure that you get the best deal possible. Of course, the Feds want you to give up someone else for a better deal. They have offered you one year if you roll over on someone else other than Elliott Winslow. They know that Winslow was not the mastermind,” Cabrera paused. “What do you have to say to the offer?”

Teddy Dee listened to the lawyer knowing that the Feds offer didn’t apply to him. It only was offered to “normals." More importantly, Teddy Dee knew that what he said or didn’t say to Cabrera was going to be passed on to the men that hired him to manage chaos in the shadows of the corporate world.

So, when the judge sentenced him to three years, Cabrera told him, with good behavior, that he would be out in eighteen-months, if not sooner. Teddy Dee didn’t blink. Teddy Dee looked at the beautiful Latina and smiled. He smiled and thought that this situation had changed him. He was no longer outside the “normal” life. He was a statistic, suddenly.

Yet, Teddy Dee knew things about Elliott Winslow that he had gleaned in Teddy Dee's preparation for the trip to Hawaii. There were numerous rumors about Winslow’s proclivity for transgender trysts. There had been an attempt to hide the perversion though with the Internet and social media all of Winslow’s skeletons were laid bare.

Even though the prosecution never was able to prove that he had been involved in the crime Teddy Dee was still charged with jury tampering and woke up in the minimum security prison in Hawaii named: Kulani. Teddy Dee was sentenced to two years for conspiracy to commit a crime on purely circumstantial evidence. Teddy Dee was suddenly a humdrum criminal.

Everyday, for a year, Teddy Dee thought that the corporate executives that he worked for would decide to flex a little muscle and twist some arms to free him from Kulani. Everyday, for a year, 365 days, Teddy Dee waited.

It was the beginning of the second year that Teddy Dee began to realize that the old saw: Out of sight and out of mind was truly the way of all humans. In the world of shadows Teddy Dee figured that the Feds had backed off and the Honolulu police had the stronger case. The feds, Teddy Dee figured, had shut down any escape for anyone trying to work a deal. So, if Teddy Dee had Hawaiian blood in him, he might get a slap on the wrist. Not having Hawaiian blood in him he figured that he was going to do time.

Again, sitting in Kulani, as a fall guy, Teddy Dee realized that he should not and could not take his incarceration personally. This is business. The only solace he had that kept him sharp was the fact that the corporate hire had decided to save his own skin and sacrificed the whole team. That selfish act was a no-no in business. It was a no-no in the shadows as well. He broke the cardinal rule of big business. For that Teddy Dee was hoping that he could exact justice.

As he thought of that last point Teddy Dee paused. Had he wanted to be caught? Had he sabotaged his own best efforts? He took a long moment to think about that question.

Teddy Dee had been trying to figure out a way to escape the hamster wheel that had become his life in the shadows. He had gone so far as to hire a high school student to play with the idea of freeing someone that was enslaved in a continual oppression.

Eric had suggested that losing his value might lead to those over him not willing to waste a bullet on him. Teddy Dee did not believe that. In the shadows, in the corporations, if you held a secret you were valuable. If you were valuable, then you were worth the cost of the bullet.

Teddy Dee wanted to blame his incarceration on Elliott Winslow. For, Elliott Winslow had ratted out everyone to secure his freedom despite the fact that the lawyer's trial had been thrown out based on jury tampering.

Yet, Teddy Dee knew that things were not that simple. Teddy Dee had played a part in the drama of Elliott Winslow and his fascination with transgender prostitutes. That perversion had thrown six men's lives into turmoil despite their best efforts.

The price of Elliott Winslow's freedom was not cheap. Winslow had to step down as the head of corporation of Winslow Law Firm. He had to surrender his 51% interest in the firm and resign from the board of directors. Winslow also had to surrender any holdings in businesses where he held over 45% interest.

The deal had, on its face, been seen as a definite and defining judgment against the competent and arrogant litigator but all that knew Elliott Winslow knew that he was a smart, rich kid who had endless supplies of cash and investments. The FBI, FTC, and FDA had only been able to address Winslow's holdings in the United States. Winslow was an international businessman doing business in America. The Winslow Law Firm dealt with hundreds of companies in at least ten different countries and the majority of Elliott Winslow's money was offshore. The FBI, FTC, and FDA all were aware of this but they were attempting to send a message. So, though the punishments seemed significant to the uninitiated the punishments were more like a slap on the wrist of a mischievous and bright child than a real punishment.

Elliott Winslow had sold out everyone to secure his freedom. The cruel part of the betrayal was that he had thrown his loyal security team under the bus without hesitation when the FBI came to talk to him about a taped conversation that had been recorded between him and a transgender prostitute named: Charity.

Elliott Winslow had folded like a bad hand of poker and put everything in motion to destroy five faithful men who had worked for the Winslow Law Firm a combined sixty years. There was history between Winslow and his loyal men. They had failed him and were attempting to redeem themselves after several failed efforts for a man that they respected.

Teddy Dee did not hold any such high beliefs in Elliott Winslow. He had done his job. He had been attempting to get off the big island but moving slower than usual, having changed his footprint and proximity to the Honolulu airport. All these things, thanks to Elliott Winslow, worked against Teddy Dee and the six. If Teddy Dee had stuck to his routine he would have checked out of the hotel, dropped off the rental car, and climbed on the plane long before his co-conspirators made it to the airport or any had been arrested.

Teddy Dee had taken a cab to the cliffs of Manoa. He had learned the address while in Kulani. He asked the cab to wait.

"I won't be too long," Teddy Dee told the cab driver.

The Manoa Cliff high on Tantalus, just minutes from Punahou were the home of a number of celebrities. Teddy Dee had not come to Manoa Cliff to find the star's homes. He had come to find one resident in particular; Elliott Winslow.

On the cliffside Teddy Dee walked up the solitary and secluded street closest to the cliff edge of the exclusive area of Hawaii. Teddy Dee turned around and made sure that the cab and cab driver were parked where he had left them. Reassured that the cab and cab driver were waiting Teddy Dee walked and turned to the left and around the bend to see the cove where Elliott Winslow's home sat behind a ten-foot stone wall.

The surf was crashing beneath the Manoa Cliffs and as Teddy Dee made his way to the stone walled entrance to Winslow's home.

Teddy Dee was inches from the wall of Elliott Winslow when he had second thoughts. He had only been back in the states for hours. Was he ready and willing to settle the score between him and Elliott Winslow?

As Teddy Dee stood unsure of his next move a familiar voice sounded in his head.

"This is all business, Teddy. Don't take any of this shit personally," Easton, mentioned. "Everyday, that you do something for someone else, realize that this shit is just that: shit. You don't have anything invested in it, except your work. Leave that shit, at the office. Don't let this shit bleed into your personal life, if you have a personal life."

Easton was dressed in his well fitting blue pinstriped Brooks Brothers suit. He had his classic Patek Phillipe wristwatch on his wrist. He was wearing black Italian leather boots.

"Remember, that you have to get through this shit, everyday," Easton announced. "The bigwigs don't really care if you lose a limb, are blinded, or get imprisoned. They are paying us to protect them and their interests. So, in their heads, we are just a number on a sheet. They aren't anymore invested in us, as you are invested in the ants and bugs that you drive over everyday. Remember that," Easton had said so long ago after lunch at Jordan's and waiting for the valet to bring his brand new black Mercedes Benz to the front of the restaurant.

"If there is a problem who do we call?"

Oscar Easton smiled at Teddy Dee in answer.

"No safety net. We are only safe after the job is complete. Before, during, and sometimes after the suits can deny our work for them to protect themselves and those that are above them. If there is trouble, then say nothing. If you get in a situation and figure that you are about to be pinched, then call your handler and let them handle the rest. Do not allow anyone to retrace your work back to the company or person in the company that hired you in the first place."

"But--," Teddy Dee began only to be cut off by Oscar Easton.

"We are hired and paid to protect the corporation at all costs. Our job, whatever it is, whenever we are working, is done to protect the corporation. Don't forget that."

Teddy Dee nodded.

"Do you understand that there are billions of workers? The workers make the shadow world hum. They sell, feed, shop, plan, and work to make the shadow world. Their lives are meaningless to the shadow world and important as well. They can die and the corporation will recruit another worker before the last one dies." Easton pointed out that in the shadow world, the world most people lived in, everyone was born and expected to work. In the normal world people worked and their self worth was measured by the work they did. There were no non-workers in the corporate world. Those that did not work were killed and removed for the good of the corporate world. The rules were simple.

Working in the corporate world was a 24-hour process. There was no work from sun up to sundown. In the corporate world the sun did not set on work. Workers worked in shifts. They worked day and night. They worked tirelessly. They worked with the belief that what they did was for the betterment of the corporate world. Of course, the worker believed that the work they did was for themselves and that their work was important to the world and the corporate world. Yet, everyone in the corporation knew what mattered. Some of the workers deluded themselves into believing that what they did for the corporation was essential work for the corporation and their work was important as a result. They were deluded. All workers and work done by workers was interchangeable by any other worker. The essential work was done by the heads of corporations that few saw or understood.

If a worker got sick and died no one cared except the workers that had to pick up the slack because of the inconvenience of the death. Workers mourned workers. Workers mourned workers because it affected the workday and workload.

Just above the workers were the corporate blooders. Corporate blooders were the guardians of the corporation. The corporate blooders protected the doors and secrets of the corporation. There were not a finite number of corporate blooders in any corporation. As a result of the limit of corporate blooders they were the third most important part of the corporation.

Corporate blooders were better than workers. The camarilla, retinue of the head of corporations were the next rung up in the corporate world. The camarilla by definition and importance was more essential than the corporate blooders. Within the camarilla were the board of directors, the Vice Presidents, and CFOs, CEOs, and CCOs. The head of the corporation was the top of the corporation hierarchy.

A corporate blooder, the leader of the foot soldiers in the corporation, there were never more than five in a corporation. There were never more than one hundred blooders working in the shadows. Corporate blooders were dangerous people. Their numbers had to be regulated. Men like Teddy Dee and Oscar Easton were sent to tear off the heads of those foolhardy enough to try and threaten the corporation in anyway or worse to try and steal from the corporation. Corporate blooders were the corporations shock troops. The corporate blooders were the loyal samurai of the corporation.

They were paid for their loyalty and unflinching willingness to do whatever was necessary to protect the corporation. Corporate blooders went to war for the corporation. There was no job that a blooder would not do for the corporation. Like the samurai of old the corporate blooder was a loyal and self-sufficient one-man army. They were fearless and unblinking in the face of danger. Corporate blooders guarded and protected, killed and threatened for the head of corporations and the camarilla. They were the closest to the camarilla and the heads of corporations. Corporate blooders were an open secret in the corporate world. Paid off books their budgets were unknown. Their perks were beyond imagining. Yet, being a corporate blooder was a solitary life and few noted or cared when they died.

Being so close to power the corporate blooders learned corporate secrets that could cripple Fortune 500 businesses. The death of a corporate blooder in the corporate world was a sad moment and a moment of relief for the heads of corporations. Secrets died with corporate blooders. It was a complex and intricate social dynamic in every corporation.

"Understand corporate blooders are finished with a knock at the door or text to meet somewhere for a drink. The most common end of a blooder happens when a stranger on the street simply walks up and double taps us in some alleyway," the older man said. Easton looked at Teddy Dee with his dark eyes and smiled. "Our end is never pretty or dignified. It is done to send a message. They, the higher ups, the heads of corporations, the Presidents, CEOs, CFOs, CCOs, Vice Presidents, want us all to understand where the true power is located. They, the big wigs, decide that we no longer are able to do our jobs and then suddenly we are hunted and tracked down like rabid dogs and shot in the streets like common criminals." Easton paused, "I think that the worst part of it all is knowing your time is up and being locked out of the corporation." Easton paused.

"They lock us out of the corporation?"

"Yeah. Locking you out of the resources that you have used is the ultimate insult to injury. If your time comes do not expect help to come from anyone. Don't expect the higher ups to be your friend. You are not friends with anyone in the corporation. You are just an essential part of the corporation but always replaceable."

Easton had explained time and time again that the worst part of being a part of the shadows and being a corporate blooder was that corporate blooders were cannibals in a barrel. "Being a corporate blooder you give up everything to gain more than you can imagine. You know the candle that burns twice as bright lasts half as long. Just know that in this shadow world, you are a target of the other corporate blooders. It is worse than dog-eat-dog. It is shark devour shark in the shadow of the corporations where you are being watched and tested for weaknesses. The corporate blooders circle and wait for you to stumble and attack. When they attack their attack is savage and brutal. The attacks are tests. Pass the test and survive. Fail the test and die."

Fail the test and die?

Had Teddy Dee failed the test? Hadn't he failed the test? Why wasn't he dead?

"Acta non verba. You know that not everyone is built for shadow work," Easton pointed out in Teddy Dee's memories.

Teddy Dee studied Oscar Easton carefully in his memories. Teddy Dee remained on the bench and watched as Easton stopped and turned around about ten feet away from his Teddy Dee. Oscar Easton repeated what he had said before: "Acta non verba." It was the last thing that he said to Teddy Dee for another two years.

Teddy Dee did not know what Oscar Easton said or more importantly what it meant. All he knew was that he had taken the step toward a better life.

Yet, when Teddy Dee turned 39 all the work that he did, all the security measures that he had put in place, all Teddy Dee's years of building his reputation in the dark world of big business was suddenly at risk, Teddy Dee's own security, was put in jeopardy. Forty had been a moment in time that made Teddy Dee rethink, for a moment, what he was doing. What had he accomplished? What had he done in his life?

Teddy Dee had a bout of doubt and in that brief moment, like the Grinch that stole Christmas, he grew a heart. Teddy Dee grew a conscious. He had a moment of self doubt. Was his life meaningful? As a corporate blooder there was no philosophy. There was no need to reflect. Teddy Dee, like all corporate blooders, was paid for his loyalty. Growing a conscious in Teddy Dee's line of work was perilous. Everything that mattered was suddenly in jeopardy because Teddy Dee hadn't followed the rules.

"You cannot get lazy in the shadows, Teddy," Easton explained. "There is all this gold and honey and pussy and power at arm's reach," Easton said sipping a Belgian beer. "That's the trap. That is the distraction that makes you let your guard down. When you feel like you have made it that is the moment that you need to work even harder. You have to be alert. Making it is not the end. Making it and taking it and then remaking it is the goal."

The shadow world of corporations, though few knew of it in any other name other than above the hum of the world was an open secret that most did not believe existed. It was a place of myths, lies, deception, obfuscation, and smoke and mirrors. No one attached to the real world could imagine a place just on the other side of streets that they walked down that held so much wonder.

The shadows of corporations were magnificent and cruel. It was exquisite and cutthroat. There were great riches and continual backstabbing in the great palaces and mansions that the lesser gods of the shadows resided. Some familiar names had been part of the shadow world of corporations. There were rumors that the shadows of corporations had something to do with the Illuminati. Anyone that knew anything about the shadows of corporations knew that the veiled mystery that was the Illuminati was a children's fairytale compared to the highly guarded and incredibly secret shadows.

Too often, when Teddy Dee thought about what he did in comparison to the bigger picture of the shadows of corporations he always found himself feeling smaller than his six foot four-inch frame and two hundred and forty pounds. The shadows of corporations were a construct that seemed ever expansive.

It was seven families, initially, that had wrested power from the governments by investing their sizeable treasuries in gold, silver, and copper. They, the seven, had been ahead of the technology boom. They had been ahead of the housing bubble burst. They, the seven, had invested in gold, silver, and titanium when the world seemed to waver.

The plane landed. Elijah and Teddy Dee took a shuttle to the domestic terminal. Teddy Dee purchased the plane tickets. They had eight hours to kill.

"Eight hours to kill, E," Teddy Dee said. "Think that I will go to see an old friend."

"I'll just stay here and heal up," Elijah said his shoulder still healing from Japan.

Teddy Dee exited the airport and took in the Hawaiian weather. It was still dark. It was not yet three in the morning.

Teddy Dee caught a taxi to the Pali highway and the Ko'olau Range. The twisty road and green hills of the Ko'oalu Range gave way to the exclusive residences of the rich and famous. Teddy Dee asked the cab to wait.

"I shouldn't be long," Teddy Dee announced.

Teddy Dee walked up the quiet and gated neighborhood that few Hawaiians knew existed. The black giant walked up and around the winding road to find the home that he had dreamed of finding while in Kulani Correctional Facility.

He stood at the entrance to Elliott Winslow's luxury home. He thought about how easily it would be to go in and kill Elliott Winslow. All he had to do was climb the wall and bang, zip, a hundred-yard sprint to the main building and Elliott Winslow would be found dead in his shower or his pool. Death by accident.

Teddy Dee thought about the satisfaction of killing Elliott Winslow as he studied the large main house that had been the temporary governor's residence years before. It was situated on the Ko'oalu Range high over Nu'uanu Pali State Wayside Park, just minutes from Honolulu. The brilliant lights of the city were visible as Teddy Dee considered what he was contemplating.

Teddy Dee paused, thinking. He was a wanted criminal. Teddy Dee, not by name, had been linked to the death of Hiro and Tanaka Fujinaka. He could not go back to Japan, probably. Teddy Dee considered. He sounded like a fool. There was no description of him or Elijah.

Then, as soon as he thought of Elijah and his tenuous involvement in Elliott Winslow's chaos his anger returned. Elliott Winslow was a nagging loose thread that he had pulled and instead of pulling and stopping the unravelling the unravelling had become worse. Teddy Dee had left Kulani Correctional and Hawaii and began the whole fiasco that led to Japan and the death of Hiro and Tanaka Fujinaka. So, as he stood looking at the outer walls of Elliott Winslow's exclusive estate Teddy Dee tried to push down his emotions.

This was not personal, he lied to himself. This was business. He had been robbed. Teddy Dee had lost two years of his life because of Elliott Winslow. Twenty-four months had been taken from Teddy Dee by Elliott Winslow. He wanted revenge. He wanted his two years back.

Nothing personal.

"Strictly business. Nothing personal." When Teddy Dee was growing up in Chicago he used to hear this saying over and over. Teddy Dee thought that there was a song made about it. It didn't make too much sense to Teddy Dee at the time. Teddy Dee supposed that he didn't understand the phrase because he didn't understand business.

In business, good business, there was a callousness to the business model. The employer doesn't hire someone because they are family. The employer hires someone because they are qualified. The employer doesn't fire someone because they won't put out. The employer fires someone because the person is a terrible employee and not because they feel threatened by the employee's intelligence.

So, to do well in the business, Teddy Dee had to distance personal feelings from his business practice. This was perhaps one of the hardest rules to adhere to regularly.

Being the fall guy was another bitter pill to swallow. It was a part of the business of the shadow world. For all the benefits there were disadvantages to the shadow world as well. So, Teddy Dee had learned, reluctantly, that he should not and could not take his incarceration personally. That was business.

The only solace he had that kept him sharp was the fact that the corporate hire had decided to save his own skin and sacrificed the whole team. That selfish act was a no-no in business. It was a no-no in the shadows as well. He broke the cardinal rule of big business. For that Teddy Dee was hoping that he could exact justice.

Killing Tanaka had given Teddy Dee some satisfaction. The elimination of Marvin Harper, the mercenary, had been necessary. Eliminating the Germans was essential. Yet, Elliott Winslow was the one person that had not had his comeuppance. Allowing Elliott Winslow to live and breathe seemed unfair.

Teddy Dee couldn't kill the Germans again. He couldn’t kill Marvin Harper any more. He couldn’t kill Tanaka again. He wanted to make Elliott Winslow suffer for the betrayal that had cost him two years in Kulani Correctional.

He scaled and dropped over the wall and did a hundred-yard sprint to the main building. The surf was crashing beneath the Pali Highway and as Teddy Dee made his way around the main building looking for a way inside. Looking for entry, he paused. Sitting in the sunken living room was Elliott Winslow and his wife watching television. They were smiling and talking about something.

He could break into the house and snap Elliott Winslow’s neck before he could sound an alarm. Yet, the woman, Elliott Winslow’s wife, was the real obstacle. She would be an unsuspecting witness and then what? Was he to zap her as well? Were his hurt feelings enough to kill an innocent woman? Had Teddy Dee sunk to the depths of an uncontrolled and savage street thug?

Teddy Dee leaned against the wall that separated him from Elliott Winslow and justice, or what Teddy Dee viewed as justice. He closed his dark eyes and covered them with his scarred hands. Teddy Dee took a few breaths and reminded himself that living in the shadow world of corporations had never been about justice. He was a shit eater. He did what others were not willing to do.

So, then and there, Teddy Dee decided that killing Elliott Winslow was not a good thing to do suddenly. He could not say what the reason was exactly. If it was business, he rationalized, then he should be paid for punching Winslow's ticket. Teddy Dee knew that was true. It did not satisfy his hurt and desire for some sort of justice. Maybe, Teddy Dee thought, in this crazy world of shadows, someone would need Winslow silenced and he might be tagged as the button man. Teddy Dee knew that the shadow world did not work that way. There was no justice in the shadow world of corporations. There was only power and the lack of power.

Teddy Dee did not have the power to silence Elliott Winslow. He had the physical strength to end Winslow's life but he did not have the power to stop the blowback of Winslow's murder on himself and others. So, he chose not to exact revenge on the man that had orchestrated his near death and incarceration. Teddy Dee had issue with Elliott Winslow and not his wife or children.

Teddy Dee pressed himself from the wall and turned on his heels to leave the compound. He padded past the car that was Elliot Winslow's and left his calling card. The card was blank. On it though was his thin and fine script initials: TD. Beneath it Dandridge had written Elliott Winslow a message: "You are lucky. Luck runs out, though."

The cab ride back to the airport was one that Teddy Dee anticipated and dreaded. As the cab navigated the winding road of Pali Highway Teddy Dee closed his eyes and tried to think about what lie ahead. He was heading back to California and then to Atlanta where he would make sure that Bethany Rogers and the Rogers were safe. He would contact Samantha Morris and try and arrange a meeting in South Dakota. His life was farcical.

Elijah was seated and waiting for the plane to depart in the airline lounge. Teddy Dee met him inside the exclusive high mileage sanctuary. Teddy Dee sat down next to Elijah who was drinking a beer.

"You want one," Elijah asked.

"Think so," Teddy Dee admitted, suddenly hungry. He picked up the menu and looked over the choices. "Think I want to eat something, before the flight."

"Sure," Elijah agreed.

The waitress of the airport lounge came by and Teddy Dee ordered a cheeseburger and fries.

Seated next to him was the near mute Elijah Graham. Elijah turned to Teddy Dee and looked him up and down for a moment trying to decide something.

"Did you kill him?"

"No," Teddy Dee said, with a shake of his head.

"Why not?"

"I think I'm done with all that now," Teddy Dee said, suddenly tired.

"Yeah, huh," Elijah agreed and fell silent in the lounge.

After eating the cheeseburger and fries Teddy Dee pulled out his laptop and read an e-mail sent by Asami Fujinaka. Teddy Dee thought briefly to delete the message before reading it. Instead, he opened the file and read it.

To: Teddy Dee
Fr: anonymous123113751971114111
Subject: puppet
Dear Teddy,
This is a little late.
Sorry.
I have been really busy. Thank you for all your hard work.
You were so invaluable.
Remember, you have your life to lead.
Don't come back to Japan or I will have to get mean.
Oh, Signet Industries may have a name change.
Everything old is new again.
If you are interested.
Stocks should go up.
Way up.
Insider information.

Your friend.
Nausicca of the Valley Wind Asami

Chapter Thirty-Four.

It was April in the Badlands, when Teddy Dee arrived. It was cold and there were light flurries, as he stood watching the planes take off or arrive. The temperature was in the low thirties. It was cold but not bone chillingly cold that the body hurt from the savageness of the temperature. Teddy Dee was wearing a black and old and battered, insulated and zippered motorcycle jacket, black jeans and motorcycle boots. He was extremely warm.

Gone were the suits, ties and lace up leather shoes, Teddy Dee thought absently. Gone was so much that had been his life, for the last decade. Teddy Dee smiled at the mild discomfort he felt, not being in a suit and tie, that moment at the small South Dakota airport.

He had flown in from Los Angeles and brought with him just a small leather carry-on. Teddy Dee had not planned on being in South Dakota long. He checked his Rolex watch and twisted his lips on his dark face, thinking. He was in South Dakota after a seemingly endless battle with powers greater than himself. The trip to South Dakota was a bucket list item. It was also a reward. He was there to see Crazy Horse. If he had time he would go and see Mount Rushmore. He had never seen either.

"Thank you for coming, Mister Dandridge," Samantha Morris smiled as Teddy Dee turned and found the beautiful and curly haired administrative assistant leaning against the counter of an unused kiosk. Teddy Dee smiled. He smiled and his smile was that of a boy that cannot hide his affection for the girl that has won his heart.

Samantha Morris was dressed in a fur collared three quarter length jacket, jeans and knee high boots. In her left hand she was twirling a pair of oversized sunglasses. Her hair was pulled back into two French braids. On her dainty ears were a pair of cascading diamonds.

"I thought you were coming on a later flight," Teddy Dee managed, longing not to begin the conversation for fear that beginning it would mean the inevitable end of the conversation and moment.

Samantha Morris moved and the air around her shimmered as she did. Teddy Dee tried to commit every detail of the reddish brown beauty to memory. He watched every movement of the svelte and lithe beauty longing to stop and hold the moment between them just a little longer. In his mind, Teddy Dee imagined that this meeting was the greatest moment in his life.

He longed to suddenly take out his camera, on his phone, and take hundreds and hundreds of pictures of Samantha Morris in South Dakota. It was a ridiculous thought but one that he entertained in his head. When this was over, and it would be over inevitably, he wanted to look back and recall everything that his mind had been unable to catalog in some way.

"Didn't want to be too predictable," Samantha Morris smiled, mischievously.

Teddy Dee smiled at Samantha Morris and her response.

Teddy Dee had spent years trying not to have feelings bleed into his business and with the sight of Samantha Morris all that reservation disappeared. Teddy Dee was drawn to Samantha Morris.

"What brings you to South Dakota, Miss Morris," Teddy Dee smiled, easily, broadly as if he were thirteen and just discovering the opposite sex.

"I was in town and have never been to Mount Rushmore or Crazy Horse," Samantha Morris smiled. "Thought I might go and see them today. After that, I don't know," the green eyed beauty smiled. She quickly added, "What brings you here?"

Teddy Dee loved the slight Southern drawl of Samantha Morris. It made her unique in Minnesota. That drawl made her unique everywhere.

Teddy Dee listened and cataloged the accent. He had listened and instantly thought of mint juleps and katydids and all of the beauty of the south and its rich history as this twenty something woman with shoulder length hair spoke. He could not help myself from smiling.

"Downtime," Teddy Dee said, knowing that Samantha Morris knew the reason that he was in the Badlands.

Teddy Dee studied Samantha Morris and took in her neatly manicured fingernails. There was a blue acrylic on her otherwise clear fingertips. The only evidence of her youth sat there on her fingers.

"Are you hungry?"

"No, I'm fine."

Teddy Dee smiled at Samantha Morris and her choice of words.

"Well, I suppose that we can go to one of the monuments then," Teddy Dee began awkwardly. "Do you have a preference which one you want to see first?"

"Always wanted to see all those Presidents," Samantha Morris smiled and dazzled.

"Well, Mount Rushmore it is," Teddy Dee said grabbing her small piece of luggage. The two walked slowly from the airport to the rental car parking lot. Teddy Dee had rented a Cadillac XTS for the journey. He popped the trunk and placed Samantha Morris' luggage in the gigantic trunk. His small carry-on sat beside her small piece of luggage.

Teddy Dee was about to climb in the car when he stopped himself and went to open the door for Samantha Morris. She smiled and folded herself into the Cadillac XTS. Teddy Dee closed the door and walked around the rear of the Cadillac and when he arrived at the driver's door he found that Samantha Morris had opened the door for him.

"Thanks," Teddy Dee said as he climbed in behind the steering wheel and started the engine. He punched in the destination that he wanted to arrive at on the GPS system of the Cadillac XTS and waited for it to give the best route and directions. Samantha Morris sat in the passenger seat comfortable and not stiff or ill-at-ease. That, ease, delighted Teddy Dee.

"You know that there are eight Crazy Horse locations," Samantha Morris said in the quiet of the car's interior.

"I did not." Teddy Dee smiled. "I know of the one here. Is there one in Las Vegas?"

"Yes," Samantha Morris nodded.

Teddy Dee paused.

"Do you want to listen to music? You play with that part of the car. I'll drive," Teddy Dee said, putting the Cadillac XTS into gear.

Teddy Dee and Samantha Morris drove to Mount Rushmore. The drive was spectacular as Samantha Morris talked about the flight, her family and Teddy Dandridge.

"You know that I had to check you out," Samantha Morris admitted.

"I would not expect less."

"Do you want to know what I found?"

Teddy Dee shook his head; no.

"No?"

"No."

"Why not?"

"I suppose, because I know me. If there are things that you found out that are bad, then they couldn't have been too bad." He paused, driving through the National Forest. "You are here. If you found out things that are good. You are still here."

"Yeah, I guess so."

Samantha Morris found a R&B station and allowed the music to fill the Cadillac XTS. Teddy Dee did not mind. The music reminded him of his mother and aunt. They loved Motown and Marvin Gaye and The Temptations.

"You like music?"

"I don't like all music."

Samantha Morris smiled at Teddy Dee's response.

"Hey, I have a question," Samantha Morris said as Teddy Dee pulled into the parking structure for Mount Rushmore. The temperature had fallen into the twenties the higher up they drove. There was snow on the ground in thick patches.

Teddy Dee listened.

"Barry Granger told me that you arranged that lunch with you and me long before the day that you asked me. Is that true?"

Teddy Dee nodded.

"Why did you feel that you had to arrange the lunch?"

Teddy Dee smiled.

"I am a realist. I look at you and know that you are out of my league. I didn't ask you to lunch to get in your pants. Granger thought that was what I was asking, at first. I wasn't. I think that I told you that you are this brilliant, beautiful and bright person and I just wanted to sit down and get to know you. No strings attached."

Samantha Morris nodded and slipped her arm around Teddy Dee's gigantic bicep as they made their way up the great walkway toward the four historic heads on Mount Rushmore.

"You know that I don't just catch flights to South Dakota for just anyone?"

"Did they play that earlier, on the radio?"

Samantha Morris laughed. It was a tinkling of crystal. The sound was bright and delightful like Samantha Morris.

Samantha and Teddy Dee made their way carefully up the ice covered walkway to the iconic monument. Samantha Morris held Teddy Dee's hand as they moved slowly to the railing of the monument and found themselves in front of the immenseness of Washington, Jefferson, Roosevelt and Lincoln. The sight was impressive.

"Can I take a couple of pictures of you, for scale," Teddy Dee lied.

"For scale?"

"Yes, to get a better perspective of the size of the monument," Teddy Dee lied.

"Are you lying?"

"Yes," Teddy Dee admitted.

"If you want to take a picture of me or with me, just ask," Samantha Morris smiled.

"Okay, can I take a picture of you and one with you?"

Samantha Morris pursed her lips, thinking. She smiled as Teddy Dee seemed horrified that she might say: no.

"Of course, I did fly all the way here," Samantha Morris laughed.

Teddy Dee asked a tourist to take pictures of them. Teddy Dee took several pictures of Samantha Morris. Surprisingly, Samantha Morris took his phone and took a few pictures of the both of them.

The pair after taking pictures retreated to the gift shop.

Teddy Dee smiled once inside.

"Do you still have your elephant?"

"Of course, that was the first elephant that I ever received that sang to me."

"See anything that you like?"

Samantha Morris smiled. She walked around the gift shop and brought Teddy Dee a plush buffalo purse. It was a gag gift.

Teddy Dee bought the buffalo purse and gave it to Samantha Morris.

"Thanks, Teddy, I didn't get you anything," Samantha Morris said, feigning sadness.

"You are enough."

Samantha Morris opened her mouth and closed it. She smiled and blushed.

"Want to try and see Crazy Horse? We still have daylight."

"Okay," Samantha Morris smiled.

The pair headed back to the parking lot only to see eight mountain goats walking around the parking lot.

"Look," Samantha Morris screamed like a child, suddenly. She was pointing to three mountain goats that are eating on the side of the parking lot exit. Teddy Dee followed her outstretched hand and saw the three mountain goats.

"We are in the mountains, I suppose," Teddy Dee reasoned.

"That is wild. I mean, I have seen them on television and in documentaries, but up close and right here," Samantha Morris was suddenly giddy. "Wild."

Teddy Dee handed Samantha Morris his phone and instantly she took hundreds of pictures of the mountain goats.

The mountain goat moment was over after five minutes. The mountain goats just mosey on and away from the parking structure.

"That cannot happen all the time," Samantha Morris decided.

"Yeah, I can't imagine that happens all the time."

They laughed as Teddy Dee put the car in gear and drove away from Mount Rushmore.

Samantha Morris played disc jockey as they drove. She liked the R&B station and after a couple of failed attempts at trying to find another station that was better she turned it back to the station and enjoyed the drive.

"Thanks for my purse."

"Thanks for coming to South Dakota."

Teddy Dee was not a great conversationalist. He never imagined himself incredible or mildly interesting. But, Teddy Dee was a listener. He circled back to a topic that Samantha Morris had dropped earlier in the day.

"Now that we are on our way to Crazy Horse can you tell me all eight of the other Crazy Horses in the states?"

"Very specific," Samantha Morris stated with a slight smile. She was enjoying herself. She seemed completely relaxed and that made Teddy Dee relax as well.

"Well, there is a Crazy Horse in Las Vegas. I think that is a club. There is a Crazy Horse in San Francisco. That one is a bar. There is a Gentlemen's Club in Nashville named Crazy Horse. There's an antique store in Bedford named that. There is a racing track in Maine called Crazy Horse too." Samantha Morris paused. "How many is that?"

"Six," Teddy Dee said.

"Okay, I know that there are eight. Let me think for a second."

"Take your time. We aren't close."

The entrance to Crazy Horse Memorial is impressive in its simplicity. There are signs everywhere. As they drew nearer to the monument the more signs appeared. By the time that Teddy Dee turned onto the road that led to the monument he and Samantha Morris were ready to see the Memorial that had been commissioned and begun in 1948 and still was unfinished. The Crazy Horse Memorial was the largest mountain carving in progress and when completed would be the largest mountain carving on earth. It dwarfed Mount Rushmore. The Crazy Horse Memorial also was a privately funded endeavor by the seven Lakota tribes.

"Sadly, the tours to the memorial have ended, for the day," the park ranger explained. "You are more than welcome to look and take pictures but the workers are out and it is not safe for any visitors to be near the memorial."

"Bummer," Samantha Morris said.

"It's okay," Teddy Dee said. "I just wanted to see it. Going and climbing on the arm would have been nice but that's a bonus."

"Do you want to get something to eat?"

Samantha smiled.

They ate at the snack bar at the Crazy Horse cafeteria.

"So what do you want to do now?"

Teddy Dee shrugged his shoulders.

"Well, I guess we can take some pictures and go to the gift shop."

Teddy Dee smiled at Samantha Morris and her ideas.

"Come on, you love taking pictures. You also love going to gift shops."

The two went to take pictures. They took pictures at the Native American museum. They took pictures at the artist studio. They took pictures of the artist model of what Crazy Horse Memorial was going to look like when completed.

After all the pictures Teddy Dee and Samantha Morris went to the gift shop.

After the gift shop Teddy Dee and Samantha Morris climbed back in the Cadillac XTS and headed back to Rapid City.

"Have to warn you that Rapid City may be a little slower than Minneapolis," Teddy Dee said as they drove on the freeway and prepared to head for Rapid City.

"What are our sleeping arrangements?"

Teddy Dee smiled.

"Teddy?"

"We have separate rooms. Nothing sneaky or underhanded on my part."

Samantha Morris smiled at Teddy Dee's words.

"When do you go back to Minnesota?"

"In the morning."

"Just a quick turnaround," Teddy Dee asked, happy to be with Samantha Morris but sad that the moment would end in a few hours.

"Just a quick turnaround," Samantha Morris agreed.

Teddy Dee took Samantha Morris to dinner. The selection was limited. So, Teddy Dee selected Minerva's. They were sitting at a small local restaurant.

"You know that you are an unusual man," Samantha Morris had to admit.

"I've been told that before."

"Thanks for inviting me."

"Of course."

Samantha Morris ate Potato Risotto, a salad and washed it down with a glass of wine.

Teddy Dee had salmon, a salad and a Belgian beer.

"I have been meaning to ask you something that happened in Minneapolis but I just don't know how to ask," Samantha Morris said sipping her wine and nibbling at her Potato Risotto.

"Just ask," Teddy Dee said.

"Okay, the last time you were in Minneapolis I had a bit of an issue with a coworker bothering me. I don't think that you knew him but after you left that coworker came up to me and apologized."

Teddy Dee nodded.

"Did you have anything to do with that?"

"I could say that I didn't but that wouldn't be truthful. I will never lie to you, Samantha. I think that I was raised right, in ways. I protect those that matter to me. I may not be perfect. I have flaws. I heard that he had been bothering you. I talked to him. I convinced him that you did not like being bothered. That was it."

Samantha Morris nodded. She did not speak. She studied Teddy Dee silently.

After dinner Teddy Dee drove Samantha Morris back to the hotel.

"It's still early," Samantha Morris pointed out.

"It's still Rapid City," Teddy Dee retorted.

"Yeah, there is that."

"We can drive around if you want," Teddy Dee smiled. "We haven't seen Rapid City until we have seen the Rapid City Walmart."

The pair went to the Rapid City Walmart and walked up and down the aisles and watched as people stared at them.

"I'm bored."

"Me, too," Teddy Dee lied.

After Walmart Teddy Dee drove back to the hotel. They sat in the lobby for a few minutes.

"I'll drive you to the airport in the morning. I'll meet you here at eight o'clock.

Teddy Dee climbed to his feet and went to his hotel room. Samantha Morris went to hers.

The next day Teddy Dee woke early and drove Samantha Morris to the airport.

"You are definitely not what I expected," Samantha Morris smiled and leaned forward and gave Teddy Dee a kiss on the lips. She pulled back only to feel his strong hands holding her.

Teddy Dee kissed Samantha Morris with all his heart. He was passionate, but not lustful in his kissing. Teddy Dee held her in his arms and allowed Samantha Morris to hold on until she again backed off. When she pulled back Teddy Dee reluctantly released the diminutive woman and smiled.

For a moment, the two just looked at each other. There was the high school awkwardness of two people that suddenly found themselves infatuated with the other that made the kiss special. Teddy Dee looked at Samantha Morris with new eyes. The ash blonde beauty fluttered her eyelids and smiled and blushed. In that moment, Teddy Dee felt again that he did not want that moment to ever end.

"Thank you," Teddy Dee said awkwardly.

Samantha Morris smiled, suddenly holding onto Teddy Dee's gigantic bicep. She pressed her frame into Teddy Dee and was not surprised to find that she could not move him even if she wanted. He was a solidly built chunk of scarred stone.

"Maybe, when you come back to Minnesota, we can go back to the museum," Samantha Morris offered.

Teddy Dee turned and left Samantha Morris on the departing side of the airport. He walked to the small outdoor parking lot and headed for his rental car. In the periphery of his eyesight he noticed a man moving toward him quickly. Teddy Dee braced himself and turned to face the man.

The man had a knife and attempted to stab Teddy Dee in the chest. Teddy Dee avoided the first attack. He sidestepped the attacker and immediately checked his surroundings. The parking lot had maybe a dozen cars parked in it at the moment. Yet, where Teddy Dee had parked there were maybe three cars. No one was near except for Teddy Dee and the attacker.

The silent battle took place out of the view of anyone that might be able to help, if Teddy Dee needed help. The knife wielding attacker slashed and stabbed at Teddy Dee but no attack was successful. Teddy Dee allowed the attacker to stab at him and as he did he used the attacker's momentum against him. Teddy Dee punched down on the attacker's inner elbow and wrist causing the knife to go pin wheeling toward one of the three cars near Teddy Dee. Unarmed and unsure, Teddy Dee went to work on the attacker.

It was a methodic chopping down of the attacker. Teddy Dee began at the the biceps, then the elbows, then his kidneys and groin. The attacker wilted like a flower in the blazing sun of Teddy Dee's attack, finally stopping the entire attack with a punch to the attacker's quadriceps that put the one-time threat on his knees.

Teddy Dee walked away from the attacker. Teddy Dee folded himself into the interior of the Cadillac XTS and started the engine. He drove away from the airport wondering had he inadvertently put Samantha Morris in danger.

He tried to think who was behind the attack. He was in South Dakota. Who still had him in their crosshairs? Who wanted him dead?

Teddy Dee parked his car and, as was his routine, he made sure that no one was waiting for him to climb out of the car. He made his way toward the hotel and at the entrance to the hotel Teddy Dee saw a man dressed in a black trench coat, business suit, snap brimmed hat and glasses. His hands were in his coat's pockets, and that one thing put Teddy Dee on edge.

The stranger moved forward and angled toward Teddy Dee. The movement made Teddy Dee hesitate. He was suddenly unsure if he should look for cover or retreat. Teddy Dee chose to hesitate, not noticing the kill team moving toward him from behind.

The stranger was none other than Nigel Hillman. Hillman was a blooder that Teddy Dee had run into, from time to time, in the near decade of working in the world of shadows.

"This job is relentless," Nigel Hillman admitted in the parking lot. They were near the entrance but not close enough that anyone seemed to notice.

"Yeah, but what else can we do?"

"Anything, everything," Hillman suggested. He was a butter yellow corporate arm breaker and looked like he should be walking up and down model runways, instead of in the backrooms, alleys and hotel rooms where Teddy Dee often found himself.

That day, in South Dakota, he was dressed in a checked alligator green suit with matching green collared shirt and tie. On his feet were the same alligator green leather brogues. Hillman had done a couple of years in college before he signed on for the shadows.

"Not me," Teddy Dee admitted. He watched the button man cautiously. There was never a time to be more defensive than when meeting someone working in the shadows. Teddy Dee kept Hillman squarely in front of him constantly watching his hands and feet for any attack.

"This life is for dead men," Hillman stated. "There is no way out, once you get inside this fucked up world."

"Yeah, but you knew that when you stepped into this madness. We weren't lied to about the future," Teddy Dee responded.

"Yeah, I know," Hillman said. "I'm simply realizing that in less than two or three years all the people that I knew or saw are gone."

"It's a grinder," Teddy Dee pointed out. "We aren't meant to last. We work until we cannot work anymore and then someone younger and more capable takes our place."

"I know all that, but it doesn't make it right. I suppose that I expected somehow to figure a way out," Hillman breathed. He seemed suddenly tired and old.

Teddy Dee watched Hillman closely. If Hillman was going to do something it might be in that moment. He suddenly seemed desperate, frustrated and unsure.

"You know that Tucker was retired last month? Bennett was retired the month before that. Penn was retired three weeks ago, I think."

Teddy Dee listened and tried to figure out how Hillman knew this information. Teddy Dee did not move. He wanted to wait and see what Hillman was planning.

"You know that the end of this story is never where you run off into the sunset with the girl, all happy." Nigel Hillman seemed suddenly sad. "Our story ends with someone walking up to us, that we do not recognize, and them putting two in the back of your head. They strip you of your wallet, your cellphone and maybe your watch and call the police to report that they heard someone screaming. The police show up and find you dead."

"Damn, Nigel, you are a little macabre."

"I don't make this up."

"What do you mean?"

"Read the papers," Nigel Hillman said stopping as two others that Teddy Dee had not noticed until too late stepped forward and stabbed Teddy Dee in the side and chest. The attacks were precise and fatal.

Teddy Dee winced and for a second wanted to scream but the stabbing to his side had hit his lung and made screaming suddenly impossible. He reached across his body and tried to apply pressure to the stab wound that caused the most pain; his left lung. Teddy Dee knew there was little that he could do to defend or fight off the three men in the dark of the parking lot in South Dakota.

Teddy Dee turned to the first assassin stunned, surprised, shocked that he had allowed anyone to get that close. Teddy Dee knelt, suddenly unable to breathe. He placed a hand on the cold ground and tried to regain his strength. Teddy Dee knew that the fight was not over until it was over.

The assassin, holding the blood covered blade was already stepping back to admire his handiwork. As Teddy Dee turned the second assassin had appeared and Teddy Dee suddenly had no strength or power to defend or attack. The second assassin stepped forward and meticulously took his time and stabbed Teddy Dee in the chest two or three times only to step back and admire his work; knowing that he had sealed Teddy Dee's fate.

Teddy Dee closed his eyes to the pain and the attack. He wanted to tell someone that he had been concentrating on Hillman and missed the two assassins sneaking up on him. He wanted to grab one of the assassins and say something to him. Suddenly, nothing he wanted to say mattered.

"Hillman was the distraction," Teddy Dee mouthed but no one heard.

Hillman stepped forward and lifted a foot and tapped Teddy Dee's shoulder and watched the corporate blooder tip over like a turtle on its back. Teddy Dee was suddenly a tortoise struggling on his back under the sunless sky of South Dakota. Teddy Dee, for the life of him, had no strength to turn over or to climb back onto his feet. Nigel Hillman bent down and looked at the dying Teddy Dee at his feet.

"You look sad, Teddy," Hillman said. "We're the bogey men that everyone is afraid of, and now you are just...," Hillman trailed off, straightening up.

Teddy Dee lay on the ground trying to breath. Suddenly, he was struggling to pull air in or push carbon dioxide out.

"Make the call," Hillman said.

The last thing that Teddy Dee recalled was lying on the ground in the cold of South Dakota and three men standing over him. Hillman, the one dressed in a black trench coat, business suit and snap brim hat leaned down and smiled. He whispered a phrase that harkened back to a time that Teddy Dee had thought was just ancient history.

The other two men, the assassins, looked around cautiously and then walked away and out of Teddy Dee's line of sight. Hillman towered over Teddy Dee. He smiled his Cheshirely smile and narrowed his dark eyes. In the distance there was the sound of a police siren.

"The death of a blooder," Teddy Dee recalled Oscar Easton saying long ago. "Is never something pretty or delicate. We go out the way that we came into this world of shadows. There is always violence. There is always blood."

Hillman, in his business suit, loomed over Teddy Dee and drew out his Sig Sauer, aimed and fired three silenced shots: one in the chest, one in the face and one into Teddy Dee's heart.